T0209334

Books by Dan Hayden

THE GAME WARDENS
THE GAME WARDENS, Book 2, Danger's Way
THE GAME WARDENS, Book 3, The Game Warden's Bullet
TALL SHIP SAILOR

TALL
SHIP
SAILOR

DAN HAYDEN

TALL SHIP SAILOR

iUniverse books may be ordered through booksellers or by contacting:

iUniverse
1663 Liberty Drive
Bloomington, IN 47403
www.iuniverse.com
844-349-9409

ISBN: 978-1-6632-2404-0 (sc)
ISBN: 978-1-6632-2403-3 (e)

Library of Congress Control Number: 2021911118

Print information available on the last page.

iUniverse rev. date: 07/09/2021

PREFACE

This story was inspired from real life and from someone who was a tall ship sailor. Some of the scenarios are as they actually happened, and some have been fictionalized either because some of the details have slipped away through the years or the author felt they weren't pertinent to the story's cause.

The story's character, Scott Muldoon, is modeled after someone with a different last name, whom the author knows and has had the opportunity to work with for several years. One of the reasons I chose his story is because of his exemplary leadership skills that he obviously accrued through the years, some of which came from his time and experience as a sailor.

Although, Scotty Muldoon's character model and fellow shipmates were previously involved in various hi-jinks normal to young men in their late teens and early twenties, actual escapades of that sort were minor enough not to warrant arrest, detention, or incarceration. Any insinuations to that extent are fictitious or are a fabrication of the author's imagination.

The story, Tall Ship Sailor, is taken from a combination of several sailor's experiences at sea including a smattering of some of my own. In support of Scotty's character, one of the sailor's personalities was injected with some of my own personality traits. It would be interesting to see if some of you that know me recognize that. In any case, feel free to enjoy the outcome.

Finally, I'd like to pay tribute to the musicians that sailed on the famed ocean liner Titanic. The first names and first letter of the last names for the Tall Ship Sailors are taken from those gallant men.

Please note, there are still several youth Explorer associations that exist for the education and betterment of young sailors as well as a few Tall Ship Sailor programs (otherwise named) that are actual state, federal, or privately funded programs for the rehabilitation of troubled youth.

Dan Hayden
Author, TALL SHIP SAILOR
April 2021

DEDICATION

This book is dedicated to friend and colleague, Scott Krawczyk who patiently offered many of his Tall Ship memories for the production of this book.

It is good to have an end to journey toward,
but it is the journey that matters in the end.

Ernest Hemingway

ACKNOWLEDGEMENTS

Mr. Robert Hathaway, Fishing Boat Captain
Nancy Jean II, Carver Massachusetts

Captain Bruce Goulding, USN (Ret.)

Mr. Scott Krawczyk, Sailor
The wooden schooner Truant, Sea Scout ship,
Gloucester, Massachusetts

CHAPTER ONE

The little harbor of Stone Water in Gloucester, Massachusetts was a quiet cove set inland from the rough Atlantic Ocean. It lay protected from some of the harsher weather by a circle of forested land that came to surround it on three sides with a small inlet that opened to the sea. Nestled between two salt marshes and bordered on its perimeter by boardwalks, boat slips, and shops of all kinds, a wooden schooner rested, lashed to its moorings, its sails down and devoid of human activity.

The sixty-foot schooner, Defiant moved easily with the waves that occasionally rolled under her hull. She was an older ship and her sails showed several years of use and repair. Her hull revealed wooden slats with obvious gaps in need of caulking and painting. Two wooden masts rose skyward from her wooden decks that supported a gaff rigged arrangement when she was under sail.

Today the ship was quiet as she rested in her slip, the sail space from bow to stern was bare, and her sails reefed until the next sailing opportunity. The main mast was the tallest with upper and lower spars hinged at the mast with sail hoops to accommodate raising or lowering. The forward mast was shorter and supported a smaller sail area.

Defiant's bow swooped up from the water line to a large timber or bow sprit that protruded out in front of the ship. A line, referred to as a bowsprit shroud, hung loosely from its spar and nearly touched the quiet surface of the harbor's water. At the stern of the ship was the captain's station or helm, as the sailors called it. The helm was the business end of the ship and was where she was steered from. Most of the ship's operational decisions were made there when she was underway and was the prime station for the ship's captain and first mate.

To a regular passerby, the ship seemed as if it was a lonesome thing, abandoned and forgotten. The disarray of normally taut lines and sheets that hung loosely from their spars suggested the ship had been inactive and somewhat neglected.

A traditionally active sailing vessel, normally full of human activity, was now quiet and dormant, aching for action and people to occupy her decks. The wind from the busy harbor whistled by her wooden masts and through her hundreds of lines, making an eerie sound. The gentle rocking of the ship creaked in unison as the waves lapped against the wharf's old wooden piers. The Defiant waited. Soon there would be an opportunity.

▽

Scott Muldoon and his gang of streetwise buddies sat in an unoccupied boxcar that sat idle in a nearby train yard. The group of boys were from nineteen to twenty-two years old. Scott, at age twenty leaned against the open door of the car, smoking a cigarette as he listened to his friends plan to steel hub caps from a new corvette parked near the local beer factory. The corvette made its first appearance outside the factory three days ago, so the boys thought the car belonged to a working visitor or someone at the factory who had got lucky. George Kelly, the oldest of the group at twenty-two looked up at Scott, "Hey, Scotty. Get over here. You're gonna' be part of this too. What do you think so far?"

Scott shrugged his shoulders and blew a puff of smoke out of the box car's door. "Whatever, man. Just get it together. I'm not going until everyone decides on the same thing."

George squinted his eyes, looked at the other four boys and stood up. "Well, give us some input. You're just standing there letting us do all the work."

Scott shook his head slightly from side to side, blew a puff of smoke out the door and tapped his cigarette, letting the ashes fall on the box car's floor. "We need to agree on what time of day...not when you guys are available. You also need to consider other things...like when that car is there, who's around, who could be watching...stuff like that."

George appeared confused and looked back at his group of guys sitting on the floor. Everyone kept silent. George turned back to Scott. "Okay, we got nothing so far. What do you have?"

Scott flicked the cigarette out of the boxcar's door, "The next best thing is to just do it...now, before you guys get it all screwed up. Just run in there, get the hub caps, and get out. Everyone takes a different wheel." Scott looked at the group with a serious face. "Get 'em off and run for it. Meet back here in an hour...and don't everyone run in the same direction."

The other four boys sitting on the floor said nothing but nodded their heads in agreement. George looked up at the boxcar's ceiling as if in deep thought and grimaced. "Now?" He turned back to Scott. "I mean it's broad daylight."

Scott jumped from the car's door and landed on the rock ballast by the train tracks. He turned around to look back into the boxcar's door. "Let's go. Roger and Teddy, get the right rear hub cap. Percy and Wally…the left one. George, you get the right front, and I'll get the left front." Scott was already walking toward the factory. The boys in the boxcar looked at each other in a questioning way.

George watched Scott walk away. "He means it. Let's go." The boys picked up their tire irons and screwdrivers and jumped from the idle boxcar, tripping over each other as they chased after Scott.

When they were all together again Scott said, "Okay, there's the factory…and there's the 'vet.' When we get within one hundred feet, I'll say now, and we charge the 'vet.' You don't look to see who's watching, who's coming…nothing. Just get your hub cap off and run."

The boys picked up their pace as they approached the waiting corvette. It wasn't stealth as one would think of a wolf stalking a deer. It was just fast, uncoordinated, and deliberate. They looked like part of an inner-city gang on their way to a rumble walking with determination and their tire irons in plain sight. The boys walked over the scrub brush and sand that separated the factory from the train yard. Scotty picked up the pace then shouted, "Now!"

All six boys were on the corvette in just a few seconds. Scott was the first to reach the car, and to his horror, the driver was still in the driver's seat watching their approach. George saw the car's occupant and shouted to Scott, "Shit, the guy is in the car!"

Scott went right for his assigned hub cap. "Forget him. Get your hubcap off." The boys focused out of fear and of getting caught. The driver rolled up his window and locked his doors. Muffled expletives could be heard coming from within the confines of the corvette. The boys began to smile as they began to enjoy the driver's obvious anxiety and frustration about what was happening to his vehicle. They knew he was too frightened to get out and had to endure what they were doing to his car.

Within a few minutes the hub caps were off and the group of budding thieves were running back toward the train yard but in different directions.

Scott was the first to return to the boxcar. He had been in a dead run since the heist and had circled around the train yard before returning. He threw the coveted hub cap up into the boxcar and climbed the ladder rungs on the car's exterior. Scott sat on the floor in the car's doorway and leaned against the sliding door. He looked at his watch. It was almost two hours since they had left to get the hub caps. It was unseasonably hot for April, and even hotter inside the boxcar. He rested his head against the door frame and closed his eyes. A small intermittent breeze brushed against his face and moved his reddish blonde hair. Scott wondered why he had agreed to such a meaningless and criminal act. It wasn't even fun. He opened his eyes and looked at the corvette's hub cap lying on the floor. He didn't even care about it.

Suddenly there were voices coming from outside the boxcar. He craned his head around the door's opening to see Percy and Teddy walking alongside the car. Teddy carried one hub cap and Percy was bragging about how easy the heist was. They came up to the door and Scott helped each boy into the car. They too were sweating and complaining about the heat. Scott craned his head outside the car again to look for the other three boys. He leaned back into the car, "Have you seen the others? Where's your partners?"

Teddy threw his hub cap on the floor next to Scott's. "I saw Roger run by the station master's office. Don't know what he was thinking but he was running like I never saw him run before. I heard the station master yell something to him but Roger just kept running."

Scott looked concerned, "Do you think he caught him?"

Without looking up Teddy said, "I don't know but Roger looked real scared. He kept looking back to see if the station master was chasing him."

Scott thought for a moment, "What about George? Anybody see where he went to?"

Percy and Teddy shook their heads to indicate they hadn't. Scott glanced back out the door to see Wally trotting alongside the tracks but coming from the opposite direction the other boys had come from. "Here comes Wally and he's got his hub cap." As Scott watched Wally approach, something looked wrong.

Wally got to the Boxcar's opening and threw his hub cap up into the car but made no attempt to climb in. Instead, he briefly stopped at the opening to catch his breath. "You guys gotta' get out of there. I think one of the station master's guys grabbed Roger. He's probably gonna' rat on us."

Teddy and Percy started to get up but Scott didn't move. "Where is George?"

Wally was starting to leave the doorway. "Come on. We gotta' get out of here!"

Scott reached out and grabbed Wally's arm. "Wally, where is George?"

Wally stopped again and looked at Scott. "He was right behind Roger when the station master stepped out of his door. I don't know what happened after that."

Suddenly, the sliding door on the opposite side of the boxcar slid open. Surprised, the four boys turned to look across the car. The station master and the track sheriff stood there with Roger and George in tow. The four boys made a move to exit the car but two more track sheriffs appeared, one coming from each end of the idle box car. The station master smiled and said, "Don't even think about it. We have your names and we'll go visit your folks if we have to." Wally shook his arm loose from Scott and ran from the car. The station master nodded at the other two sheriffs now standing by the doorway occupied by Scott, Teddy, and Percy. "Let him go. We'll catch up with him later."

Embarrassed, Scott looked back at the three hub caps that lay on the boxcar's floor and shook his head.

CHAPTER TWO

Scott's father Sean, paced the living room floor. Mary, his wife sat in a rigid pose as she watched her distraught husband walk the floors of their home in Natick, Massachusetts. Her hands covered her mouth as she held back tears. Sean spoke as he paced, "I don't know what to do, Mary. Scott is just getting into more and more trouble. He says he's sorry and then it's something else. Something completely different…like he's just exploring or something. He's a smart kid…he knows better and knows what the consequences are."

Mary took a deep breath and offered an opinion. "Sean, it's exactly as you said. He's exploring. None of these things he's done or tried are bad things. They're small infractions…okay, against the law, but not major. Our boy is a good kid. He's just at an age where he's testing things. Maybe he's bored with what his life is about, but he's never done anything malicious…hasn't hurt anyone or robbed a bank."

Sean stopped pacing and looked at Mary. She was a slight woman and very plain with short brown hair. Sean looked her straight in the eyes, "Yeah, not yet any way. This whole new behavior is heading down the wrong road." Sean paused and looked out the room's picture window. "You say he's bored with his life and everything else. Well, he's not interested in going to college."

Mary interrupted her husband, "At least not yet, Sean. He may go that route. He needs some time."

Sean heard Mary but continued to look out the window as he spoke. "Ah, shit...time. I don't buy that. I didn't have any time to even think about it when I was his age. I got out of high school and went right to work, and then paid room and board until I could live on my own. You're coddling him, Mary. The boy needs to grow up."

Mary was nervous. She was afraid of what Sean might impose on Scott. "Sean, he is working... at the beer factory. The night shift is a tough shift and then he has all day to hang around. He's bound to get into something. The only kids around at that time of day are the five he got into trouble with. Okay, they're not the pick of the lot, but they are company for him."

Sean turned from the window and faced Mary again. "Yeah, those five guys that hang around the train yard. They sit in an old abandoned boxcar and smoke cigarettes. I'm telling you, Mary he's headed for trouble."

Mary dropped her head and wrung her hands as they lay in her lap. The room was quiet for a few minutes as the concerned parents searched their brains for an answer. Finally, Mary broke the silence. "What do you suggest, Sean? We've given him a good home. He's never wanted for anything. He's not had the best but it's been a good life for him."

Sean looked back out the window before answering. "Mary, first it was breaking into an abandoned factory and vandalizing the place. Then it was writing graffiti on the turnpike's overpass, then starting fires in the city dump…this time was hub caps… off a corvette of all the cars he could have picked. What's it going to be next time…the whole car?"

Mary was still watching the floor and shook her head. "Yes, yes, I know all that. Where are you going with this?"

Sean turned to face Mary once again and waited for her to raise her head and look at him. "I have to be tough…we have to be tough. The next time I'm going to find some kind of program we can get him into. We'll have to send him away… for a long time, until he learns."

Mary put her head in her hands and began to cry, silently sobbing to herself. Sean walked up to his wife and put his hand on her shoulder. "He's our only son, Mary. We have to do this for him."

CHAPTER THREE

Scott and his pals from the boxcar spent the next month doing community service for the town of Natick, Massachusetts. Some of the older folks in town thought the boys got off lightly but twenty-year old boys have a lot more on their minds besides picking up trash alongside highways and secondary roads. They were required to put in an eight-hour shift, five days a week for one month. Their tools included a metal grab stick, a plastic bag, and gloves. The job was monotonous and painfully boring. To add to the drudgery, the judge ensured that all the boys were spread out around the town so they wouldn't have the luxury of each other's company. It was a long day and especially uncomfortable when it rained.

The day finally arrived when their penance came to an end. It took only a few days before the delinquents were back at their boxcar smoking cigarettes, telling stories, or playing cards. Boredom soon began to infiltrate the boys' minds. The thought of something they hadn't done before or would like to do, eventually became a favorite topic.

It was a Wednesday afternoon and the boys had climbed the exterior ladder that ran up one side of the boxcar for access to the roof. The six lads laid on the roof of the boxcar soaking in the warmth of an early May afternoon. The sky was clear and the sun cast its newly sharpened rays on the six scantily clad bodies on the metal roof awaiting an early suntan. Occasionally, an airplane from a nearby airport passed overhead, its sleep-inducing thrum getting louder as it passed overhead and then slowly faded into the distance.

Scott fought to keep his eyes open and watched an old propeller driven airliner pass overhead. He wondered if the passengers could see them from their seats, high overhead. He thought it might be fun to paint some kind of sign or message on the roof, next to their bodies like, For Sale or SOS. Maybe something vulgar would be fun…like a picture of giant middle finger pointing skyward. What were they going to do? Those people were high up in an airplane headed someplace faraway. Scott smiled to himself as he thought about how he could piss them off and there was nothing they could do about it.

All the boys had other things on their minds. Roger broke the silence on the roof. "Hey you guys. How long do you think it would take us to get to Boston on one of these trains?"

Teddy answered without opening his eyes. "You need money for a ticket moron, and we don't have any of that."

Roger, sat up and scanned the train yard. "We won't need any. We'll jump trains and never have to even touch the ground."

That statement got everyone's attention. All of the boys sat up focused on Roger. Percy shook his head, "You can get arrested for that and I'm not gonna' spend the rest of the summer picking up trash."

Scott smiled at Billy. "What do you have in mind, Rog?"

Roger got on his knees to balance on the slanted roof. "We figure out which trains…and I mean freight trains headed for the Boston area. We can get that schedule from the dispatch office over by the station master's office. It's posted. Anyone can look at it."

Scott was interested and leaned in toward the conversation. He prodded Roger, "Go on."

Roger continued, "We write down the times and which cars are on which tracks headed for destinations that can get us close. When we've taken one train as close to our next drop off point, we jump onto the next train. That should happen in or near the train stations so we'll be going pretty slow. We jump from one boxcar to another so we won't lose any time." Roger paused and looked at the group. "Of course, there will probably be a few times where we'll have to jump off a moving train and run to catch up with another already moving train… but again, they should be moving fairly slow at those parts of their schedules. When we get there, we'll go get a beer in some Boston bar and then work our way back here the same way." Roger raised his arms in the air with his palms facing up. "Simple."

Wally laid back on the car's roof, "You're nuts. We're not old enough to drink yet. We need an ID card for that. Somebody push him off the roof."

Scott stood up, "No, no, I think he might have something there. Let's do it!"

CHAPTER FOUR

It took a week of planning and timing their visit to the dispatcher's office so as to stay out of the station master's sight but the boys soon had their train schedules. Tomorrow was Wednesday and everything was in place. Scott had asked for the night off in case he was late coming home, the others made excuses with their parents about going to a late ball game or having to meet with friends. Most importantly, the train schedules worked out great. If all the connections were on time, they could make Boston in about ninety minutes. There was only one rough spot in the plan. Jumping trains in Wooster Station was tight. The cars would be moving and the boys would have to jump off one train and run alongside the new train, grab the ladder handle and swing up onto the car's platform which was positioned over the car's coupling to the next car. If they waited for the last car and failed to board, their transit to Boston would end there.

$\triangledown$

It was Wednesday, seven o'clock in the morning and the boys waited on the far end of a long sweeping curve for the first freight train headed for Boston. Their position was hidden from the train's engineer by some small storage buildings.

Right on schedule, the 715 bound for Boston came steaming up the tracks and began its wide turn to the northeast just outside the old trainyard. As the train started to pick up speed, the boys pressed closer to the tracks but not so close as to expose themselves to anyone watching from the train or otherwise.

In minutes, the train was upon them and the would-be stowaways watched for an accessible ladder handle on the side of one of the upcoming boxcars. Scott was closest and raised his hand as a signal to be ready. There was too much noise from the train so words were not even a consideration.

The train now moved at about ten miles an hour and was picking up speed. Scott saw the car he was waiting for and slowly began pumping his hand in an up and down fashion. As soon as the car was just ahead of his position, he ran for the front of the car, stepped on a metal running board and jumped as he reached for the ladder handle. Scott had a good grip and swung his feet up onto the platform attached to the forward part of the car. The car coupler that linked the cars together was directly below the platform. Scott reached for the next ladder handle and landed on the platform. He motioned for Roger to go next. The other four boys ran alongside the train taking their turns getting onto the car's platform. George, the oldest, tripped on some loose railroad ballast as he leapt for the running board. He made it to the running board but the stumble had rendered him off balance. He got one hand on the ladder handle but his legs swung out in front of him. The handle was still slippery from the sweat of the other boys and George lost his grip. From on top of the platform the other five boys watched in horror as George disappeared between the two boxcars. There was a hideous scream and all five boys on the platform froze.

Scott held onto the metal railing at the front of the platform and thought he felt the train begin to slow. Then Teddy shouted, "Scott, the train is slowing down. We gotta' tell someone about George."

Roger immediately retorted, "Not me. I'm out of here." He started for the ladder handle that he used to get onto the platform, and Scott stopped him.

"Stay put. George may be alive and need us. The train is slowing for some reason so we have to find out how to get some help."

As it turned out, the train's conductor, Clancy Miggins had spotted the group of boys as they ran alongside the slowly accelerating train and radioed up to the engineer to stop. He hadn't realized one of them had fallen between the cars and thought he just had some stowaways. Once the engineer had begun to slow the train, it would take about a quarter mile to come to a complete stop and that was only because of the slow speed they had been at.

Conductor Miggins made his way up the line of coupled cars and saw part of a disfigured body alongside the tracks. It looked fresh from the bright blood. He stepped off the slowing train and looked underneath. Someone was under the train and lay motionless. It appeared to be a young male, obviously dead.

Miggins raised his radio to his mouth and reported the victim. The engineer called the track authorities and soon the area was populated with emergency vehicles, flashing lights and police cruisers. The track had been shut down.

Miggins approached the fear frozen boys as they watched the emergency vehicles, flashing lights, and emergency personnel rushing around in front of where they stood on the boxcar's platform. "What do you guys know about this?"

The boys were confused and still in shock at the same time. They stood without saying a word. The Conductor stepped up to the side of the boxcar, "I asked you boys a question. Someone has been killed here. What happened?"

Just then the station master appeared. "Oh, these guys again."

Miggins turned to see the Station Master. "You know these guys?"

"Yes, I do. They're trouble makers." The station master looked from the frightened boys back to the angry conductor. "What where they trying to do…jump the train?"

Miggins looked back at the boys standing on the platform. "Well, I watched them do that from the caboose as we pulled out of the yard. The last one to jump must have lost his footing and fell under the car. That's when I radioed the engineer to stop the train."

The station master held the boy's attention with an icy stare. "You did the right thing, Clancy. We already have one fatality and there could have been more." The station master beckoned to the boys, "Come on down from that platform. The track sheriffs are on their way. You're going to spend the night in jail and your parents are going to get hit with some mighty pricey fines. Aside from trespassing, there is also impeding a train schedule. The judge will be dealing with you guys, except this time it won't be Community Service."

The track sheriffs pulled up to the scene in two cruisers. The station master hailed them as they exited their cars. "Right here officers. Take these five into the Natick Police Department, book 'em, and hold them for questioning…and call their parents. We have a fatality here too."

The track sheriffs collected the boys as they climbed down off the boxcar's platform, cuffed their hands behind their backs, and ushered them into waiting cruisers. Scott stared out the cruiser's window as he thought to himself that it couldn't get much worse than this.

CHAPTER FIVE

Sean and Mary Muldoon sat in a private office at police headquarters after a terse discussion with the prosecutor regarding Scott's future. Mary sat at a small table with her head buried in her hands sobbing quietly. Sean was pacing the floor again. "I told you, Mary…the next time he got into trouble we were going to find some kind of program to get him into. Well, here we are. He is going away…some place far away so those friends of his won't have any further influence on him."

Mary looked up and suddenly became strong. "Sean! You heard the judge…it's not up to us. After the hearing, he will be sentenced according to the magnitude of his crimes. We'll have to go along with that. There is no…choices." She stood from her chair. "You don't seem to understand. This time someone was killed. It might have been an accident but still, there was loss of life." Mary sat back down shaking her head.

Sean walked over to the window. "Then, so be it. The boy has got to learn."

▽

Scott Muldoon, Teddy Brinks, Wally Hanley, Roger Bower, and Percy Tuttle stood before Judge Lowe after a detailed and embarrassing hearing. The judge was very serious and strict with the five youths. "Stand up straight when I speak to you." The judge paused and told them what laws they had broken. "The charges are Criminal Trespass, Impeding a Train Schedule, and Wrongful Death."

Teddy and Roger actually broke down a few times as the judge outlined what they could be facing for punishment. He detailed what years of incarceration would be like, the possibility of hard labor, how a criminal record would influence any kind of job opportunity, and what their parents could be looking at in restitution.

When the boys' fear and anxiety was apparent, Judge Lowe raised his gavel as if to pass sentence. Everyone in the room held their breath, but the gavel didn't come down. The judge lowered the gavel and placed it gently on its side. Then he addressed the boys.

"Gentlemen, approach the bench so I can look into your eyes." The boys looked over at their parents who nodded at them to do as they were told. When they were all standing in front of their prosecutor, Judge Lowe took a deep breath and began. "Look at me...right at my face!" Roger decided to look at the front of the tall bench instead. The judge roared, "I said – look at me!" The boys were nervous and visibly shaken.

The entire court room was silent. The parents were as nervous as their sons. Judge Lowe paused for an uncomfortable minute to assure the court that he was in control of everything, including these young lad's futures.

Finally, Lowe began as he stared into the youthful faces of the condemned boys. "I have looked into each of your past histories. I have read all about you and your families, where your parents work, where you went to school, and what kind of students you were." The Judge paused. The boy's eyes were locked on him. They dared not move. "I've read about your histories after high school and what you've been doing since you graduated." The judge looked down at the boys, slid his glasses to the tip of his nose and peered over them as he looked at the boys. He cleared his throat. "You guys are all very intelligent individuals. Guys that had…and still have an opportunity to make something of yourselves, so…in lieu of sending you to the state jail for two years, I am sentencing the whole lot of you to a Tall Ship Program in Gloucester, Massachusetts." The judge looked back down at the boys. "You are all sentenced to hard labor aboard the schooner Defiant for a period of one year where you will be required to work on the ship as its captain sees fit, and you will respect him as your superior as well as your surrogate parent. You will eat, sleep, and live on this schooner and live by the laws of the sea as your captain outlines them for you, on a daily basis. Any deference from this sentence will be directly reported to me in a timely manner and will most assuredly cause additional months or years to the aforementioned sentence." The judge raised his gavel and smacked it hard against the wood sound block, "Case closed!"

The court room was in shock. Some had heard of such programs for youths that were too old for detention and too young for prison with regard to the crime that had been committed, but this was the first time they'd witnessed sentencing of the program first hand.

Mary Muldoon glanced quickly at her husband. "Sean, Scott's never even been on a boat!"

Sean smiled as he watched the bailiff escort the five youths from the courtroom. "It's a ship, Mary. A schooner is a tall-masted sailing ship."

CHAPTER SIX

Scott and his boxcar compadres were placed on house arrest until the fateful day arrived when they were to report for duty on the schooner Defiant. The car trip from the Muldoon's house in Natick, Massachusetts to Gloucester Harbor seemed shorter than times past, when the family had visited the famous place. Scott was nervous and excited at the same time. His parents, in the front seat of the car, said nothing as they drove to meet the ship that would be Scott's home for the next twelve months. Everyone had the same tormenting fear, but no one had as yet said it aloud. The thought of these five streetwise city boys roughing it out on the open ocean under old-time sailing techniques was a little hard to fathom or accept.

Eventually, the road sign everyone worried about finally appeared, "Welcome to Gloucester, Massachusetts." Sean cleared his throat and kept driving. As they neared the harbor, a tribute to all sailors and fisherman appeared in the center of the seaside town. It was for those who were lucky enough to have returned from the sea and also for those that weren't as lucky. It portrayed a statue of a young sea faring sailor, behind a ship's helm, in rain gear, apparently in a storm. As the family passed the statue, Mary's heart sunk even lower when she read the inscription carved into its base. In bold letters was, THEY THAT GO DOWN TO THE SEA IN SHIPS.

Mary began to sob and hid her face from Scott and Sean. Sean knew what his wife was going through and reached over and patted her gently on her left leg. Scott's eyes were wide open as he tried to take in all the sights appearing around him. To him, it was as if he was about to begin a new adventure. The nervousness disappeared but the excitement escalated. Still, no one uttered a word.

Scott watched as they approached the last part of the seaside town's street. They turned down a narrow gravel road that ran between a salt marsh and an old wooden wharf. Almost at once, tall masts could be seen reaching in a straight line for the clouds. They were like giant arrows that pointed toward the sky. Then more of the masts became visible with their lower portions exposing spars that held the sails in place when underway.

Scott's heart began to race. *It's a real sailing ship...and I'm gonna' be on it!* They drove down the narrow gravel road and took another left toward the piers. The ship was partially hidden by a large berm or levy between the wharf and the road. Scott wondered what the ship looked like. He could only imagine from the sea stories he'd read about and pictures he'd seen of the old whaling ships. Finally, they drove up a ramped drive in the berm and the schooner was in plain view...right in front of them. She was in dry dock. She had been hauled out of the water for repairs and placed in a wooden, framed structure that supported her on all sides, and kept her hull from touching the ground. Tall grass grew up and around the bottom of the ship. Scott's heart sank.

Sean Muldoon stopped the car by a sign that said NO VEHICLES BEYOND THIS POINT. He turned around and looked at Scott. When Scott's eyes met his, Sean Muldoon said, "Well, here it is son. Your new home."

Mary eyed the dormant ship with a degree of glee. "Oh, it won't be bad, Scott. I'm sure they'll put the boat in the water at some point. It looks like they're working on it, and then maybe they'll take you guys out." Mary had a hard time containing her happiness with the idea Scott may just be working on old sailing ships, not sailing them. She thought, *That must be what the judge was alluding to when he said 'hard labor.'* After witnessing the condition of the Defiant, she was sure of the judge's meaning. Her boy would be toiling with wood and tar and sewing sails. Going to sea was not even a consideration in Mary's mind. She chuckled to herself, *How could it be anything else? After all, they're just boys.*

Scott got out of the car and stood in the tall grass. A stiff, cool breeze made his light jacket flap and rearranged his hair immediately. The ship sounded as if it were whistling as the wind blew through the spaces between the masts and loose rigging lines that dangled from the spars and moved with the cool sea breeze. The ship was sleek enough and looked like it would only ride a few feet above the water when it was underway. He walked toward the stern of the ship and stopped. Scott would remember the vision in front of him for the rest of his life. Painted on the port side of the ship's stern, the name DEFIANT, stood out in bright, white bold letters.

Suddenly, a man appeared from below the deck of the ship. It was the schooner's captain, Thomas Murdock. He hailed Scott and his parents. "Ahoy, there! I see you've found the Defiant." Scott's parents waved back and forced a smile.

The man walked to the deck's railing at about the middle of the ship or amidships, as sailors called it. "You must be the Muldoons. I had a description of the car you'd be arriving in." Sean Muldoon waved and nodded in an affirmative way to indicate they were. "Regular crew is out to lunch about now. You're the first of the Tall Ship Sailors to arrive. How about a tour?"

Scott walked back toward his parents. He got right up close to the schooner's hull and let his hand slide along its wooden planking as he walked. The wood was fairly smooth but showed a lot of gaps between the slats that made up the hull. The hull was dingy, obviously in need of painting or staining and looked like the charcoal grey was at one time a dark black color. The sea could be very hard on any vessel and removed paint and caulking on a daily basis.

The smell of salt, glue, tar and marine paint filled Scott's nostrils. It was a good smell…at first. It would become one that he would detest in due time. Soon Scott reached the ramp that led to the schooner's gangway, or entrance to the ship. His parents left the car behind and met him there. Everyone stopped and looked up at Captain Murdock as he stood above them on the schooner's deck.

"Come on up folks. Grab hold of that rope by the ramp to steady yourself and walk on up." The captain was a medium sized man, with short brown hair, and a close-cut beard that covered the lower cheeks of his face from his sideburns to just under his jaw. Only his cracked and smiling lips were exposed to the New England sun.

The Muldoons reached the top of the ramp and another white hatted man appeared beside the captain.

He walked up to the gangway's ramp and stopped the trio before they set foot on deck. It was one of the regular crew, First Mate Jordan Smith, otherwise known as Smitty. He put his hand up to indicate he wanted them to stop. Smitty leaned forward and murmured to the Muldoons. "It's maritime tradition that you ask for permission to board a ship before setting foot on her deck."

The Muldoons once again looked confused. Sean whispered back to Smitty, "But he asked us to come aboard for a tour."

Smitty smiled and said, "I know, but it's still the appropriate thing to do. Everyone that boards the Defiant today will be doing the same thing."

Mary asked, "What do we say?"

Smitty smiled and faced Scotty. "You are the sailor here. This is your responsibility. Look the captain in the eye and say, 'Permission to come aboard, sir.' He'll nod at you and say, granted."

The trio stood there for a moment not knowing what to do. Smitty prodded Scotty. "Go ahead, he's expecting it."

Scotty turned toward the smiling Captain Murdock. "Permission to come aboard, sir."

Murdock nodded. "Granted." Captain Murdock tipped his captain's hat, "Come aboard, folks."

He walked over to Scott and said, "You must be Scott," and extended his hand.

Scott nodded his head and remained stoic, "You can call me, Scotty."

The captain jumped at Scott's brash reply. He faced Scott squarely and announced in a stern tone. "You are now on my ship laddie, and of this moment, are one of my sailors. You'll call me Captain or Skipper from here on. Is that understood?"

Scott didn't like the captain's tone. "What are you gonna' do if I don't...keel haul me?" Scott quickly glanced at his embarrassed parents hoping for a smile.

Captain Murdock smiled warmly at Scott and stepped closer to him. "Well son, I might have to, once we get the Defiant underway. She's in dry dock right now, but we'll be launching her in about a month." Then he added, "I don't take kindly to wise guys, so I'd hate to think you're looking to be handed all the worst chores on the ship."

Mary Muldoon put her hands to her mouth. Captain Murdock appeared to be a man who wasn't very lenient and now he confirmed Mary's worst fears. Scott would be a sailor on the ship and the sentencing included more than just repairing old sailing vessels.

Scott's father intervened in the conversation between Scott and the captain. "Uh, excuse me Captain, but did you say you'd eventually be taking the boys out for a ride on the schooner once they get it seaworthy?"

Murdock was surprised at the confused parent's question. "Excuse me, Mr. Muldoon! Didn't they outline what Scott and his buddies from the boxcar would be doing for the next year?"

Sean and Mary looked at each other, equally confused. Sean replied, "No sir. Just that he'd be doing hard labor aboard the schooner, Defiant."

Captain Murdock stepped closer to the couple. "Mr. and Mrs. Muldoon, the Tall Ship Sailor Program is hard labor. It's designed for troubled youths. These sailors will be refitting the ship, making repairs…everything it takes to get her back in the water and underway again, under my sole direction. They are required to perform every task the old way and with the old kind of tools…just like they used in the 1800s…and once they get the ship back in the water, they'll have to sail it the old way. That means climbing the rigging, setting sails, hauling up the anchors by hand, swabbing the decks, and a multitude of other things that make the ship go…all of them requiring human elbow grease. Hell, if there's no wind and we need to get out of the harbor, I'll have them towing the Defiant with one of those dinghies you see stacked on her stern."

Sean and Mary each gave Scott a quick glance. Scott remained relaxed and showed no emotion as he leaned against the rigging, or ratlines, as sailors referred to them. Murdock gave everyone an opportunity to ask a question or comment but the three landlubbers were so taken aback, no one knew what to ask. Murdock continued, "Folks, this is not going to be a pleasure cruise…not by any means. It's a lot of hard work and if these guys don't do their jobs, the ship won't go. Plain as that. They are going to be in storms at sea and have the living shit scared out of them, but when they come to realize they can make this sailing thing happen, using the skills I teach them, it will be a revelation. They will begin to see themselves differently."

Mary still covered her mouth with her hands. "Where will you be taking our boys during all these trips to sea?"

Murdock smiled warmly at the concerned mother. "Part of the program is to visit various ports of call along the East Coast and maybe even south to the Chesapeake Bay area if the weather is cooperating." He paused and glanced at Scott to see how the youth was taking all this. "You see, Mrs. Muldoon, these boys are sailors now in the Tall Ship Sailor Program. They are repaying a debt to society. They will have work uniforms, and they will have dress whites for the summer. When we visit a port of call, that port will usually be expecting us. We will be on a schedule. The boys will be doing demonstrations on the equipment, how to make easy repairs to the sails for instance, and when they go ashore, which is called liberty, they will be wearing their dress whites. The Tall Ship Sailor Program will be demonstrating to the public about the positive opportunities in revitalizing wayward youth."

Murdock paused a bit to let everything sink in. Once everyone seemed to be on the same page, he spoke directly to Scott. "We'll go below and I'll give you a quick tour of the ship. Your bunk is up by the bow and you can just throw your things on it for now. I've got more of your shipmates due within the hour so let's get to it. Once everyone is here you guys will be assisting the regular crew with quirking and caulking the hull."

Since time was getting short, Sean asked, "You mentioned regular crew, Captain. Is that to say there are seasoned sailors aboard also?"

The captain had already started to go below the main deck hatch. He stopped and looked up at Sean. "Yes, sir. I have three regulars. One is the cook. The other two include First Mate, Jordan Smith or Smitty, that you just met, and one deck hand." He smiled and went below.

Sean looked at Mary and raised his eyebrows. "Well, it looks like the captain will have more help than just a bunch of green kids who have never been on a ship before."

Mary ducked her head as she went below. "Let's hope so."

▽

The tour began at the top of a set of an extremely steep stairs that descended from the main hatchway slightly aft of amidships. Captain Murdock referred to it as the aft hatch and ladder, and walked ahead of Scotty and his parents. At the bottom of the ladder was a dimly lit passageway, narrow and cramped, that exuded a damp, musty odor that permeated every space below deck.

As the Muldoons followed Murdock, they found it necessary to walk single file since the passageway was purely functional and not meant for an easy stroll. It was apparent the idea of comfort had never been a consideration.

Murdock walked by one of the larger spaces and pointed to a very narrow wooden doorway. The polished red oak door had a gold plate that hung from its upper panel. Inscribed on it were the words, in bold capital letters, CAPTAIN. He nodded at the door and said, "My quarters." The tour group followed until the captain pointed to the port side. "That's the head, and most important space on the ship."

Mary looked back at her husband and shrugged her shoulders. Sean whispered in her ear, "That's the ship's toilet, Mary."

The group of four began to approach the forward part of the ship. A wall seemed to cut the ship in half and had an open doorway on its left end. A ladder was attached to the wall to the right of the port opening, but at the center of the ship. As they got a little closer, Murdock pointed up the ladder, "This ladder leads to the forward hatch." He turned and looked at his visitors. "It's also a secondary way out of here in case of trouble."

The group remained quiet and took in the surroundings of the ship's wooden belly. Various ropes and items hung from every useable and unoccupied nook and cranny. Murdock stopped at the doorway that led to the bow of the ship. He looked at Scott and smiled. "This is the crew's berthing area. Since you're first on the ship you get your choice of bunks." He stepped aside so Scott could pass through the opening.

As Scott entered, Murdock stopped him and put his hand on Scott's right shoulder. "Scotty, I advise you to choose well. The upper bunks are preferred on sailing ships…for reasons that you'll come to find out."

Scott eyed the captain curiously and stepped into the crew's sleeping space. There were two sets of upper and lower bunks positioned on each side of the bow's bulkhead. Scott chose one of the upper bunks on the port bulkhead, closest to the bow's extreme point.

Captain Murdock folded his arms and smiled approvingly, "Good choice, son. I think you'll be happy with that."

Mary also had her arms folded in front of her chest as she looked about the tiny and cramped sleeping quarters. The bunks were actually part of the ship's interior wall or bulkhead, and because it was in the bow, was curved with the shape of the ship. In the center of the room was a lonely lantern that dangled from a rope line hung from a wooden beam. There were no portholes, as anything made of glass couldn't be tolerated in this section of the ship. The other side of their bunks was the bow's exterior hull, and is where the ship would be breaking through the oncoming seawater, and in some cases, ocean swells.

Murdock pointed to the wall they had all just passed through to enter the crew's sleeping quarters. "There you have the ship's galley and crew's mess, folks."

Everyone turned around to see a very simple kitchen with pots and pans hanging from the ship's overhead timbers. The stove top was blackened more than it should be from countless applications of grease, and its oven below had a glass window in it that had a crack that ran from one corner to the other. A rustic wooden table was bolted to the floor with long bench seats that ran along both sides and separated the galley from the sleeping space. The table sported numerous cuts and gouges from years of use and collisions with the surrounding kitchen equipment.

Murdock noticed the concern on Mary's face. "This can be a very chaotic room at times, Mrs. Muldoon. You must realize this is the absolute front of the ship...the pointy end, so to speak. At times, this bow area will dive right under the waves as the ocean swells try to pass over the ship." Mary had moved her hands from her chest to cover her mouth again. Murdock continued. "Some of the crew's personal belongings tend to fly across the room in the worst weather but we try to get them to remember to stow everything, or at least lash down anything loose, every time they get out of their racks."

No one said a word. Scott didn't think much of the situation and kind of liked the idea he had one of the top bunks.

Murdock said, "Okay, let's go back down the same passageway we just came up and see the storage area and engine room. There are two more bunks back there in the event we have overnight guests."

Mary grabbed the captain by the arm as he passed. "There is an engine? You have an engine on this boat?"

Murdock stopped and smiled. "Yes, Ma'am. It's all the way back in the stern. It powers the one propeller we have. We only use it in dead air or emergency conditions." With that, he moved past Mary and led the party aft to the storage area and finally to the smallest room on the ship which housed the Defiant's only diesel engine.

As the Muldoons and the captain emerged from below deck, several people stood on the grass berm where they had left their car. Captain Murdock glanced quickly at the group of people standing by their cars, then nodded at Scott. "Do you know any of those people, Scotty?"

Scott hauled himself up the final few steps of the steep aft hatchway and peered over the port side. There were four more vehicles parked next to the Muldoon's car. Scott recognized the cars immediately and the people who stood beside them. "Yes, sir...I know those people." It was Roger, Teddy, Wally, Percy, and their parents. Scott smiled for the first time since he first saw the Defiant.

Murdock smiled. "All of them, Scott?" He had been expecting the boys from the boxcar...and their parents, and one more from Portsmouth. He knew the presence of his buddies would help him to relax a little.

Scott focused on the crowd of people. "Uh, I don't know the kid on the far left, next to the red car."

Murdock nodded his head. "That is Jack Clark. He's from Plymouth, and is the sixth Tall Ship Sailor. He'll be sailing with you guys too."

Murdock walked over to the ship's port lifeline and hailed the group. "Ahoy there! I'm Captain Murdock. Please approach the ship at the ramp amidships. The first mate will see you aboard."

Smitty stopped painting and went over to meet the group. He was obviously informing them of appropriate boarding courtesies, just as he had for the Muldoons. The captain waited patiently by the ship's gangway.

CHAPTER SEVEN

After the second tour of the Defiant's interior, this time given by Smitty, Murdock asked the new sailors to bid their parents farewell. He ushered the parents to the gangway. "Okay, folks. Say your good-byes. The boys have work to do."

Murdock moved over to a place near the ship's helm and watched as mothers cried and hugged their sentenced children. Fathers stood straighter than they had to, and when the time was right, gave their sons a quick handshake and said as little as possible.

One by one, the parents reluctantly turned from their confused sons and left the ship. Murdock moved forward again and stood behind the line of sailors that lined the side of the ship. "Okay boys, wave to your folks and smile. You're going to see them again…in about a year."

Murdock gave the new sailors another thirty seconds…just long enough to see the parents enter their cars, then addressed his new crew. "Okay gentlemen, turn around." The sailors did an about face to see Murdock staring at them in a severe way. His arms were folded against his chest and his legs spread shoulder width apart. He began, "Welcome aboard lads. As you have all heard, I am the captain of this ship. I will be your boss, your parent, and in some cases your worst nightmare from this point on. You will do as I ask, when and where I say... without question. Anyone who strays from my rules will face consequences." Murdock paused as he looked each sailor in the eye. "It can't be any other way. This is a sailing ship, gentlemen. A real sailing ship, and we will be taking her out to sea. If you don't work as a team, it could mean disastrous consequences. There are too many to list, but just to name a few...you can cause her to founder and roll into the sea, too slow on letting out the sheet lines and you can destroy her sails - which is our only propulsion, falling asleep on watch up in the crosstrees can result in a collision with another ship, especially in the fog." Murdock paused for effect. "That's right, sailors. There is no radar on board. We sail the old way. Just like the sailing ships of the 1800s when there weren't any engines. We are only as good as you guys make us. If any of you fail, we all fail."

Murdock had everyone's attention. "One more thing. You are going to be sailors and you need to know the terminology. This is a ship, not a boat! There are no ropes on this ship... only lines, and if they're attached to a sail, they're called sheets." Murdock paused to see if the boys were getting his point. He continued, "Doors are hatches, stairs are ladders, the floor is the deck, and the ceiling is the overhead." Once again, he paused and took delight in the new sailors' confused expressions. "You'll get more on terminology as we go along." He held their gaze in his for a few more moments. Then in a loud and demanding voice said, "Everyone get below. Louis, the cook, is down there issuing your work clothes. Stow your gear on your bunks, change, and get back up here. You're going to be quirking and caulking for rest of today, and beginning tomorrow…the rest of the week. It's 2:00 PM now - we'll work until 6:00 PM and then get down to the galley for supper. That's all. Go!"

The boys scrambled for the aft hatch at the stern of the ship. Only two remembered there was one closer that led straight down to the crew's quarters. Scott and Jack Clark, from Plymouth got their work clothes first.

Louis, the cook, was a big man and didn't appear to be very friendly. He looked at Jack, murmured to himself, "medium," and shoved a pair of blue jeans and a light blue button-down shirt into his stomach. Jack got the message and wanted to get away from the surly cook as soon as possible. As he turned to leave, Louis snarled, "Hey, you're gonna' need these too," and tossed him a pair of white deck sneakers. Jack dropped the sneakers on the floor and Louis barked at Scotty. "C'mon, get over here, sailor. What size are you?" He looked the youth up and down, "Yup, another medium." Louis turned to the bunk area, grabbed another pair of jeans and a shirt, and threw them at Scotty. Scotty caught the clothes as Louis threw a pair of deck shoes at him. "If they don't fit, bring 'em back."

Louis turned back to the pile of clothes on one of the lower bunks. "Next! Let's go, you guys! Get in here. I don't have all day." One by one, the new sailors took their place in front of Louis to get their work clothes.

The sailors hastily dragged their clothes away, and in some cases kicked their loose deck sneakers ahead of them, and stumbled out of the galley to go change. When the last sailor received his clothes, Louis shouted after them. "Get those work clothes on as quick as you can and get up on deck for your work assignment. The first mate is waiting."

CHAPTER EIGHT

Scott and the other five sailors lay on their backs under the Defiant. There was about two feet of space to get between the ground and the bottom of the ship. Smitty called it the keel and it was a little deeper than on most ships. It was weighted and helped to stabilize the ship in windy conditions.

Smitty had positioned the boys at various locations along the bottom and sides of the ship so as to give everyone their own working area and ensure all the affected areas were getting attention. Scotty looked at the wooden hull. It consisted of slim wooden planks that were bent to form the shape of the ship's hull. Between the planks were gaps that occurred with time and exposure to the salt water. Constant pounding in heavy seas also contributed to the situation and as Smitty had pointed out earlier, was usually a yearly chore. That meant that this was the last time the crew would have to perform the miserable task.

Scotty held a wooden mallet in his right hand and a roll of cotton caulk inside his work apron. The end of the cotton was pounded into the gap between the cedar slats with an iron. The iron was best described as an iron chisel with a wide flat end. The user pushed the cotton caulking between the slats with the mallet and iron with two taps of the mallet so the cotton was wedged between the planks. Once the cotton caulking was firmly placed in the gap, a second iron was used, called a making iron, which was used to drive the caulking just below the hull's surface. A white seamer compound was then applied over the caulked seam with a putty knife to smooth out the gap and fill the space between the caulking and the water side edge of the planks.

The technique allowed the planks to move against each other as the boat tried to twist when underway while keeping the sea water out. The movement is actually a sawing action of one plank against the other and allows the hull to flex. Once the seamer dried, the surface was sanded to smooth the hull's surface. The entire process was all by hand and extremely monotonous.

Jack Clark was under the boat too but on the opposite side of the keel Scott was under. "Hey Scotty, are you as bored as I am?"

Scott continued to tap the cotton caulking into the gaps. "Yeah. This sucks! My hands and wrists are getting kind of sore, and laying on this gravel isn't helping either."

Smitty was standing near the starboard side keeping an eye on the boy's work and heard Scott's comment. "Keep going, Mr. Muldoon. Hopefully, you'll only have to do this once in your sailing career. It's not going to hurt you. Wait till you see the result of all your efforts in about a week."

Scott and Jack looked at one other and Jack mouthed quietly, with a disgusted look, "Another whole week of this shit?"

It was as if Smitty anticipated Jack's comment. "That's right, Jack. A whole week to get good at it, maybe two to finish the job. If she leaks, we'll have to pull her out of the water and you guys will have to do it all over again." Smitty smiled as he spoke to the boys who couldn't see him from under the ship.

▽

The hours of monotony dragged on. Finally, it was 6:00 PM. A bell clanged somewhere on the ship. The boys were starving and getting sore from all the compromising positions they had been in to get access to specific parts of the hull. Scotty glanced quickly at Jack, "What the hell is that?"

Jack put his hand up as if to quiet Scott. Jack listened and seemed to be counting the number of times the bells clanged. "Eight bells! We're done!" Jack rolled out from under the Defiant's hull. "Come on, Scotty, get up. Eight bells! Shift is over. It's six o'clock!"

Jack, having grown up around Plymouth Harbor in Massachusetts, knew the signal and threw his irons and mallet on the gravel under the ship. "Supper time! We are done for the day, matey. Let's go eat."

The two boys scrambled up the ramp to the gangway and almost dove for the forward hatch's ladder that led to the galley. The other four boys saw Jack and Scotty's reaction to the bells and came running from the stern of the ship. Teddy, Wally, Roger, and Percy raced for the aft hatch and made their way up the long narrow passageway.

The cook, Louis Baltrone, stood in the passageway, his massive frame too large to stand squarely in the galley's entrance. He wore a white tee shirt that seemed too small for his hairy chest and a dirty white apron over his greasy jeans. His hands were placed firmly on his hips and a cigar hung loosely from the corner of his mouth as he squinted at the hungry youths. "You guys are right on time. Where are your tools?"

Everyone seemed confused and glanced at one another for some kind of answer. Scotty spoke up, "Excuse me, sir. The captain said dinner at six, so we rushed right down here."

Louis grabbed one of the skillets that hung from an overhead beam and spit into it. "It's supper, not dinner! No one eats around here until all the tools are stowed." He made a point of looking the group over for effect and raised his eyebrows. "I see no one brought any tools with them."

The boys shrugged their shoulders and stared at the mean looking cook. Louis bellowed like an angry navy chief. "Well, go get 'em and stow 'em in the tool locker over there." Louis turned and walked back into the galley hiding a wicked little smile. The hungry sailors turned, tripping over each other to find the fastest way back on deck to get their tools.

Louis threw the skillet onto the stove and lit the gas. The newly deposited saliva just sat in the warming skillet. He spoke aloud as if someone was in the galley with him. "Skillet's not hot enough yet, anyway." Louis shook his head in frustration. "It's the same way with every one of these crews - just leave everything around." He nodded his head. "They're gonna' learn, by god – or they won't eat."

CHAPTER NINE

After supper, the new sailors had their free time. They could do whatever they wanted or go wherever they chose, as long as it was on the ship. Most of them were too tired to be interested in anything except sleeping or sitting on deck, topside. Wally and Roger napped in their bunks. Percy sat at the galley table reading a dirty magazine, and Teddy busied himself writing a letter to his parents. Scott was topside and lay on the canvas cover of the port side dinghy and watched an orange sun set behind the quiet town of Gloucester. His head was propped against the dinghy's gunnel and his legs were crossed at the ankles. Jack was asleep in a heap of sails piled against the deck rail next to Scott's dinghy.

Smitty, the Defiant's first mate, stuck his head up from below to check on the boys. One look at Scott and Jack confirmed that everyone was too tired to try anything, like leaving the ship, so he went back below to report to the captain.

He walked to the captain's door and knocked once. A muffled, "Come," came from behind the oak door. Smitty walked in and Captain Murdock nodded. "Good evening, Smitty. What are the boys doing?" The first mate reported the activity of the four sailors in crew's quarters and the two at the stern, topside.

"I think we tired them out, Cap." Smitty pulled up a chair and sat in front of Murdock's tiny desk.

Murdock smiled. "Good. We have to give them a taste of what it's going to be like living on board a ship. I've been going through their records. None of these guys have ever been on a boat, let alone a ship." Murdock paused, "Except for one of them. Jack, from Plymouth, Massachusetts. Looks like he grew up around Plymouth Harbor and he's got some sailing experience… or at least some knowledge from one of those youth programs by the name of…," Murdock paused while he leafed through Jack's file. "Here it is…, the Young Men's Sailing Association."

Smitty raised his eyebrows. "Well, that explains it."

Murdock looked up from his file. "What do you mean?"

Smitty went on. "When we sounded eight bells this afternoon, Jack and Scotty were working right next to each other and dropped their tools as soon as the bells hit eight. They were first to the galley to report for supper. The others didn't know what the bells were and only responded because they saw Jack and Scotty get up and run." Smitty grinned. "I watched the whole thing from the bow."

Murdock smiled. "Are Scotty and Jack getting along?"

Smitty nodded. "It appears that way, Cap. They worked next to each other all afternoon, talking and complaining. Looks like they're bonding."

Murdock was still perusing his personnel files. "How about the others?"

Smitty nodded his head. "They'll be okay. They look like good kids…complain a lot, but they did their work. I didn't see any goofing off."

Murdock was still glued to his paperwork. "How did it go when they met Louis?"

Smitty laughed. "Oh, yeah. They're terrified of that guy. They couldn't get away from him fast enough, and they ate everything he slopped onto their plates without a word."

Murdock finally looked up from his reading. "Sounds like a typical crew. Keep an eye on them and let me know about anything out of the ordinary."

"Okay, Skipper. Will do."

Murdock nodded. "That will be all, Smitty. Have a good evening."

Smitty rose from his chair, bid the captain a good night and left the cabin.

▽

Topside, at the stern, Jack awoke in a heap of sails scheduled for repair. He looked over to see Scott lying on the canvas that covered one of the two dinghies at the stern of the ship. "Hey Scotty, are you awake?"

Scott was focused on the sunset. The beautiful hues of red to orange with a mix of gold was mesmerizing. The breeze that had accompanied them all day was gone for the moment, and the temperature was just right. He was tired. It was a good tired but he was comfortable and didn't want to move. "Yeah, I'm just chillin' out. Watching the sun go down is pretty cool. I've never seen so many colors mixed together. It's real pretty."

Jack climbed out of his tangle of sails and stood up to lean against the dinghy Scott rested on. "Pretty entertaining, huh?"

Scott had his arms folded behind his head. "Yes, it is. I never realized something so quiet and slow moving could be so interesting."

Jack nodded his head as he placed his arms on the dinghy's gunnel and rested his chin on his clasped but sore hands and began to watch the sunset too. "Well, I'm glad you like it because there is no television or radio on this ship. We're gonna' have to find things to entertain ourselves…just like you're doing right now."

Scott turned his head from the sunset. "No TV?" He thought about that for a minute. "Oh well, I guess that makes sense. But, I gotta' tell you, I'm too tired to care right now. The sunset is good enough for me."

The sun began to disappear behind the distant hills and buildings. Jack looked up into the darkening sky. "Wait until the stars come out. I guarantee you've never seen a light show like the one you're about to see."

Scott looked up. The stars weren't visible yet. "Ah, I've seen stars before, Jack. What's the big deal?"

Jack turned around to face the harbor and looked into the dark sky. "It's different out here, Scotty. There are no trees or buildings…just ocean. No light pollution from street lights or restaurants. Just open blackness." Scott turned to look in the same direction as Jack. "Clear nights with a full moon are really special. It's like you can see forever and all the different star constellations are visible. If you look at them long enough you can see the different animals, mythological people, and objects the ancient Greeks and Romans saw."

Scotty was still watching the sky. "Are you talking about things like the Little Dipper?"

"Yeah, that's one of them but out here, they're bigger than life." Jack pointed into the sky. "Look, the stars are beginning to come out." He pointed north. "Always look for the North Star. It's due north but is higher or lower in the sky depending on what time of year it is. You can find the Big Dipper and the Little Dipper easy once you find that."

Scott nodded his head, "Yeah, I can see it now. It does look bigger than what I've seen before."

The boys were quiet for a while and stared at the dark sky and the brightening stars. They let their minds wander as the stars entertained their thoughts. Finally, Jack turned to Scott. "What are you thinking about? You seem like you're in deep thought."

Scott was still concentrating on the stars and dark sky above. "I'm thinking about what brought me here."

Jack quickly added, "Hey, man. I wasn't asking about that. You don't have to talk about it."

Scott ignored Jack's comment and continued, "One of the guys that hung with me and the other four that are below right now, was killed while we were jumping a train about a month ago. Lost his footing and slipped under the cars."

Jack didn't know what to say but he felt he had to say something. "Sounds like it was an accident, Scotty."

Scott turned and looked at Jack. "It was, but we never got to say good bye. He was with us one minute and then…gone. Just like that." Scott paused a moment, "He was the oldest by one year. He wanted to be the last one to make the jump to ensure no one would be left behind." Scott paused again and looked back up into the sky. "None of us have talked about it since it happened…at least not to one another."

Jack said nothing for a while. The two shipmates just watched the stars twinkling above. Finally, Jack broke the silence. "You guys have to get that out in the open. It's got to be bothering them too."

Scott turned to look at Jack. "Think so?"

Jack pushed away from the dinghy and walked toward the deck rail. "Absolutely! You guys have to pick a night and just talk about it. Let everyone say what's on their mind. Just let everyone get it out. I think you'll see a change in everyone after that."

Scott looked back into the sky. "Yeah, that's a good idea. Maybe I'll bring it up some night after supper."

Not much was said after that. The sky had become black and the stars showed like white sparks of various shapes and sizes scattered about its veil.

Jack patted Scott on the shoulder. "I'm gonna' turn in old buddy. Smitty said breakfast is at 6:00 AM and I to want get some time in the rack before that awful hour comes."

Scott jumped off the dinghy and shook off the stiffness he'd gotten from lying down for such a long time. "Yeah, me too. After breakfast, we'll be looking at a whole eight hours of quirking and caulking." He shook his head from side to side. "Gawd, almighty!"

CHAPTER TEN

It was the first week of June and the Tall Ship Sailors worked hard. It was as if they were watching each other and taking strength from that. No one gave in to the heat, the monotony, or the soreness. Eventually, Smitty would grab one or two of them from under the ship and give them a different task. Wally and Teddy were brought to the bow to clean the anchor winch and grease it. Percy was pulled away and brought to the stern to mend sails. Roger was brought below to sort out the signal flags and wash the ones that needed it. Everyone was kept busy while Smitty kept reminding them it was less than three weeks to their launch back into the harbor. If the ship wasn't ready, Captain Murdock would keep her in dry dock until he felt she was seaworthy.

One morning, Smitty came looking for Scott and Jack. The sun was shining and there wasn't a cloud in the sky. He found the two boys back on the ground caulking the bow. "Yo, Scott

Muldoon and Jack Clark! Up on deck!" The boys knew it was another chance to get away from the godforsaken caulking job. They threw their mallets and irons on the gravel and ran for the gangway's ramp.

Smitty stood waiting with his hands on his hips. When the boys were on deck he said, "There's barely a breeze today, boys…and the sun isn't bad yet. We're going aloft." Scott looked confused but Jack nodded his head in compliance. Smitty noticed the frown on Scott's face. "I want you guys to follow me up those ratlines to check the rigging."

The other sailors watched as Scott and Jack were given their assignment, snickering quietly to themselves.

Scott looked up into the masts and tangle of lines that controlled the sails. "I don't even know what to look for, Smitty."

Smitty nodded his head and pointed to the deck rail amidships where the ratlines were secured. "I'm going to show you what to look for and how to fix it." He pointed to a new sailor that stood on the starboard side holding onto the rigging with his right hand. "That's Josh McGivney…the Defiant's deckhand and one of the regular crew. Just arrived this morning so he could sail with you guys this summer. Now that he's here we can get this job out of the way." Smitty looked over at the two nervous youths.

"Jack, you're going up the starboard side with Josh. Scotty will be with me. Just think about every move you make and make sure you have a good grip and good footing before you do anything." Scott and Jack were wide eyed and felt a bit leery but couldn't back down in front of the rest of the crew. Smitty smiled. "Relax and concentrate on what you're doing and why. You might even like it."

Smitty nodded at Josh, "Okay, let's do it. Main mast first."

▽

Smitty climbed up on the deck rail with one hand on the leading edge of the main mast's ratline. "Okay, Scotty. I'm going up. Watch where I put my hands and feet. Do just as I do. Grab the rat lines where I do and put your feet on the same ropes I do." He looked down at Scott who watched with intense focus and realized Scott was wearing cutoff jeans. He turned to look to the starboard side to see Jack was wearing the same thing. "I wish you guys were wearing long pants today. Try not to miss a step because your leg will go right through the ratline's opening. The ratline is made of rough hemp and will scrape your leg up pretty good." Smitty turned and began to climb.

Smitty was about halfway up and looked back down at Scott. "Okay, Scott. Come on up."

Scott did as Smitty instructed, and climbed up on the deck rail and grabbed the ratline's leading edge. He put one foot on the ratline's first crossover rope and froze. Scott was only six feet off the deck but being that the entire ship was in dry dock and basically sitting in a wooden frame to keep it off the ground, made it seem that much higher.

Smitty shouted down to Scott. "That's it, Scott. The height of the ship off the ground makes it seem higher than it is. Just look at each place you're going to put your hands, then your feet. Once you start climbing, you'll get the feel of it. Keep going."

Scott looked away from the ground and up toward Smitty. He'd always been a little skittish when it came to heights but knew he could push through the uneasiness. He held tight to the ratline and moved his right foot up to the next cross over rope. His right hand reached up to the next higher crossover rope and he pulled his body weight up the ratline. He noticed that at least half of the work required upper body strength as the ratline collapsed a few inches under his body weight. The cross over ropes under his feet bent in a downward direction as he stood on them, as did the ropes he grabbed with his hands.

The rope hemp in his hands was very coarse and slippery at the same time. Rope by rope, Scott raised each foot to the next crossover rope followed by the opposite hand reaching for the rope above him.

Scott was just below Smitty when he told him to stop. "Okay, hold here for a minute. See those lines that are coming up from the deck rails?" Scott nodded to indicate that he did. "Those are shroud lines. You have to watch for any frayed lines or slackness. Everything has to be taut. If it's not too bad we can 'whip the line' until we can replace it." Scott looked confused. Smitty explained, "We can take some smaller line, like paracord, and make a loop over the frayed area, wrap the chord over the frayed area and chord, draw the end of the chord back under the wrapped chord and pull it taut. Basically, putting a splint on the frayed line." Scott still looked confused. Smitty smiled. "Forget about it for now. I'll show you once we're back on the deck. You might have to make that repair when we're under sail and in choppy seas…up here in the rigging." Smitty pointed to the space around them. "Since we're in dry dock right now, we'll replace any frayed lines we see, so we won't have to deal with it when we're under sail." Scott wondered how there was room for the sails with so many lines running through the sail spaces. Smitty pointed to the main mast. "We need to check those pulleys…make sure they're not bound up."

Smitty looked back down at Scott. "Okay, let's keep moving." The two sailors moved slowly up the ratlines stopping to inspect the rigging in high wear areas. During one of their stops, Scott looked to starboard to see how Jack was doing. He and Josh had climbed higher and were nearing the crosstrees… the closest thing to a crow's nest on a schooner. It consisted of two horizontal wood timbers each secured to opposite sides of the mast. The cross trees provided an area where the sailor could sit by wrapping a leg around one of the timbers while holding onto nearby rigging or the main mast's extension that was bolted and secured to the lower section.

Josh reached the cross trees and moved to the side so Jack could climb ahead and move onto them. Jack got into position easily, wrapped one leg around one of the timbers and held onto a nearby rigging line.

Jack shouted down to Scott. "Hey Scott, this is cool! What a view from up here!" Then he looked down to see that the deck seemed disproportionately small. "The deck looks so much smaller from up here."

Josh smiled. "Yeah, it's an optical illusion. The narrow hull directly below against the wide area of ground around the ship throws it off. It's exaggerated even more when you're at sea and there is nothing but water around the ship."

Smitty and Scott arrived below the crosstrees that Jack sat on. Smitty looked out to the horizon and up at the sun. "Your turn in the crosstrees will be the next time we come up, Scott. The sun is beginning to come on hard and the breeze is picking up. I think that's enough for today."

Scott was grateful and ready to descend. Smitty looked at the boys, "Okay, same thing going down. Just think about each move and be deliberate. Go slow and have a good grip as you go down, except this time you'll be leading with your feet."

The two pair of sailors descended the ratlines without incident. When Scott jumped from the deck rail back onto the deck, he felt a surge of satisfaction and accomplishment. He looked aloft to where he had been on the main mast, smiled, and murmured, "I did that. I really did that."

Smitty overheard Scott's remark but pretended he hadn't. He jumped down from the railing and put his hand on Scott's shoulder. "Tomorrow we'll do the foremast," and walked away. "See me at the bow in ten minutes. We'll have a quick lesson on how to whip a line."

Jack jumped down from the starboard side deck rail and walked up to Scott. The young sailors looked at each other for a moment and then back up into the rigging. They realized things were different now. They were going to have to do things they weren't comfortable doing for the good of everyone on board and for the ship. Slowly, they were beginning to understand, it was about something bigger than themselves and their own wellbeing. Their lives, their responsibilities...and most of all, what they were about, were changing...quickly.

CHAPTER ELEVEN

The day came to a close as the sun began to drop in the western sky. Another workday on the Defiant was almost done. None of the Tall Ship Sailors wore watches so telling time by the sun's position in the sky was getting to be an artform. Finally, there it was, eight bells clanging from the ship's bell...the end of another shift. Various cheers and expletives came in answer and could be heard from all over the Defiant. Cries of glee came from beneath the hull, some came from the deck, and some came from within the ship – wherever the boys were working at the time. Words and phrases like 'Yahoo,' 'YESSSS,' and 'Yeah Baby,' floated about the landlocked ship.

Tools were hurriedly collected and stowed in their appropriate lockers followed by a quick trip to the head for clean up before the meal. One by one, the crew piled into the galley and sat at the long bench table that separated the crew's sleeping space from Louis' cooking area.

Louis stood by his gas stove and leaned against the galley's pantry as he watched the sailors push and shove for a position at the table. Once everyone was seated, there was the usual good-natured banter that accompanied every meal. Louis raised the large soup spoon in his right hand and struck it repeatedly against some of the empty pots that hung from a timber above the stove. "Alright, knock it off!" The galley became silent in an instant. Louis threw the spoon into a small sink. "We're gonna' have company after supper tonight. The regular crew is gonna' be down here, including the captain, for a short discussion after the meal, so don't mess the place up. When the captain walks in here, you guys will be sitting at the table. Stand up until he waves at ya' to sit back down."

Louis continued, "Once you finish your supper, pass your plates to the end of the table." Louis looked over at Roger. "Roger, you're doing KP tonight. Collect the dishes and get 'em into the sink. You can wash 'em later. Teddy and Wally clear the table and sweep the floor. Percy, get a pot of coffee going. Jack and Scott get the white navy mugs and napkins, and put 'em at the head of the table." Louis stared at the quiet group for a moment. "Got it?" Everyone grunted or nodded that they did. Louis continued, "Okay, you have 30 minutes to eat. They're in the captain's cabin right now. Just eat your supper, do what I told ya,' and don't make a mess."

Louis turned back toward the stove and started slopping food onto empty plates. "Percy, get over here and start passin' this stuff out."

The boys ate heartily and immediately went about the assigned chores Louis had outlined before the meal.

At 6:30, Captain Murdock walked into the galley followed by the regular crew, Smitty and Josh. Louis had never left the galley. A small brown beagle followed Josh and sat next to him once everyone was inside the cramped crew space.

The young sailors stood when the captain walked in and sat back down when he signaled them with a wave of his hand. "Good evening, gentlemen. I hope you guys had a good supper." He paused a moment and scanned his youthful audience. The boys all nodded or smiled. Murdock continued. "Before we begin, I'd like you all to meet the Defiant's regular deckhand, Josh McGivney." Josh smiled and nodded his head at the group of young sailors. Murdock went on. "He came aboard this morning and has already worked with a few of you today. He is your information source about everything that goes on topside." Murdock went on, "Scotty and Jack climbed the ratlines with him and Smitty this morning." He glanced over at the two boys. "I bet that was an adventure." The boys smiled back and nodded their heads but offered no comments.

Captain Murdock cleared his throat and looked over at the beagle sitting at attention next to Josh. "The dog's name is Burt and is also regular crew. He belongs to Josh and makes every sail with us. He also holds the illustrious title of Ship's Mascot." Murdock put his hand up as a cautionary gesture. "Have fun with Burt. He's great company. All I ask, is that you don't mention the phrase, 'abandon ship.' Burt will take action immediately and jump into the sea...no matter where we are or what is going on."

The young sailors laughed and snickered. Murdock's face stiffened. "Seriously, gentlemen. We are going to be in some situations for sure. If he jumps, and we're in a storm or trying to get out of the way of an oncoming freighter, I'd hate to have to leave him swimming for his life." The laughing stopped immediately.

Murdock smirked at the crew and raised his eyebrows. "Okay, to get on with ship's business, "I wanted to go over the ship's schedule with you and what the plan is for the next couple of weeks."

Murdock walked to the head of the table and sat down. Louis nodded at Percy to get the brewed coffee and fill the mugs. It was apparent there wasn't enough room at the bench table, so with one ugly sneer from Louis, two of the young sailors got up and stood by the starboard bulkhead.

Smitty smiled and thanked the generous sailors as he and Josh took seats on either side of the table, adjacent to Murdock.

Murdock took a sip from his coffee mug and began. "We've been in dry dock for about a month and you guys have been working on the Defiant for two solid weeks now." He panned the room and smiled. "I'm happy to say I have been given favorable reports from the first mate and he feels you are all coming along very well with your assigned tasks. If we can keep this pace up, I plan to launch the Defiant on the third Saturday in June. If we get out into the harbor with no problems, we'll spend the day checking the bilges for leaks, running the sails and pulleys...just general checkout." Murdock paused and asked, "Any questions?"

Percy raised his hand. "I have one, Captain."

Murdock nodded, "Go ahead, Percy."

"Where are the bilges and what are they?"

"They're down below, Percy. They are the space between the lower deck and the very bottom of the ship...the keel. If we get any leakage from outside the hull, the water will pool there. Some of you guys will be below watching that area to see if we're taking on any water."

Murdock noticed some of the young sailors looked a little nervous at the mention of taking on water. "Don't worry about that, though. A little water is normal. After a while, the water will make the wooden hull swell and close up the gaps. We also have a couple of bilge pumps down there to pump it out into the sea."

Murdock paused for more comments, but the crew remained quiet. "So considering everything goes according to plan, we'll set sail for Plymouth Harbor in Massachusetts, around the middle of the following week. It's due south and about a day's sail from here, if we have good seas and good wind. The ship's hull speed is about eleven knots under the best conditions." He paused and smiled. "We'll probably get about nine out of her. That's about ten miles per hour in landlubber lingo." Murdock continued, "Plymouth is a 45-mile run as the crow flies – which would be about a five-to-six-hour trip if we have the wind to our stern and favorable currents. We probably won't have that luxury, so if we're sailing into the wind, we'll have to keep tacking, almost doubling our sailing distance, and considering the current, I'll add a couple of more hours. I'm figuring on a ten-to-eleven-hour trip."

Murdock paused and took a slug from his coffee mug. "Once we get into Plymouth on Wednesday...or Thursday, we'll use that time to get set up in the harbor and be ready for tours and on-board demonstrations for the public. Friday night you guys have a four-hour liberty in town – 6:00 to 10:00 PM." At the mention of free time and off the ship activity, the young crew broke out into almost uncontrolled excitement but Murdock cut them short, "...and that liberty will be supervised by the first mate."

The raucous banter died suddenly and Murdock added in a serious tone. "This is not a pleasure cruise, gentlemen. You'll be working your asses off all week and through the weekend. Use that liberty to decompress and relax. Come Monday morning we'll be setting sail for...," Murdock paused a moment and looked up to the overhead. "Well, that one is a surprise. For now, let's just concentrate on getting her back in the water."

The captain stood from the table and took one last swallow from his coffee mug. "That's all. Good night, gentlemen."

Louis looked at the sailors and motioned with both hands for them to stand. Murdock put the mug back on the table and left the galley. Smitty and Josh followed close behind.

The galley remained quiet for about thirty seconds after Murdock left. Louis stood by his stove and watched the young sailors. By the look on their faces, he knew they were excited but apprehensive at the same time. He'd seen so many crews go through the same routine during his years on board the Defiant. This one would be no different. The cook pulled out his large soup spoon again and struck a few of the pots hanging above the galley. "Okay, listen up! Roger has KP and the rest of you help to clean up the galley...dishes, cups, and silverware have to get dried and stowed. The floor has to be swept and the table gets washed down. I better not see a one of you outside this galley before it's cleaned. Get to it."

Louis turned his back to the crew and pursed his lips. He knew what was going to happen next and didn't want to hear it. He hung his spoon next to the pots and left the galley.

When it was safe, Roger slapped his hand on the table. "In two weeks, we'll be out on the town! Just two weeks, guys."

Teddy spoke up. "Don't get so worked up, Rog. Smitty is going to be with us everywhere we go...and you know he's not gonna' let us go to any of the good places."

Percy leaned into the table and joined the conversation. "Smitty is an okay guy...he's cool. I think he'll give us a little freedom. Let's just ask him to take a walk and we'll meet him back at the ship in two hours."

The table of sailors continually offered their opinions and schemes as to how they could get Smitty out of the way. Scott sat at one end of the table and listened, not offering an opinion. Finally, Jack stood up and put both his arms out with his hands down, gesturing everyone to be quiet. "Guys quiet down!" He pointed toward the galley door, "Do you want them to hear what we're talking about?"

The galley became quiet once again. Jack stood up straight in an all-knowing way. "I'm from Plymouth, guys. Plymouth Harbor to be exact." The boys started grinning and looked at each other anticipating what Jack was about to say. Jack continued, "I know the place like the back of my hand and I'll show you a good time but you guys are going to have to play along."

Scott sat back and leaned against the ship's bulkhead smiling and shaking his head from side to side.

Percy looked confused. "What do you mean…play along?"

Jack continued. "We go on liberty in our nice clean dress whites and go wherever Smitty wants to take us. We behave as gentlemen and make a good show of it. It'll be a nice, quiet Friday night In Plymouth Harbor."

The table of sailors started grumbling and waving their hands at Jack. Jack put his hand up to stop the commotion. The room quieted again. Jack bent over the table and leaned on his forearms. "Friday night…we're just going to do what they expect of us. We're going to be good little boys that night." Jack paused and stood from the table, "It's Saturday night that I'm looking at." He waited until all eyes were on him. "I heard Captain Murdock and Smitty talking this afternoon. Murdock may have a date on Saturday night and it's the regular crew's night off. If we play our cards right, there may be an opportunity. Just forget about it for now and don't talk about it, especially around Louis…he's got good ears. For now, just get this place cleaned up so Louis doesn't have another fit. We'll talk more when we figure out what's happening on that night."

CHAPTER TWELVE

Captain Murdock and the Defiant's regular crew sat in the captain's cabin following their meeting with their young sailors. The cabin was dimly lit and supported by a single lamp that hung off the starboard bulkhead near the captain's desk. There were a set of shelves that ran along the bulkhead behind the captain's desk chair and also along two of the interior walls that were home to various reference manuals, chart books, and hand carved figurines. The captain's bed, which was referred to as a rack, was secured to an interior wall adjacent to his desk, and a file cabinet was wedged between its foot and the bulkhead.

Smitty sat before the desk in a solitary wooden guest chair and Josh McGivney sat on Murdock's rack. Louis stood by the door.

Murdock motioned to Louis, "Please close the door."

When the cabin was secured, Murdock looked at his men. "I think it was a good meeting with the boys. They at least know what to expect and how it's all going to unfold. As always, I'm depending on the three of you to watch everything they're doing when we launch." The regulars nodded with blank stares. They'd been through the same process several times with other crews and weren't expecting any surprises.

Murdock continued, "I know you guys figure it's pretty routine by now but that's usually when something unexpected arises."

The regulars remained quiet so Murdock continued. "When we get into Plymouth and the ship is secure, get the boys up to speed with on-deck demonstrations and topside tours, and who's assigned to which one. Switching assignments is not allowed. Spend the middle part of Thursday on how to present to the public, etiquette, and so forth." Murdock looked across the desk at Smitty. "Take them for a good tour of the town on Friday night and treat them to a nice restaurant for dinner… everyone at the same table." Smitty nodded in compliance and Murdock turned back to Louis. "I'm giving you the night off, Louis but I expect you to be back on the Defiant for the night. The boys should never be alone, especially through the night."

Louis nodded his head. "I was planning on it, Skipper. Don't have any plans for that night anyway. It's Saturday night that I won't be back on board."

Murdock smiled, "No problem. Saturday night is regular crew's night off but that is our problem. I have a date that night with my ex-wife." He paused while everyone smiled. "There may be some reconciliation if all goes well, so it's an important night for me. Normally, that would be my night to stay on board with the boys but I probably won't be getting back until early morning. Can any one of you stay on board for me that evening?"

There were a few awkward moments of silence and finally Smitty spoke up. "I've got them the night before, Cap and I already made plans for Saturday evening."

Murdock nodded his head. "Okay, Smitty."

Josh shrugged his shoulders. "Sorry, Skipper. I have a wedding to attend. I'm locked-in for the night."

Murdock grimaced, "Well, I understand gentlemen. This whole date thing kind of snuck up on me yesterday. I've had to blow this lady off the last two times we were in port," Murdock paused and looked a bit sheepish, "…and as you all know, she's kind of special."

There was a moment of silence and Murdock turned his attention back to Louis. "Do you think we can trust these guys to stay on board the Defiant for a few hours unsupervised? I'll just cut my date short by a few hours."

Louis leaned against the cabin's door and folded his arms. "These guys are no different than the rest, Skipper. They're twenty-year-olds and they got drinkin' and women on their minds."

Murdock put in, "I know that but they're too young to drink. They have to be twenty-one to get into a bar…they'll get carded, and they know it."

Louis pursed his lips. "Uh, Skipper…with all due respect. When I said these are twenty-year-olds, I also meant that they'll try anything."

"So, you're saying we can't trust this crew?"

Louis stood up straight. "No, sir. I didn't say that. I'm just sayin' they're young and stupid, and by that particular night, they'll have been tied to this ship for four weeks. All they've been lookin' at, is each other, and all they've been doing is working on this ship."

Murdock tapped his pen on his desk. He said nothing but looked thoughtful for a few minutes. No one offered a word. Finally, Murdock broke the silence. "As I told them before, this is no pleasure cruise, but it might give them the wrong idea if we let them think we can't trust them. They know they're on board to pay a debt, and it's our job to get them thinking along a different line. I think we're going to take the chance. They know the consequences."

Smitty pursed his lips and shook his head.

Murdock noticed the gesture since he was sitting right in front of him. "What's on your mind, Smitty?"

"Uh, well, Skipper. You just said the boys shouldn't be on board alone, especially at night."

Murdock returned Smitty's remark with a serious frown. "I said, 'especially through the night.' I'll be back before 1:00 AM, but if you guys think…as my crew, that it's a risk, I'll cancel the date."

The pressure was back on the regular crew again. Smitty stared at the floor and Josh shifted in his position on the captain's rack.

Louis finally broke the silence. "Okay, Skipper. I'll come back from The Mayflower's Fancy until you get back from your date. As soon as you're aboard I'd appreciate you lettin' me know so I can leave again."

Murdock leaned back in his chair and smiled. "The Mayflower's Fancy? Isn't that a flop house and bar at the lower end of town?" Everyone began to snicker at the captain's suggestion.

Louis was quick to reply. "No, sir! It ain't a flop house! It's a bar! We drink and shoot pool there. There's a few guys owe me some money, but I can get away for a few hours." Louis' defensive demeanor suddenly softened. "I'll do it, but it's gonna' cost ya,' Skipper."

Smitty turned and eyed Louis. "Really, Louis? Are you making a deal with the Captain?"

Murdock interrupted. "It's okay, Smitty. He's doing me a favor and it is his night off. It's personal and not ship's business, so I'll hear it. What is it, Louis?"

Louis shrugged his shoulders. "Well, Skipper. I'm changing my plans, as well as a few of the guy's plans down at The

Mayflower, so I figure it ought to be worth a whole weekend off…when we get into Mystic."

Murdock agreed. "Done."

Smitty addressed Murdock. "The boys don't know about Mystic yet do they, Skipper?

"Nope. I started to say something in the meeting but dropped it. I want it to be a surprise. It'll be a reward for all their hard work. Make sure that stays between us." Murdock panned the room and everyone nodded in compliance.

Murdock slapped the desk top with his hand. "Okay, it's settled then! Louis is coming back to watch the boys while I'm gone for a few hours Saturday night, the 24th." He looked back at Louis. "That's Saturday, June 24th…Louis. Pencil that in your date book. We have a lot of work to do before then. Dismissed, gentlemen."

The regular crew bid the captain a good night and left the cabin.

CHAPTER THIRTEEN

The weekend passed without incident and the boys seemed to display more enthusiasm and interest than usual. Smitty watched the young crew go about their daily tasks without grumbling or delay. There seemed to be less chatter and horseplay during work assignments and the level of bickering had subsided appreciably. Smitty continued his rounds and shrugged his shoulders. He finally decided the change in behavior was because the boys were happy to be getting the ship in the water soon, and away from this landlocked position on the harbor's bank.

All of the assigned tasks had been completed and the young sailors' work was beginning to show signs of improvement. Smitty began to feel good with the idea that his training and attention to the crew's work was beginning to pay off. He felt that if things continued, as to what he witnessed today, the Defiant's launch on June 21st or 22nd would surely happen.

It was late afternoon and the day had been a hot one. Smitty looked to the western horizon as the sun began its dive for the day. A thick cloud cover began to move across the sky and seemed to close on the horizon as if a large grey curtain was closing on the peaks of hills far off to the west. Only a sliver of visibility remained between it and the earth. The lower end of the cloud cover was darker at its bottom and contrasted with the last available rays of the setting sun. A band of bright red highlighted the sky closest to the bottom of the cloud and dissipated into lighter colors of orange, and finally to yellow. It was a typical sunset for the hills beyond the harbor town of Gloucester.

First Mate Jordan Smith took a deep breath and inhaled the crisp sea breeze that arrived to cool the day. He drew the fresh salt air into his lungs as he watched the setting sun. It was the end of a perfect day. The crew was coming along nicely, and on schedule, there were no altercations or mechanical problems, and if all went well, they would be leaving this place soon. He closed his eyes and took in another deep breath. It was comforting to know it wouldn't be long before he'd have all this and the feel of a rolling ocean under his feet.

The familiar eight bells clanged signaling the end of the work day. Smitty opened his eyes and watched as sailors from all over the ship raced to the tool lockers in preparation for supper. He smiled and stepped back so the ship's deck railing was at his back and let the boys race for their meal. They had earned it today.

$\triangledown$

The boys sat in the galley as Louis slopped chipped beef and mashed potatoes onto their plates. "Percy, get over here and pass these plates around." He turned around to look at the table of tired sailors. They were too quiet. "Some of you guys get off your butts and get the drinks and silverware. Wally, get the cups from the pantry. C'mon let's go, guys. I ain't your mother."

The boys obeyed. Finally, the meal was on the table but the room remained quiet. Louis stood by his stove with his arms crossed. *Somethin' ain't right here*, he thought. The grizzly cook watched the hungry boys for a few more minutes. "Okay, finish up and then clean the galley. Roger and Teddy have KP. I'll be in my quarters." Louis stared at the young sailors for a few more moments, shook his head and left.

When they heard Louis' door slam shut, Scott walked over to the galley door and looked down the single passageway. "Okay, he's in for the night."

Teddy pulled one of the dirty table cloths from the laundry bin and hung it over the galley's entryway. When everyone finished their chores, they sat back down at the table. Jack stood at one end of the table and placed a tattered sheet of paper down where everyone could see it.

Jack glanced at the galley entrance and spoke in a low tone. "Okay, guys. Let's start working on a plan for next Saturday night in Plymouth. It's regular crew's night off. One of them has to stay on board to watch us. I'm figuring it'll be Louis."

Teddy was first to respond. "How can you figure on that, Jack?"

Jack continued, "Process of elimination. Murdock has a date and someone has to fill in for him. Smitty will have had us the night before, so that leaves Josh or Louis. Murdock knows Josh doesn't know us that well yet and that might be a problem, so that leaves Louis."

Everyone considered Jack's thinking and shook their heads in agreement. When Jack felt he had everyone's attention again, he continued. "It's going to be Saturday night in Plymouth Harbor. That means it's gonna' be busy and probably noisy. We're going to wait until who's ever on board, gets distracted… like falling asleep or something. We'll take turns peeking in his door. Whoever it is, will keep it open because he's supposed to be watching us. Just don't get caught."

Jack went on, "If it is Louis, we'll wait until he falls asleep or something and make our move. We have to be gone before Murdock gets back on board."

Teddy spoke first. "How is that going to happen? Louis is going to be watching us until the captain gets back. We don't have a chance."

Jack smiled, "Louis is a big drinker...if you haven't figured that out yet. He's probably going to have a few pops while he's here waiting on Murdock. I'm figuring Louis is going to be really impatient until Murdock comes back to switch with him."

Wally interrupted, "What do you mean switch?"

Jack continued, "Louis isn't going to stay on board, on his night off...if there is someone else here to watch us."

Everyone nodded in agreement. Jack took a moment and looked at the group. "We're going to have to watch him when he's in his quarters. Hopefully, he'll have a few pops and fall asleep while he's waiting. When he does, we'll head up the forward hatch ladder and leave."

Teddy shook his head. "Jack, even if Louis doesn't hear us, Murdock is going to know we're gone when he gets back aboard."

Jack nodded in agreement. "Only if he checks on us... and he won't have a reason to, since Louis was supposed to be watching us. But if he does find out, we'll be long gone, and he won't know in which direction. Plymouth is a big town."

Percy cautioned. "Jack, we're going to be pretty conspicuous in our dress whites. All he has to do, is ask anyone on the street if they've seen six sailors in white uniforms...and they'll tell him what direction we went in."

Scott leaned against the starboard bulkhead with his chair tipped back on its rear legs. "Percy, we're not wearing our 'whites'...only jeans, tee shirts and sneakers that night.

Baseball caps if you want, but nothing that says Defiant or has anything to do with sailing."

Jack scanned the room. "Remember, we may have to change some of the plans when we find out exactly what's happening that night. Everyone got it?" Everyone nodded that they did. "Okay, then. Don't talk about it again until our next meeting."

CHAPTER FOURTEEN

Tuesday morning found the boys going about their assigned chores on and around the ship. It was June 13th and the sun continued its climb into a bright, blue sky. The air temperature hadn't risen yet and the breeze that came off the harbor was moderate but strong enough to cause a whistling sound as it passed through the rigging.

Captain Murdock came on deck and looked up into the rigging. The breeze came from the ship's port side and felt moderate, at best. He called Roger over from the bow and sent him below to have Smitty come topside for a word. A few minutes passed and Smitty's head poked out from below the aft hatch. He panned the area until he located the captain's location. Smitty slid the aft hatch slider back and came up on deck. "Hey, Skipper. What can I do for you?"

Murdock was by the stern railing and behind the ship's

dinghies. He motioned with a nod of his head for Smitty to join him at the aft end of the ship.

Smitty walked up to Murdock. "What's up, Skipper?"

Before he answered, Murdock took one last drag on his cigarette and flicked the butt over the side and onto the gravel below. He turned around and looked aloft, into the rigging. "I want to dry sail her today, Smitty. The wind is just strong enough to catch some wind. Let's get the boys on deck and give them some experience raising and lowering the sails. I want them to know which sheets (lines) operate the sails. Have them practice daily until we launch, unless the winds get too strong."

Smitty smiled, "You mean until the ship starts to move in its cradle?"

Murdock nodded his head as he began to walk away. "Yeah, just don't scare them too much. A little movement is okay…just don't have anyone up in the crosstrees."

Smitty answered as the captain walked around the stowed dinghies. "You got it, Skipper. I'll give them a good time."

Murdock raised his hand in the air as he headed for the aft hatch. "We launch on June 17th, set sail for Plymouth on the 21st…carry on."

Smitty looked at the calendar on his watch's wrist band and murmured, "Shit, the 17th, that's Saturday. I have four days to get the boys to know the sails and sheets."

$$\triangledown$$

Smitty walked over to the ship's bell and rang it three times. It was the crew's, 'Attention All Hands' signal. The boys dropped what they were doing and came running from all areas of the ship. Smitty stepped back and draped his left arm over the helm as he watched the crew gather before him. Josh, the Defiant's regular deckhand came from below and stood next to Smitty.

Once all the Tall Ship Sailors had arrived at amidships and settled down, Smitty began. "Good morning, sailors!" Everyone's heart sunk. Their experience was that it was never good when the first mate began a discussion in that way. "Everyone get their sneakers on and be ready to hustle. Today we're going to dry sail the Defiant. It'll be as if she was in the water. We'll be raising and lowering the sails, and setting the jibs, just as if we were underway."

The boys looked confused. Everyone, except Jack Clark, was confused about sailing a ship still in its dry dock cradle.

Smitty smiled at the expressions on their faces. "I can't tell you how important it is that you do things when and how I ask. The captain told me to push it without tipping her out of her cradle, so expect the ship to be tipping from side to side… but if you hustle and react when I say, we'll be able to keep her from going over."

Smitty looked over the worried crew. The entire lot of young sailors were confused and showed some animosity. Smitty knew he had to get the boy's attention so they could realize the seriousness of the dry sail. "We'll be doing it all day, over and over again…and probably for the next few days, so you're going to be working your asses off. Remember, do what I say when I tell you, and we'll be able to keep her in the cradle." Smitty paused for effect then shouted, "Okay, get over your fears and let's do it. No one is in the crosstrees or on the ratlines today."

The young sailors' eyes were glued to him. He stepped away from the helm and pointed at specific sailors as he called sailing stations. "Percy and Teddy, to the bow. Jack and Scott, go amidships. Wally and Roger, to the stern."

The boys scrambled to their assigned positions, and Smitty and Josh walked to the Defiant's beam. Smitty went to Port and

Josh went to starboard. Smitty began to describe the scenario, and which sheets and sails would be involved. "Okay, Sailors!" Smitty shouted above the sea breeze. "The situation is…we are in the water and docked, and need to push off the pier. At this moment, the wind is coming off the port bow, so it's going to try to push the bow to starboard, toward the harbor and backward…like going in reverse. In this circumstance, it's called our windward side."

He pointed at the two sailors in the bow. "Percy and Teddy… ready on the bow moorings." The two boys went to the Defiant's port bow and put their hands on the mooring's lashings. Smitty cupped his hands around his mouth. "That's right! When we actually prepare to get underway and I call, 'Cast off the bow lines,' you would loose those lines and throw them aft of the ship but onto the pier." Smitty looked to amidships and pointed to Jack, Scott, and Josh. "You guys get on the mainmast halyard and be ready to raise the mainsail. Josh standby the mainsheet." The first mate then turned to the boys in the stern. "Wally and Roger, ready the stern moorings. When I say, 'Cast off the stern lines,' let go the lines and let them fall on the pier."

Smitty turned back to amidships and pointed to Jack and Scott. "We've got to 'Get Way On.' The sails are our engines so when I say 'Raise the mainsail,' free the halyard from the cleat on the mainmast and pull down hard. The halyard is the line that is running vertically along the main mast. There's a pulley further up the mast to help you raise it, but it'll take the both of you to do it. Try to work together on that or one of you may be taking a ride aloft."

Scott was standing next to Jack and whispered. "What is 'Way On?'"

Without taking his eyes off the first mate, Jack murmured, "It means to get the ship moving through the water."

Smitty raised both hands into the air to get everyone's attention. "When they begin to raise that sail, the ship is going to start to move forward…slowly at first, then faster. For today, because we're still in dry dock, the ship will only heel to starboard, so expect it. Just keep listening for my commands."

He looked back to the sailors in the stern. "The bow moorings will have been cast away at this point. When you see the bow begin to fall away from the pier, cast off the stern moorings. The mainsail will fill with more and more air, so Josh will need to trim it by holding onto the mainsheet." Smitty explained that is the line that controls how far the mainsail can travel from side to side. "It's too hard for a man to hold alone, so those blocks (pulleys) take the pressure off who's ever controlling it. When the sail is all the way aloft and full, I'll tell Josh to secure the mainsheet and lash it around the line cleat that's secured to the deck rail."

Smitty stopped for a moment and observed the young crew. They all held their positions and eyed him fiercely. "Alright sailors, at this point we should be getting underway. I or the captain will be at the helm and steer the ship away from the pier." He walked to the centerline of the ship and stood next to the mainmast. "Everyone know what to do?"

No one wanted to be the one to ask a question and Smitty knew there had to be at least a few. "No questions? Okay good, because we've got six more sails to learn and what all their lines do. I'll know who doesn't understand when we start." He paused and looked about the ship. "No matter, we're going to be doing this for the rest of the day," he stopped and glanced at his watch. "Yup, six more hours to be exact."

Smitty walked back to his position on the port beam. "Okay, all hands to sailing stations! This time the mainsail goes aloft." He smiled as the crew ran to their assigned stations.

The young sailors went through Smitty's deck exercises several times in the next few hours. Every time the mainsail was raised the Defiant shuddered in her cradle and tipped to starboard. The ship answered the crew's actions as if it was a live beast straining to free itself of its landlocked restraints. Wood creaked and rigging lines vibrated, causing the boys to stop and look aloft to see what was happening. Smitty watched for the distraction and shouted, "Keep working! Do your jobs and don't pay attention to the shudders or the creaking. It's a sailing ship...it's normal."

Smitty began shifting sailors to different sailing stations so everyone would experience all the stations. He also demanded quicker responses to his commands and when he switched their sailing stations, everyone was required to run to their new position.

It became obvious the boys were tiring. The sun was high in the sky now and the temperature had risen considerably since they started their sailing exercise. The boys work shirts were soaked through and their reaction times were beginning to slow. Smitty went to the port beam, climbed up on the port railing and held the ratlines with his right hand as he shouted to the crew. "Okay, sailors. Take a break. Get some water and take twenty minutes to rest up." The boys collapsed where they were and slumped against the nearest stationary object. Smitty roused the boys again. "No good, sailors. Get amidships and get some water. Louis brought up a bunch of water bottles for you. Make sure you thank him later."

Slowly, the crew made their way to the much-needed water. Smitty kept his perch on the deck rail and watched as the tired youths drank and rested about the deck area. "This is only practice, gentlemen. Better get a handle on it. What would you do if we were in a storm? Hell, we're not even in the water yet."

Scott and Jack sat on the deck with their backs against the main mast. Scott took a sip from his water bottle and murmured to Jack. "I didn't think it was going to be this much work."

Jack didn't look up either. He put his bottle down on the wood deck and let his head rest against the wooden mast. "This is nothing, Scotty. We're not reefing the sails, climbing the ratlines, or a hundred other things yet." He paused to take another sip of water. "Smitty is just busting our asses right now. Remember we only get underway once per trip. Once we're underway, it's just sailing along under a constant wind. Unless, we have to tack or come about, we'll just be at sailing stations. It's mostly the guy at the helm steering the ship asking for corrections here and there. Don't worry, it'll all fall into place."

A few more minutes passed and the peacefulness was interrupted with Smitty's booming voice. "Okay sailors, on your feet. We're going to fly the jib next...right after we raise the mainsail. You have another three hours before chow." He looked over the tired group. "Scotty and Jack get up to the bow. Percy, you're going to help fly the jib with them. Wally and Roger, get to amidships for the mainsail, and Teddy go aft."

When all the sailors were at their sailing stations, Smitty once again set the scenario. He described the situation as the ship was already underway and gaining speed. Smitty shouted from his place on the deck rail. "We want more speed. We're only doing eight knots and our maximum hull speed is 11 knots, so we gotta' get more sail aloft. We're going to fly the jib sail. Be careful with it...there are actually three of them, but we'll only fly one for now. If you're on the wrong side when it catches air, it'll knock you over the side." Smitty paused and looked to the two sailors on the mainmast. "On my command, raise the mainsail as fast as you can." He looked forward again to Scott, Jack and Percy. "When that main sail gets to the top, I'll tell you to fly the jib sail. Scott and Jack...grab the foremast halyard and pull for all your worth." He pointed at Percy. "When that jib gets to the top of the foremast, cleat its halyard to the foremast. The lead edge, called the luff, is already attached to the headstay so you have to be alert. If you don't time it right the sail will fill and pull you over the side."

Percy's eyes looked like saucers at the thought of being flung over the side. It was a ten-foot fall from the main deck to the gravel base that supported the Defiant's cradle and would be exaggerated by the force of the wind.

Jack noticed Percy's fear and called to him as he stood ready by the bow railing. "Don't worry, Percy. I'll tell you when to cleat it." Percy merely nodded his head and offered a weak smile.

Finally, it was 6:00 PM and the customary eight bells clanged accompanied by whoops of glee and colorful expletives. Smitty had since climbed down from the deck railing. "Watch your terminology gentlemen. There's a lot of folks walking the boardwalk, some of whom were watching your performance this afternoon. Let's keep it clean."

Smitty leaned against the deck rail, tired but satisfied with everything the boys had learned and experienced today. It was a dry sail, but no one had got injured, and most importantly… the Defiant was still in her cradle.

CHAPTER FIFTEEN

The Defiant's crew trained on the sails and rigging for the next three days. Smitty and Josh had brought the young crew through the handling and use of all seven of Defiant's sails. He created several scenarios for the inexperienced crew and tried to make it as life like as possible.

The boys took their training seriously and worked hard. There were some bumps and bruises during each dry sail and it became obvious the crew was getting proficient at some of the more basic sailing tasks. Smitty had begun to throw different scenarios at the boys to see how they responded, and now, by the third day, were getting comfortable with the ship's tipping and moaning. The boys were tired and were beginning to forget or ignore some of Smitty's warnings from earlier in the week.

The breeze had stiffened considerably and deck hand Josh McGiveny approached Smitty and quietly suggested they quit for the day or until the wind died down. By now, the boys had rocked the ship in its cradle to some terrifying angles, such that the hull would need to be repainted at some of the contact points where it had been secured to the temporary frame. Murdock hadn't been happy about that but it had been his call to push the dry sail.

Smitty looked up into the rigging. "Nope. The boys are getting used to the tipping, the sails swinging across the ship, and all the noises. We have to keep going. We launch tomorrow and I want to be ready."

Suddenly, a shrill cry was heard from the bow. Both Smitty and Josh shifted their attention to the front of the ship. Roger and Wally were struggling with something over the port bow railing. Smitty cupped his hands and shouted in their direction. "Percy! Where is Percy? He was assigned to the bow this time."

Josh turned from Smitty and ran to the bow. Percy had been blown over the port side again and was hanging by a safety strap attached to his belt. Josh looked over the port railing and saw Percy hanging by the back of his belt with his head pointed toward the ground. He reached over the side, grabbed Percy by the belt, and hauled the young sailor back onto the deck. He turned Percy around and grabbed him by both shoulders. An embarrassed Percy Tuttle turned to face the concerned deckhand. Josh shook the sailor as if to wake him up. "Percy! You gotta' be more careful, damn it! You've been blown over the side three times this week. If that happens at sea, you're gonna" be shark shit! We just can't turn around and go pick you up."

Mortified, Percy dropped his head stared at the deck. No one laughed or cracked a smile. The crew just watched as Percy was admonished before his entire crew. Josh turned the slightly built sailor around looking for cuts and abrasions. The boy was only five feet, six inches tall and weighed one hundred thirty pounds.

Josh caught himself and took a deep breath. "What happened this time?"

Percy began to explain. "The wind shifted, Josh. It was coming over the starboard side and I was holding the jib sheet waiting for the sail to get to the top of the mast. All of a sudden there was a puff from the port side so I thought it was going to blow the jib sail back to starboard."

Josh prodded Percy to finish his explanation. "Go on."

"So I changed my position…and I still haven't got the timing down on when to cleat the jib sheet. I kept waiting for someone to tell me, and the next thing I know I got hit with the sail and I'm over the port side."

Josh straightened up and folded his arms in front of his chest. "So you learned not to react to the puffs. Sounds like some wind got behind the jib sail and died. The original wind from starboard immediately followed the puff and knocked you over."

Percy nodded in agreement with his head down.

Josh continued, "What makes you think someone is gonna' tell you when the jib is at the top of the mast? You're supposed to be watching the jib sail when it goes aloft…and you were on the wrong side of the jib sail anyway."

Percy began mumbling something and Josh's temper flared again. "Speak up, boy! I can't help you if I can't hear you."

Percy suddenly blurted his answer out of frustration. "I was watching! The wind shifted I told you…all of a sudden, from starboard to port. It happened so fast and I had a good hold of the jib sheet."

Josh acted as if he didn't believe the boy. "If you were watching, you would have seen the switch when the jib hit the top of the mast. Never react to the puffs."

At that moment, Percy became a different person… someone he never dreamed of being, and lashed out at Josh. "Sometimes I can't see it…okay? The sun's glare on my glasses blocks everything out. Usually, someone tells me when the jib gets to the top…and then sometimes, it's already too late. I was watching, and then all I got was glare. That was when the wind shifted and the sail filled with air, and pushed me over the port side."

Percy went from aggressive to suddenly passive again. "I suppose that means because I wear glasses, you're going to take me off the bow station." He looked into Josh's eyes in a pleading sort of way. "Please don't take me off any duty, Josh. I can do whatever anyone else on this ship can do. Just give me another chance."

Josh's heart melted. He realized they were pushing the boys too hard and had forgotten about Percy's glasses. He sat on the deck rail and put his huge arm over Percy's shoulders. Josh was quiet for a moment and quietly murmured. "That wasn't your fault Percy. That was my fault. I'm gonna' get you some clip-on sunglasses so that won't happen anymore. They'll fit right over those glasses you're wearing right now. What do you think about that?"

Percy nodded his head and smiled. "Thanks, Josh. Thanks a lot."

▽

Captain Murdock sat back in his desk chair and listened to the regular crew's concerns about the crew's readiness with regard to tomorrow's launch. Smitty sat in his usual place in front of Murdock's desk, Josh leaned against the cabin's right interior bulkhead, and Louis took his usual place by the cabin door.

Smitty pursed his lips before he spoke, then offered his opinion. "I think we should give the boys a few more days, Skipper. They're coming along but we've had some problems that concern me that could turn into big ones, if I don't get them ironed out before we go to sea."

Murdock pulled his corncob pipe from his mouth and blew a circle of smoke to the overhead. "We're only launching the Defiant into the harbor tomorrow, Smitty. We don't set sail for Plymouth 'til until next Wednesday, the 21st." Murdock smiled at the first mate and asked, "What could be so bad that would make you want to stay in dry dock?"

Smitty was quick to reply, "I didn't say that I wanted to stay in dry dock, Skipper. We're okay to launch tomorrow as long as we stay in the harbor and just shake down the Defiant. I'm talking about delaying our trip to Plymouth for a few days... just until the boys are a little more comfortable in their sailing responsibilities." He paused and added, "I may also need to restrict certain personnel from some of those responsibilities... for their own good."

When Smitty offered that information, Murdock glanced at Josh and caught him shaking his head from side to side as he stared at the floor. "Josh, you're shaking your head. What is it?"

Josh looked up. "Excuse me, Skipper?"

Murdock continued, "I saw you shake your head when Smitty mentioned restricting some of the boys from specific sailing responsibilities."

Josh stood up straight as he spoke to Murdock. "With all due respect, Skipper...I am the ship's assigned deckhand. I experienced some problems with one of the boys...that is specific to him only. Smitty witnessed those problems, and I told the boy I would get him through it. Smitty is only coming from his position as a first mate."

Murdock's face began to redden. "Okay, listen up! It appears you two know something, and are not telling me the whole story. One of you better get it out or there will be hell to pay."

Smitty remained seated and rose his right arm with fingers spread as if to say, 'This one is yours, Josh.'

Josh began. "Well, Skipper...it's Percy Tuttle. He's a good kid and has a lot of heart. He tries his damnedest, but he's just not getting it. Aside from that, it's his size. He's only 5 feet, six and all of 130 pounds. During the dry sail, he got blown off the ship four times, and on another occasion took a short ride up the mainmast when his partner slipped and dropped the mainmast halyard. Luckily, I caught him by the ankles before he went too high."

Murdock leaned over his desk and eyed Josh with a severe glare. "Are you saying, that because of his size, he's a detriment to the ship and to himself…because he can't handle the sails?" Murdock paused not taking his eyes off Josh, "Because if you are, I'll take Percy off the ship's list and he'll go straight to a land-based facility to finish up his time there." Murdock's glare seemed to fill the room with a new tension. Everyone was uncomfortable.

Louis started, "In Percy's behalf, Skipper…," Murdock cut him short as he raised his hand and continued with Josh. "What's it going to be, Josh? Is he Tall Ship Sailor material or do I put him off the ship?"

Josh was sweating through his shirt. "Skipper, I said I'd get him through, and I will. We'll figure it out."

Murdock sat back from his intimidating lean across the desk. "If that is your decision…," Murdock paused and glanced at Smitty and revised his statement, "If that is what 'both' of you say, then he stays on board the Defiant…but he will have every responsibility the others do. Is that understood?"

Smitty turned to look at Josh and each nodded at one another. Smitty turned back to Murdock, "We'll get him through, Skipper."

Murdock was silent for a few awkward moments then made a statement of his own. "Okay, Percy remains in the Tall Ship Sailor program. If he gets hurt, killed or lost at sea…it is your responsibility." Murdock held his glare a few more moments. "Is that understood?" Both Smitty and Josh nodded. Murdock raised his hand in the air and waved in the direction of the cabin's door. "Launch tomorrow at 7:00 AM. Dismissed!"

CHAPTER SIXTEEN

Launch Day for the Defiant had finally arrived. The boys were dressed in their work clothes and ready on deck at 7:00 AM sharp. The day was overcast and the cloud bank appeared darker at the bottom. For now, the sea breeze brought a chill with it and a dampness rode inside the salt air.

The young crew milled about the main deck nervously awaiting their launch instructions. The captain and regular crew had not yet appeared on deck, escalating the boys' anticipation of events to come.

Scott and Jack stood at amidships by the starboard railing. They looked out over the harbor watching ships and sailing vessels of all kinds and sizes prepare for their departures of unknown destinations. The wind had picked up and was steady, but the overcast sky made it feel much cooler.

Jack broke the silence. "How are you feeling about today's launch, Scotty?"

Scott answered without turning from the harbor. "It is what it is. I'm just going to do what they tell me. Hell, we practiced all week and today is the big test. Hope we don't wreck her on the first time out."

"We won't." Jack smiled and turned his head to look aft, past the Defiant's stern. "See that portable ramp they moved up the berm last night? That's called a slipway." Scott turned his head to the ship's stern. A work ramp with train tracks on it rose out of the harbor's tidal river and up to Defiant's stern. Jack pointed to the slipway. "They're going to align that slipway with the cradle the Defiant is resting in right now, and remove the adjustable stanchions pressing on her hull. Once the stanchions are removed, she'll settle into the cradle. The dockyard hands will give Smitty a cable to attach to the stern to pull the ship and cradle down that slipway. They'll roll down the slipway's tracks into the water and the ship will float off the cradle and slide right into the back bay. Then Murdock will get us back on board to get her out into the harbor."

Scott nodded his head. "Sounds pretty simple."

Jack stood back from the railing. "Oh, it's simple enough, but it's a lot of weight to move. Once that momentum gets going in one direction, it's hard to stop. They just have to make sure everything is balanced and lined up."

Just then, the Defiant's regular crew and captain came up from below through the aft hatch. Smitty was first to appear. As soon as he stepped on deck he looked forward for his young crew. He rang the ship's bell three times, raised his right arm in the air and twirled his hand in a clockwise fashion. The crew recognized the gesture and headed aft for a crew's meeting.

When the entire crew was at Defiant's amidships, Captain Murdock began, "Good morning, sailors. Today's launch is upon us. As you can see, we're lined up with the slipway, and the dockyard hands are in place and ready to roll." He smiled at the young crew. "You guys will be happy to hear that you will not be a part of the launch. I want you to disembark and follow Louis to the harbor's main wharf…at the northern part of the harbor. It's across from Popeye's Bait and Tackle Shop. Any questions?" The group remained silent.

Murdock nodded his head. "Okay, fine. You may stay here to watch the Defiant get wet, then head right for that wharf. We'll meet you directly."

Murdock turned and waved his hand in the air. "Everyone off the ship. Regular crew, prepare for launch."

The boys stayed around long enough to watch the regular crew brace for Defiant's ride down the slipway. Josh stood in the bow by the foremast, Smitty was amidships on the port beam, and Murdock stood by the helm. On Murdock's command, lines were cast off and launch positions assumed. Then, with a wave of his hand, Murdock signaled the dock yard gang to remove the stanchions. The Defiant settled into the cradle that had held her high and dry for the past few months. The next signal came from a yard hand by the slipway. He pointed to the ground and the slipway's winch was engaged, and tugged at Defiant's stern.

The big schooner began to move down the slipway…slowly at first, then faster, until her stern crashed into the calm water of the back bay. Her stern went under for a moment followed by a huge gush of water that rose high into the salt air from both sides of the hull. The stern popped back up and the bow followed with violent but graceful force. The Defiant was afloat and ready.

$\triangledown$

The Defiant's young crew followed Louis north along Gloucester Harbor's western perimeter until the boardwalk began to curve around to the northeast. Louis walked alone, ahead of the group and said nothing…although he kept an ear tuned to the boys' conversations.

The boys pushed and shoved as they walked and got a little noisy in anticipation of their first sail…even though it would only be in the harbor today.

Louis finally spoke up. "Cut the shit, you guys. You're supposed to be sailors. People are watching."

Everyone went back to silently following their cook until the famous Popeye's billboard appeared. Louis turned right and continued down to the next wharf. The dock side area was huge but offered only a small space for the Defiant to tie up. There were two lobster boats on one side of the free space and a large fishing trawler on the other. Getting the Defiant in would be tricky enough but getting out under sail could pose a problem.

About twenty minutes passed and Louis pulled the cigar from his mouth. "There she is," and pointed to the southeastern part of the harbor.

Everyone pushed toward the edge of the pier and looked along the harbor's eastern side. Pushing out from behind moored fishing boats and other vessels of all sizes, the Defiant's bow could be seen making her way toward their wharf.

The boys watched quietly and admired the scene Defiant portrayed as she approached. Her sails were still down (baremasted) and she showed a small bow wake as she got closer. Her two masts looked tall and stately as the ship passed between other moored vessels. She moved quietly and serenely, and appeared to be gliding down a long corridor of moored vessels that appeared too narrow for her passage. People working the docks and walking along the boardwalk stopped to admire the scene as she slid easily over the smooth water.

Wally suddenly exclaimed. "She's moving pretty good without her sails."

Louis turned around to meet his gaze with a frown. "She's on her one Diesel engine, noggin head. It's probably one of the few times you'll see her under motorized power."

In a few minutes the Defiant had loomed up in front of the crew and Captain Murdock could be heard shouting mooring commands to the regular crew. Josh and Smitty ran about the port side of Defiant and threw mooring lines to the dock yard hands awaiting their approach. Murdock eased the big schooner in with her port side to the pier. A boarding ramp was laid across the pier to the Defiant's gangway, and when she was secure, Murdock waved the boys aboard. No one dared to move until Louis crossed the ramp first.

▽

The ship's bell clanged three times and Smitty gave the accustomed crew's signal at amidships again. He shouted above the breeze that had increased to a moderate level. "Let's go, sailors! Move it, move it, move it! We only have fifteen minutes to get out of this slip."

The boys stood in front of Smitty awaiting their instructions. Murdock said nothing and stayed behind the ship's helm. "Listen up! We dry sailed this maneuver with the wind coming at us from the port bow. Unfortunately, the wind is coming from the stern's port side today so we're going to do it all in reverse."

The look of horror could be seen on each sailor's face. Smitty saw the reaction but ignored it. "Don't worry. It's all the same stuff…we'll just be doing it differently. After we cast off the bow lines, we'll fly the jib sail to pull us out and away from the pier. When she starts to move forward and the guy in the stern sees the gap open between the bow and the pier…cast off the stern lines." Smitty glanced back at Murdock who gave him a nod of approval. "Percy, Wally and Teddy in the bow. Jack and Scotty ready on the mainsail. Roger…ready the stern lines. Sailing stations, GO!" As the young crew started for their sailing positions, Smitty stopped one of the sailors. "Percy, one moment please." Percy ran back to Smitty, who looked into the boy's eyes with severity. "Percy, we have to get out of this tight parking place. The jib is the way to do it and you're quicker than those other guys up there. I need you to make this happen. Can you do that?"

A smile crossed Percy's face. "I can do that, Smitty."

Smitty kept the serious tone on his face. "Good. Get to it." Percy trotted off to the bow and Smitty glanced back over his shoulder to where Murdock stood behind the helm. Murdock nodded approvingly and cracked a small smile.

Smitty gave the orders to leave the pier and the boys reacted as they had practiced. The bow fell away from the pier as planned, and everyone held their breath as the bow team flew the jib sail. Percy timed it perfectly. The jib filled with air and began to pull the Defiant from the pier. Roger cast off the stern moorings and the Defiant eased out of the tight slip space and into the harbor.

Smitty smiled to himself and shouted, "Raise the mainsail." The mainsail rose quickly, filled with air, and heeled the Defiant over to starboard as she picked up speed. "Steer for clear harbor. Ready to shake her down, Skipper."

Murdock steered for a quiet place in the harbor and away from any boat traffic. Then he nodded to Smitty, "Shake her down."

Smitty looked fore and aft and shouted above the wind. "Okay, sailors, shakedown time. I want three of you below in the bilges. Check to see if we've got any leaks. Teddy, Jack, and Wally, get below and check it out. One forward, one amidships, one in the stern. GO!" The three sailors disappeared through the forward and aft hatches.

When they got below deck, Jack sent Wally to the bow area and Teddy to the stern, while he watched the bilges below the middle half of the ship. A few minutes passed and Teddy came running from the stern area with his eyes wild with fear. "Jack, we're sinking! There's water coming in from either side of the keel back there. I gotta' go tell the captain."

Jack grabbed Teddy by the arm as he tried to get around him to climb the steep aft ladder. "Whoa! Hold on there, Teddy. Is it pouring in like a faucet?"

Teddy tripped and stumbled into the ladder. Jack still held him by the left arm. "No, not like a faucet, but there's water in the keel space below the floor boards. I can hear it and see it sloshing around down there."

Jack nodded his head. "We're not sinking, Teddy. That's normal. Some of it came in when they launched her and there is some that just seeps in between the hull planks. After a while the wooden hull will swell and close those gaps. The bilge pumps will take care of the rest. As long as it's not knee deep, we're good." Jack let his arm go.

Teddy put one foot on the ladder to the aft hatch. "I'm gonna' tell the captain anyway."

Jack walked toward the bow. "Go ahead, but he's going to laugh at you."

Teddy ran up the ladder and disappeared through the open hatch.

The rest of the shakedown went without incident and Defiant passed her test as being seaworthy. The young sailors felt a great satisfaction and a sense of accomplishment knowing that what they had worked on for so long and so hard had paid off. Their ship was afloat and ready for what the sea and winds could give them. The only person that felt some bruising that night was Teddy, and he paid dearly for his reaction in the bilges when everyone met for supper that night.

CHAPTER SEVENTEEN

Sunday morning found the Defiant's young crew going about their general duties above and below deck, only now the ship was afloat. They were moored to a pier in a safe harbor so there really weren't any waves to speak of...or any large enough to be noticeable on a ship the size of Defiant. The sensation of being afloat was definitely apparent as compared to being in dry dock, but unfortunately, their time in the harbor would not count toward attaining their sea legs.

The smell of hot coffee wafted up through the forward hatch and seemed to travel the length of the ship. Somehow the mix of coffee, salt air, a partly overcast sky, and a gentle roll of the ship, instilled the romance of the sea and inspired a feeling of comfort and belonging in all of the young sailors. The Defiant was their home now and the aspiring sailors were becoming accustomed to it. Their new life was harder but preferable to what they had known before. It may have been because everyone shared a common burden and everything was more easily understood under those guidelines. The general feeling among the boys was that everyone was equal. No one was any better than the next guy. They all had the same job and everyone had to abide by the same rules.

It was just past 7:00 AM and Smitty stepped out on deck from the aft hatch. He rang the ship's bell three quick times to get the crew's attention. Once everyone was assembled amidships, Smitty began to line out the crew's activities for the next few days before setting sail for Plymouth. "Good morning, sailors. I'm glad to see you guys are up and about, and getting your chores done." No one spoke. They knew the sooner Smitty said what he came to say, the sooner they could go to breakfast. Smitty smiled as he began. "As you know, we have three days of downtime before we set sail for Plymouth, so we'll be swabbing the decks, doing some painting here and there…especially in some of those places that got banged up during the dry sail, and we'll be taking her out of the harbor in a day or so to get a little sailing experience." The boys all paused and looked at each other. Smitty continued. "We'll pick a decent day where we have a moderate wind and the chop isn't too bad. Once again, you will all be experiencing every sailing station."

Smitty reached down and picked up a white cloth bag that had the words US MAIL printed on it. "We have our first mail call." The boys all began to smile and express their satisfaction. "You guys are allowed mail once a month and it looks like everyone got some. When I call your name, come and get your mail and go below to the galley for breakfast. Your assignment for today is to write a letter to your folks or next of kin, girlfriends…whatever…and if you don't have any of those write me or the captain a letter, but everyone has to write a letter today. Other than that, today is Sunday and you guys have earned a break, so you have the entire day off." Everyone whooped and cheered. "Smitty continued, "Don't get too excited. You still have to stay on the ship...so write your letters, and rest up. I'll be below in the captain's cabin, should anyone need anything."

The day seemed to pass quietly. Some of the sailors stayed below and read magazines or slept. Around 2:00 PM, loud voices could be heard above the harbor's breeze and Defiant's creaking and groaning. The noise had awakened Scott from a sound sleep. He opened his eyes and stared into the overhead eighteen inches from his face. Percy, Teddy, and Roger stopped writing their letters and listened to the muffled disagreement coming from outside, on the Defiant's port beam.

The banter was growing louder and more agitated. Percy threw his pen down on the galley table. "What's going on out there?"

Scott raised his left arm in the air as if to silence Percy. "Shh, quiet. It sounds like a woman, and she's sounds pissed."

The boys listened a little longer. The conversation was coming from the pier and from someone standing above and a bit aft of where Scott lay. Scott broke the silence. "It sounds like Smitty up there and some lady is giving him some shit."

Just then Jack came pounding through the galley's entrance. "Hey, Scotty. It's your mother up there. She's arguing with Smitty, and says she has a right to see you before you go off to sea."

Scott turned in his bunk and sat up with his legs dangling. "Really? Is my father there too?"

Jack came into the galley and sat on the table. "I don't know what your dad looks like but there is a guy standing near a parked car watching the whole thing. That could be him."

Scott shook his head and jumped down from the bunk. Jack put his hand up in front of Scott. "Hold on there, shipmate. Smitty sent me down here to tell you to stay put. There are a couple of cops up there too. I think somebody must have notified the harbor police about the disturbance."

Scott stared at the deck for a moment. Jack watched him closely and knew he was considering going topside despite what Smitty had said. He reached out and put his hand on Scott's shoulder. "Look buddy, we have our instructions and your parents have theirs too. They just can't come out here and demand to see you."

Scott started to put on his sneakers. Jack continued, "In a way, this is like our floating prison. We have our rules that can't be broken. Remember what Murdock said on our first day? If we step out of line, we take the risk of getting put off the ship…and then it's a land-based reformatory." Jack paused. "I don't know about you but I'll take this crap any day rather than go to some big detention center and have to become some badass's girlfriend."

Scott turned and looked at Jack. He reached into his foot locker and pulled out a slip of paper, wrote a few words on it, and handed it to Jack. "Take this topside to Smitty. Tell him to give it to my mom, and tell her I just wrote it."

Jack smiled, "That's my boy." Jack left the crew's quarters and took the slip of paper to Smitty. After a few minutes, the bantering above subsided and Smitty said something that was in line with a parting phrase.

Scott leaned on his bunk with his head resting on his forearms. After a few minutes, Scott climbed back up onto his bunk and turned his back to the open crew space. Percy began to say something but Teddy grabbed him by the shoulder and silently shook his head from side to side.

$\triangledown$

Scott slept all afternoon and woke up to the ship's bell. It was dinner time. Scott lazily started down from his bunk as everyone else began to seat themselves at the galley table. The activity was interrupted by Smitty's head poking through the galley's open entrance. "Hey, Scotty. Can I see you in the captain's cabin for a few minutes before chow? It'll be quick."

Scott rubbed his eyes and jumped down from the bunk. "Yeah…sure, Smitty. I'll be right there."

Smitty disappeared back into the dimly lit passageway. Scott started after him and Jack caught him by the arm. "Be cool, man. Just listen to what he has to say."

Scott nodded his head and followed after Smitty. When he got to the captain's cabin the door was open and Smitty sat behind Murdock's desk.

Smitty looked up and smiled, "Come on in, Scotty. This will be quick. Have a seat, then you can go eat."

Scott took the seat in front of Murdock's desk and dropped into it. Smitty began, "As you know, your mom was here today. She said she needed to see you before your first cruise." Smitty paused and eyed Scott for a moment. Scott had no reaction and blankly stared back at the first mate. Smitty continued, "There are restrictions, so I couldn't let her come aboard or allow you to see her. Visitations are strictly limited under the rules and regulations of the Tall Ship Sailor Program. Do you understand?"

Scott sat stoically and listened to the first mate. He understood full well why Smitty had acted in the way that he did and needed no further explanation. "I understand, Smitty. You don't have to say anything else."

"Well, I wanted to thank you for your cooperation under the circumstances and I also wanted to assure you that you did the right thing." Smitty paused and added, "I do have one question, if you don't mind."

Scott nodded his head. "Sure, what is it?"

"What did you tell your mother in that note Jack gave me? She read the note and stopped arguing immediately. Then, she told me she was sorry to have bothered me. What did you say that caused her to change her mind so suddenly?"

Scott shrugged his shoulders. "I told her I appreciated her coming out to see me but the ship has rules. I also said that this is my home now and I'll be fine. Please go home."

Smitty listened to what Scott had said and understood why his mother had tears in her eyes as she left. Smitty nodded, "Okay, Scott. Thank-you, but one more thing." He narrowed his eyes, "What about the letter I asked each of you to write today? Everyone has passed theirs in except for you."

Scott rose from his chair and answered Smitty on his way out the cabin's door. "You gave it to my mother this afternoon."

CHAPTER EIGHTEEN

Sean and Mary Muldoon left Gloucester Harbor and drove out to the highway that would take them back to their home in Natick, Massachusetts. The car was quiet. Neither spoke for quite some time. The car passed old and beautiful seaside towns, and romantic places of history, that otherwise would cause a passerby to stop and explore, or at least take a picture. Today everything that passed outside of the car's windows was merely a blur. The houses, shops and restaurants went unnoticed. Everything seemed black and white. Mary's beloved son had told her to go home.

Of course, she understood the rules set forth by the court and the Tall Ship Sailor Program but under the circumstances, felt they might bend a little. Just long enough for her to see Scott and maybe hear his voice.

Mary sobbed quietly to herself for the first part of the trip, but once they were on the highway, the tears began to dry. Sean

97

knew better than to say anything. It was Mary's idea to drive out to meet the Defiant and he understood her feeling. Scott was always going to be her little boy and no matter how big or, or smart, or old he got, she would always be his mother. The worry, and caring characteristic of a mother's love, was forever. She had no intention of explaining the real reason for her visit. She only knew she had a limited time on this earth and merely wanted to see her son for what could have been the last time. The doctors were unsure of how long she had left to live but Mary was fearful that by the time Scott had finished his time on the Defiant, it might be too late. She wanted to hear his voice one last time and maybe hear that characteristic laugh of his. She wanted to look into his blue eyes one last time and see that twinkle that always gave her the message that everything would be okay. She realized that was more than she could ask for but hoped for it anyway.

Sean finally broke the silence when he turned onto Highway 90 South. Mary had suffered inside of herself long enough. Softly, he prompted his wife. "Mary, we need to discuss what was in that message Scott wrote to you."

Mary heard Sean's words but had no interest in answering. He waited a few minutes for her reply and asked again. "Mary, what was in that note? Let's get it out into the open. I need to know. He's my son too."

Mary turned and lashed out at Sean. "How dare you say, 'my son too.' You couldn't wait to get him out of the house!"

Sean tried to interject, "Mary, I was only…," Mary cut him off. "Every time he got into trouble, all you could think of was where we could send him until he straightened out. Lucky for us, Judge Lowe was a fair man and saw the good in him…and put him in a program that wasn't too far from home."

Sean swallowed hard. He missed his son too, but wasn't the type to show it. He only wanted what was best for Scott but didn't know how to go about it. The family wasn't well off, by any means, and Sean had neither the ways or means of putting Scott anywhere. Mary was right. They were indeed lucky that Scott's case had been presided over by a judge with good insight.

Sean drove on for a while and pulled into a rest plaza to get a couple of coffees. When he came back to the car, he placed Mary's coffee in the console next to her and continued their drive homeward. Occasionally, he snuck a glance over at his wife who blindly watched the world pass outside her window. The coffee's aroma permeated the car's interior and eventually Mary picked it up and took a sip. She held the cup in both hands rather than return it to the console. Sean realized she was beginning to relax. She was drinking the coffee.

The sign for the Massachusetts turnpike came up and Mary looked at Sean. "You're right. I'm not being fair. You should know what Scott said in that note." Mary took a deep breath and read the note to her husband.

Sean kept a serious face as he drove and paused a moment before he spoke. "Scott knows we are aware of the program's rules and I think he knows better than to think we just took a Sunday drive all the way up to Gloucester to say hello. He's a smart kid, Mary. I think he was trying to diffuse the situation."

Mary put her coffee down. "What do you mean?"

Sean continued. "He knew there was nothing he could do and I'm sure he could hear your discussion with the first mate, so I think he just wanted to get you out of there before the harbor police took you downtown." He glanced at Mary. "You do realize, the harbor police know what kind of ship the Defiant is and what her purpose is? Part of their responsibility is to watch that ship and who's around it, just as prison guards keep an eye on a prison." He paused, "We were out of line Mary."

Mary turned in her seat and looked forward as she brought the coffee cup back to her mouth. She thought for a moment and nodded as she looked through the windshield. "But he said that's his home now. Has he forgotten us? Is he saying he likes living on a damp, dingy old ship rather than being at home with us?"

Sean cracked a smile for the first time since they left Gloucester. "No, he's not saying that, Mary. He's your son, and he knows how you worry. He's trying to tell you he's okay, and for right now," Sean stopped to make a point and glanced at Mary again, "that is his home."

Mary put her hand up to her mouth, "But, he told me to go home!"

"Mary, Scott knows that ship is watched by the local law enforcement. He was getting you out of the way before they decided you had made enough trouble and took you down to the police station for interfering with a state sanctioned incarceration." Sean paused again and added, "He gave you a message to back off for your own good and I'm sure it killed him to look like the bad guy. I'm proud of him for that."

Mary suddenly realized the meaning in Scott's note and began to cry again. "I need to see him, Sean. They don't know how long I have. It could be three months or three years. What can we do?"

Sean thought for a moment. "Well, they're sailing to Plymouth Harbor in Massachusetts. Maybe we can go to the authorities and explain the situation. They might grant us a few minutes with him but are you going to tell him about the A L S?"

Mary shook her head from side to side. "No! I just want five minutes to see him and remember him that way."

Sean nodded his head. "Okay, I'll call the Tall Ship Program on Monday."

CHAPTER NINETEEN

Monday morning at Gloucester Harbor was sunny and warm, but breezy. Today would be the legendary sea trial for the boys as well as the Defiant. The wind was out of the southeast, but steady, and the Defiant had sailed out of the protected harbor without a hitch. The boys were right on their game and Smitty couldn't have been prouder. As the Defiant left the harbor entrance, each sailor remained at his assigned sailing station. Captain Murdock stood behind the helm and steered the Defiant for open sea and away from any boat traffic.

The ocean swells were at about two to three feet with a fair distance between crests and approached Defiant from the starboard side. At first, the gentle rolling motion was very noticeable to the young crew, but everyone on board seemed to adjust as the ship slid over the top of each swell. Murdock scanned the horizon and there were no white caps. He smiled knowing this would be a great sailing experience for his young crew. He called for the mainsheet to be winched in until the mainsail showed no luffing. Jack and Scott were amidships and cranked on the mainsheet winch. As the sail came in closer to the ship, it filled with air and blossomed white against the clear blue sky. The ship responded and heeled over to port as the Defiant picked up more speed.

Murdock heard a series of stutter steps behind him followed by a thump and selective expletives. Wally had lost his balance in the stern when the ship heeled to port, and skidded across the deck until finally colliding with the port side dinghy. Murdock smiled and shouted over his left shoulder, "You okay there, sailor?"

Wally was embarrassed by the slip and collected himself quickly. "Uh, yeah I'm okay, Captain. I didn't expect the ship to heel over so quickly."

Murdock smiled but never turned around, "You'll learn."

Smitty walked the deck and instructed the boys to stay at their sailing stations. Their job was to keep the sails tight. The captain would take care of the rest.

The Defiant had one jib sail flying and the mainsail was hauled in tight. They had finally left the last harbor buoy behind and Murdock requested the foresail to be raised. Jack and Scott hustled over to the foremast's halyard, loosed it from its line cleat, and began to pull. Josh stood by the young sailors and helped ready the sail. The foresail unfurled and rose from its boom, as its sail hoops slid up and along the wooden mast. Defiant picked up more hull speed causing ocean spray to splash over the bow as she plunged through the swells, soaking the boys tending the jib sheets.

Murdock continued on an easterly heading until he felt the crew was comfortable with their new experience at sea. Everyone began to settle down and adjust sheets and lines as the sails called for it, without having to be told. The sight of land diminished with each minute until the coast was barely visible. Murdock tried to keep them on a course they would be sailing two days from now and knew they'd have to be turning south soon. He shouted over to Smitty, "Prepare to come about."

Smitty stood at amidships at the ship's centerline and shouted above the wind. "Prepare to come about!"

The boys knew the order meant that the ship would be changing direction and the two large sails, the mainsail and the foresail booms, would be swinging horizontally across the breadth of the ship. The boys on the bow prepared to un-cleat the jib sail and crouch under it until it flew over them before cleating it to the opposite side. Percy paid special attention to the shifting of the jib.

Murdock glanced at the crew's positions and shouted, "Coming about," as he swung the helm over to starboard to point the Defiant ninety degrees to the direction they had just come from. The sails responded and slowly moved to the opposite side of the ship. The crew was relieved. They had never come about before and were shocked to see the maneuver was a slower and more predictable response than they had figured on. Their biggest concern was to keep the sails tight and not get pushed over the Defiant's railings.

The rolling motion of the ship had increased as the Defiant sailed further out to sea. Because of her new direction, she rode almost bow to stern, along the top of a swell and then slid into its bottom, until the next swell carried her back up to its crest by the port side. The sudden change was evident in some of the boy's reactions.

Roger was in the bow with Teddy and Percy. Teddy noticed Roger began to look a little funny. "Hey, Rog. You okay?" Roger suddenly turned away and leaned over the port side to lose his breakfast. Choosing the windward side was a learning experience for the young sailor. To Roger's surprise, a new swell broke against the Defiant's port side dousing Roger's face at the same time. The impact knocked Roger back from the rail and onto the deck.

Teddy watched Roger's experience and suddenly felt sick himself. Luckily, Teddy chose the starboard side to release his lunch. The ship was sliding down the side of the previous swell and to Teddy, looked as if the ocean was coming up to swallow him. He leaned forward in horror as the ocean's surface rose to meet him and suddenly fell away again. Percy Held Teddy by the back of his belt and had his other hand on a lower shroud line. "I got you, Teddy. Hang on."

Murdock and Smitty watched the antics from the helm and smiled at one another. The boys were figuring it out and what was more important...they were watching out for one another.

The Defiant sailed on for another few hours tacking back and forth, at an angle to the wind. Smitty called it being close-hauled. The boys were getting pushed around as they hadn't acquired their sea legs yet but hung in there and stayed at their stations.

Satisfied with the day's performance, Murdock gave the final course correction and turned into the southerly wind for a gentle turn to port until the wind was at their stern. The ride home would have the wind at their back with following seas.

Smitty walked around to each sailing station stepping around puddles of vomit and loose sailing caps. "Okay boys, we're headed home. You can take a break now. It'll be straight in on this wind, right to the pier. When we get to the harbor entrance, Josh and I will drop the foresail." He looked over at Jack and Scott, "Be ready on the mainsail. That's still your responsibility." Then he shouted to the bow station. "Keep that jib up until we're almost at the pier. Then we'll drop it and dock her with the engine."

The young crew stayed at their stations and relaxed. The gentle rolling of the sea under them and the warm sun on their faces was sleep inducing. The movement of the ship caused by the swells was actually soothing and the schooner surfed the swell's rolling motion instead of fighting it. Some of the boys were lulled to sleep by the motion and rested on the hard, wooden deck or against the wet railings.

Smitty was satisfied with the day and let the crew rest until the first harbor buoy appeared.

▽

Louis stood in the galley with his hands on his hips. He had cooked a hearty dinner for the crew and all they wanted to do was lie in their bunks. He reached up and grabbed his favorite soup spoon and whacked a few of the metal pots hanging from the overhead. "What in hell is this? I slaved all afternoon to make you guys a decent dinner...trying to cook down here while the ship heeled over one way, then another, and you don't even have the decency to come to the table?"

One by one the crew climbed out of their bunks and stumbled over to the galley table. Louis hung the spoon back up. "That's more like it. At least make believe you appreciate it."

The crew sat at the table and merely pushed the food around their plates. Everyone was too tired and sore to eat. Eventually, they began to discuss the day sail. Wally rubbed his shoulder. "I don't know about you guys but I got beat up pretty good out there today. I still don't know how to time it when she heels over like that. I kept getting slammed into the dinghies, and once I almost went over the side."

Teddy chimed in, now that someone else admitted the roughness of the sea. "Yeah, me too. When Murdock came about that first time, I was hanging over the starboard bow and losing my breakfast. I thought for sure I was going in until Percy grabbed me by the belt."

Jack began to laugh at the stories, and soon they all had one or two stories to share. The atmosphere in the room relaxed considerably as everyone began to share their experience of the day sail.

Scott joined in with the table humor. "I don't think I could have winched in the sails one more time. It's a two-man job, and Jack and I were constantly in each other's way." He stopped and looked over at Jack. "Do you realize how many times your elbows caught me in the ribs when we were sheeting in a sail?"

Jack laughed and shook his head. "Yeah, I do. It was about as many times as your elbows got me."

The bantering continued while Louis leaned against his stove and smiled. He nodded his approval as he left the galley. "Clean the place up before you go to your bunks."

Eventually, each sailor cleaned up after himself and retired to his bunk. Jack's bunk was beneath Scott's, so he reached up knocked on its wooden bottom.

Scott answered, "Yeah, what's up?"

Jack murmured. "You okay about yesterday? You know… your mom coming out here and all?"

Scott paused before answering. "Yeah. It was a little tough at the time but I'm good now. I just can't understand why she and my dad drove all the way out here. They know the rules."

Jack was falling asleep and barely heard Scott. "Aww, you know how mothers are," and fell asleep.

Scott continued to stare into the overhead until the day's activity had taken its toll. The crew's quarters were quiet.

CHAPTER TWENTY

Sean Muldoon held the telephone's receiver close to his ear and carried the phone by its cradle with his other hand. The long telephone cord trailed behind him as he paced the living room floor.

Mary Muldoon watched her husband anxiously. "Has anyone answered yet?"

"Yes, Mary. I'm on hold."

Mary pressed her husband further. "Well, what is happening? Are you speaking to the correct department?"

Sean continued to pace and ignored Mary's question. There was no sound inside the phone, no music, just silence. "Sean, it's been five minutes! Maybe you were cutoff."

Sean's patience was growing thin and he was about to admonish his wife when a voice on the other end cut him off. "Corrections. Special Programs Department. Sergeant Braddock speaking, can I help you?"

Sean silently mouthed to Mary that someone was finally on the line. "Yes, hello. This is Sean Muldoon. My son, Scott Muldoon, has been sentenced to the Tall Ship Sailor Program for Youthful Offenses and I have a few questions."

There was a short pause on the other end of the phone and the voice replied. "This is a state sponsored program sir, and is affiliated with the State of Massachusetts Corrections System. I cannot divulge or provide any information about your son over the phone."

Sean was quick to reply, "I understand all of that, but we have extenuating circumstances and need to appeal for special permission to see our son. We're not sure quite how to go about it and that is what this call is about."

The unemotional voice answered rather dryly. "I understand Mr. Muldoon. Most every parent that has a son or daughter in the program has the same interest, and I commend you for that but as I told you at the start of the phone call, I cannot give you any specifics about your son, where he is or may be going. This program is a sanctioned form of incarceration and is subject to all the same rules and regulations as that of a land-based reformatory."

Sean rolled his eyes. "Okay, I got it. I don't need to know any of those things. I just want to see if I can get permission for his mother and me to visit him. His sailing schedule was provided to us at the outset of the sentence. We know where he is and where he's going, but we need to have a planned visit with him."

Sergeant Braddock was skeptical, "What is the name of his ship?"

"He's on the schooner Defiant...out of Gloucester." Sean hoped the sergeant might be relenting.

Braddock again queried Sean. "Do you know the name of his captain and where the ship is now?"

"It's Captain Thomas Murdock and the ship is berthed in Gloucester Harbor. They'll be sailing for Plymouth Harbor on June 21st."

There was another pause on the other end of the phone. "Please provide his sentencing date and judge or prosecutor that presided his case."

Sean answered all of the Braddock's questions and without concurring with Sean's answers, Braddock asked one more question. "What is the reason for your unscheduled visit?"

Sean was beginning to sweat through his shirt. "His mother has recently been diagnosed with A L S, which is life threatening, and she just wants to see him. The doctors can't tell us how fast or slow things may happen but we thought it prudent that she see him before the year's sentence is satisfied."

"What is A L S, Mr. Muldoon?"

Sean explained, "It stands for Amyotrophic Lateral Sclerosis, better known as Lou Gehrig's disease." Sean paused and looked at his wife, and picked his words carefully. "It comes on quickly and may be slow to start or can be quite aggressive. We can't be sure yet."

"Well, Mr. Muldoon, I'm sorry to hear of your wife's sickness. I have looked up the information you just provided, and you are correct about the Defiant's schedule. I will have to run this request by my superiors before I grant your request."

Sean raised his eyebrows as he looked up at the living room ceiling. "Okay, Sergeant. We would appreciate any cooperation you may be able to provide." Meanwhile, Mary was livid. Sean kept signaling her with one hand to remain silent.

The conversation ended with a promise from Sergeant Braddock that the Muldoons would get a phone call regarding the unscheduled visit sometime in the next week.

Sean hung up the phone and closed his eyes while rubbing the back of his head. When Sean didn't offer any more information, Mary asked, "When will they let us know?"

"Some time in the next week, Mary."

Mary began to get upset again. "Why are they giving us so much trouble? I just want to see my only son for about twenty minutes…and maybe for the last time." Mary dropped her head in her hands and began to cry again.

Sean came over and sat next to his wife to console her. "They're good people, Mary. They won't deny a mother that privilege. You'll see." Sean stroked Mary's short brown hair and hoped he was right.

▽

Waiting for the call back from the Youthful Offenses Program was long and painful. Tuesday, June 20th came and went. Thursday morning started slow with Mary sitting at her kitchen table and staring blankly into a cup of coffee. Sean had long since gone to work.

Suddenly, the telephone rang and Mary was shocked back into reality, knocking her coffee cup over as she reached for the telephone. "Hello?"

The voice on the other end of the phone began. "Good morning. This is Sergeant Braddock from the Tall Ship Sailor program for Youthful Offences. Who may I be speaking with?"

"This is Mary Muldoon, Scott Muldoon's mother."

Braddock began, "Mrs. Muldoon, the Youthful Offenses Program authorities have reviewed your information and have found that the information your husband provided on Monday, June 19 was accurate and in line with our records as to who you are. In line with that, I'm afraid we could only grant a very limited time for you and your husband to see your son in Plymouth Harbor. There are also restrictions applied to the visitation. As we mentioned in our last phone call, the ship and crew are on a tight schedule with sailing responsibilities, demonstrations and tours, allowing little opportunity for visitations."

Mary's heart was pounding. "Okay, okay. Whatever…as long as I can see him for fifteen or twenty minutes."

Braddock continued. "The Defiant will be moored in Plymouth Harbor the night of June 21st. You may visit Scott on the eve of Saturday, June 24th at seven PM. The restrictions are that you may have twenty minutes with him at the stern of the ship. There will be deck chairs set up for the three of you and one of Defiant's regular crew will have to be standing by… probably the ship's cook, Louis Baltrone or Captain Murdock."

Mary was elated. "Thank you so very much. We'll be there and make sure not to overstay our allotted time. Thank you again."

Braddock continued, "Scott will not be advised of the visit until you arrive at the pier. We are very serious about not setting any precedents. This program is reformatory based and we must be strict.

Mary replied, "I understand. I'm just grateful for the opportunity."

Braddock added one more thing as a parting comment. "Mrs. Muldoon. Do not attempt to board the ship without the assigned escort and it is our hope you do not disclose to Scott the real meaning of your visit. It could hamper his progress in the program and his work on the ship."

Mary was quick to reply. "Oh, no. I wouldn't do that. I just want to see him and hear his voice."

Braddock thanked her for her time and hung up.

Mary slowly placed the phone back in its cradle, smiled, and began to cry. She knew it may very well be the last time she would see her son.

CHAPTER TWENTY ONE

A cool, damp air filled the crew's quarters in the Defiant's bow while the boys slept. There was a pungent, salty aroma from the sea that seeped into the stillness while the darkness was barely broken by light from a small gas lantern that hung from an overhead timber. The dim light in the cramped sleeping space was just enough to highlight the silhouettes of six bunks and a galley table. Small creaks and groans from Defiant's skeleton worked in unison with the waves that rolled under her keel. In the distance, a fog horn bellowed its lonely warning.

The room was dead quiet. Occasionally, the quiet was interrupted as someone shifted in their wooden bunk or coughed in their sleep. Blue jeans and dirty work shirts hung from the bunk's edges and mingled with blankets meant for its occupant, and sneakers littered the floor around the galley table. The boys had been too tired to pick up the area before lights out and planned on getting that done before Louis came in to start breakfast.

The ship's bell clanged followed by a gruff voice coming up the passageway. It was Louis. "Let's go. Everyone up and outa' those racks. Sun will be up in ten minutes." He walked into the galley and grabbed his favorite soup spoon, running it across every pot and pan that hung from the overhead. When his eyes adjusted to the dim lighting, he saw the unkempt conditions. "What in hell is this? Clothes all over the damn place, sneakers in my galley, shit on the galley table." Louis walked along the stacked bunks and whacked the wooden bunk frames with his spoon. "Get this place cleaned up before breakfast. I ain't cookin' in a shithole like this." Louis turned and threw his spoon across the room and left the crew's quarters.

The boys woke with a start and jumped out of their bunks, bumping into one another as they scrambled to collect their belongings and straighten up the living space. If it wasn't clean in the next fifteen minutes, the idea of breakfast would be forgotten, especially if Louis was nursing one of his famous hangovers.

After a few minutes, the crew's quarters and galley were beginning to take shape. Scott walked over to the galley entrance and peered down the ship's passageway. He turned around to the rest of the boys and smiled. "He's gone back to his cabin. Let's cook breakfast ourselves and make him some of that strong coffee he likes so much. Maybe he'll ease up on us and get us a good supper tonight."

The boys weren't crazy about Scott's idea because that meant they'd have to clean up again but they knew anything was better than to have Louis on the warpath.

Percy made the strong coffee just the way Louis liked it, Jack scrambled eggs and bacon, Scott set the table and the others cleaned up the dirty dishes as Jack made them.

Just as the last plate of eggs was placed on the table, there was a loud slam from down the passageway. Louis was on his return trip to the galley. The boys hurried to their usual places at the table and listened to Louis' heavy footfalls as he neared the galley.

Suddenly, Louis was in the entryway. He was obviously taken aback. The crew's quarters were spotless, breakfast was on the table, the dishes done and put away, and on the small counter, by the gas stove, was a steaming mug of black coffee that said LOUIS on it.

Louis looked around the quiet crew space and nodded his head. The boys waited with anticipation for his reaction. Finally, he spoke. "The coffee better be good or you're all in deep shit." He walked past Percy and patted him on the shoulder before grabbing his mug. Louis raised the mug to his mouth, and before drinking, eyed the boys with one brow raised. Louis took a long pull from the mug and slammed it back down on the small cooking counter. "Not bad. Eat your breakfast. Captain wants to see you guys after chow." Louis turned back toward the stove and poured himself another mug of the hot, black stuff."

▽

It was seven o'clock in the morning and the ship's bell clanged three times…short but loud. Jack was pulling on his work jeans and heard the familiar signal. "Let's go guys. That must be the crew's meeting Louis was talking about. Don't want to be late for that too. We can only hope Louis didn't tell the skipper about the mess he found this morning. That's all we need."

Roger was the slowest of the sailors to dress. "Aw, what are they going to do to us? I'm getting damn tired of the 'hurry up and do it' stuff. It's not like we're getting paid or anything."

Scott finished dressing and walked over to Roger. "You could be in prison, Rog. God knows what would happen to a green twenty-year old in a man's prison, so quit complaining." Scott picked up Roger's dixie cup (sailor's hat) and threw it at him.

Jack was on his way out of the galley entrance and glanced at Roger. "It can only get worse if we get Louis and the captain pissed off at the same time…and if I have to do extra chores because of your lazy ass, there is most definitely going to be a problem."

Roger finished dressing and picked up his hat. "Okay, okay. I'm right behind you guys. Tell the captain not to start without me."

Murdock waited until the entire crew was present amidships and patiently watched Roger stumble across the deck, tucking in his work shirt and trailing untied sneakers.

"Can we start our meeting now Roger, or is there something else you need to do?" Murdock was straight faced and serious.

Roger was unaffected by the captain's comment and didn't catch the sarcasm. "No. I'm good, Skipper. Go ahead."

Murdock raised one eyebrow at the remark but kept stoic. "Well, thank-you. See me after the meeting please."

Murdock continued to glare at Roger until the atmosphere began to get uncomfortable and shifted his attention to the rest of the crew. "Tomorrow we set sail for Plymouth Harbor. I want you guys on deck, dressed in clean work clothes…the issued ones. The light blue work shirts, blue jeans and white sneakers. No mixing and matching stuff like you've been doing. Everyone has to look the same. We're sailing into Plymouth Harbor and people will be watching. I want us to look sharp… like sailors. There will be a lot of people waiting for the Defiant as we are on their schedule as one of the tour ships. This is an event, gentlemen. It's a maritime exhibition of tall ships, sort of like a floating museum.

That means some people are going to want a tour of the ship…like school groups and such. We are expected to do different demonstrations like how to raise the sails and which sails do what. I expect that all of you can talk about those things, by now." He turned his attention to Percy. "You'll be in the bow talking about the perils of the bow team and what happens up there."

There were a few snickers from the crew and Percy's face began to flush but Smitty slapped him on the back and smiled. "You're going to be great, Percy. Some of the things that have happened to you up there have never happened to most people because they have never sailed on a schooner before."

Percy forced a weak smile. "I'll do my best, Smitty."

Murdock let Percy finish and continued. "That's right boys. You guys have already done things on this ship most people will never do. You repaired an ocean-going schooner, helped to refit her to be seaworthy, and even dry sailed her while she was still in dry dock…and I'll tell you now, that took a lot of balls." Murdock paused to let the compliment sink in. "The regular guy on the street may dream about getting on a sailing ship like this but will never even get to set foot on its deck. That being said, an event like Plymouth Harbor, where there will be all kinds of sailing ships, will prompt people to be curious and encourage them to explore." Murdock paused a moment and continued, "These are the people that are going to be our focus. The Tall Ship Sailor program is designed to educate people about the old ways…sailing tall ships. Sailing takes skill and knowledge of the wind and water as well as that of the ship. We want you guys to hold demonstrations all day long about that. Those days will be, Friday and Saturday, and you'll be in your dress whites. Be courteous to the people you are talking to and just talk about what you know and what you've done so far. Smitty will assign people to specific demonstrations and associated times.

Murdock scanned the crew. "Are there any questions?" There were none so Murdock nodded his head and finished. "If you guys perform on the sail to Plymouth, the way you did on our day-sail yesterday, I'll be more than pleased. I've been watching all of you and know you can do this. It's going to be about a ten-hour sail. You'll be tired, so tomorrow night get a good sleep and be ready for Friday."

Murdock started for the aft hatch to go below and turned to look at the boys. "Remember, when we're in port and tied up to the pier, don't leave the ship! Not for any reason." Murdock stared at the boys for a moment so they got the full impact of his meaning, then turned and disappeared down the aft hatch ladder.

CHAPTER TWENTY TWO

June 21ˢᵗ arrived in Gloucester, Massachusetts and the schooner Defiant set sail for Plymouth Harbor, a day's sail to the south. Defiant motored out of the busy seaport propelled by their one diesel engine as there was little room for the schooner to maneuver with a Wednesday morning's boat traffic. Departure from their slip was uneventful and the crew tended their assigned sailing stations anticipating Captain Murdock's order to raise the sails.

Defiant approached the final harbor buoy and headed for open ocean. Seas were rough at four to five feet and approached from the southeast, remnants from a tropical storm the night before. Winds were out of the east and moderate.

The bow team of Percy, Wally and Teddy stood fast at their sailing station and held onto the rigging lines as the Defiant slid over the crest of each swell and drove down its other side, plunging the bow into the oncoming trough of the next swell.

Smitty stood on the starboard rail with one hand on the ratlines and shouted above the wind, "Life jackets!" He turned toward the stern and repeated the order. The boys looked to the foredeck's sea locker where the life jackets were stored and tried to time it so they didn't have to let go of their handholds for too long.

Percy saw the concern on the boys' faces in the bow. "Okay you guys, I'll get 'em. Just hang on until the skipper comes about. He won't raise the jib now. We're headed straight into the wind." Percy let go of his hold on the starboard jib shroud line just as the Defiant's bow rose from the previous swell's trough. The bow suddenly pitched skyward slamming Percy against the sea locker in front of the foremast. Percy got on his hands and knees and desperately grabbed hold of the locker's handle as the bow continued to rise to the crest of the next swell. He knew it would only be a moment before the bow would pitch down again, so he held tight and braced his feet against the bottom of the starboard deck rail. Just as the bow pitched over again, the momentum pulled Percy away from the sea locker and caused him to turn its handle, spilling its contents onto the foredeck. Percy held onto the locker's handle as he rolled about the deck and shouted to his bow team. "Grab the jackets before they go over the side!"

Captain Murdock was at the helm and Smitty stood next to him awaiting orders. Both men watched the bow team struggle to keep their positions. Murdock leaned toward Smitty. "Look at the boys in the bow. They're really putting up a good fight."

Smitty answered as he watched the bow team slide about the deck scrambling for their life jackets. "They are doing that, Skipper." He watched for a moment longer and added, "They do look a little scared though."

Murdock replied as he watched the chaos in the bow. "We're not making much way against these swells with the one prop. The swells are kicking our ass at this slow speed. We're going to have to switch to sails pretty soon."

Smitty nodded. "I agree. We're taking water over the rails amidships too. Jack and Scotty are up to their knees in it when we're in the trough."

Murdock motioned to the stern with a turn of his head. "How's Roger doing in the stern?"

Smitty looked aft to see Roger positioned between the two dinghies with a death grip on their life lines. He smiled, "Roger's okay. Looks a little scared but he's got a good grip on those dinghies."

Murdock smiled, "I have a little surprise for Roger when the seas calm down. Keep him in the stern for now."

Smitty had an idea of what Murdock's plan was and grinned, "Aye, Skipper."

Just then, the Defiant's deckhand, Josh popped his head up from the aft hatch. "Excuse me, Skipper. The Diesel is running pretty hot. It's over speeding every time the stern comes out of the water." Josh's report was due to the swell's effect on the stern of the ship. In heavy seas, the Defiant's stern was the last part of the ship to experience an oncoming swell. Consequently, as the ship rose to the top, the propeller and drive shaft would clear the water and turn faster because of no water resistance.

Murdock nodded at Josh. "Thank you, Josh. Come topside now and get to amidships." He turned to Smitty. "Prepare for a turn to starboard."

Smitty climbed the deck rail once again and shouted to the crew. "Prepare for a turn to starboard! Ready the mainsail!"

Murdock watched the sea ahead. As the Defiant climbed the next swell, he began to turn the helm over to starboard. When Defiant crested the next swell and began her slide down, she was already at an angle to the oncoming swell, now on her port bow. He pushed the engine to full throttle and as she crested the swell ordered, "Mainsail!"

Jack and Scott pulled hard on the mainsail's halyard and Roger came forward from the stern to help. From the distant horizon, the mainsail seemed to rise out of the sea, and moved quickly to the starboard side as it caught the wind. Josh tied off the mainsheet and the ship immediately increased speed, riding up the next swell, and at a forty-five-degree angle to its approach. When Murdock felt the ship surge forward, he turned to Smitty, "Sails only now," and reached down to kill the power to the Diesel.

The Defiant gracefully rode the waves now and pointed due south in the intended direction of travel. She rose at an angle to each oncoming swell cutting its crest with her bow and slid down it's backside into the trough before continuing its climb up the next one. Josh stood by the mainsheet and made corrections as the ship crested the swells to eliminate any luffing in the sail. Before long the ship had settled into a rhythm with the sea and wind.

Murdock called Josh over. "We're pretty smooth now. Go down and check on Louis and the dog…and tell Louis to send up some hot coffee."

Josh looked at the captain in surprise until Murdock let out a small laugh. "Tell him I said that anyway."

Defiant continued to sail a southerly course. The wind was moderate but steady and came across her port side heeling the ship over to starboard as she sailed over the shimmering blue water. Smitty called it 'sailing on a reach.'

In an hour or so, Murdock handed the helm over to Smitty. The seas were calming, and the wind was changing its direction. Now, it approached from more of a southerly direction, so Defiant began to sail into it, but at an angle. Smitty shouted to Josh, to get her close-hauled. Scott and Jack watched as Josh winched in the mainsheet so the ship could sail as close to the wind as possible without luffing the mainsail and stay on the intended course. The boys were learning.

Before going below, Captain Murdock visited every sailing station and talked to the sailors stationed there. He asked them how they were and what they thought of the last two hours. Before moving to the next sailing station, he told the boys what a good job they had done and how he appreciated their efforts, especially in such rough sea conditions.

By noon time, Defiant had been under sail for five hours and was off the coast of Boston, about halfway to Plymouth. Murdock came topside again as Smitty began sending the crew to lunch in shifts of two. "How's it going up here?"

Smitty was at the helm turning it one way, then another, to keep the ship on course. "Everything is good, Skipper. The boys have been tending their stations and making adjustments as I call for them. The seas have flattened out considerably, and the wind has shifted again. It's out of the southeast now, so we're sailing close to it. I have to keep tacking but it's not so bad without the swells."

"Murdock nodded his head. "Call me an hour after the crew finishes their lunch shifts. I have a special assignment for Roger."

Smitty smiled as he watched the sea ahead of Defiant's bow. "Okay, Skipper. That'll be about an hour from now."

Murdock nodded at the first mate and turned to go below again. "Carry on."

The Defiant continued on its southerly heading for Plymouth Harbor. The wind remained steady but was lighter and the sea had calmed considerably. When the seas flattened out and the wind dropped off, Smitty ordered the foresail raised. The maneuver went without incident and the increased sail area increased the Defiant's speed making up for the lighter winds.

Soon, the coast of Norfolk, Massachusetts could be seen in the distance approximately ten miles off the starboard bow. The boys had finished their lunch shifts and it was time to get the captain back up on deck. Smitty called Scotty over to the helm. "Scotty, take the helm while I go below please." The surprise and fear were both evident in Scott's face. Smitty smiled, "Don't worry, you'll be fine. Just keep her straight, watch that compass in front of the helm and keep the sails full. If one of them start to luff, turn the helm a little until the sail fills again. Just keep making those kinds of corrections while keeping us pointed in the same general direction."

Scotty' eyes seemed to pop out of his head but he wasn't going to let Smitty think he was afraid. "Okay. I'll do my best, Smitty."

Smitty patted him on the shoulder. "It's easy. Everyone else will be at their sailing stations and Roger is in the stern, in case Jack needs any help. Just watch the compass and keep the sails full. I'm going below to get the skipper."

Scott managed a nod back at the first mate. Smitty smiled, "Keep an eye out for any ships that come across your bow. Holler if that happens, okay?" Laughing to himself, Smitty turned and disappeared into the aft hatch.

Smitty arrived at Murdock's cabin and knocked once. A voice from within answered, "Come in."

Smitty walked in and smiled. "Scotty's got the helm. We have clear, flat seas, and no ships in sight."

Murdock rose from his chair. "Where is Roger?"

"He's assisting Jack amidships." Then Smitty cautiously asked, "Are you really going to do this, Cap?"

Murdock headed for the cabin's door. "Absolutely! First of all, it's tradition and second, Roger has to learn some respect when speaking to his captain. His behavior at the crew's meeting this morning made up my mind as to who was going to get the bucket of water."

Smitty came up from the aft hatch followed by Captain Murdock. They walked over to the helm and watched Scotty as he steered the Defiant over the flat, blue sea.

Murdock put his hand on Scotty's shoulder. "You're doing a fine job, son. Just keep her pointed straight." Murdock looked over Defiant's starboard side. "See that spit of land out there, Scotty?"

Scotty squinted through the haze and nodded.

Murdock continued, "That's Norfolk. When you're steering the ship, always look for landmarks. It'll help you navigate." Then he turned to amidships and shouted, "Roger, I need you back here."

Roger was sitting on the deck and leaning comfortably against the port railing. He rose slowly as if it was an effort, and sauntered back to the helm area. "Yeah, what's up?"

Murdock handed him an old wooden bucket with a line of rope attached to its handle. "I need you to get me some water. Put your life jacket back on and go back to amidships and drop the bucket over the side. Bring the bucket back to me when it's full. Can you do that?"

Unbeknownst to Roger, Smitty was already tying off the end of the rope to the stern railing. Roger took the bucket from Murdock. "You called me over here just to get a bucket of water?"

Murdock nodded his head staring blankly at the lad. "Yup. This bucket is very special to me. I've had it since I was a sailor…like you. I don't want to lose it and I know you're pretty strong and that you won't let it go. Just drop it over the side and get the water please."

Roger shrugged his shoulders and walked over to the starboard railing not realizing the rope on the bucket was tied to the stern of the ship. He calmly reached over the railing while holding the heavy wooden bucket by its handle and dipped it into the sea. Immediately, the water rushing by the ship at, ten knots, grabbed the bucket from Roger's hand. Roger sensed the sudden pull and tried to resist it, refusing to let it go, and held tighter. Almost instantly, Roger went over the side following the wooden bucket into the cold Atlantic Ocean. He didn't have far to fall since the ship was already heeled to starboard.

Murdock smiled and calmly said, "Man overboard."

The Defiant continued to sail on and Scotty looked wild with surprise. Murdock turned to Scotty. "Steady as she goes, Scotty. We'll reel him in once he gets behind the ship."

Roger instinctively held onto the bucket. It looked as if the ship was leaving him behind. He held onto the bucket tighter than he had held anything before. The small sea swells slapped him in the face and water went up his nose and into his mouth as he gasped for air. The boy was terrified.

Finally, the line of rope reached its end and became taut, dragging Roger and the bucket behind the ship. The Defiant, literally towed Roger through the water as long as he held on to the bucket. Roger coughed and spit seawater. "Help! Stop the ship! Don't leave me! Please! Stop the ship!"

The rest of the crew watched Murdock's face. There was no emotion. He watched Roger struggle with the bucket, making his own wake inside of the one Defiant left behind. The boys began to look at one another with concerned expressions.

Finally, after Roger went under a few more times, Murdock sent Smitty and Josh, to the stern. "Reel him in."

As Roger neared the Defiant's stern, Smitty yelled out to him. "Hey Roger, this is how we troll for sharks. We drag the bait behind us, just like this." The entire crew watched in horror but at the same time, was on the verge of laughter. As the two regular crew hoisted Roger out of the sea, Josh looked the boy in the eye as he tried to catch his breath. "That was just like being shark bait kid, glad you made it back aboard," and so, a new knick-name was born.

Murdock took the helm from Scotty and told him to take Roger below for a change of clothes. "Hey Scotty, get Louis to give him some hot coffee. He'll need that to warm up."

Roger walked, wet and frozen, to the aft hatch and never gave the captain the satisfaction of seeing his face, so Murdock stopped him. "Roger!"

Roger stopped to listen, not looking up. Murdock continued. "In the future, when you address an adult or a superior, I suggest you choose your words wisely." The captain paused and then continued when the boy looked up. "From now on, be on time, tuck in your shirt, and tie your shoelaces." Murdock paused and mentioned one more thing to the boy before he disappeared down the aft hatch. "Get some dry clothes on and a cup of something hot. Be back up on deck in thirty minutes."

There was no emotion on Roger's face. He was shivering badly and nodded his head as if to agree. Then he turned away from the captain and followed Scotty to the aft hatch on his way to the crew's quarters.

Smitty stood next to the captain with pursed lips. Murdock turned toward him and calmly said. "Learning the hard way is tough for everyone involved. One good thing is that a lesson like that will never be forgotten."

CHAPTER TWENTY THREE

Captain Murdock stood behind the ship's helm and glanced at his watch. Then he scanned the horizon and looked at the sails. It was late afternoon and the wind was getting lighter. If they were going to get the ship into Plymouth Harbor before nightfall, they had better make some time.

Murdock looked over to Smitty standing by the starboard beam. "Smitty, fly the jib. We have to make some time. It's getting late in the day."

Smitty climbed up on the starboard railing and pulled himself up by the ratlines. He shouted forward to the quiet bow team of Percy, Wally and Teddy. "Bow team, on your feet! Prepare to fly the jib sail!"

The boys in the bow thought they had it made at this point. Although, they had endured a tough day on the bow, they hadn't had to fight with the jib all day. They sat on the deck and leaned against the bow railings and relaxed. They were sore from being knocked around earlier in the day and had hoped to cruise into Plymouth without a call for the jib. The boys jumped to their feet at Smitty's order, somewhat surprised.

Percy looked aloft to see the pennant flying at the top of the foremast. He noticed the wind was still coming from the southeast. He made a mental note to himself. *The jib is going to fill on the starboard side. Better get myself over to port.* "Guys, get ready on the halyard and jib sheet. She's gonna' fly over the starboard side." The boys adjusted their positions and waited for Smitty's next order.

Smitty waited for the boys to get into position and shouted, "Fly the jib!"

The tired bow team hoisted the jib sail as fast as they could. The triangular sail rose from its sail locker at the prow of the ship and began to fill with air making a loud snapping sound as the sail went taut. Percy timed the jib opening perfectly and tied it's sheet off to a cleat on the foremast.

The Defiant surged forward as a result of the extra sail area. The ship heeled a small degree over to starboard and cut through the calm sea majestically. Murdock smiled to himself as he was reminded of that old, familiar feeling…the one that a sailor felt when all the sailing conditions were in harmony. Defiant seemed to glide along the ocean's surface, propelled by an invisible force accompanied by a slight rolling motion under the ship, that enhanced her momentum. It was a tall ship sailor's moment.

The boys felt the phenomenon at each of their stations. It was a moment to stop and consider what was happening right under foot. The ship's cruising speed climbed above normal yet there were no blustery winds to deal with and the power was free…no fuel required. The ride was smooth and comfortable and all they had to do was watch their sails and watch for other ships.

Smitty interrupted the serenity. "Scotty, get up into the crosstrees and bring the glasses with you. Keep an eye ahead of the bow...port and starboard, and tell me what you see." Smitty knew they were getting close to the entrance of Cape Cod Bay and wanted Scott to give him an unprejudiced opinion of the up-and-coming landmarks. He looked aft and called Roger. "Take Scotty's place amidships with Jack."

Scott ran over to one of the equipment lockers and grabbed a pair of binoculars. He hung them around his neck and began his climb up the port ratlines.

Smitty watched from the starboard beam. "That's right Scott. Take your time and make every step a deliberate one. Don't watch the water passing below...it'll only throw off your balance."

Scott was a little nervous. The only other time he'd climbed these ratlines was when the ship was in dry dock. They hadn't been afloat or underway. Now, he tried to focus. *Don't look down*, he told himself. He continued his climb toward the crosstrees near the top of the mainmast, picking his handholds as he went. He felt the ship moving beneath him and the wind encircling his exposed body. At first, it was unnerving but he pushed on. Scotty climbed higher and began to get the feel and rhythm of the ship. The light, cool wind became a welcome visitor and the nervousness disappeared.

Scott arrived at the crosstrees, about forty feet above the deck. He was happy to see it and welcomed a place to sit. He lifted himself up by one of the shroud lines and swung one leg over the tiny lookout station. When he felt secure, he wrapped the other leg under it and gently tightened his legs around the horizontal structure. He let his body feel the ship's roll and went with it. The sway and roll of the ship were much more pronounced up in the crosstrees and Scott squeezed his legs tighter as he straddled them.

Still holding the shroud line, he reached down and grabbed the binoculars and raised them to his face. Focusing the lenses, he held the binoculars in one hand and scanned the sea ahead of Defiant's port bow. A tiny spit of land seemed to reach out toward him. It was far off to the southeast but it was land. He dropped the binoculars to his lap and shouted down to Smitty. "I see sort of a hook of land off the port bow…like it's reaching out into the sea."

Smitty looked over to Murdock at the helm and smiled. "I think he's got Provincetown."

Murdock nodded as he steered. "Probably Race Point Light."

Smitty waved back to Scotty and pointed to starboard, "Now starboard." Scott carefully brought the glasses back up to his face. Once again, he focused the lenses and saw what looked to be a lighthouse. He shouted back down to Smitty. "I think I see a tall smokestack and a lighthouse."

Smitty smiled again, as Murdock responded. "That's Plymouth Light. Sounds like we're approaching the channel. We should be seeing a channel marker buoy soon. Tell him to watch for that and brown water. Once he sees that, tell him to come down. We'll be able to see the other landmarks from down here."

Smitty relayed Murdock's instructions up to Scotty. The young sailor was beginning to feel the chill of the open ocean but tolerated the discomfort since it was a new and exciting assignment. He felt he could put up with anything for another hour.

Scott shouted back to Smitty, "What is brown water?"

Smitty and Murdock glanced at each other and smirked. Smitty cupped his hands about his face and replied. "It means shallow water…sandbars. That's why the water looks brown."

Thirty minutes passed and Scott was getting cold and stiff up in the crosstrees. He shouted down to the first mate.

"Yo, Smitty! I see brown water off the starboard bow and a channel marker just outside it. The marker is about 1000 yards to starboard."

Murdock heard Scotty's report and acknowledged it before Smitty could relay it to him. "We're in the channel. I see the marker buoy. That buoy is a tricky one. The shallows are closer to it than you think and the current can push it toward the coast. We'll keep this course as long as the wind accommodates us, and come about to starboard when we get to the harbor entrance."

Smitty shouted back up to Scott, "Good job, Scotty. Come on down. We have our bearings now." Scott waved to Smitty to signal he understood. Smitty saw the signal and added, "Loosen up a little before you come down. Stretch your legs, arms, and fingers. You've been sitting there for about an hour. You don't want to be stiff climbing down those ratlines."

Once again, Scotty signaled that he understood Smitty's instructions.

Defiant fell off a few more degrees to starboard and sailed due south for another hour. The new course allowed for the wind to come across the port side with the opportunity of increased speed, and visual contact with the Massachusetts coast. It also allowed Murdock to start his approach toward Plymouth Bay. They would have to make the turn into the bay before getting to Plymouth Harbor to dock.

The boat traffic became busy once inside Cape Cod Bay. It was approaching 5:00 PM and fishing boats, freighters, and pleasure craft were all heading for the harbor. It was dinner time. Murdock shouted over to Smitty. "Lookouts!"

The busy approach to the harbor required lookouts positioned on the bow, amidships and in the stern. Since the crew was still at sailing stations one of the bow team members was responsible to watch for traffic dead ahead of the ship. Jack and Scott watched for vessels approaching from either side, and Roger looked aft for anything approaching the stern. Maritime rules are that a ship under sail has the right-of-way, although assumptions are made, and right-of-way rules are no longer of consequence.

It was mostly the larger vessels Murdock worried about. The freighters just keep coming no matter who's right-of-way it is. They give the smaller ships a few blasts on their horns never making a course change or reduction in speed. This part of the bay was strictly a defensive sailing area.

Murdock kept the Defiant on a course parallel to the narrow causeway that separated Duxbury Bay and Cape Cod Bay, and about a half mile off its beach. The wind was still strong but getting a little puffy because they were between two land masses. He summoned Smitty to the helm. "I have Plymouth Light at about five hundred yards off our starboard bow. The wind is still out of the southeast so I'm gonna' try to beat that freighter approaching us from a quarter mile off our port bow. I want to get the Defiant in there before he gets close to the entrance. If we get stuck behind him and he slows for harbor traffic, we're going to have to drop the sails and go back on the engine."

Smitty watched the freighter as it approached off their port bow. "You have the right-of-way, Skipper." Smitty paused as he watched the oncoming freighter. "If he doesn't slow once we get in front of him, he could run right up our ass. You know how those guys are."

Murdock nodded. "Yes, I do. So I'm going to come about as soon as we get past Plymouth Light and the channel marker. We still have plenty of blue water (deep water) there. It's going to be a tight and fast turn so let the sails out further when I begin my turn into Plymouth Bay."

Smitty pursed his lips. "You realize you're risking a jibe situation and the boys haven't experienced that yet."

Murdock continued to watch the oncoming freighter and the channel marker buoy. He knew a jibe was a possibility if too much of the wind was allowed to get behind the sails. A sudden puff could cause the mainsail to violently blow the mainsail across the beam of the ship and over to the port side. The action would almost instantaneously heel the ship over from starboard to port and drop the port beam toward the water, knocking the crew around with dramatic results.

Murdock looked into Smitty's eyes. "I do realize that, Smitty. That's why I want you to let the mainsail and the foresail out almost until they're at ninety degrees to the ship. That way, we'll keep the wind in the turn. As I start to bring the ship around, begin sheeting in to half that distance so the wind doesn't get behind the sails. As soon as the turn into Plymouth Bay is complete, drop the foresail. We'll leave the jib and mainsail up until we see what the harbor traffic is like."

Smitty nodded his head as he watched the Defiant approach the channel marker. He turned to the crew and gave the order. "Prepare to come about. Sails out to starboard."

The freighter kept coming on. There was no question she had spotted the Defiant but it appeared she hadn't slowed yet. The bow team saw the big freighter and its massive bow that seemed pointed right at them. Wally looked at Percy. "That ship is coming right at us. By the time we finish this turn he's going to be right on our ass."

Percy watched the oncoming ship and had his concerns as well. "We have the right-of-way and we are under sail. The skipper knows what he's doing."

The Defiant passed Plymouth Light and as soon as she was abeam of the channel marker Smitty shouted, "Coming about to starboard. Sheets out on the mainsail and foresail. We'll be running before the wind."

Jack and Scott let the mainsail out as the Defiant showed her stern to the wind. Josh and Roger followed with the same action for the foresail. The Defiant's forward momentum brought them around and as the ship completed its turn into the harbor, Smitty once again climbed up on the port rail and ordered, "Bring the sheets in by half their travel. Keep them tight. Ready to drop the foresail."

The turn was executed perfectly. Smitty shouted above the wind and harbor noise. "Sheet in the foresail and drop it." Josh and Roger were moving fast and got the foresail down and secured to its boom.

The boys' focus was on the freighter now. Wally had been correct. The freighter was bearing down on the Defiant with alarming speed. It was a clear case of harassment at this point. The big ship began to blow its horn...five short, continuous blasts followed. There was a momentary pause and then five more short blasts bellowed from the freighter. Her bow was now about one hundred feet astern of Defiant. Everyone looked worried except Murdock and Smitty.

Smitty was closest to Scott and noticed the concern on his face. He smiled at Scott. "Don't worry. We're in the harbor entrance and he's almost there too. He knows he's going to have to slow any moment now or he'll have the Harbor Master to answer to. He's just putting on a big show to let us know we cut him off."

Almost as soon as Smitty finished speaking, the freighter began to slow and began to fall behind. Smitty smiled and winked at Scott. The entire crew was relieved.

Smitty walked back to the helm area and nodded at Murdock. "Nice turn, Skipper. Right on the money."

Murdock still looking ahead of the Defiant's bow chuckled. "Yeah, thanks. Let's hope the freighter doesn't follow us to our slip.

CHAPTER TWENTY FOUR

The Defiant ran before the wind with her mainsail out half of its total travel and the wind was light to moderate. She was making her way to the end of Plymouth Bay and Murdock spotted Bug Light (Duxbury Pier Light) off the port bow. The freighter they had cut off had slowed for harbor speed, and began to fall behind the Defiant.

Jack stood next to Scott as they watched the Massachusetts coast close in on them from three sides. "See that peninsula coming out of the southwest…behind the lighthouse?"

Scott looked over the port railing and past Duxbury Light and nodded his head.

Jack smiled. "Plymouth Harbor is just the other side of that. They are expecting us so there is already a slip assigned to us. The skipper will sail for that and moor us up for the night. We're almost there."

Then the call from the port railing came, "Prepare to come about, port side."

Another minute passed and the call was, "Coming about, port side." Defiant began a long slow turn to port as she passed west of the lighthouse. The mainsail stayed in position except now the wind was crossing over the ship's port side. Murdock shouted over to Smitty as he stood on the railing. "We'll keep her on a beam reach until we close on the pier. At two hundred yards drop the mainsail and take her in on the jib sail."

Smitty nodded and replied, "Aye, Skipper." Then he turned and shouted to Josh stationed near the foremast. "Josh, come aft and prepare to drop the mainsail." Josh hurried over to help Jack and Scott. They still had some time but would have to work fast when the order came. The big gaff rigged sail would need to be sheeted in when Murdock made the turn toward the pier. As soon as the huge sail closed on the center of the ship, it would be dropped and folded over on its boom.

The ship sailed into Plymouth harbor for a few more minutes and Murdock shouted to Smitty. "There's our pier!"

Smitty jumped up on the port rail again. "Sheet in on the mainsail and drop it."

Jack and Scott pulled furiously on the mainsheet as Murdock angled the boat a little to spill some wind from the sail. The pulley squeaked and groaned with the pressure from the wind, and when the sail was directly over the ship, Josh instructed Jack and Scott to drop it. Moving as fast as they could, the two boys ran over to the mainmast and let the halyard loose from its cleat, dropping the mainsail. Smitty's attention was on the bow team, but shouted to Jack and Scott first. "That's good enough for now. Just secure the sail to the boom. We'll furl it and tie it to the boom when we get in."

The Defiant kept its way on for a few more minutes as Murdock steered for the pier. Smitty shouted to the bow team. "We're taking her in on the jib. When we get close to the pier, we'll drop the jib and let her coast in. Be ready on the bow lines to tie her up."

A captain should be familiar enough with his ship to know how long his vessel will keep way on after the sail is dropped. In this case, Murdock still had the small jib flying. As expected, the Defiant gradually slowed but continued toward the pier. The wind came over the starboard stern after Murdock's last turn and the bow team anxiously awaited the captain's order to drop the jib. The Defiant had slowed appreciably and was about fifty feet from its slip when the order came, "Drop the jib."

The bow team dropped the small sail and with the last amount of ship's momentum left, Murdock angled the schooner up to the pier. Smitty shouted from his perch on the railing. "Ready on the starboard bow lines!" The ship coasted in slower and closer and the next order was, "Lines ashore!" He turned aft and shouted to Roger in the stern. "Stern lines, now!"

Line handlers patiently waited on the pier to receive the Defiant. They caught the mooring lines as the boys threw them, and secured the ship. The Defiant and her new crew had completed their first cruise. They had made it.

▽

The boys were tired but proud of the day's sail. They were sore from the heavy seas earlier in the day and most of the way to Boston, but they had prevailed. Each sailor had remained at their posts and followed the first mate's instructions and accomplished a forty-five-mile sail over open ocean. They experienced coming about in heavy seas and also the wondrous feeling of 'sailing the troughs.' They had witnessed navigation by landmarks and the importance of marker buoys, and to finish off the day, experienced right-of-way threats first hand.

Some of it had been downright frightening and some of it enlightening.

Louis had cooked up a big meal but the crew was too tired to eat. They sat at their galley table, ignoring their food and shared their experiences of the day. The boys had worked so hard to get to Plymouth where they would secretly plan their getaway for an unsupervised night on the town, but for now, their thoughts remained on the day's sail.

Percy shook his head back and forth. "I never thought we'd get out of Gloucester Harbor this morning. Those swells that came over the bow were huge. I didn't think we'd ever be able to raise the jib under those conditions."

Teddy laughed, "I know! I couldn't find enough handholds to grab onto and when I did, they were wet and slippery."

Wally smiled and said, "Well, thank god for Percy. When he wasn't rolling around the foredeck, he at least got us our life jackets."

Percy came back, "Yeah, and I have a hundred bruises and twice as many splinters in my ass to prove it. You're welcome, you bastards."

The banter was all in good fun and a feeling of bonding as a crew grew stronger. Not just a group of young men who had known each other before but as an organized team with a specific goal in mind.

The room began to grow quiet and Wally glanced down the length of the table to see a quiet Roger. He couldn't resist the temptation to mention Roger's 'out-of-the-ship experience.' If it didn't come up now, it would come up later. "I think the highlight of the day was when Roger took the bucket over the side." He glanced at Roger, "What do you think, Sharkbait?"

The entire room exploded in laughter. Roger shook his head from side to side and waved Wally off as if to dismiss the thought. Teddy added, "Yeah, that fits! Smitty did say that's how we troll for sharks."

Scotty and Jack sat at the end of the table adjacent to Roger. Scotty, eyed Roger and reminded him. "I warned you about showing the captain some respect. I learned that on my first day aboard. Murdock is not the kind to mess with. Now you have a nickname."

Roger said nothing. He just smirked at Scotty and let the boys have their fun. The nicknames and possible scenarios began to build, but Roger had learned his lesson. He just sat at the table and frowned, as the crew had their fun at his expense.

Eventually, Jack had enough. "Alright, cool it! Roger screwed up today and paid the price for it. Do any of you have any idea of what that must have felt like being towed behind a ship at sea? Roger didn't realize the line was attached to the stern. Murdock set him up. And if that wasn't enough, he really was shark bait. There are sharks out there, and one could have been following him for all we know." Jack paused as the boys had stopped laughing and listened open-mouthed, as Jack spoke. "The captain took a real chance in teaching our shipmate here a lesson…but it could have backfired."

The room was uncomfortably quiet for a minute and Jack continued. "You guys seem to forget. This is nothing but a floating reformatory. We're here to pay a debt to society and if one of us steps out of line with the regular crew, we're going to pay for it. Our sentence is to learn…the hard way."

Finally, Percy broke the silence. "Hey Scotty, what in hell did you do to get chosen to climb the ratlines while we were under sail?"

Scotty shrugged his shoulders. "I don't know. Maybe I showed my inexperience or nervousness with it when we were in dry dock. Like Jack said, it's our mission to learn…however and whatever it takes."

Jack added, "Yeah, it could have been that, but they let you steer the ship when Roger was in the water. I think they see something in you, Scotty."

The room went quiet again, but only momentarily. Wally reminded everyone about the freighter. "How about that freighter that came down on us? I couldn't believe Murdock pulled that one off."

The freighter scenario created a whole new conversation and everyone, including Roger, offered their opinions or possible outcomes. The bantering continued but this time it was about the crew as a whole and how they would handle it... together.

CHAPTER TWENTY FIVE

The morning of Thursday, June 22 found the crew's quarters dark, quiet and accommodating six sleeping sailors. As usual, the sun began its climb out of the east, rising above the sea's horizon in a red and orange ball. At first, the ball appeared as a rounded glow above the sea's horizon. Slowly, as if cautiously, the glow became circular and finally took the shape of a sphere as it cleared the flat horizon. Its rusty colored rays of light reached across a pale blue sky and reflected against a huge expanse of dark water, as if reaching toward the tiny harbor. It was dawn in the port city of Plymouth, Massachusetts. The ever-brightening fingers of light found the Defiant moored to its pier and tried to find their way through the schooner's wooden hull. The ship resisted the intrusion and the crew's quarters remained a dark space inside the ship's bow.

Suddenly, the lantern hanging above the crew's galley table came on accompanied by loud banging. Louis, Defiant's cook, beat the pots and pans that hung from the galley's overhead timbers with his large soup spoon. "Everybody up! Let's go, let's go, let's go. Out of those racks!"

Louis walked by the galley table and began pulling blankets off the people they covered. In some cases, he shook a leg or an arm that hung off of a bunk. In any case, he made his presence known. There were moans and grumbling coming from bunks that moments before had been dead silent. Louis replied to the complaints with more raucous banter. "I don't want to hear it. You guys have work to do before breakfast."

Some of the boys slid out of their racks feet first, hitting the deck with a thud while others seemed to move in slow motion. Louis turned up the gas on the galley's lantern and the room brightened, causing everyone to squint as they tried to find their clothes. There was bumping and stepping on other people, until the sleepy sailors began to find their way across the tiny berthing space.

Louis started the gas stove and the aroma of freshly brewed coffee began to permeate the entire area. "You guys get a couple of slugs of this into ya' and get up on deck. Check the bow and stern lines, open the fore and aft hatches, and swab the deck. When that's done get back down here for breakfast. You got twenty minutes. After breakfast we gotta' get her ready for tomorrow's guests and you guys have to get your assignments for the day." The boys stumbled all over the crew's quarters as they rushed to dress and get their cup of coffee. The clock that hung over the galley entrance said 5:30 AM.

One by one the boys filed out of the crew's quarters. It wasn't long before they realized there was more to the increased amount of stumbling and loss of coordination. They had been sailing for the most part of the week, including yesterday's eleven-hour day sail. Apparently, the boys had finally got their sea legs and were accustomed to walking on uneven decks and adjusting to the roll of the sea's swells as the ship moved over them. Now in a quiet harbor, their inner balance had been influenced, and the crew had a hard time walking without anticipating the ship's movements.

Louis watched the boys file out of the ship's galley. "You guys look like you've been drinking for Christ's sake." He singled out one of the boys. "Percy, hold onto something if you can't walk straight."

Wally was closest to Louis and replied. "It's all of us…not just him, Louis."

Louis laughed and bent over forward with his hands on his thighs. "That'll teach ya' to sit around after a day of hard sailin.' You guys finally got your sea legs and just sat around last night before lights out. Your balance is off…that's all. It's goin' to feel funny walking on a level deck that ain't movin' but you'll shake it off after a while." Louis went back to preparing breakfast, laughed again and said aloud, "Rookie sailors."

Up on deck the boys went about their chores. They were amazed to see the number of standing puddles of old vomit that had mixed with seawater. The odor was horrendous and the appearance, just as bad. The idea of breakfast soon became a memory as they swabbed the deck.

Jack spoke to Scotty as they worked. "It must have been pretty rough up in the bow. What a mess up there!"

Scott smiled, "Yeah, I noticed. I'm surprised Smitty or the captain let us go below without cleaning it all up."

Jack replied. "That was probably another lesson for us. They probably wanted us to see what happens if we don't take care of it. Besides, do you think any of us were in any kind of shape to do anything once we got moored up?

Scott nodded, "I know. We barely had enough strength to get below."

Jack reminded Scott. "Remember, we gotta' have a crew's meeting about Saturday night. It's already Thursday and Smitty is taking us off the ship tomorrow night, so we have to get everything finalized tonight."

Scott smiled. "I'll start passing the word."

▽

The day promised to be a busy one. After breakfast, the decks had to be swabbed a second time and there were some painting tasks that needed attention. Everyone was busy cleaning the ship, above and below decks. Louis pulled out the ceremonial pennants and some of the boys had the opportunity to raise them to the top of the fore and main masts. It was a statement to the maritime community that the ship was in the harbor for a purpose.

Around 11:00 AM, Murdock came up from the aft hatch followed by Smitty, and rang the ship's bell three times. The crew had assembled amidships in record time, probably a result of Roger's experience behind the ship the day before.

Murdock began, "Welcome to Plymouth Harbor boys. Now you can say you've made the same entrance as the Mayflower did four hundred years ago when she landed the pilgrims here at Plymouth Rock." Murdock pointed north in the direction of the tourist site. "After lunch clean-up is complete. You each have different assignments for Friday and Saturday. Guests will be coming aboard to learn about life on a sailing ship and how it sails. These people are tourists and are to be treated with the utmost of respect. Most of them will be here out of curiosity and some of them will have read about the Tall Ship Sailor Program. They don't know anything about you personally or why you're here, so please do not feel defensive. Be friendly and sociable. Just talk about what you know and if you can't answer a question, tell them you just completed your first cruise yesterday, and talk about that. The mission of this program is to show society about the opportunities for youth rehabilitation. They'll be looking at you guys with a critical eye so show them the kind of men you really are. Make us proud."

The crew took lunch together as the ship was moored and there was no need for shifts. Louis busied himself about the galley while the boys ate and engaged in small talk. Finally, the moment came that Jack and Scott had been waiting for. Louis turned and addressed the table of sailors. "Okay, boys. Finish your lunch and clean the place up before you go topside. I have some work of my own to get done. I'll be in my cabin and I'll be listening to what's going on up here. No screwin' around... understand? You gotta' get topside to get your assignments for tomorrow and Saturday. Smitty will be waitin' for ya' by the aft hatch in thirty minutes." Louis gave the group one last serious stare, turned, and left the galley.

The boys watched in silence as Louis left. After a minute or two, Scott got up and went to the galley entrance. There was no sign of Louis. He turned to the watchful eyes of his crewmates and gave them a thumbs up.

Jack began, "Guys, we're going to discuss our sneak-away tonight after dinner. It's our quiet time so the regular crew will leave us alone. We discussed this before we left Gloucester, but I want to go over it again tonight just to make sure everything goes smooth. Remember, they can never know we left the ship. That means we can't leave any clues to show that we left and we have to get back here before they do." Jack paused a moment for effect then reminded the crew. "Don't talk about it. They'll overhear you."

Everyone smiled and nodded in agreement.

▽

After lunch the crew meandered to the Defiant's stern and met Smitty by the aft hatch. Smitty held a clipboard in his hand and seemed to be checking things off a list. Eventually he looked up at the group of sailors. "Everyone here?" A quick glance confirmed the crew's attendance. "Good. These are your assignments for the next couple of days. I'm going to have you at the sailing stations you sailed here with. I don't need three guys in the bow at once, so Percy, Wally and Teddy will take turns, two at a time. Talk about when to fly the jib, how you do it, show them the different lines, pulleys and cleats. Tell them about your experience coming out of Gloucester in heavy seas. Make it a fun thing. When one of you isn't on the bow, I want that person by the aft hatch to give a tour of the ship below decks."

Smitty checked off more items on his clipboard. "Jack and Scott are at amidships and will discuss the lines, their names and what they're used for in raising the mainsail and foresail." He paused and looked at Scott. "Scotty, you're the only one so far to have been up in the crosstrees, under sail...talk about climbing the rigging and what it looks like from up there, and how you sighted those landmarks coming into Cape Cod Bay."

Roger sat quietly near the helm awaiting the worst. Smitty turned and smiled at the quiet sailor. "Roger, you don't have to talk about the bucket ordeal. That's ship's business. Talk about the mooring lines, how to pull away from a pier or coast into one, and the timing required to heave those mooring lines. You can also talk about quirking and caulking and how all of you had to lay under the ship for two weeks stuffing the gaps in the hull's planking."

Smitty finished the assignments and reminded the boys. "You'll be in your dress whites...and look smart. No slouching or laying around. Stay at your stations until we have no visitors, or eight bells is rung. When it's the end of shift we'll pull up the gangway plank and lock the deck rail." He looked at the quiet group. "Any questions?" No one said anything so Smitty quickly added, "Okay, good. Be on deck at 8:00 AM in clean uniforms and ready to accept the public. You'll do fine."

After the meeting, Smitty dismissed the boys to their quarters to rest up, get their clothes in order, and think about what they wanted to say during their presentations. Most of them thought about their plans on getting off the ship Saturday night. Everyone was excited and anxious, but no one rested.

CHAPTER TWENTY SIX

Louis stood with his back to the galley's stove and watched the boys eat their dinner. It was quiet for once. There was none of the usual banter, insults, or goofing around. Everyone just ate their dinner or pushed their food around their plate. *Something is up,* he thought. *I cooked them one of their favorite meals and they don't seem to care.* Louis watched a few more minutes, then in his usual loud and annoying tone asked, "What's wrong with you guys? I finally cooked you spaghetti and meatballs and no one is eating."

Percy looked up. "Uh, It's good Louis. Just thinking about tomorrow. You know...meeting the public and everything?"

The others took Percy's cue and looked up, nodding their heads in agreement. Scott added with a smirk, "We're not used to all that cleaning either, and trying to iron our dress whites was a nightmare. I thought that was the cook's job."

Scott's comment took Louis off balance. His face began to turn red as he reached for his large soup spoon. "You know Scotty, that's a shitty thing to say. I might only be the cook, but I'm the guy responsible for what you eat, so be careful, sailor."

Scott smiled back at Louis. His distraction had worked. "Sorry, Louis. I was only fooling with you."

Louis hung up the soup spoon, glared at Scott, and nodded his head. "Yeah, well supper is over. Clean the place up and then you guys can have your quiet time. No one goes topside tonight." Louis turned and walked out of the galley.

Scott rose from the table and walked over to the galley's entrance as soon as Louis was out of ear shot. He peered down the dimly lit passageway. No sign of Louis. Smiling, Scott turned to the waiting table of sailors and signaled with a thumbs up sign.

Jack spoke quietly. "Okay, cover the galley's entrance with a blanket."

Wally was closest to the bunks and reached over and pulled a blanket from a lower bunk and threw it to Scott. Scott promptly hung it over the entrance.

When the blanket was up and covered the opening, Jack said quietly. "Scotty, stay by the entrance. Give us a warning signal if Louis starts up the passageway."

Scott, just nodded and gave Jack a flip of his hand.

Jack began, "Okay, guys. We have to be careful. I think Louis suspects something is up. We're giving him that impression with our behavior. He knows us better than the other three and would be the one to recognize any differences in the way we act. Just be yourselves when he's around. It's his job to watch us whether we have something going on or not."

Jack looked around the table. He had everyone's undivided attention. "Okay, we've been through this a few times already but let's do it one more time just as a refresher." He started with the sailor closest to him. "Percy, Louis likes you the best, so if he sees you out in the passageway, he's less likely to suspect something. When Murdock leaves, and Louis takes his place, Louis is probably going to have a few beers in him. Watch Louis' cabin door. Get right up to it and wait for him to start snoring. When he's finally asleep, get back here and let us know. One by one, we'll climb up the ladder to the forward hatch. It's right outside the galley entrance and far enough from Louis' cabin where he shouldn't hear us. Scott, your first up the ladder. Get over to the gangway rail and leave it locked. We'll just climb over it. Slide the gangway plank across to the pier and wait. Once we're all off the ship we'll take the gangway plank and hide it behind those barrels they have stacked out there. When we come back, we'll just slide the plank up to the gangway and come back aboard." Jack looked at the rest of the boys sitting at the table. "Teddy, you're next. Stand by the ladder and count to 100. That should give Scotty enough time to get to the pier. Climb up the ladder and quietly get over to meet him. Wally, you're next, then Roger, then Percy. I'll be the last up to make sure there are no problems."

Jack looked at the smiling group. "Everyone got it?"

Everyone acknowledged that they did. Jack added. "When we come back, we'll just do it in reverse." He reminded Scotty, "Just be extra special careful about putting the gangway plank back. We can't risk waking Louis."

Percy asked, "Where we going anyway, Jack?"

Jack smiled, "I'm going to show you the town. I know a few girlie bars that I can get us into."

Percy looked confused. "We're all under age, Jack. No one here is twenty-one yet."

Jack chuckled. "I know some bouncers at a few of the bars around here. They'll let us in. Just bring an extra ten bucks with you. Follow my lead and don't flash the money around."

Percy looked thoughtful for a moment but slowly nodded his head as if he understood.

Jack finished up. "Okay, that's it. Remember not to wear anything that mentions sailing, or has the word Defiant on it. Keep it simple and don't talk about it, especially after we get back."

Scott took the blanket down and the boys continued with the rest of their quiet time as if nothing was afoot. Teddy and Wally retired to their bunks to read, Roger sat by his bunk and wrote a letter to his parents, and Percy had a small length of rope and practiced tying a bowline knot that he was going to use as part of tomorrow's demonstrations.

Scott and Jack stayed where they were at the galley table. Scott started to reminisce about how different life had been just two months ago. "I never even thought about being on a sailboat, never mind sailing on a tall ship like the Defiant."

Jack smiled and looked into Scott's eyes. "Do you like it, Scotty?"

Scott was unprepared for such a question. Up until now, it was something he had no choice in. "Uh, like it? What part?"

Jack replied. "If you love sailing, you love everything about it. Yeah, there are some crappy parts that come with it, but if sailing on a ship gives you that special feeling…that certain sense of satisfaction of using the wind and your knowledge of sailing, to get the ship to do what you want, then that feeling will outweigh the bad parts."

Scott thought about lying on his back under the Defiant while she was in drydock, quirking and caulking her hull planks, scraping off old paint and slapping on new paint. He thought about the hard, wooden bunk he slept on every night, and Louis…like a den mother looking over his shoulder every minute of his off time. Then he thought about his first day sail out of Gloucester, followed by the eleven-hour sail to Plymouth. He remembered the feel of the sea as it rolled under the ship, the spray that came off the wave crests and the feel of the ship as it responded to his efforts with the halyards and the mainsheet lines. He thought about the way the ship heeled to the leeward side and picked up speed as he pulled the sails in tighter. It was like the ship was answering back in its own physical way and spoke to him, with its creaking and groaning timbers.

Scott raised his eyebrows and looked up from the table. "I guess I do like it…a lot. I guess it just kind of grew on me without me realizing what was happening."

Jack smiled and slapped him on the arm. "I knew you did. I'm from the harbor here and grew up with this stuff. It's in my blood. I noticed you were a natural as soon as we started working together." Jack reached into his shirt pocket. "That's why I made this for you." He handed Scott a rope bracelet, braided with three different coils of line. "It's called a grommet. Traditionally, a sailor is presented with one of these after his first successful, long cruise but I'm giving it to you now because of how far you've come…from riding an old boxcar to sailing a tall ship. I have to tell you Scott, they just don't let anyone take the helm like they did you, when we were dragging Roger through the water yesterday."

Scott took the rope bracelet and put it on his right wrist. "Wow! Thanks, Jack! This means a lot."

Jack said, "Don't take it off. It's a rite of passage. When another sailor sees that, he'll know you've completed a long journey on a tall ship and done something great while doing it."

Jack reached out and shook Scott's hand. Unbeknownst to Jack and Scott, the other sailors had been watching the exchange between them but didn't let on. They all thought the gesture was fitting and felt good about it. An air of friendship and camaraderie filled the crew's quarters and everyone was content to pass the night in each other's company.

CHAPTER TWENTY SEVEN

It was Friday morning in Plymouth Harbor. The boys were up on deck and stood at amidships, in their clean and crisp dress white uniforms. They were shoulder to shoulder, about a foot apart in the 'at ease' position, awaiting their guests for the day. It was an impressive sight, as behind the young sailors, was a clean and sparkling schooner. The ship's hull was a dark chestnut color with a white gunnel, all of which was highlighted by the light brown masts that protruded skyward from her decks.

Defiant was bare-masted as she sat moored to the pier. Her skeleton was exposed outlining all the sheets, lines, and pulleys that worked the now absent sails. Rigging lines went fore and aft from the bow sprit to the ship's stern and ceremonial pennants flew at the top of her tall masts. The mainmast was the tallest, just forward of amidships, and supported the mainsail and a topsail, that normally occupied that sail area, when underway.

The foremast, just aft of the bow, was shorter and supported a top sail and a lower fore sail, also triangular in shape. Two headstays, attached to the Defiant's bowsprit rose at a severe angle to the top of the foremast and could support two large jib sails. The smallest one was secured to the forestay and foremast, upon which her cotton sails hung when underway. The jib sail set up was an integral part of the schooner's 'gaff rig.'

For the day's demonstrations, the sails remained furled to their spars, booms, and stays for viewing purposes. The crew had tied them up neatly and cinched them to their spars and stays so they couldn't collect any wind.

Forward of the aft hatch, where the ship's meetings were held, Louis had set up a refreshment area with coffee brewing and anyone's choice of fresh donuts. The Defiant was ready for the public.

Scott stood next to Jack and in a sideways gesture asked, "Did they say when the first group would be arriving?"

Jack looked at his watch. "I heard Smitty say the first group would be here at 9:00 AM. It's 8:55 now."

Scott looked out beyond the pier and onto the wharf. The people traffic was beginning to build but it was still pretty light. After all, it was a Friday morning and many people were still winding up their work week. Scott glanced behind the row of sailors to see Burt, their beagle mascot, sitting in his most attentive position on the amidships cabintop.

Jack smiled and said to Scott, "Hey, here comes some folks now. "Tell Burt to abandon ship."

Scott's face momentarily went serious. "Shh! The dog will hear you! That's all we need is for Burt to jump off the ship.

A group of five people walked up to Defiant's gangway ramp and hailed the sailors. "Ahoy, sailors! You must be the lads doing the tours! Can we come aboard?"

Smitty stepped from where he stood at the end of the row of sailors. "That we are, sir. Permission to come aboard granted. Please hold onto the ramp railing provided, and watch your step."

Three men and two women boarded the Defiant and stood before the crisply dressed sailors. The man that had hailed the sailors was somewhat overweight with greying hair that sneaked out from under something that resembled a 'newsboy cap.' A mustache of the same color adorned his plump face. "I am Gerald Risner, Chairman of the Tall Ship Sailor Program for Youthful Offences." Risner looked the row of sailors up and down. "I haven't attended one of these in a while, but the weather is good today and I wanted to see what these...sailors, are made of."

Smitty stepped forward and shook Risner's hand. "Of course, Mr.Risner. We can start with our bow team and those sailors will escort you to the next sailing station when they're done."

Risner nodded in agreement, so Smitty called the first two sailors. "Percy, and Wally! Please escort Mr. Risner and his group to the bow and explain the bow team's purpose and what goes on at your sailing station."

The boys nodded and stepped out of the receiving line, and greeted the new arrivals. Percy was first to greet the group. "Good morning. I'm Percy Tuttle and this is Wally Hanley."

Risner was surprised at the smallish looking sailor. "You're kind of small to be up in the bow aren't you, son?"

Percy straightened up and looked Risner in the eye. "I'm the best, sir. I'm the bow team leader." Percy paused a moment and added, "Please follow us to the bow."

Risner shot Smitty a surprised glance, smiled, and then winked at him.

Teddy also fell out of line and headed for the aft hatch. Smitty glanced back at Risner and nodded in Teddy's direction. "That's Teddy Brinks. He's the third man on the bow team and will be waiting for you at the aft hatch for a tour below decks once your circuit of the ship is complete."

The groups of guests began to come quicker as the morning burned on. By late morning, the guests on the wharf had grown to a crowd patiently awaiting their specific turns. Smitty started using the odd man from the sailing stations, to go out onto the wharf to bring up the next party.

After lunch, the boys came back out on deck and took their position amidships to greet new guests. Slowly but surely, a group of young women, probably from the local college, walked off the wharf and onto the pier. Giggling and prodding each other, made their way up to the Defiant's starboard side.

The boys watched the girls approach and imagined all sorts of things. Jack whispered out of the side of his mouth. "I got the one, third from the right, if they come aboard."

The girls just stood there ogling the young sailors in their new uniforms. Finally, one of them shouted, "Hey, sailor boys! Can one of you guys come down here and walk us up there? We want to see the ship."

All six boys went for the gangway at the same time until Smitty stepped in front of them. "Hold it, hold it, hold it. The girls only need one of you to bring them up." Once the boys resumed their position in line, Smitty looked at the man closest to the gangway. "Roger, please go down there and bring the girls aboard." Smitty shifted his attention back to the line of sailors. He quietly reminded the anxious crew. "Women love a man in uniform. Be professional. I'll be watching."

Once the girls were on deck, an awkward moment ensued. One of the girls noticed Burt sitting at attention on the cabintop and broke the ice. "What a cute little dog! Is that your mascot?"

Percy was thankful for the question. "Yes, he is, Miss. That's, Burt. He sails with us and basically follows us around the ship when we're working or just hanging around…sleeps with us too." Again, the silence resumed. Quickly, Percy added,

"Let's go to the bow and I'll show you what we do up there. Burt will probably follow us up there too."

It was late in the afternoon and there were no people waiting on the pier so all six of the sailors thought they would take the opportunity to escort the five girls through the ship. Smitty stood by the helm and addressed his boys. "Sailors! Sailing stations! The girls will get their turn to visit your station." The boys paused as they listened to their first mate and slowly returned to their sailing stations. Burt followed Percy and the girls to the bow.

When the college girl contingent got to the bow, Percy began to explain the function of the bow team and the jib sails. One of the young ladies eased her way up to, and uncomfortably close to Percy. She grabbed the sailor's tie and playfully flipped it back and forth in her hand. "Can I keep this, handsome? I'll wear it when we go into town later and tell everyone the bowman on the Defiant gave it to me."

The girl was almost a foot taller than Percy as she gazed promiscuously down at him, their bodies almost touching. Percy didn't know what to do. His face began to redden as he stared up at her.

When he didn't answer, she took his sailor's hat from his head and put it on her own. "That's okay. I'll just take the hat instead."

Station by station, the girls flirted their way through the ship. When they approached the aft hatch, Roger stood waiting to bring them below for a tour of the Defiant's interior.

Roger introduced himself under the watchful eye of Smitty. "Hi girls. I'm Roger. Would you like a tour below decks?"

The girls all giggled and the tall one wearing Percy's hat spoke up. "What's down there? It looks kind of dark."

Roger smiled. "It's where we eat and sleep, the galley, and our one engine. There is some storage spaces and the head. The captain's cabin is down there too."

"One of the girls asked what's the head?"

Roger chuckled. "That's what they call the bathroom on a ship, except there is no bath…just a toilet, sink and a tiny shower."

The girl's face reddened a little. Another one of the college girls started for the hatch. "Of course, we want to see all that."

Roger extended his hand out in front of the aft hatch entrance. "Hold on. I'll go first. The ladder is pretty steep and it's kind of dark down there."

The hat girl peered down into the aft hatch. "It looks like steep stairs to me."

Roger turned and replied just before stepping into the dark hatchway. "Stairs on a ship are called ladders Miss, and all doorways are referred to as hatches. We do have a vertical 'ladder' up near the bow that is just outside the galley and comes out on the foredeck, just aft of the foremast. I'll show you when we get up there." He turned and started down the aft hatch. "Be careful, and hold onto the side rails." One by one, the girls entered the aft hatch and followed Roger below decks.

It was dimly lit in the long passageway as Roger started the tour from the engine compartment, followed by the regular crew's quarters, and worked his way past the head and stopped at the captain's cabin. "This is ship's headquarters…where the captain lives. We don't go in there unless we're in trouble or he has something special he wants to tell us. He's in charge of everyone and everything on the ship."

One of the girls giggled and asked, "Did you ever have to go in there, Roger?"

Roger nodded to indicate that he had. "Uh, yes. I have. Been in there once or twice."

Finally, the tour got to the Tall Ship Sailor's quarters. "This is where we eat and sleep. Right inside this bulkhead is the galley, or kitchen, as you'd call it. That table is where we eat, and our bunks are forward of that attached to the ship's bulkhead on either side."

All but two of the girls ran past Roger, ignoring the galley, and climbed up into the bunks. One of the girls left standing in the entranceway, panned the room and asked, "What is that musty odor?"

Roger smiled. "We don't even smell it anymore but that is from the humidity and stale air that gets into the wood timbers down here." Upon hearing that, two of the girls climbed down from the bunks immediately.

The girl remaining was in Scott's bunk and was obviously taking in the whole scenario. "These bunks are curved...not straight like a regular bed."

Roger laughed. "Yeah, we complain about our crooked bunks all the time. It's because they're attached to the pointy end of the ship. It saves space."

One of the girls, still standing in the galley's entranceway, held her hand over her nose. "Okay, I'm done. Let's go back up on deck."

Quickly, Roger asked. "Aren't you the one who asked about the stairs?"

She answered with her hand still over her nose. "Yes, why?"

Roger took the opportunity and lied, "Well, that passageway is one-way only. We have to exit here." He pointed to the forward ladder that led straight up to the foredeck. "That's the only way out. So, you're all going to have to take turns climbing straight up."

The girls all looked at each other and shrugged. Roger picked the girl with Percy's hat. "Okay, you're first. Go hand over hand and push the hatch open over your head as you get to the top."

One by one, the girls climbed the vertical ladder from below decks. The sly sailor stood at the base of the vertical ladder and smiled as he watched five sets of beautiful legs and short panted butts climb straight up over his head.

Once they were topside, Roger led the girls back to the gangway so they could debark the ship. Smitty stood by the gangway and thanked them for coming. He noticed there was one girl wearing a sailor's cap as she walked down the gangway ramp. He smiled and nodded his head.

▽

The day had been a long one. It was a little nerve racking at first, but eventually became routine. The boys discovered areas in the guest discussions where they could add to the demonstrations by talking about their own experience and anticipate the questions. After eight hours of tours, they were ready for a break.

Eight bells rang and the boys started for the aft hatch, and some for the forward hatch. Smitty called everyone back to amidships. When everyone was present, he smiled and said, "Good job today, sailors.!" He paused and looked seriously at the tired crew. "I suppose after a day like that you're too tired to go out for dinner."

Everyone answered at the same time, in one way or another, but they were all definitely interested in getting off the ship.

Smitty laughed and said, "I thought so. Go get cleaned up and keep your whites on. We're going to get a fine dinner at one of my favorite restaurants and maybe take a stroll around town. We'll leave in half an hour and be back at 10:00 PM."

The group of six Tall Ship Sailors escorted by their first mate had debarked the Defiant and walked leisurely through the small port town of Plymouth Harbor. The contingent drew a lot of attention as they walked amongst tourists. They were an impressive looking lot as they walked in their dress white uniforms. There was at least one instance where someone exclaimed, "Look, Honey. There's the sailors from that schooner we went on today." The boys began to feel special and walked holding their heads high.

Smitty was proud of his new crew and smiled as they walked through the harbor town. He looked at the boys as they walked and noticed one of the boys in particular. He pulled Percy aside. "Where is your sailor's hat?"

Percy's face flushed red. "Sorry, Smitty. One of the college girls took it."

Of course, Smitty already knew that but hadn't known which one of the boys' hat she had walked off with. "Did she take it or did you give it to her?"

Wally was walking next to Percy and intervened. "Ah, that chick had the hots for our bowman here. I think she just wanted a souvenir. She swiped that hat right off his head after snuggling up so close to him I thought they were gonna' kiss."

Everyone laughed and Smitty looked back to Percy. "Why didn't you just ask for it back?"

Teddy was at the back of the group. "Are you kidding? She was about a foot taller than him. I think he was afraid of her."

Everyone broke into laughter again. Percy turned and shot Teddy an ugly glance. "I guess I should have, Smitty. I'll pay for it."

Smitty chuckled and patted Percy on the shoulder. "No. That's quite alright, sailor. We have more hats. You should be proud that she chose to have your hat out of five other possibilities."

Percy straightened up, turned toward Teddy, and flipped him off.

The boys walked a few more blocks. It felt good to be walking amongst people and buildings again, and to have the sensation of solid ground under their feet again. Smitty pointed across the street. "Okay, we're here, guys."

They stopped and looked across the street. The sign above the door said Savage Sam's. Smitty let the boys take it in and prodded, "Let's go eat."

Savage Sam's was a typical harbor restaurant. It was on the west side of the harbor and provided its patrons with a fine view of the water and the vessels it accommodated. The theme for the interior of the establishment was nautical. Lobster buoys and fish netting hung from the ceilings and walls. Items like ship's bells, wooden helms of all sizes, and lobster traps adorned shelves and corner tables. Most of them were authentic, having been recovered from old shipwrecks or purchased from ships and boats headed for the scrap yard. The interior was dimly lit with ship's lanterns on each table and nautical style candle sconces that hung from the walls. The walls were of distressed wood planking made to look as if they had once been used as a ship's bulkhead planking.

There were two floors, and of course, the boys insisted on the upper level. Their table of choice was in the dining area that cantilevered out over the marina.

"There's a good view of the Defiant, boys." Smitty pointed to a dockside area north of where they sat. Up a little further was the Mayflower II, an exact replica of the tall ship that transported early pilgrims to America in September of 1620. Mayflower II sat quietly at its mooring, also awaiting visitors.

The boys drew a lot of attention from the restaurant's patrons and the waitresses. A lovely young lady, who identified herself as a journalist for a local newspaper, approached the sailor's table and asked if she could take a few pictures. Smitty politely rejected the offer but told her she could write an article on the boys' stay in Plymouth and what their assignment was as long as none of the sailor's names were mentioned. She agreed and spent a few minutes speaking to each of the boys and what their job was on the Defiant.

Finally, the long-awaited dinner, that wasn't cooked by Louis, was over. Smitty paid the bill and took the boys for a stroll through the town. It was now dusk and darkness was setting in fast. Smitty took them along a narrow, bricked walkway that took them past Mayflower II. The boys took in the sleepy harbor town. It seemed quainter and more countryfied than Gloucester. Vintage homes of antique architecture adorned the hills that rolled down to the docks, and shops of various purposes offered their wares along the street's way. It was a quiet night and although the boys preferred to stay out longer, fatigue had begun to set in. Smitty led the group in a loop back to where Defiant sat quietly moored to its pier.

Smitty stopped Defiant's crew at the gangway ramp. "Well, that's it boys. It's almost ten o'clock and you guys have another busy tour day tomorrow. I think you all needed that time away from the ship and some exposure to the public. I want everyone in the crew's quarters after you board and lights out in one hour."

The boys all nodded and thanked Smitty as they crossed the ramp to Defiant.

Smitty stood on the pier and watched the crew as they approached the aft hatch and reminded them. "Hey! Get some sleep…and don't leave the ship."

Smitty watched until the last sailor disappeared through the dark hatch. When he was satisfied that all hands were safely below, he boarded Defiant and went below to his own cabin.

CHAPTER TWENTY EIGHT

Saturday June 24th had finely arrived. The 'sneak-away' would be tonight, but first there was still another eight hours of tours and demonstrations on the Defiant. Scotty climbed up the ladder that led to the foreward hatch and poked his head out. It was 7:00 AM and the pier was devoid of would-be tourists. He climbed down and went back into the crew's quarters. The boys were getting ready for the day and slipping back into their dress white uniforms. They all looked up when he came around the galley entrance. "No people yet, but it's only 7:00 AM. I figure it'll be busier than yesterday, being Saturday and all."

Jack smiled as he made his bunk. "I hope we get more of those girls in from the local college."

Just then Smitty appeared in the galley entrance behind Scotty. "I think there's a good chance of that happening, Jack." He looked over to Percy and tossed him a sailor hat. "Percy, I only have one more in that size so choose wisely, if you feel the need to give this one away."

Percy who had been seated on a lower bunk tying his shoes, reached up and grabbed the hat from the air. The room erupted in laughter. "Thanks, Smitty. It'll have to be the girl I'm going to marry this time."

Smitty grinned and nodded at the group. "I'm proud of you guys. You did well yesterday. We received some great reports about all of you and how you were such gentlemen." He glanced backdown at Percy. "There was one marriage proposal for you but I canned it because you're not available for another ten months."

At first the young sailor looked surprised but realized Smitty's dry humor and went back to tying his shoes, "Yeah, right…okay, Smitty."

There was more kidding and fooling before Smitty interrupted. "Seriously, you guys did great. After yesterday, you pretty much know what to expect, so just relax and have a good time. The captain will be on board today so look sharp." Smitty paused a moment as if in deep thought and added, "I'm off for the day…and tonight. The captain will be on board until after dinner and then Louis will be back from liberty early to watch the ship. Don't worry, he'll just be on board…just stay out of his hair."

Smitty turned to walk out of the crew's quarters and stopped. He turned around and looked at the busy group of young men. "Remember one thing. Do not leave the ship for any reason. I don't care how beautiful they are or what they say to you." Smitty paused and stared at the group for a moment to let the order sink in.

The boys merely stared back at Smitty, not saying a word, and nodded.

▽

Finally, eight bells rang throughout the ship and the last guests of the day were headed for the gangway entrance. The boys began disappearing through the aft and foreward hatches. Captain Murdock was standing by the helm and noticed the abrupt change in behavior. *Boy, they're not wasting any time getting below tonight. Must be hungry.*

The boys hurried to the crew's quarters and started changing to street clothes. Louis was still on liberty and Murdock would be leaving soon. As they changed, Teddy asked, "Hey did Louis leave anything for dinner?"

Wally pointed over to the small refrigerator in the corner of the galley. "Oh yeah. He said to tell you guys there are ham and cheese grinders in the fridge for dinner."

Jack saw that the boys looked as if they were rushing. "Hey guys, just slow down. We don't want to make anyone suspicious, so just act normal. If Murdock or Louis happen to come in here, everything has to look routine. We can't do anything until Louis comes back from liberty. Even then, we have to wait until he hopefully passes out, so stop rushing. Go grab your grinders and eat. We have plenty of time."

$$\triangledown$$

Sean and Mary Muldoon had left Natick, Massachusetts early to catch Scott and have their twenty minutes with him as scheduled. They had only been in the car for fifteen minutes and Mary was getting anxious. "Sean, can't we go a little faster? We only have twenty minutes with Scotty and I don't want to be late."

Sean rolled his eyes, "It's only about an hour and twenty minutes to Plymouth Harbor, Mary and our meeting is scheduled for 7:00 PM. We should be right on time."

Mary was still nervous. "What if we get tied up in traffic or get a flat tire? We'll miss the meeting and I don't think they would consider another one."

Sean kept his eyes on the road. "We'll be there in a little over an hour, Mary. I know you're anxious but calm yourself knowing you'll be seeing your boy in about an hour."

Mary sat back in her seat and offered one last bit of advice. "Keep in mind, Sean. Scotty doesn't know about the meeting yet. He won't be told until it's confirmed we are on the pier. They may just cancel it if they think we're not coming and then he'll never even know we tried."

Sean allowed a grin to cross his face but didn't answer.

CHAPTER TWENTY NINE

Saturday night had arrived and Captain Murdock stood by the Defiant's gangway awaiting Louis' arrival. Murdock had just come from below after commending the boys on another successful day of tours and demonstrations. After bidding the boys a good night, he went topside to meet Louis for a change of shift.

Murdock glanced at his watch. It was 6:15 PM, time for him and Louis to switch shifts. The captain began to pace the deck. On his second pass by the gangway, he saw Louis making his way down the wharf in no apparent hurry. *Aww, shit! Is he drunk? I'll have to call Katie and tell her I have to cancel.*

Louis sauntered across the pier and over to the Defiant's gangway ramp and noticed Murdock pacing the deck. "Hey, Skipper! I'm here…a little late, but I'm here. Get on your way and give Katie a kiss for me. Permission to come aboard."

Murdock stood by the gangway with his arms crossed. "Granted." He waited for Louis to get on board and stepped in close to him to see if he was intoxicated. "Louis, are you drunk?"

Louis stepped back a little surprised. "Not at all, Skipper. I did have a few, and that's probably what you're smellin' but I was just biding my time until I had to leave. Shot a little pool. That's about it."

Murdock was very skeptical. "Louis, I can't leave you with the boys if you're under the influence. If something happens it would mean your job and maybe worse."

Louis stepped closer to Murdock. "Skipper, I'm good... really. I'm just in a good mood. Won me a few bucks at the pool table and I too have a date when I go back to Mayflower's Fancy tonight."

Murdock scrutinized Louis and the way he spoke. He wasn't slurring his words or stumbling around. "Let me see you walk forward to the cabintop and back."

Louis seemed to walk fine, so Murdock said, "Okay, I'll take your word for it. If you let me down Louis, there will be hell to pay."

Louis began to redden a little. "I swear, Skipper. I'm okay... maybe a little tired, but that's it."

Finally, Murdock relented. "Fine! Listen to me. Scotty's parents are due here at 7:00 PM. That's forty minutes from now. It's an approved and private meeting between him and his parents, and they are not to be disturbed. I do, however, expect you to stay topside and in sight of the group for the entire twenty minutes they have been allowed. Scotty doesn't know about it and is not to be told until they arrive at the pier. Is that understood?"

Louis had become more serious as he listened to the captain. The smile he boarded with had long since left his face. "I got it, Skipper. It'll all be fine."

Murdock stared into Louis' eyes. "See that it is, Louis. I put some deck chairs out here for the three of them. See that they're comfortable. It's very important that they're not disturbed." When Louis said nothing, he nodded at the cook and made for the gangway ramp.

Louis watched the captain leave the ship and looked at his watch. It was 6:30. He smiled and thought. *I got thirty minutes before they get here. I just need a few minutes to myself and then I'll put on some coffee for them.* Louis went to his cabin and lie on his bed. In two minutes, he was fast asleep.

Percy had been waiting to hear Louis' footfalls in the passageway. When he heard him open his cabin door, he crept up to it and waited. At the first sound of any snoring, Percy hurried back to the crew's quarters. "Okay, he's asleep. Let's go."

Jack was first to speak, "Okay, it's 6:40. Get ready by the ladder. Scotty, you're first." The boys started for the foreward hatch ladder but Jack stopped them. "Remember, it's still daylight. Don't act like you're sneaking off the ship. People are still out on the pier. You're in street clothes, so from a distance you could be tourists. Just walk off the ship. Try not to look conspicuous."

The excited sailors went to their positions. Scotty climbed the ladder and went topside.

$\triangledown$

Sean and Mary Muldoon were stopped in traffic just outside the main road into Plymouth Harbor. Mary opened her window and tried to look out beyond the line of cars ahead. "I can't even see the beginning, Sean. Just pull over onto the shoulder and pass everyone on the right...other cars are doing it."

Sean shook his head. "Nope. Not doing that. That's against the law and if a cop catches one of those guys, he's going to make him sit there a while before he even writes the ticket, just to prove the point."

Mary looked desperate. "We can't even call anyone to let them know we might be late. I don't see a telephone booth anywhere."

Sean tried to reassure his wife. "Mary, it's 6:40. We still have twenty minutes. Normally, we'd be ten minutes away. Just relax."

Suddenly, Mary noticed some activity up ahead. "Oh! It looks like the traffic is starting to move again. There's a big tanker truck moving to the side of the road. Oh please, God. Let it be him that was causing the problem."

▽

Jack was the last to climb the forward ladder. He took a step into the passageway toward Louis' cabin and could hear the snoring from where he stood. Feeling as if they had the sneak-away made, he turned and climbed the vertical ladder to the foredeck. Jack looked to the gangway. Everyone was standing on the pier, waiting for Jack to cross the gangway's ramp.

Once across the ramp, Teddy and Wally unhooked the ramp from Defiant and rolled it to the side of the pier and behind some large storage barrels.

Jack turned and walked toward the wharf. "Let's go see some sights, boys." The others, feeling as if they needed that permission, followed him.

CHAPTER THIRTY

Sean Muldoon sped down the narrow roads leading to Plymouth Harbor's wharves. It was 6:55 PM. Mary leaned forward in her seat and instinctively pressed her feet against the floor, as if it would make the car go faster.

"Oh, I just know they're going to cancel the meeting. "Tears began to stream down Mary's face. I'm never going to see my Scotty again. I just know it."

Sean came around one of the secondary street corners so fast that he drew attention from pedestrians on the sidewalk. "Mary, look…up ahead. There's the Defiant's mainmast."

Rising above the shops and restaurants was a white top mast with a Jolly Roger flying at the top. It was the Defiant's pennant and signature amongst the ships in her class. Mary's heart began to pound as she pressed her face closer to the window.

Sean pulled up to the wharf and parked illegally near the entrance. The anxious parents wasted no time and exited the car as soon as it came to a hurried stop. They raced across the wharf and ran down the short set of stairs to Defiant's pier. As Sean had promised, the wooden schooner Defiant sat moored to the pier, her black hull and white gunnel stood out among the various fishing boats and recreational craft. The majestic Mayflower II filled the background north of Defiant.

Sean and Mary raced up to Defiant's gangway, but the boarding ramp had been pulled. Mary was out of breath. "Sean, they closed the ship and pulled the ramp. It's cancelled."

Sean scanned the ship. "It can't be cancelled. Look over there. The deck chairs they said they'd provide for the meeting are still on the stern." Sean frantically looked around the area. Finally, he noticed a small version of a ship's bell lashed to a railing for visitors that came for tours. He walked up to the bell and rang it. He rang it three times at first. There was no response. Sean rang it three more times. Still no response.

Mary began to cry. "Oh Sean, we missed the meeting."

Sean shook his head from side to side. "No, we didn't Mary. It's just 7:00 PM now." Sean began ringing the bell furiously and shouted at the same time. "Hello? Anyone on board? Hello?"

Finally, the aft hatch canopy slid open and a drowsy Louis poked his head out of the dark opening. "Hello! Can I help you?"

Sean shouted back. "Yes. We're the Muldoons…Scott's parents. We're here for a twenty-minute meeting with our boy."

Louis' head began to clear. Now, he remembered Murdock notifying him of the meeting with Scotty and his parents. "Oh, of course. Please come aboard. I'm Louis, the ship's cook. I'll go get Scotty."

Sean shook his head. "We can't. There's no ramp to crossover with."

Louis looked puzzled and came over to the gangway. *Hmmm, that's strange.* He looked around and saw the ramp behind some barrels. "Oh, someone must have stowed the ramp. Hold on. I'll get it."

Louis jumped the three-foot gap between the Defiant and the pier and rolled the gangway plank into position. "Sorry folks. The boys must have closed it up, knowing they'd be in tonight. The first mate took them out on the town last night for dinner."

Sean and Mary crossed over the gangway ramp and went over to the deck chairs. Louis waited until they were seated. "I'll go get Scotty. He should be up in a minute."

Louis disappeared into the aft hatch and hurried to the crew's quarters. He came to a dead stop at its entrance and spoke aloud, as if someone was there. "What in hell's name?"

The room was vacant. He walked out of the galley entrance and peered up the foreward hatch ladder. The hatch was still open. "Those little bastards!" Before going topside to give the Muldoons the news, he checked all of the compartments below deck. The boys were gone.

Once again, Louis' head appeared at the aft hatch. The Muldoons were staring blankly in his direction anxiously awaiting their son's appearance. Louis paused a moment, then walked slowly over to amidships and sat in one of the deck chairs. "I don't know what to say, folks. He's not here. None of the boys are on board."

Sean Muldoon looked surprised and confused at the same time. "I don't understand. I thought they weren't allowed off the ship...ever."

Louis pursed his lips. "They're not, Mr. Muldoon. Not unless they are accompanied by one of the regular crew."

Mary was visibly shaken. She stared into Louis' eyes as if hoping. "Well maybe the captain or the first mate took them out again."

Louis shook his head in a negative way. "No, Ma'am. The captain is off for the night and the first mate is out of town. Our deck hand, Josh is at a wedding."

Mary became angry. "Well, you seem to know where everyone is except for the boys that you're supposed to be watching!"

"I'm sorry, Ma'am. This is not like them. I fell asleep for a few minutes and they must have taken that opportunity to jump ship."

Sean tried to defuse Mary. "Alright, alright." Then he leaned forward in his chair and into the cook's eyes. "I understand, Louis. Boys will be boys. What do we do now?"

"I'll call Captain Murdock and we'll go lookin' for them, sir." Louis thought for a moment. "You know... a bunch of college girls came aboard yesterday and were very taken with our boys. I can't help but think they made plans to meet somewhere around here." Louis paused a moment and looked at the worried parents. "I can't say that I blame the boys either. They have been tied to this ship for four weeks now. They've been working on it, cleaning it, and have had a couple of rough days at sea. They're only human."

Mary stared into Louis' being as if her gaze were daggers. "You sir, I take it, were supposed to be watching them... correct?"

Louis nodded his head sadly. "I take full responsibility, Ma'am."

Mary stood from her chair. "I'll have your job, mister!" Mary walked to the gangway and debarked the ship.

Louis looked up at Sean. "I'm sorry, sir. There is no excuse."

Sean looked back at Louis and patted him on the shoulder. "I understand, Louis. These boys didn't get here by playing by the rules. I'll talk to Mary, and as I said, boys will be boys."

Sean rose from his deck chair and turned back toward Louis before he entered the gangway. "Just find them, Louis. Just find them and contact us as soon as you do."

CHAPTER THIRTY ONE

When the Muldoons left, Louis locked up the ship and pulled the gangway ramp again. He decided to go look for the missing sailors before calling Murdock. Plymouth Harbor was a small town and he knew all the popular places. He thought he'd find the boys first, get them back on board, and then call the Muldoons. If Mrs. Muldoon was okay with it, maybe they could leave Captain Murdock out of it.

Louis walked the streets for three hours and concentrated on the younger people's hot spots. There was no sign of the young sailors. He even tried a local hotel that was said to be a house of ill repute. Still, no sailors. Louis looked at his watch. It was 10:15 PM. He grimaced and thought, *Better call the captain. I did my best. I'll probably lose my job over this but it's the right thing to do.*

Louis found a telephone booth near the wharf, called Murdock, and explained the situation. Murdock remained silent and just listened. Finally, Louis was done and had admitted his shortcomings. Still, there was silence on the other end of the phone. Louis cautiously asked, "Uh, Skipper are you still there?"

Murdock answered in an even, flat tone. "Yes, I am Louis. I was wondering when you were going to call me about this."

Louis was confused. "I don't understand, Skipper. I went out lookin' for them and checked most of the likely places. When I came up empty, I figured I'd better call and let you know."

Murdock replied, "They're in jail, Louis. As you know, the port authority is always notified before we enter a harbor. We are, in effect, a ship of detention, so the right people have to be put on notice."

Louis was surprised the boys had been corralled so quickly. "But, Skipper. I went right out looking for them. I was after them as soon as the Muldoons left."

Murdock had a calm and stern tone. "The town constable was called by a local establishment because a few of the boys were ordering beer...large amounts of it. One of them, I guess Roger, had passed out and hit his head on a bar stool... split it open actually, and had to go get stitches. When the ambulance arrived, the EMTs asked for Roger's identification. He was still unconscious, so Scotty reached into his pocket and gave it up. They found the whole lot was under age so the bartender called the sheriff mainly to protect his own ass. Five of them were escorted right to jail, and Roger was driven there later. The sheriff called me to let me know they're all in a group holding cell and wanted to know when I'd be by to pick them up."

Louis was stunned. "I'll go down there now and take them back to the ship. There's no reason to ruin your night too."

Murdock answered quickly. "No need. I told the sheriff to keep them overnight. Let them experience a night in jail. I guess they're all sick and puking their guts out. I'll pick them up in the morning and make them walk back to the ship."

Louis added, "You realize that's a couple of miles from the ship....right?"

Murdock answered flatly. "Yes, I do. I want you to go back to the Defiant and stay there. We'll talk about your part in this later, sailor. That's all." The line went dead.

Louis hung up the phone and slowly walked back to the ship. He no longer had any inclination to return to Mayflower's Fancy. He wondered if he still had a future on the Defiant.

▽

Katie drove Murdock back to the ship the next morning, at 9:00 AM. She walked with him up to the Defiant's pier and kissed him on the cheek. "I had a good time, Tom. Are you sure I can't give you a ride to the police station?"

Murdock grabbed his ditty bag from the back seat and slung it over his shoulder. "Nah. I'm good, Katie. I need to walk off some of this frustration before I see the boys."

Katie had her arms folded in front of her and gave him a serious look with one eyebrow raised. "Before you go off on those boys, try to remember what it was like when you were that age. If my memory serves me right, I think you may have had some of the same experiences when you were a young sailor."

Murdock smirked and allowed the tiniest smile to cross his face. "That was a long time ago, Katie."

Katie walked up to him and hugged him as she looked up into his blue eyes. "That's true but you were still a spirited young man with normal needs and desires. I'm just asking you to try and put that into perspective."

Murdock nodded his head as he drew away from her. "I get it, Katie. But these guys left the ship. It's like breaking out of prison. I'm going to have to punish them. After all, this is a reformatory based program."

Katie gave him another kiss on the mouth. This time it was a long one and they embraced for a while longer. "I'm just asking you to remember what it was like."

Murdock picked up his bag and turned toward the ship. "I'll keep it in mind."

Katie watched her captain walk up to the Defiant and throw his ditty bag over the railing. The bag landed just ahead of amidships near the cabintop. He checked his watch, waved to Katie and headed for the police station.

The little harbor town of Plymouth included a small police station with a small staff of sheriffs and a group holding cell for drunks, and other small time law breakers that could house the offenders for twenty-four hours. Murdock walked up the fieldstone walk and entered the station. The desk officer recognized Murdock and smiled. "Good morning, Captain. I guess you're here for your boys?"

Murdock nodded, "Yes, I am. Where are they? I want a word with them before you let them out."

Sheriff Jones nodded. "Of course. They're through that set of double doors. Let me know when you're ready."

Murdock pushed open the heavy oak doors and walked down a short corridor. The odor of urine and vomit permeated the entire area. He came up to the holding cell and stood there looking at his disheveled crew. There was only one toilet and sink, and a narrow bench that hung from two of the cell's walls. Some of the boys sat on the bench slumped against the walls, two sat in separate corners, and Roger was asleep face down on the cold floor.

No one had seen him yet, so Murdock took the opportunity and barked out a loud greeting. "Good morning, sailors!" Everyone was startled at the sudden breach in silence. Roger remained asleep on the floor. The boys were embarrassed and said nothing. They had no excuses for why they were there.

Murdock noticed they all looked pale and tired. Their clothes were wrinkled and stained, and no one had found a comb yet. Murdock continued, "I know you're all feeling pretty crappy right about now and what I have to say may not sink in the way I want it to, so we'll discuss that part when we get back to the ship. Right now, I want you guys to stand up, pick Roger up off the floor, and wake him up. You have a two mile walk along the wharfs before we get back to the Defiant. Maybe, by that time, you'll have sense enough to understand what I have to say."

The walk back to the ship was tortuous. It was a gloomy and overcast day to begin with. The only good thing was the sobering effect the cool sea breeze and smell of the salt air had on the boy's condition. The holding cell had been stuffy to say the least, and overcrowded with six young bodies. However, the clean air did nothing for the headaches and nausea they experienced. Roger's head and whole body ached from the fall and collision with bar stools and a hard floor.

No one spoke as the group walked along the wharfs. Captain Murdock led the way and intentionally kept a moderate pace. Every now and then, one of the boys stopped and ran to the wharf's edge to vomit. Murdock was aware of every stumble and vomit stop, and urged the group to keep up. No matter who was sick, Murdock repeated the same words. "Keep walking, he'll catch up. We need to get back to the ship. Let's go."

Finally, the Defiant appeared in the distance, sitting quietly at her pier. The boys drew a huge sigh of relief when they noticed it. The final hundred yards seemed to be the longest and most uncomfortable. Murdock continued to lead and walked down the short stairway from the wharf to the Defiant's pier. He anticipated what was about to follow, and again smiled to himself. Murdock had already reached the bottom of the stairs when the boys started down them. Their balance was still off from the night before and they had to think twice about negotiating the steep stairs. Wally was at the rear of the group and tripped on the second step down. It was an uncontrolled stumble causing him to tumble into the rest of the boys. The fall resulted in a domino effect and everyone but Jack was knocked over and lie tangled together at the base of the stairs.

Murdock heard the group fall, among various expletives and name calling. He stopped and stood looking at the tangle of sick sailors. "Get up." The boys were slow to move. He repeated his order but louder and more demanding. "On your feet! Now!"

The boys had never heard that tone from Murdock before and struggled to get up. When Murdock saw they were responding, he turned and continued toward the ship and shouted over his shoulder, "Whoever is not with me when I get to the gangway, will spend the rest of the day on the pier with Louis…and in the sun."

The boys struggled to regain their coordination and helped the ones who were having more difficulty. Murdock saw what was happening, and with his back to the group allowed a smile. *They'll remember this one.*

The captain found the gangway ramp and rolled it into position. He pointed toward the ramp, "Get below and get cleaned up. I want all of you topside in an hour. Anyone not there will be confined to quarters for three days. Move."

The boys struggled up the ramp and held onto the wire life lines they had always ignored.

Murdock watched the boys board the ship. "Let's go. You have a long day ahead of you."

CHAPTER THIRTY TWO

It was noon time, but there wasn't anyone on board that felt like eating lunch. Murdock waited for the boys at amidships. They all arrived together so as not to leave anyone behind. "Sit down, boys. I don't want anyone puking on my decks."

The boys found their way down to the deck and tried to get comfortable. Murdock paced the deck in front of them for a few minutes and began. "I'm very disappointed. Leaving the ship is one thing but sneaking off when I was away is something else." He stopped and looked at each one of them. The boys kept their heads down. Murdock continued. "How many times have I reminded you not to leave the ship...not for anything? So now, you have lost my trust. I can't have a crew that I can't trust." He walked over to the port railing and looked out over the harbor for a moment. "We are a team on this ship. You must have felt something like that over the last several weeks, and through the rough seas we sailed through to get here, and then you pull something like sneaking off the ship. Did you think I wouldn't find out?" Murdock turned and stood facing the embarrassed sailors. "I hate to put it this way sailors, but this is a floating reformatory…a ship of detention. You are here to hopefully learn something or at least learn how to be a better person. What you guys did, was akin to breaking out of jail so there are going to be consequences."

Murdock began pacing again and let the boys think about that for a moment before he continued. "I had a little surprise for you guys and I kept it a secret until now. The regular crew was so excited about it, they wanted to tell you back in Gloucester, but I wouldn't allow it." He stopped pacing and faced the boys again. He had their attention now. All six sailors watched Murdock with nervous anticipation. "We have been invited to be in the Parade of Tall Ships in Mystic Harbor, Connecticut. It's the first, in one hundred years, and we were going to be a part of it." The news brought some smiles to the pale faces. "It's next weekend…but now we can't go because you guys left the ship."

Jack stumbled to his feet. "Wait, Skipper. It's my fault. It was my idea…my fault. Don't punish the whole crew for something I instigated."

Murdock remained stoic. "Sit down, Jack. I don't care. You all went ashore." Murdock paused and looked at the deck for a moment, then back at the crew again. Everyone's eyes were glued to the angry captain. "I have to recommend that your sentences are to be extended by another three months for pulling a stunt like that." He paused again and without looking at the boys said, "Everyone is back on duty as of this moment. I've already cancelled the tours and demonstrations for today. Break into teams of two. Swab the decks, paint the railings, and pull all the spare sails out of the hold, and wash and repair them. When that's done, report to me. We're working until 6:00 PM. Maybe you'll have an appetite by then. That's all."

Murdock started to walk to the aft hatch and stopped. "Scotty! In my cabin in ten minutes."

Scott looked surprised and nodded. "Okay, Captain."

$$\triangledown$$

Scott stood outside the captain's cabin and wondered what Murdock could possibly want to speak to him about. He knocked on the oaken door. A gruff, "Come," responded from the other side. Scott opened the cabin door to find Murdock flipping through a pile of paper on his desk. Without looking up, Murdock said, "Come in Scotty, and take a seat."

Scott sat in front of the captain's desk awaiting the worst. Finally, Murdock looked up. This time there was no smile. "Scott, I understand your parents had been out to see you when we we're still in Gloucester, and then again last night."

Scott began to interrupt but Murdock held up his hand. "Let me finish." The captain paused as he read through another document. "These papers are all about you, Scotty. Your parents came to Gloucester for an unscheduled visit which is against the rules in a program like this. I'm told you did an admirable thing to defuse the situation, and I appreciate that. However, they appealed to the Youthful Offenses Program to see you here in Plymouth Harbor, and were granted twenty minutes of time on the ship, scheduled for last night at 7:00 PM." Murdock paused as he stared into Scott's face.

Scott asked, "Why wasn't I told about this? I would have been here."

Murdock put the visitation documents back down on the desk. "You were not to be told until your parents showed up at the pier. This is a reformatory program, Scott. No frills, no special treatment. Anyway, it's not yours to question. It came from the Tall Ship Administration. You're lucky they granted that time for you."

Scott sat bolt upright in his chair. "What happens now? Do my parents know what happened last night?"

Murdock nodded his head several times and finally said, "Unfortunately, they know you left the ship without permission and were informed of your detainment at the local police station."

Scott's heart sunk as he slumped in his chair. Murdock reacted quickly to Scott's reaction. "Sit up straight, son. I have every right to put you off this ship, and to let your parents know the meeting was flawed by your hand, and further visitation is cancelled." He paused again and cleared his throat. "However, under the circumstances, I suggested your parents come tonight at 7:00 PM. They stayed overnight in Plymouth with that hope in mind. They also realize that if Louis is reported to the administration, any future visitations would also be cancelled, because punishment would now be out of my hands."

Scott added, "I guess we got Louis in trouble too."

Murdock replied, "Louis is another matter. That is between Louis and me. So as far as you're concerned, this is your one and only break. If you blow it again, I'll have no recourse than to put you off the ship and you'll be admitted to a land-based facility until your sentence is satisfied. Is that clear?"

Scott reached across the desk to shake Murdock's hand. "Thank you, Captain. I really do appreciate it."

Murdock ignored the hand and did not return the gesture. "Scotty, keep your nose clean and do what you're told. You know the rules. Be on deck at amidships at 7:00 PM. That's all."

Scotty left the cabin and saw Louis waiting in the hallway. Their eyes met for a moment and Louis brushed past Scott without a word. Scott walked slowly toward the aft hatch and strained to hear what might be going on with Louis.

There was a muffled greeting and then he heard the captain say, "Hello, Louis. Close the door and have a seat." The cabin door slammed shut.

Ship's Cook, Louis Baltrone sat in front of Murdock ready for his reprimand. He had already begun to pack his bags fearing the worst. Murdock sat back in his chair and eyed the burly cook. Louis was obviously uncomfortable and couldn't think of anything worthwhile to say.

Finally, Murdock broke the silence. "I'm disappointed, Louis. After everything we've been through…after having had so many of these crews together. I trusted you with my vulnerable crew," Murdock paused, "and they ended up in jail. What have you got to say for yourself?"

Louis sat in front of the captain with his head lowered. "It's my fault. When do you want me to leave, Skipper? I'm pretty much packed. I just hope you have someone to step in right quick. Those boys need a cook and someone to keep reminding 'em about things. They're comin' along but they ain't there yet."

Murdock looked surprised. "Is that what you think? That I'm going to fire you…or do you feel that you can't handle these young men any longer?"

Louis looked up, "Well, it's my fault they got into trouble. I was supposed to be watchin' them."

Murdock leaned forward in his chair and across the desk. "I appreciate you saying that, Louis. But it's not just your fault. It's all of our fault. Obviously, the boys had planned their…sneak-away well in advance. It was well orchestrated to the point where they knew when you and I were changing places." He paused and added, "Smitty and Josh work closely with all of them daily, and never picked up on a thing. I never detected anything that may have been going on either. This particular mix of boys is dangerous. When you have a mixture of intelligence and mischievousness, it's a whole different ball game."

Louis looked sheepish. "Are you saying that I'm not fired?"

Murdock remained stoic. "I can't fire you under the circumstances, Louis. You were supposed to be on liberty. You came off your personal free time to do me a favor. I do appreciate that. However, I am disappointed in what happened and I know it won't happen again, but I still want you as the ship's cook."

Louis sat straight up in his chair and smiled for the first time. "Thanks, Skipper. That means a lot. You do know, that I think a lot of those boys…more than any crew before them." Louis looked away for a moment and added, "I don't know why. That's just the way it is."

Murdock finally smiled. "I know that, Louis. We all feel that way. This crew is different and we all got a little too comfortable with them. I think we can consider this a warning sign as to how we perceive the crew, especially for sailors of this age."

Louis looked a little confused. "I don't know how else to be, Skipper. I treat them the same as I've treated every other crew. I don't know what to do different."

Murdock nodded. "Nothing, Louis. Just be yourself. Smitty and Josh were notified of the ordeal and will be back on board tonight. We'll have a meeting about this and how we'll approach it." Murdock paused again and shuffled some papers in front of him. "That's all, Louis."

The rest of the day was uneventful. The boys kept busy with Murdock's original set of tasks. Around 3:00 PM Jack went below to report they had completed his original request. Murdock looked up at Jack from his desk and nodded. "Thank you, Jack. Tell the boys to stay out of the rigging for today. I want everyone to come below and clean all the spaces down here, including the crew's quarters. We've gotten a little sloppy lately and this is an opportunity to get back on track. From now on, beds are to be made every morning and everyone's belongings stowed in their personal footlockers. No excuses."

Jack nodded, "Okay, Skipper. I'll tell them."

Jack turned to leave the room and Murdock stopped him. "Hold on a second, Jack." Jack turned to face the captain again.

Murdock was curious. "How are they doing up there?

Jack looked confused, "Well, like I said, they completed everything you asked them to do this morning."

Murdock shook his head, "No, no. How is everyone feeling?

Jack raised his eyebrows. "Oh, I think they're doing a lot better. Roger has had to go hang over the side a few times, but now it's just headaches. Everyone is just looking forward to getting back to their bunk."

Murdock nodded his head. "Okay, get things straightened out down here and that'll be the day. After dinner tonight, everyone needs to write Louis a letter of apology for sneaking off on him the other night. The letters have to be on my desk before lights out. That's all."

"Yes, sir." Jack turned and left the cabin.

Finally, six bells clanged. It was a more welcome sound than it had ever been. The boys slowly put things away and walked to the galley. Although Louis had prepared a large pot of chicken soup, everyone only sampled the hot liquid with a few spoonfuls, so as not upset the cook. Then, everyone thanked Louis and retired to their bunks.

Louis understood, and for once said nothing. The cook saw they needed to get some rest and said over his shoulder as he left the galley. "Just let that pot cool for a few hours. I'll be back to put it away later."

Scott was sound asleep in his bunk and someone shook his left leg. "Scotty, on your feet. You have visitors, topside. Captain's waiting."

Scott opened his eyes. It was Louis. The cook stood there and waited until Scott slid out of his bunk and followed him to the aft hatch.

Scott said nothing to Louis and climbed the steep ladder to the stern. When he stepped out on deck, he turned to look forward and saw his parents standing next to Captain Murdock by some deck chairs. He came around the port side and his mother shot him a huge smile. Sean just smiled and nodded at his son. Murdock stood there quietly watching with his hands clasped in front of him.

Scott smiled back but was cautious. He knew his parents were aware of what happened last night and was unsure of how his parents felt. He came around the aft hatch and walked up to his mother first.

Mary stepped in close to Scott, gave him a huge hug, and just held him for a minute. Sean cleared his throat and offered his right hand to shake, as he put his other hand on Scott's right shoulder.

Scott thought to himself, *They don't seem angry. Maybe they'll just let it go for now.* He was in no mood for more reprimand.

Murdock saw that everyone was happy to see each other and began to step away from the group. "Excuse me folks. I'll let you have your time alone together. Have a seat on the deck chairs. I'll be on deck, forward of the cabintop, if you need anything."

Sean and Mary were oblivious to Murdock's words. Their focus was on their son's presence and the changes in his outward appearance. He looked leaner but stronger, his face was a deep tan, his sandy colored hair was sun bleached a shade lighter making him almost blonde, and his hands had become very rough.

Scott took hold of his mother's arms and gently eased her away, and shook his father's hand. "It's good to see you guys. I thought it would be next year some time, but this is great." Scott motioned to the deck chairs.

Once they were all seated, Sean leaned forward in his chair and asked, "Scott, what has it been like. You look totally different from seven weeks ago."

Mary interrupted, "You look pale. Have you been eating right?"

Scott smiled as he answered. "Everything is fine. I'm learning a lot of things I never even thought about before," he glanced at his mother, "and we have a cook who is responsible for what we eat."

Mary's face suddenly turned serious and she looked off in the distance. "Yes, we know. We met him."

Scott felt the tension but changed the subject. "So, what brings you guys here? How did you ever get permission for this meeting? The rules stated no visitations."

Sean glanced quickly at his wife and Mary began to explain. "As you know, we came to Gloucester before you were scheduled to sail here...to Plymouth." Scott nodded that he remembered. Mary continued, "Well, I just thought life is too short to be deprived of seeing my son for a whole year. After all, what you boys did wasn't that bad."

Sean interrupted, "Mary...,"

Mary ignored Sean, "If George hadn't got killed, the Wrongful Death charge would not have been an issue and you boys would be back living your lives again." She paused and thought for a moment. "We're getting older and I just wanted to see my boy. That's all."

Sean hurriedly added, "And, you know how demanding your mother can be!"

Scott nodded his head and took what his father said at face value. "Well, everything is fine and everyone is getting along. My best friend is one of the Tall Ship Sailors from this town. His name is Jack Clark." He lifted his left wrist to eye level and showed them the grommet Jack had made him. "He gave me this after our sail from Gloucester. It's a sailing tradition to get one of these after completing your first long cruise, especially if you did something out of the ordinary."

Mary picked up on what Scott said. "Oh, and what was it that you did that was different?"

Scott thought quickly. He remembered he wasn't supposed to talk about Roger's tow behind the ship. "Oh, they let me steer the ship for a while, and as we were approaching Cape Cod Bay, sent me up into the cross trees to watch for landmarks."

Sean nodded his head as he stared at the deck. Eleven hours of hard sailing on a tall ship, Scott. I admit, I didn't think you had it in ya.' I'm impressed son."

Scott smiled but didn't say anything. Mary, however, shot Sean a dirty look. "Sean! How could you say such a thing? This is our boy, Scotty. He can do anything he has a mind to." She turned back to Scott, smiling.

Sean couldn't hold back any longer. He had to ask about the sailors and their night out on the town. "Scotty, I'd really like to know how your night out on the town went. You know… finally getting back out among the public and such."

Scott began to turn red before he realized his father was asking about the night with Smitty, or maybe it was just a trick to get Scott to admit what had happened after the sneak-away. Scott smiled and said, "We had a good time, Dad. We walked off the ship and it felt like total freedom. We also felt like we were a spectacle because we had to wear our dress whites. That drew a lot of attention, but Smitty brought us to a cool restaurant…kind of a sailor's sports bar, called Savage Sam's. We had a great dinner and then took a walk around the town before going back to the ship."

Sean was staring into Scott's eyes. He was waiting for Scott to offer information about the following night and the trouble they had gotten into. When it was apparent Scott was finished, Sean asked, "Anything else?"

Mary shot Sean a severe glance.

Scott pursed his lips and shook his head. He knew where his father was going with that question. "Uh, nope. Plymouth is a nice little harbor town. I may even consider moving back here someday."

Sean smiled and realized his boy was growing into a man. He was twenty years old and some things were just none of his father's business anymore. If Scott didn't want to discuss that night and what had transpired, whether it was for his mother's sake or otherwise, it was Scott's business, so he decided to leave it alone.

Mary broke the silence by talking about Scott's sister and her latest endeavors followed by a discussion of some of the immediate relatives and how they had all asked about him.

Scott listened to his mother speak and really didn't concentrate on the subject matter. He concentrated on the sound of her voice and how she inflected on some of the words. She never spoke in a monotone way. He watched the way her cheeks puffed up, just a little, when she smiled at something she just said, and how she shook her head as if to make herself believe that something she didn't believe in, would never happen.

Suddenly and without warning they realized Captain Murdock was standing before their little circle. "Sorry, folks. I believe it's time to call it a night." He glanced at Scott, "Say your good-byes and go below please. It's time for me to escort your folks off the ship."

Scott hugged his mother as she teared up a bit. He turned away quickly and met his father's expectant stare. Scott reached out and shook his hand. "Thanks for bringing Mom out here again, Dad. I appreciate it."

Sean was taken aback as he felt as if he was considered as just the driver for this little meeting.

Murdock stepped into the group and led them toward the gangway as Scott started for the aft hatch. Mary lowered her head and dropped her gaze to the deck as the captain led her away. "Where will you be going next?"

Scott stopped at the aft hatch and turned back toward his parents before going below. He heard Murdock's reply. "We'll be spending the rest of July in Cape Cod Bay. The next port of calls are Barnstable Harbor, Wellfleet Harbor and then on to Provincetown Harbor. Depending on the weather, we may head south and make for the Cape Cod Canal and spend some time in Buzzards Bay. After that, we'll sail around the southern coast of the Cape. Weather permitting, we are scheduled for a call in Block Island Harbor. That should bring us to late August."

Mary looked concerned, "Block Island? That's pretty far off the coast isn't it? I mean, I've heard of some bad storms out that way."

The captain was a patient man. He rubbed his beard and smiled once more. "Again, Mrs. Muldoon, everything depends on the weather and the sea conditions."

Mary stopped before debarking the ship and faced Murdock. "That's a lot of sailing and demonstrations. Will you be going back to Gloucester at all?"

Murdock met her gaze and smiled as he crossed his arms in front of his chest. "After we come around the northern tip of the Cape, I'll probably sail Northeast to Boston Harbor for one more port of call and then head into Gloucester for repairs… which the boys will be tasked with. If we're still seaworthy, our schedule is to sail north to a group of islands off of Portsmouth, New Hampshire. Probably be anchoring at a little island by the name of Smuttynose. There's a lot of history…or legend there. It'll be good for the boys."

Mary looked at her husband and back to the captain. "Well, now you're into the fall. I hope the seas won't be too rough."

Murdock placed his left hand lightly against Mary's lower back as if to encourage her to depart. "The fall is an exciting time to sail. The winds will be stronger but we'll be watching for any dangerous conditions." He moved toward Mary to get her to move into the gangway.

Sean got the hint and took Mary by the hand. "Let's go, Mary. I'm sure the captain knows what he's doing." He looked at Murdock and winked. "Thank you for allowing our time with Scott."

Murdock nodded back at the smiling father. "Absolutely. Have a safe trip home."

Scott waited until his parents had debarked. He turned and descended the aft hatch ladder. *Hmm, Smuttynose. I wonder what that's all about?*

The Muldoons crossed the gangway ramp and worked their way across the pier before climbing the stairs to the wharf.

Murdock waited until the couple were at their car and followed Scott down the aft hatch ladder.

CHAPTER THIRTY THREE

Monday morning found the Defiant's entire crew of Tall Ship Sailors and regular crew on deck and at amidships. It was the widest section of the ship and could accommodate everyone when the captain only wanted to say something once. The boys stood aft of the cabintop facing the helm while the regular crew stood in a recessed part of the deck on either side of the helm.

It was 7:00 AM with a moderate breeze coming in from the northeast. The harbor was quiet for the time being and the skies were overcast. A chill was evident that required everyone to wear a sweatshirt, hoodie or windbreaker. The group remained quiet as they waited for the captain to appear at the aft hatch. Only the sounds of the ship's responses to the elements around her were evident. Wind whistled through and around the rigging, and block and tackle consistently banged against masts and spars in unison with the waves that rolled under the Defiant's keel. Wooden deck planking creaked and groaned and the pennants at the top of the main mast and at the stern, snapped their replies to the harbor's weather.

Finally, Murdock appeared on deck and walked into the space between the two sects of crew. He paced starboard to port twice before speaking, then stopped at the ship's centerline and faced the Tall Ship Sailors. "This is the first time I have seen this crew show any kind of segregation. In the past, these meetings have been informal and casual but now I see that there is definitely a line of demarcation." He stopped and gestured toward the Tall Ship Sailors. "Is this to mean you guys want to be separate from the regular crew...to be treated differently?" No one spoke. Murdock turned and looked at the regular crew. "How about you sailors? Is this what you want?"

The three regular crew shook their heads and looked at Smitty. He knew he had to say something. First mate was a lonely position. He didn't have the power the captain did, yet he was also considered one of the crew...the voice of the men, so to speak. Smitty reluctantly rose his hand. "It's not what we want, Skipper. I think there is an awkward feeling here because of what happened Saturday night. Speaking for the regulars, I can say that it's not something we haven't experienced before with other crews. We almost expect something like that to happen at some point," he paused and looked at the Tall Ship Sailors, "but the boys need to understand how many people they disappointed and inconvenienced, in doing what they did. They also need to know we understand, as their crewmates and mentors. We realize why they are on this ship. We don't hold that against them but we do want them to know there will always be consequences. Missing the Parade of Tall Ships in Mystic hurt us all, but there will be other times and opportunities. We feel the boys have paid their debt spending a night in jail, missing the One Hundred Year Parade in Mystic, and working it off yesterday on their day off." Smitty nodded to the regulars who readily nodded their heads in agreement and looked directly at the Tall Ship Sailors. "As First Mate, I can say the regular crew is over it. We are ready to move on with no hard feelings.

Murdock nodded his head and turned to face the Tall Ship Sailors. "Does anyone have anything to say?"

There was an uncomfortable moment with everyone staring into the cold deck. Scott raised his hand, "We don't want to be separate or special. I think the problem is that we know what we did wrong, and collectively feel embarrassed to the people that were trying to do right by us." Scott stopped and looked at the other five sailors. The boys nodded in agreement. Scott turned back to the captain. "We're ready to move on too."

Murdock let the tiniest smile cross his face. "Well, that's good. As I've said before, we are a team on this ship and we can't sail it without each other." He stopped and paced the deck. "Alright then, let me get to what I came up here for. We will set sail for Barnstable Harbor this afternoon, and we will be spending the month of July in Cape Cod Bay. There are three scheduled ports of call, the first is Barnstable Harbor, about twenty miles from here. The next will be Wellfleet Harbor, followed by Provincetown Harbor. Each of those calls include tours and demonstrations which include long hours. The ship must be kept squeaky clean and safe for our guests. Originally, we were supposed to sail a southwesterly course from Provincetown Harbor across Cape Cod Bay, to the Cape Cod Canal. That would have been the route we would have taken to get to Mystic, but in spite of that, we are scheduled for a call in Block Island Harbor which is an island nine miles south of the Rhode Island coast and east of Montauk Point in Long Island. That trip depends largely on weather and sea conditions."

The boys shared concerned looks with one another as they knew they were going out to sea.

Murdock saw the facial expressions and continued. "We'll be sailing through Block Island Sound to get there and It'll be a long haul, but we ought to be able to do it in two legs. If we go, we'll probably spend a night somewhere off Rhode Island and sail into Block the next day. It's about a ninety-mile cruise. From there, we'll head northeast along the southern end of the Cape, then go due north along the Cape's eastern coast. There will be one more port of call in Boston Harbor before returning to Gloucester for repairs. After that, we are scheduled for a small set of islands off Portsmouth, New Hampshire...one of which is called Smuttynose." The captain was quiet again and paced the deck. He walked from port to starboard, obviously thinking out loud, then offered a different plan. "There is an alternate plan which has us sailing north to Boston Harbor and then to Gloucester for repairs. Right now, that is the way I'm leaning. That'll be the beginning of August which is known to the sailing world as the summer doldrums. The winds are inconsistent and sometimes don't exist at all. If we get caught in that, we could literally be dead in the water. Because of sudden storms and excessive fog, we could be in peril and I don't want to be east of the Cape if that is what we can expect."

The boys seemed to appear more relaxed at the news and the captain's careful attention to weather.

Murdock stopped pacing and looked to the sky. "It all depends on the weather. We don't have radar on board or short-wave radio to give us any updates or warnings as to the latest weather forecasts, so we'll have to use the old and accepted sailing techniques...the most important of which, is to err in the way of caution."

Murdock looked at the young crew for any signs of nervousness. He knew the regular crew was seasoned and acceptable to either alternative. "Okay then, let's prepare to get underway." He looked at his watch. It was 7:30 AM. "We'll leave Plymouth Harbor at 1:00 PM...right after lunch, and set sail for Barnstable harbor. It'll be a short twenty-six-mile cruise southeast of here. It's a shallow harbor, so I want a lookout in the crosstrees and one in the bow. Who is ever in the crosstrees will look for brown water ahead of the ship. Brown water means it's shallow or there's a sandbar there. If you see anything like that, including ships approaching us at high speed or in close proximity, hail the helmsman." Murdock paused a moment. "Any questions?"

The crew remained quiet. Murdock nodded his head. "Get her ready. Set sail for Barnstable at 1:00 PM. That's all." He turned and disappeared into the aft hatch.

$\triangledown$

After lunch, the crew was standing ready at their sailing stations. Smitty was at the helm and Josh was standing-by at amidships. Louis was below securing anything to the bulkhead that could move or fall. Burt, the ship's mascot followed Louis around as he went to each space below decks.

Murdock appeared on deck precisely at 1:00 PM. He stood at amidships on the ship's centerline and looked up at the pennants that flew at the top of the main and fore masts. The wind was coming out of the northeast…over the Defiant's starboard side. He raised his hands to his face and cupped them around his mouth. "We're going to swing off the wind! Raise the small jib sail and cast off the bow lines. Hold the stern lines!" He turned toward Smitty, "Helm, give me hard over and fall off to port."

The Defiant's jib sail caught the light breeze and pushed the Defiant's bow out to the port side and away from the pier while her stern lines kept her anchored to the mooring. Murdock watched the bow and turned to the stern. The entire ship pivoted on the still secured stern as the bow responded to the wind and the rudder's position. "Away the stern lines! Helm, steer for open harbor."

The Defiant left its pier and slowly angled out into the harbor. As she left her berthing area, Murdock shouted above the breeze, "Mainsail!"

Josh helped Scotty and Jack raise the huge triangular sail and the ship began to get way on. Murdock looked over to Smitty at the helm, "Steady as she goes, Smitty. Once you get out into the harbor, go north and make a starboard turn in front of Duxbury Light. Make for Cape Cod Bay and then south to Barnstable Harbor."

Smitty held the helm with both hands and smiled. "Aye, Skipper."

Murdock turned and went below through the aft hatch.

The schooner Defiant was once again underway as she began her exit from Plymouth Harbor. Smitty swung the helm over and sailed her close to the northeasterly breeze, and just as the captain requested, made a starboard turn at Duxbury Pier Light. The strength of the wind increased noticeably as the Defiant left the protected harbor in Plymouth and entered Plymouth Bay.

The day had become sunny with scattered clouds and the seas were light to moderate. Once they passed south of Plymouth Light, Smitty swung the helm over hard to starboard to catch the ever-stiffening northeast wind, and sailed into Cape Cod Bay. The ship now ran before the wind with seas approaching their stern quarter. Smitty smiled and thought, *Got a good wind behind us and following seas. Should make good time on this leg.* He looked ahead and knew his voice would carry with the wind, "Bow! Raise the second jib sail!" Percy and Teddy scrambled about the bow pulling the number two jib out of the sail locker while Roger clipped it to its halyard and headstay. The sail rose from the deck and snapped loudly as it opened like a blossoming flower.

Smitty looked up at the pennant atop the mainmast. The wind was directly behind them now. He turned the helm slightly so the wind was at a slight angle to their stern and ordered the foresail aloft. There were more snapping sounds as sail cloth was consumed with wind. The masts and spars moaned and creaked as the ship realized the new stresses imposed by natures invisible force. The ship began to heal to starboard and began to develop a rhythm as the swells rolled under her keel and pushed her along a southeasterly tack. Defiant was sailing at her maximum hull speed of eleven knots.

Down below, Murdock felt the increased speed and the heel over to starboard. He left his cabin and came topside. He went aft and approached the helm. Smitty was looking aloft checking the sails and pennants. Four of Defiant's seven sails were under power. "In a rush?"

Smitty dropped his gaze to see Murdock standing in front of him. "No sir. Just taking advantage of a good sailing day. The ship is responding beautifully…conditions are perfect, and we should be able to sail all the way in on this breeze."

Murdock smiled and looked about the ship. "Yeah, these are good sailing conditions…for sure."

Smitty kept his eyes on the sails and the area ahead. "The current will be with us at least until we get to the Cape Cod Canal…then we'll be fighting a cross current. I figure we'll be getting into port about 3:00."

Murdock rubbed his beard. "Okay, good. Once we get around Sandy Neck Light, sail for our pier. Same place as usual…South Pier and south of the harbor entrance. We should be moored up by 4:00 PM. Let the boys get her secured and ready for the next couple of days. We'll be a tourist attraction until Wednesday evening and sail for Wellfleet on Thursday morning."

Smitty absently nodded, "Okay, Skipper."

Murdock started for the aft hatch. "Call if we get near any brown water or boat traffic. I'll be in my cabin doing the boy's evaluations."

Smitty answered without taking his eyes off the horizon. "Aye, Cap'n."

▽

"Brown water ahead!" It was Roger's turn in the crosstrees. He looked down toward the helm and cupped one hand around his mouth and shouted louder. "Smitty! Brown water ahead!"

Smitty heard the call. "How far ahead?"

Roger could see Smitty was shouting something back at him but couldn't make out the words. He pointed at his right ear with his free hand and shook his head. Smitty shouted above the breeze to no avail, so he took both hands off the helm and spread his arms apart with palms facing up, indicating confusion.

Roger got the message and called. "Fifty yards, dead ahead."

Once again, Smitty let the helm go and spread his arms with hands faced inward.

Roger held onto one of the shroud lines and bent toward the deck. "About thirty yards wide."

Smitty felt as if his heart had climbed into his throat. *Fifty yards? At this speed I'll be there in about fifteen seconds!* Smitty scanned the horizon quickly. *Some boat traffic on the port side…not enough room to get around the sandbar.* He looked aft and saw a fishing boat off the stern quarter, but far enough away.

He thought quickly, *Right now, the sand bar is dead ahead. I'll fall off to starboard about twenty degrees just enough to get around it. I hope Roger estimated its width correctly.* He shouted to Jack and Scott, "Let the mainsail out until she starts to luff." Smitty swung the helm over until he saw twenty degrees on the ship's compass in front of him. The bow slowly responded and began falling off to starboard.

Up in the crosstrees Roger watched the Defiant's bow as it moved away from a collision course with the sandbar. The ship was approaching the brown water fast. It was going to be close. He grabbed onto the shroud lines near his shoulders and held on.

Smitty held the helm tightly. Further course adjustment would put them in peril with approaching boat traffic off their stern quarter. He held his course and waited. There was a sudden thud off the port side followed by a shudder. The defiant had grazed the edge of the sandbar. The entire ship seemed to vibrate for a few seconds, and then they were clear.

Roger felt the same vibration which was more pronounced in the cross trees. He held his breath as he watched the Defiant sail past the brown water's extreme edge. Once clear, the ship seemed to lurch forward and go back to its normal rhythm.

Smitty looked aloft, as Roger gave him a thumbs up signal. "Don't let us get that close again, Roger. Use your binoculars if you have to."

Roger drew a sigh of relief and gave Smitty another thumbs up.

The entire crew began to relax and began to focus on their sailing stations again. Suddenly, Captain Murdock burst through the aft hatch. He looked from side to side and then walked over to Smitty. "What in hell happened? It felt like we hit something."

Smitty's face was stoic. "We did, Skipper. We nudged the edge of a huge sandbar that crept up on us. We're past it now... shook the shit out of the ship and rigging but it looks as if everything is okay."

Murdock looked up in the crosstrees. Roger was in position and peered through his binoculars watching the open ocean. "What was Roger doing? Why didn't he see the brown water? I warned everyone about that."

Smitty grimaced as he moved his head to the side. "He did see it, and he reported it, Skipper. The problem was that he didn't see it until we were fifty yards away. I had about fifteen seconds to maneuver with boat traffic to port and one approaching from astern."

Murdock didn't let up. "That's not what I asked, Smitty. Why didn't he see it coming? Wasn't he paying attention?"

Smitty shrugged. "It could have been the glare on the water, Skip. I don't know. He paused and looked Murdock in the eye. "He did warn us and we got clear."

Murdock continued to stare at Roger in the crosstrees. His jaw was set and one eye squinted shut. "Once we get into port, get Roger in the water with snorkeling gear. I want him to check for damage…and then get me a damage report."

Murdock shook his head from side to side, turned and went to the aft hatch. He turned and looked back at Smitty. "I want that report before supper…on my desk and typed." Murdock turned and went below again.

$$\triangledown$$

The Defiant sailed into Barnstable Harbor without further incident. Roger had come down from his perch, as the Defiant approached the harbor's entrance, and helped to secure the ship to the pier. Smitty watched the boys as they secured the mooring lines and glanced at his watch. It was 4:20 in the afternoon. Some of the sailors started to go below to wash up before supper.

Roger was in the stern talking to the harbor's line handlers. Smitty walked over to the port rail and called him. "Roger! Roger Bower!"

Roger turned his head and seemed surprised. Smitty motioned him over to the port rail.

"What's up, Smitty? I was just shootin' the shit with those line handlers."

Smitty looked out into the harbor. "Yeah, I know. That's okay. I need you to get some snorkeling gear and go down to check out the port side where we hit that sandbar."

Roger's face dropped. "Now? The day's over, Smitty." Roger paused and a curious smile crossed his face. "Oh, I get it. This is about the sandbar collision. I did my part. You're the one that hit it."

Smitty turned from the railing and faced Roger. He looked at the young sailor and thought, *you ungrateful, little bastard.* "Get that snorkeling gear on now before I throw you over the side without it. Move it, mister!"

Roger's face dropped again. He'd never seen Smitty lose his cool like that, let alone raise his voice. He ran for the deck locker and grabbed the snorkeling gear while Smitty waited.

Under Smitty's direction, Roger dropped over the side and into the cold, dark water of Barnstable Harbor to look for the damaged hull planking. Smitty kept vigil above the snorkeling sailor and pointed out specific areas of concern. Roger said he saw what looked like straight cracks in the middle of three rows of planking. The cracks looked to be about sixteen to twenty-four inches long and some of the cotton caulking looked as if it was spilling out.

After thirty minutes, Smitty was satisfied and threw a rope ladder over the side. "Okay, it appears there's only minor damage to three rows of planking and the loss of some paint. Come on up and get cleaned up for supper."

Roger climbed the rope ladder and slid over the railing. He was covered with seaweed and other pieces of flotsam. The boy shivered as he glared at the first mate. Smitty returned the gesture with a sarcastic smile. Seawater dripped from the young sailor as he walked to the deck locker. Roger stowed his snorkeling gear and headed for the aft hatch. *I get blamed for everything on this ship.*

Before he went below, Smitty reminded the dripping sailor, "Roger, there are consequences in life…either because of your actions or because of what you say. Don't be afraid to take ownership." Smitty paused and met Roger's glare. "Think about that." Roger's facial expression didn't change. He turned and disappeared into the aft hatch.

CHAPTER THIRTY FOUR

It was supper time on the Defiant. Roger was the last one to take a seat. Teddy noticed the late arrival. "Hey Rog, this is a first. You're usually the first one to supper."

Roger murmured something under his breath and sat at the end of the galley table. His hair was still wet and uncombed. His shirt tails hung outside his jeans and he was barefoot. Louis walked up to the table and crossed his arms in front of him. "You don't show up to my table like that, Mr. Bower. You know the rules. Tuck in your shirt, get some shoes on, and comb your hair...or you don't eat." Louis was unaware of the extra duty Roger had just pulled with Smitty.

Roger slammed his glass down on the wooden table and stood up. "That's fine with me. I don't need any crap from you either." He turned and walked out of the galley and headed for the forward hatch.

Teddy and Percy rose to go after him, but Louis raised his right hand as if to halt their effort. "Leave him be for now. I'll talk to him later."

An awkward silence enveloped the room. Finally, Scott broke the silence. "Hey, Louis. So, I guess it's the same thing for the next couple of days...tours and demonstrations again?"

Louis was drying one of the large pots. "That's the plan, but it's all based on the weather. We got a weather front coming in late tomorrow morning. Supposed to be a lot of rain, so you guys will be right down here, in your quarters, if you're not topside talking to visitors."

Percy asked, "Are one of you guys going to take us out on the town again?"

Louis didn't answer but looked up from his pot with a surprised look. Percy continued, "You know, so we can see what Barnstable is like."

Louis continued to work on his pot and answered Percy without looking at him. "This ain't a pleasure cruise, Percy. It's not about showin' you guys each port of call. That was something the captain did for you guys 'cause he was proud of you. Most crews don't get that." Louis paused a minute and hung the pot from one of the overhead timbers. "If you guys aren't topside working with visitors or working on the ship, you'll be right here in crew's quarters. That's just how it's gonna' be for a while."

The crew muttered their dissatisfaction and Louis smiled. "You should know by now that if you screw up on this ship, you will pay for a long time. I hope you guys have Playboys or some kinda' readin' material. This could be a long couple of days."

The cook wrapped his dish cloth around another wooden timber as he headed for the foreward hatch ladder. "I'm goin' to get Roger. You guys are in for the night."

Louis got to the top of the ladder and stuck his head out through the hatch. He spotted Roger on the starboard bow leaning over the railing with his head down.

The cook came up on deck and stood for a moment. "Hope you're not thinking of throwing yourself overboard. The water is cold down here in Barnstable."

Roger turned around and nodded. "Yeah, tell me about it."

Louis walked toward the boy. "Okay, what happened? You were late for supper and showed up half dressed, not to mention that lousy mood you're in."

Roger turned around and told Louis what Smitty had him do when everyone else went below for supper.

"Is that supposed to make me feel bad for you, sailor?"

Roger was shocked. "He made me do the damage check and he's the one who was steering the ship."

Louis smiled and shook his head. "You still don't get it do you?" We all hit the sandbar. You were our eyes in the crosstrees. We're blind without someone as a lookout. There's no radar or sonar on board. We're sailing like they did in the old days. That's one way of making it a little tougher...and scarier for you guys. Our job is to show you guys what real life is all about...the hard way. It's the crux of your rehabilitation on this ship."

Louis stopped for a minute to let all that sink in. "The regular crew is the best at what they do and that's why they have been approved to sail in open ocean on a vessel like this with six green sailors as crew. If you think that was Smitty's fault than I know you weren't watching things. You should have seen that sandbar a lot sooner than you did," Louis paused for effect then continued, '...and did you see what kind of maneuvering he had to do with the boat traffic that was around us? Roger, there are right of way rules out here. You just can't swerve in front of someone, like drivin' a car. You cause a collision out on the ocean and ships can sink, and people can die. What Smitty did with such short notice was amazing. You gave him about fifteen seconds to make it happen. If I know Smitty, he probably covered your ass in front of the captain...and if I know the captain, it was him who told Smitty to send you over the side."

Louis turned to go back below and Roger stopped him. "Wait. Murdock was on deck?"

Louis stopped, "Yeah. I saw him go topside to see what happened. He would have asked Smitty what happened and if the lookout had warned him. Since the captain hasn't spoken to you, it looks to me like Smitty covered for you. Murdock ain't no pushover either. He knows what happened and sent you over the side so maybe next time you'll pay more attention."

Louis bent down to get into the forward hatch. "Okay, Roger. I said my piece. Get below. No one is allowed topside tonight." He paused before his head disappeared through the hatch, "...and get over yourself. It ain't all about you." His head disappeared into the hatch and the cook was gone.

Roger waited for Louis to descend the forward hatch ladder and took one more look at the darkened harbor. Mooring lights reflected off the black water and stars twinkled in the sky. He took a deep breath and followed Louis below.

Tuesday morning arrived overcast and breezy. The boys were on deck at 7:00 AM ready to attend tourists. Because of the impending weather, Murdock had given the crew permission to wear their best work clothes in lieu of their dress whites. Anticipating the arrival of at least one guest, the sailors stood ready at their sailing stations. By 8:30, not a soul had visited the pier. Granted, it was a weekday but it was the height of vacation season, so Murdock felt there could possibly be a few stragglers looking for information.

Murdock came up on deck and checked the weather. The sky was heavy with dark clouds and the waves grew in size as they rolled into the harbor. The first mate and captain conferred for a while as they walked toward the bow. Murdock walked aft and disembarked the Defiant while Smitty went to the helm and rang the ship's bell three times.

The boys knew the familiar signal. It was time for a ship's meeting. Everyone went aft and Smitty dismissed them for the day. "That's it for the day, sailors. There's a tropical storm coming in, so get everything lashed down, and close all the hatches. It's going to be high winds and horizontal rain. Once everything is secured up here, you guys are to go below and find something to do. We'd like you to write some letters to your families or any special people in your lives. After that, you are on your own time. Stay in the crew's quarters and see me in the captain's cabin if you have any problems. I'll be on board for the rest of the afternoon."

The crew followed through on Smitty's directions and secured the ship for the storm. The part that took the most focus was everything below decks. Looking for anything that could be knocked loose was always frustrating and time consuming. After an hour of closing up the ship and checking the mooring lines, Defiant was ready. One by one, each sailor headed for the crew's quarters to ride out the storm.

The regular crew had all gone ashore on separate errands. Josh had taken Burtt with him to a marine supply store to look for rigging supplies. Louis had gone into town to pick up some groceries and replenish their water supply and Murdock had gone to check in with the harbor master and local sheriff's department. The plan was to have everyone back on the ship before the storm hit.

Below decks, the young sailors tried to keep busy reading or writing letters. After a few hours, tedium began to set in as they waited for the storm to arrive, so eventually, the books were put aside and their young minds searched for more interesting ways to pass the time. There wasn't much room in the crew's quarters and the passageway that ran the length of the ship was only wide enough to accommodate people in a single file. They would have to find something that didn't require too much movement.

About mid-afternoon, Jack reached into his ditty bag and pulled out a deck of cards. "Okay, who's up for some poker?"

Scott and Teddy jumped down from their bunks and Roger sat up in his. "Really? Are we playing for money or just passing time?"

Jack sat at the head of the galley table shuffling a deck of cards. "Money, baby…or anything else you're willing to put up."

Roger got out of his bunk and reached under his mattress. He turned to the group at the table and put a bottle of vodka on the table. "Good. Then, I'm in."

Scott looked at Jack and raised his eyebrows. He looked back at Roger and said, "Rog, how did you get that aboard? You realize that is highly against the rules."

Roger slid the bottle to the center of the table. "Yeah, I know, but we're all tightened down and most of the regulars are ashore." He turned to Percy. "Sit over by the galley entrance and watch for anyone coming this way. You should be able to hear them coming long before you see them."

Percy shrugged his shoulders. "Okay, I don't know how to play anyway."

Scott went to the small refrigerator and pulled out a quart of orange juice and retrieved some glasses from a wooden cabinet. "At least we have something to mix with the vodka."

Jack dealt the first hand. "Okay, five-card draw…deuces wild. Anti-up."

The boys played and drank Roger's vodka for two hours. They were so involved with losing and winning each other's money, they hadn't realized most of the vodka was gone or that the storm was upon them. Unbeknownst to the distracted sailors, the ship's reaction to the storm had worsened and moved violently in her mooring, as the storm increased in strength.

The Defiant rocked in her mooring and kitchen utensils that hung from the overhead clanged against each other. The boys played harder as they began to write each other IOUs and shout expletives at one another. Suddenly a huge gust of wind rocked the Defiant accompanied by an incoming wave. The sudden jolt to the ship knocked Percy from his chair and onto the floor.

Percy was in a prone position, face down on the deck, and saw the light suddenly pour out of the captain's cabin. "Hey, Smitty's coming!"

The boys scrambled to clear the table of money and IOUs and Jack snuffed the gas lantern that hung over the galley table, the cabin's only light. Roger grabbed the empty bottle of vodka and jammed it under his mattress while everyone dove for their bunks. The cabin was dark.

Smitty walked into the crew's quarters and smelled alcohol in the cramped space. The boys appeared to be asleep. "Is everyone okay? We just took a huge wave from the starboard side." No one moved...no one said a word. Smitty smiled to himself. "Okay, good. I heard a chair go over but it looks like no one was in it." Smitty looked down at the deck and saw a lonely playing card under the galley table. He picked it up and threw it on the table. "Hmm, ace of spades."

Smitty took one more look around the room. "You guys have an hour or so before supper. The captain will be back about the same time, so get yourselves together. I hear there's a crew's quarters inspection before supper." Smitty smiled to himself again, turned and walked out into the passageway on his way back to the captain's cabin.

When Smitty's footfalls faded down the long passageway, Jack whispered over to Roger. "Where's the bottle?"

"I got it jammed under my mattress...near the bulkhead."

Jack slid out of his lower bunk and crawled over to Roger. "Give me the bottle."

Roger could barely see Jack's face. "What are you going to do with it?"

"I'm gonna' wait a few minutes for Smitty to get settled in the captain's cabin and take it topside."

Roger handed the bottle over to Jack in the darkness and Jack slithered back to his own bunk. He let a few minutes pass and quietly padded over to the foreward hatch ladder. He looked up the ladder and saw the hatch was closed. Before he began his climb up the ladder, he took another peak down the dimly lit passageway. The captain cabin's door was slightly ajar allowing a crack of light to shine into the corridor. Jack looked back up the ladder. *The storm is pretty bad out there. Even if the hatch creaks when I open it, the wind and thunder will drown it out.*

Feeling comfortable with his decision, Jack slowly climbed the vertical ladder to the foreward hatch, holding the vodka bottle in his left hand. When he arrived at the top rung, he pushed open the hatch. It creaked and let in the sounds of the storm, in addition to rain and wind. Jack let the hatch back down slowly. *Okay, I gotta' do this quick. It's pretty nasty out there...and dark.* He threw open the hatch and climbed halfway out. A violent wind ripped at his exposed torso and hard rain pelted his exposed skin. Jack looked over to starboard and flung the bottle as hard as he could. Just as he wound up to throw a bolt of lightning seemed to crack right over the Defiant and lit up Jack's half exposed body. It was dark again in two seconds. The bottle disappeared into the wet, black afternoon.

Jack closed the hatch as he lowered himself down the ladder. When he turned to look down, he found Smitty standing at the bottom of the ladder.

"What in hell are you doing, Jack? It's storming bad out there."

Jack was dripping wet. He stood in front of Smitty in only his blue jeans and bare feet. Water streamed down the bare skin of his upper body. "Oh, I was just checking on the storm, Smitty. It was pretty noisy out there." Jack paused for a moment and reminded himself, *Don't get too close to him or he'll smell the alcohol.* Jack stepped back from the ladder and away from Smitty.

Smitty leaned against the passageway wall with his arms folded in front of his chest. "Oh, I see…and are we safe, Mr. Clark?"

Jack knew Smitty wasn't swallowing his story. "I know no one is allowed topside this afternoon, but I was curious. It was probably a stupid thing to do, and I got soaked as soon as I opened the hatch. It seemed like the rain was coming at me sideways."

Smitty smiled back at the young sailor. "Well, yes it was a stupid thing to do and the rain was coming at you from the side. This is a tropical storm, Jack…like a microburst, but ten times stronger. You could have got struck by lightning sticking your body above the deck like that."

Jack started for the crew's quarters, "Well, I won't be doing that again. I'm gonna' go get dried off. See ya' later, Smitty."

Smitty stopped Jack before he disappeared into the dark space. "I hope I don't find anything floating around the ship or around the pier in the morning except seaweed or seagulls."

Jack's face flushed red but was unseen by Smitty in the dim passageway. He nodded and disappeared into the dark crew's quarters.

Smitty watched him go and shook his head. *Every crew. They're all the same.*

▽

The next morning, Smitty, Josh and Captain Murdock were below decks assessing the bilge water level. They had access boards pulled up in several places in the engine room, and along the ship's passageway. The compromised port hull was minor but the cracks in the hull's planking were definitely allowing water into the Defiant. Murdock watched Smitty measure the bilge water level. "It doesn't look much higher than usual, Smitty. Your damage report said there were sixteen to twenty-four-inch hairline cracks in the planking on three different rows."

Smitty stood up and faced Murdock. "That's correct, Skipper. But Roger said some of the cotton caulking was spilling out from between the planking too."

Murdock waved his hand at the problem as if to brush it away. "Ah, there's only three small cracks halfway between the waterline and the keel that will swell up and seal in a few days. They're not leaking badly enough that the bilge pumps can't handle it, so I think we can continue our sailing schedule as planned."

Smitty rubbed his chin with the back of his right wrist. "I don't know, Skipper. If we get into some rough weather, we might be taking a chance on opening up those cracks."

Murdock looked at the ship's deckhand. "What's your opinion, Josh?"

"Well, our bilge pumps are in good shape and not too old. I think we can rely on them if we need to. We can't get at the cracked planking from inside the ship, so we can't apply a temporary fix before we sail, and we have to rely on what Roger saw, as the extent and magnitude of the damage." Josh stopped as if he was thinking through what he had just listed as concerns. "I think the damage is minor enough to continue with our schedule until we finish up at Provincetown Harbor. We can send the boys down with snorkeling gear to check the cracks at each port of call. If it's getting worse, we can just sail for home."

Murdock nodded his head as if considering Josh's thought process. "So, you're comfortable sailing with the cracked planking?"

Josh quickly answered. "I'm saying we're okay for now as long as we stay in Cape Cod Bay and keep an eye on the cracks.

I feel we should blowoff the Boston Harbor call and sail straight for Gloucester for repairs after Provincetown. We'll be in open ocean at that point and we'll have to watch the weather closely. I agree with Smitty that we could run the risk of opening up those cracks if we get into rough weather."

Murdock thought for a moment and considered what his first and second officers had suggested. "Okay, we have one more day here in Barnstable. Tomorrow is going to be another crappy day…overcast with a forty percent chance of rain. I'm cancelling the tours and demonstrations, and we'll send the boys over the side in shifts to work on those cracks."

Murdock turned to Smitty. "For now, we'll just get the boys to jam some caulking and tube tar between the planks and over the cracks, and hope the bilge pumps can keep up. We'll check the damaged area again when we get to Wellfleet and make more repairs if we have to. Send Jack and Scotty over first. Get the rest of the boys busy on regular deck chores and general maintenance. We'll set sail for Wellfleet Harbor on Thursday." Murdock turned away from the two sailors and walked to his cabin.

Josh and Smitty said nothing about the captain's decision. Their feeling was evident by their facial expressions. They looked each other in the eye with raised eyebrows and shook their heads. Once the captain had disappeared into his cabin, Josh began replacing the bilge access plates and Smitty leaned against the aft passageway rail with folded arms as he considered Murdock's decision. After a few minutes he shook his head and went topside through the aft hatch. It was going to be a long two weeks before heading home for repairs.

Smitty rang the ship's bell and gave the boys the news about the cancelled tours and the decision to repair the ship's hull cracks before sailing to Wellfleet Harbor. The boys were indifferent to the news and half expected Murdock's decision. Murdock was known to push his ship and crew while keeping good judgement a priority. They knew a few cracks in the hull wouldn't deter him from keeping the Defiant's assigned sailing schedule.

Smitty considered the crew's blank stares and asked, "I'm going to need you guys to go over the side in teams of two from time to time to check on the hull cracks and maybe give them a temporary fix. Today after lunch, Jack and Scott will be the first shift. The rest of you will be on regular clean up and maintenance. The storm brought a lot of crap aboard last night, so I want it swabbed. Unfurl the sails and dry 'em out, check all the lines and shrouds and make sure everything is taut. When that's done come and see me." He looked over at Jack and Scott. Get the snorkeling gear out of the deck locker and get the repair materials from Josh. He'll be supervising that operation." He looked at the expressionless crew. "Okay, that's it. Get some lunch and get to the chores. We set sail for Wellfleet Harbor tomorrow at 9:00 AM."

Scott and Jack weren't happy about their new assignment but showed up at the deck locker to get their snorkeling gear and repair materials. Josh was waiting for them and gave them a repair bag made of netting with a cinch strap at it's opening. Inside were some hemp, cotton caulking, an iron chisel, a couple of tubes of tar, and a small squeegee.

Jack took the bag from Josh and gave him a confused look. "How are we supposed to use all this stuff while using a snorkel? The damage is way below the waterline so we really can't use the snorkels and we don't have anything to hold us in place while we're working."

Josh smiled at the youth. "The rules on this ship are to sail it and maintain it using the old ways. How do you think they would have done this in the 1800s? At least we're giving you snorkeling gear."

Scotty smirked at Josh. "Josh! Be real, man! We're going to keep floating to the surface."

Josh pointed over to a coil of rope he had placed on the deck earlier. There was a large mushroom anchor attached to one end. "I knew you guys wouldn't figure this out. Lash that anchor's line to the deck rail above your work area and then drop the anchor over the side before you start working. The anchor is heavy enough for you to hold onto and keep you from rising to the surface while you're working." He smiled sarcastically at the two boys, "Don't forget to come up for air though." Josh chuckled and walked away. "Do a good job."

Scott and Jack stared at each other for a moment, then put on their gear, dropped their work anchor and went over the side into the cold water.

The boys found the three rows of damaged planking and struggled with their materials as they tried to fill the cracks and gaps with hemp, caulking, and tube tar. Surprisingly, the work anchor worked well and after about an hour the boys were able to time their repair activity with needed returns to the surface for air. By 3:30 in the afternoon, the cool water of the harbor had taken its toll and the boys were too cold to continue. They felt the repair was complete and was as good as it could be. Whether it would work, was another story.

The two sailors removed their swim fins and threw them up onto the deck. They swam over to a rope ladder that had been dropped for them and climbed back aboard the ship.

Their fingers were so cold and numb they could barely close them around the rope rungs. When their bare skin was exposed to the breezy ocean air, they began to shiver violently. Josh waited for them at the deck rail with hot coffee and blankets. "Good show, guys. Get warmed up and go stow your gear and materials. You're done for the day. Go below, relax and get ready for supper. The rest of the crew is still working on maintenance. They'll meet you below later."

Jack and Scott wrapped the blankets around their bodies and drank the hot coffee. When the shivering began to subside, they went below through the aft hatch. The foreword hatch was out of the question, as the hatch's vertical ladder would have been too difficult to negotiate.

As they walked down the narrow passageway, the thought of leaving in the morning was comforting. Their impression was that Barnstable brought sandbars, cold water, and violent storms. It would be good to leave this place in the morning. Hopefully, the sun would return and warm summer weather would be the rule again.

CHAPTER THIRTY FIVE

After lunch on their second day in Barnstable, the Defiant cast off their mooring lines and left the harbor. It was Thursday and the wind was light but steady. Smitty was not concerned since it would be a short sail of only twenty miles. He planned on sailing with only the mainsail and the medium jib sail. They were in no hurry and the wind was out of the north. The Defiant could sail in a northeast direction all afternoon without having to tack.

As soon as Defiant passed Sandy Beach Light, Smitty called Roger from the foremast. "Mr. Bower, get up in the crosstrees. There's a lot of brown water between here and Wellfleet. Keep a sharp eye. No surprises this time."

Roger came aft from the foremast and jumped up onto the starboard railing to climb the ratlines. His binoculars hung from his neck and his red hair danced about his head as he climbed higher above the deck.

The afternoon sun was warm and reflected off the blue-green water of Cape Cod Bay. A light blue sky faded by the afternoon sun seemed to go on forever until it met a distant horizon that seemingly had no end. There was no definition of distance, especially on flat water.

The Defiant rolled with the shallow swells and soon fell into a natural rhythm with the sea. Windward was on the port side. It was light to moderate, but steady. Smitty smiled and knew it would be a straight sail probably without having to tack. He felt the afternoon sun on his face and looked about the deck in front of him. The boys busied themselves about their sailing stations. *What a difference*, he thought from their first cruise of only a month ago. They no longer had to be told what to do. They monitored their sails for fullness with respect to wind direction, watched for boat traffic, and kept their working lines and sheets organized and ready for immediate use.

He turned to look aft over the Defiant's stern. Barnstable's coast diminished as the schooner headed northeast for Wellfleet. Smitty looked aloft and saw Roger looking ahead with his binoculars, panning the horizon for any ocean-going threats that might arise to hinder their intended course. He nodded his head. *That kid has come a long way. He's really beginning to take his job seriously.*

The boat traffic was light for a weekday. Smitty scanned the immediate sea ahead, and with no warning from the Defiant's lookout, turned the helm over to starboard so the mainsail could catch more of the northerly breeze from their port side. The ship heeled to starboard and the Defiant and her crew were on their way to Wellfleet Harbor.

Captain Murdock came up from below. "Want me take it for a while, Smitty?"

Smitty shook his head, "No thanks. I got it skipper. It's a good day for sailing. No boat traffic, a nice steady breeze, and almost flat water. We should be into Wellfleet by 4:00 this afternoon."

Murdock nodded his head and looked up into the cross trees. "Roger looks pretty focused. I'm glad you put him back up there. These guys have to learn from their mistakes and not be afraid to try again."

Smitty kept his eyes forward and agreed. "I think he's learned a lot, Skipper…especially about being responsible for other people's wellbeing. It may have cost us a few broken planks in the hull, but it's all working out."

Murdock looked toward the bow and nodded his head. "Steady as she goes, Smitty. Don't forget to get Wally to go below and check the bilges. I'm going to walk the ship."

Murdock walked by the mainmast. Scott and Jack were busy coiling extra line and trimming the mainsheet. He tipped his captain's hat as he walked past the busy sailors, "Looking good, lads. Enjoy the sail."

The boys acknowledged the captain as he walked by and went back to their work. Murdock stopped at the bare foremast and rested his right hand on the halyard cleat. He looked ahead of the schooner's direction, feeling the sea roll under the ship, and watched the gentle rise and fall of the bow. Murdock closed his eyes for a moment to feel the ship as it moved over the bay. He listened to the masts and spars as they creaked with every movement. The wind always made a specific kind of whistle as it passed around the hundreds of lines and sheets that composed the ship's rigging. He kept his eyes closed, and savored the cool, fresh salt air that passed through his hair, over his body, and into his lungs.

Percy was in the bow and saw the captain in an almost meditative state. He got Josh's attention and nodded to the foremast. Josh eyed the captain for a moment and looked back to Percy with a questioning frown.

Percy asked, "Is he okay? Maybe he's seasick."

Josh shook his head. "Naw. He's just taking it all in. He's a career sailor, Percy. He's just feelin' it. He loves this."

Eventually, Murdock opened his eyes and visited the bow team. "Everyone good up here?" The boys all nodded to indicate that they were. Murdock smiled. "You know, you guys get the best ride up here. You can't experience the ship's movement with the sea anywhere better than from up here." He laughed and added, "That's why you get knocked around so much in bad weather, so enjoy the calm while you can."

Suddenly, there was a call from above. It was Roger. "We got an ultralight off the starboard bow! Flying low!"

A small ultralight aircraft was approaching the Defiant and about to cross their path. The aircraft flew at an altitude of only thirty feet off the water.

Murdock turned aft toward the helm. "Smitty, you got him?"

Smitty signaled that he did. The aircraft sounded normal as it approached Defiant's starboard bow and the pilot seemed to have it under control, so Smitty stayed his course. At that altitude, a sudden downdraft from the wind or a wrong movement of the ultralight's controls could be disastrous.

The Defiant's crew watched as the small aircraft crossed their bow at an altitude lower than that of either of the Defiant's masts. As soon as it crossed, the ultralight made a sharp left turn to pass along the schooner's port side. Within seconds, the pilot made another tight left turn to pass behind her stern. The aircraft's left wing dipped to a dangerously steep angle toward the sea as the pilot attempted to fly along the Defiant's starboard side.

Smitty kept his eye on the reckless aircraft and kept both hands on the helm to maintain course. The pilot flew so close, the smallest alteration in Defiant's course or mainsail position would likely snare the aircraft and cause it to collide with the ship or crash into the bay.

The crew watched as the small aircraft crossed the ship's bow once more and flew straight out into the bay. Someone shouted at the departing aircraft, "Hey, it's leaving. Thank God!"

Smitty wasn't so sure. He watched as the ultralight flew away from the ship and further out into the bay. It appeared as if the harassment was over. He shook his head. *That thing can't carry enough gas to fly across the bay. He's going to turn around and fly right over us.*

Just as Smitty predicted, the ultralight made another tight left turn and headed straight for the Defiant's port side. It appeared as if he was lower than the mainmast and collision was imminent. The ultralight approached directly abeam of the slow-moving schooner. Its engine noise became louder by the second as the entire crew watched, expecting the Defiant's sails to catch it, as one would catch a fly with their bare hand.

The aircraft passed over the mainmast by only a few feet causing Roger to crouch lower in his lookout position. The pilot appeared to be laughing and gave the crew a thumbs-up signal before heading back in the direction of the bay's southern coastline.

Murdock raced back to amidships and shouted up to Roger in the crosstrees. "Did you see any numbers or identification on his wings?"

Roger shook his head. "Sorry, Skipper. There were letters but he was moving up and down too much for me to make them out."

Smitty turned toward Murdock. "Son of a bitch can have his license pulled for a stunt like that. One gust of wind could have put him into our sails!"

Murdock shook his head and rubbed his beard. "Unfortunately, ultralight aircraft don't have to be registered and the pilot doesn't need a license to fly it."

Smitty was astounded. "You mean, an idiot like that can come out here and harass a sailing vessel, put her and the crew in peril, and just fly away laughing like that?"

Murdock nodded his head. "If we had the exact time and coordinates of our position, we could report it to the Coast Guard and they could go after him for harassment, but we don't have that information. We could figure it out using our maps and positioning but it would only be approximate...at best. They aren't required to file a flight plan either, so he'd be hard to track down anyway." Murdock paused and said, "Look around. No other boat traffic to witness what he did, no marine patrol out this far, and no other aircraft to report it. Just forget about it and hope he's got enough fuel to get back home."

Murdock turned back to the bow and shouted, "Okay, the show is over. He's gone. Get back to sailing the ship." He paused and singled out one sailor. "Wally! Get below and check out the bilges. Let me know if the water level has risen since we left Barnstable."

Wally dropped his coil of tangled lines and disappeared into the foreward hatch. Murdock turned and walked by Smitty as he headed for the aft hatch. "Keep Wally on bilge watch every hour. The pumps have been going since we left Barnstable, so have him keep an eye on those too."

Smitty nodded without looking at the captain, "Aye, Skipper. We're on it."

Murdock went below without further discussion.

The mood had settled topside and everyone was back to their normal routine. Wally had finished checking the bilges and passed Smitty on his way back to the bow. Smitty stopped him. "Wally, what's it look like down there?"

"The pumps are keeping everything below the level mark that the captain set. The water is still coming in but everything seems okay."

Smitty smiled at the young sailor. "Okay, good. Check those levels every hour...okay? We only have about another two hours of sailing. Make sure the pumps aren't running hot, and report to me and the captain. We'll have to go back over the side again once we dock in Wellfleet."

"Okay, Smitty." The boy checked his watch. "I'll go back below one hour from now, and maybe one more time after that. We should be in port by then."

Smitty adjusted his grip on the helm and turned it one way, then the other. "You got it. Thanks, Wally."

Wally turned and went back to the bow.

Another hour passed and Wellfleet Harbor was in sight. A long slender spit of land extended south from the upper hook of the Cape Cod land mass, and the long beaches of Wellfleet began to materialize off to the east. Smitty looked up into the crosstrees. Roger had his binoculars pointed in the correct direction, but probably didn't know what he was looking at. "What do you see, Roger?"

Roger paused before answering. "I have a long, skinny peninsula facing south and a long stretch of beaches off to starboard."

Smitty shouted back to the lookout. "Very good! Wellfleet Harbor is right in the middle of those two landmarks. We'll be coming into the shallows again so watch for brown water ahead of the ship. When we get inside that peninsula, you can come down and help with the sails."

Roger looked down to his first mate smiling, and gave him a thumbs-up signal.

▽

The Defiant approached Wellfleet's harbor entrance in late afternoon. The wind had begun to lighten up, slowing the ship's progress. Smitty looked at his watch. It was 3:45 PM. *Okay…slow, steady sail. Right on time though.* He shouted to Scotty and Jack who sat near the main mast playing cards.

"Scotty, Jack! Let the mainsail all the way out but keep it full. I want to go in slow. We have another shallow harbor ahead." Smitty looked to the bow. "Percy, trim the jib sail. Keep it full. We'll drop it after we're into the harbor."

Percy signaled with his hand and set to work on the jib sheets.

Entering Wellfleet Harbor was pretty routine aside from the confused wind that passed over its west coastline. Wellfleet lay nestled at the bottom of a horse shoe shaped harbor. Coastal winds that passed over its bayside sometimes conflicted with breezes approaching from the Atlantic coast and caused down drafts and intermittent wind shifts.

Murdock came up on deck, scanned the harbor entrance and looked about the ship's deck. The boys were busy adjusting and trimming sails. He walked up to Smitty. "How's the boat traffic?"

"Not bad, Cap. No trawlers, a few fishing boats and some lobster boats checking their traps."

Murdock looked aloft and shouted to Roger in the crosstrees. "Yo, lookout!" Roger dropped the binoculars from his face and turned aft to look down to the captain.

When Murdock had his attention, he cupped his hands about his mouth. "Keep a sharp eye out for lobster trap buoys. We have to stay well away from them. There are coast watchers that will turn us in if we disturb them in any way."

Roger nodded his head and signaled back with a thumbs-up.

Murdock turned to face Smitty. "How are the bilge levels?"

Smitty stared ahead as he steered into the harbor. "Wally has made a few trips down there and reports that water is still coming in, but the pumps have been running continuously, so the levels are staying just below our high-level mark."

Murdock nodded as he listened to the first mate. "Very well. Send a couple of the boys over the side when we get in, to assess the cracked planks. We may have to cut this port of call short and maybe skip Provincetown. Keep me advised." He moved closer to the first mate and tapped him on the shoulder. "Okay, you're relieved. I'll take her in from here."

Smitty stepped aside so Murdock could take the helm. "I told Roger he could come down when we got into the harbor."

Murdock shook his head. "Negative. The boat traffic is light enough but we have shallow water from here in, and we have a lot of lobster pots to avoid. Keep him up there until I'm ready to dock."

Smitty rubbed the back of his neck as he listened to the captain's orders. "Okay, Skipper. The helm is yours." He looked aloft and hailed the lookout. Roger looked down with a confused look. "The captain wants you to stay up there until we get past the lobster buoys and brown water. We'll call you down just before we dock."

Roger's expression was more serious now but nodded that he understood.

The Defiant continued without incident, finally sighting their mooring at the harbor's northern end. Smitty walked about the deck and pointed out the historic landmarks to the crew. Mayo Beach was off to their south as was the historic foundation for the old Mayo Lighthouse. He stopped and eyed the Town Pier as the Defiant approached. A party of line handlers stood ready on the Defiant's soon to be mooring and waited to receive mooring lines. This time he'd let Murdock call out the mooring orders. It would give him a chance to watch the boys and how far they had come in only two months. Smitty watched the activity on deck as the boys ran to and fro readying the ship for docking. He listened as the captain called out sail positioning and it reminded him of when he was a young sailor. It was men like Murdock who had taught him his trade and made him appreciate what the boys were experiencing at this very moment. It was a lot of work but it was good, satisfying work. As he watched the crew respond to Murdock's orders, he reveled in the first-hand example of what it took to land a sailing ship of this size. It wasn't the captain bringing in the ship…it was the efforts of the entire crew. Everyone had a part in the process and if one or two crewmates failed in their responsibilities, the omission would have noticeable, if not catastrophic effects on the docking. It was truly a team effort and for those few minutes every sailor worked as one and shared the same anxiety and the same concern for the same goal…and finally the glorious satisfaction of a successful docking.

The Defiant was once again at rest. The line handlers secured her to the pier's mooring cleats and the boys began to stow deck equipment and coil extra line. Murdock left the helm and went to amidships. He shouted above the slight breeze that passed over the ship. "All hands, all hands!" He paused until he had everyone's attention. "Ship's meeting in fifteen minutes. Get some water and meet amidships for the new schedule while in port. That's all." Murdock turned and went below.

The crew hustled to complete their tasks. No one wanted to be late and everyone yearned for some water, so getting their docking responsibilities completed was a priority.

Exactly fifteen minutes later, Murdock appeared at the aft hatch and looked at his watch. The entire crew was assembled and waited at the assigned area and either sat on the deck or leaned against the deck railing. Murdock looked at his crew and smiled. "That was a good cruise, sailors. Good job." He smiled again and continued, "So we had a little hiccup with the ultralight aircraft but that was good for you guys to experience. You can never tell what is going to happen at sea."

Murdock paused a moment and rubbed his beard, "As everyone is aware, we are sailing with a compromised hull. Wally has been watching the bilge levels and it appears the situation is getting worse." He looked at each sailor. "There is no cause for concern. The bilge pumps are keeping up with the situation, however we must do our part too. I'll need two of you to go over the side after the meeting, just like Scott and Jack did back in Barnstable. I want you check the cracked planking and report back to Smitty. We'll start with Jack and Scott again because they were last to see the damage and will be the best ones to compare as to what the cracks look like now."

The boys all wore long faces and expected the assignment to get worse. "After Jack and Scott report to Smitty, I want a different pair of sailors to take their places to make repairs." He looked at the group. "Teddy and Roger will drop work anchors over the side and spend the remaining part of the afternoon making new repairs to the same area."

Murdock stared into the young sailors' eyes. "Get the braces and wooden mallets from the carpentry locker." He turned back to Josh. "Look around in the repair space for some lengths of wood we can use as patches." Murdock nodded his head as he spoke, "If I get clearance to pull the ship out of the water, we'll tar the back of those wood splints and secure them to the hull as temporary patches. Once we get them in place, we'll use the braces to drill some holes through the splints and into the hull. After you drill the holes, hammer the wooden tree nails into the holes." Murdock noted the confusion on the boys' faces. "Questions?"

Percy was first to ask. "What's a brace?"

Murdock smiled. "Oh, sorry. It's an old-fashioned hand drill with a drill bit on its end. You have to push against it while rotating a crank on its body to turn the bit." He looked at the rest of the crew, "Anything else?"

Roger was next. "What's a tree nail?"

The captain explained, "Tree nails are wooden dowels used to attach two pieces of wood together. In this case, the wooden patches to the hull planking. Once they get wet and swell up, the patch will be secure."

Murdock could see the group of sailors were getting uncomfortable with the hull repair and what it might entail. He looked apologetically at the group. "Look, I know it's a dirty, shitty job but it's got to be done." He paused a moment and added, "I know...I have had to do it myself."

Smitty interrupted the well-meaning captain. "Excuse me skipper, but I think the boys are confused about the ship being in the water or in dry dock." Smitty looked at the boys, "It's a great fix, if we weren't in the water but I have to say you'd have a hard time with those braces and securing the new patches to the hull, if we were still in the water."

The captain's face flushed red. "Smitty, I said we'd only do that particular fix if I got clearance to pull the ship out of the water."

"Well Skipper, depending on what Jack and Scott report, we could just tar the cracks again and slap wood patches over them as extra insurance. It's going to be tough to push the wood patches against the hull underwater."

Murdock stared at the deck and considered Smitty's suggestion. "I agree, Smitty. You're right. Let's keep it simple. Tar and...maybe wood patches, for now. We'll check it again on Saturday and re-tar when we get into Provincetown Harbor."

Murdock continued with the schedule for the next two days. "Tomorrow, you will all be back in dress whites and attend tourists at your sailing stations for tours and demonstrations." He shifted his gaze to a different set of sailors. "Teddy and Percy will be the repair crew tomorrow afternoon. You will be relieved of tour duty early, to go over the side. If tourists ask what is going on, you may simply explain that you are making some minor repairs to the hull. Please don't use that time to go into any detail."

Murdock panned the entire group. "Saturday will be a repeat of Friday in the order I described except for another checkout in the morning by Jack and Scott. That won't be necessary since the next repair team will take that responsibility."

The captain paused and added, "Any questions?" There were none. Everyone continued to stare at the deck. "Okay, that's all." Murdock turned from the group of sailors and went below.

CHAPTER THIRTY SIX

After the ship's meeting, Scott and Jack changed into their cutoffs and came up on deck to collect their snorkeling gear. Josh had already thrown the work anchors over the side and stood by to supervise the work. The boys reported wider gaps between the cracks, but the lengths appeared unchanged. As Jack and Scott went below to change back into their work clothes, Teddy and Roger went over the side with their repair bag of hemp, caulking, tube tar, a chisel and a squeegee.

Once they were in the water, Josh waited for the boys to stuff hemp and caulking into the cracked planking. When that was complete, he handed them wooden splints with tar already applied to one side to make the patch. "Be quick about it, boys. Take them down and push them into place. Once they're in place, hold 'em against the hull for as long as you can. Take turns while your partner comes up for air. When it looks like they're stuck to the hull you can come back aboard."

The boys nodded and took the tarred splints underwater with them.

The repair team experienced the same difficulty as Jack and Scott had the day before, but soon became acclimated and completed the repairs. They finished just before dinner and went below to have supper with the rest of the crew.

Louis stood in his usual place by the galley stove wiping down pots and listening to the boy's banter, and Burt lay by the galley entrance near the starboard bulkhead awaiting the usual table scraps. Roger was the first to complain. "I hate that job! The water is so cold in this bay, and that friggin' tar gets all over everything when you try to squeeze it onto the cracks."

Teddy added, "My legs kept floating to the surface, so I was upside down while I was trying to work. It was pretty tiring."

Louis interrupted the conversation, "Wrap one of your feet around the work anchor line, you noggin head! You only need to keep one foot secured to that line and you'll be fine." He shook his head from side to side and frowned as he continued to wipe down a soup pot.

Smitty walked into the galley with a leather sack. "Hey guys. We got mail! I just picked it up from the harbor's post office. Listen up and I'll hand it out." Smitty passed out the mail as the boys ate. When the bag was empty, he started for the galley entrance, but stopped and turned around before leaving. "You guys can go topside after dinner tonight. It's a beautiful evening. Read your mail, write letters or just watch the sunset but don't leave the ship. I'll be in my quarters if you need anything. Lights out at ten." Smitty smiled and disappeared into the dark passageway.

After supper, the boys cleaned up the galley area and took their mail topside. Everyone went up the forward hatch ladder and went to their favorite deck space. Some fashioned pillows out of loose sail bags, and others sat on the deck and leaned against the deck rail's bulkhead or laid on the cabintop by the mainmast.

Smitty was right. The sky was clear and black, dotted by thousands of little crystals of light. A full moon created a beautiful sheen across the little harbor as if there was an illuminated path to the ship from somewhere out in the bay. The bright path appeared smooth and solid as there was no wind or waves to disturb the illusion.

Scott was the only sailor to stay in his bunk. When everyone was gone, he pulled out his letter and studied the envelope that contained news from home. He stared at the familiar address and the sender's name. He thought about what might be going on in their lives and what they might not tell him.

Would they be sensitive enough to relate any issues in their life that he should know about? Would they be honest with the news they were about to give him? He paused for a moment and realized he never realized how much he could miss his parents and sister...even the personality traits that irritated him. He took a deep breath and opened the letter.

The letter began with the usual salutation, followed by a 'hope you're doing well' narrative, and slowly transformed into a more detailed and family-oriented business format. It provided information on his sister's latest romance with the boy across town, to what his father's work day was like.

Scott was getting impatient, *What about Mom? I've read two pages and still no mention of her or how she is.* Finally, the last paragraph read, *"Mom has been a little under the weather lately and has had some tests done. She's back home now and seems to be doing better. She sends you her love and said you looked a bit skinny when she saw you in Plymouth, so make sure you get enough to eat."*

Scott put the letter down and considered the letter's content. *They didn't answer one question I asked in the last letter. It might just be Dad's insensitivity or that he forgot what*

I had asked in my last letter. I'll just write another one but address it to Mom this time. I'll her ask her specific questions and come right out with how I feel. I'll ask if they're holding out on family issues and explain that's like treating me as an outsider. I am still a part of the family no matter where I am or what I'm doing.

Scott stuffed the letter under his mattress and began to write to his mother. *I can't live this way. I know them well enough to know when they're holding back.* Scott lay on his stomach and wrote a four-page letter back to his mother.

Just before he finished, Jack came below to check on him. "What are you doing…writing a book?"

Scott continued writing without looking up. "Yeah. I'm writing to my mother. I feel as if they're keeping information from me. I think they're doing that for my benefit, but I need to know what's going on in the family."

Jack nodded his head. "Yeah, I've got that routine going too. You can't worry about it, Scotty. Just be satisfied that they have your best interests in mind." Jack shook his head, as if disgusted, and lay in his bunk. He was asleep in minutes.

Topside and in the bow, Percy looked up from his letter and noticed Jack was gone. "Did anyone see where Jack went?"

Teddy answered without looking up from his reading. "He went below to check on Scotty about twenty minutes ago. Scotty never left crew's quarters."

Light from the full moon allowed Percy to see the silhouettes of Roger and Wally lying face up on the cabintop. They were obviously taking in the light show above their heads. Roger lay with his hands behind his head. "I never figured there could be so much to look at in the night sky. It doesn't move, but it keeps your interest."

Wally had his head propped on a loose life jacket. "I know. It makes you think about things while still concentrating on the stars above you. That's probably how the ancient Romans and Greeks got the idea to name some of the star clusters and constellations after animals and gods."

Roger pointed up into the sky and northwest of their position. "Look! There's the Big Dipper over there! I wonder who named it and what they were thinking of when they named it."

Wally looked at the star constellation and said, "It probably came from an old sailor looking for the brightest stars in the sky to get some direction. He probably thought it looked like a water scoop."

Roger paused a moment and pointed again. "The two stars at the far end of the dipper point right to the North Star - the brightest in the northern sky. Its real name is Polaris and it's also the tip of the Little Dipper's handle." He turned to look at Wally. "Do you see it?"

Wally nodded, "Oh, yeah. I see it! I got it now."

Wally had never noticed the relationship of the two star clusters before. The boys continued with their conversation considering the history of the astronomy above their heads. They discussed topics they had never thought about before as a warm sea breeze passed over their bodies and rustled their hair. In the distance, a lonely fog horn bellowed its warning. The boys relaxed in the dark and felt privileged to experience a night like this.

Soon both sailors were fast asleep on the ship's cabintop, only to be rudely awakened hours later by an unhappy first mate. "Lights out at ten means 10:00 PM, sailors. You have two minutes to get below and into your racks before I feel an urge to write you up. Move it!"

Stiff and stumbling to the forward hatch, they realized the boys on the bow had gone below hours earlier, leaving them to their fate with Smitty. Still, it was a night they'd not soon forget.

▽

The boys were up at 7:00 AM, in their dress white uniforms, and on deck tending their sailing stations at 8:00 AM. Eventually, Smitty came on deck and walked the ship giving her a cursory inspection before allowing the Defiant open to tourists. As he passed the different sailing stations, he gave the attending sailors a quick once over. Smitty returned to amidships and glanced at his watch. The ship's walk had taken longer than expected. It was 9:00 AM. He cupped his hands about his mouth and gave the order, "All hands to the port side. Prepare to take on visitors."

The sailors rushed over to the Defiant's port side and stood in an at-ease position with their hands behind their backs. It was an impressive sight as they stood with their gaze fixed at some point beyond the ship's deck rail silently awaiting their guests. They were handsome young men, physically fit and tanned by the ocean sun. Smitty smiled and remembered himself in the same circumstance so many years ago. He was proud of this crew.

Groups of on lookers began to make their way down the Town Pier in groups of three to four people and approached with their eyes fixed on the Defiant's tall bare masts flying the ship's pennants – a jolly roger at the top of the main mast and the American flag off the stern. The ship's black hull and white stripe below the deck rail, highlighted the six sailors in their dress white uniforms, and sent an impressive message to the crowd that began to assemble on the pier.

Smitty walked over to the gangway and had Teddy and Wally slide the boarding ramp over to the pier. He greeted the growing crowd of tourists. "Good morning folks. Welcome to our day of tours aboard the wooden schooner, Defiant. Please board the ship in groups of no more than six. We'll take fifteen guests at a time and close the boarding ramp until we're ready for the next group. Please be patient and wait your turn. The sailors will take five of you to the bow, five will remain at amidships with two sailors, and the other five will go astern to begin the tours. Each tour will end right here at amidships. Kindly debark the ship and hold your conversations until you're back on the pier to avoid confusion on board." Smitty walked up to the gangway and unclipped the boarding chain. "Okay, the first groups may board." He stepped aside so the guests could come up the ramp.

Percy took the first group to the bow, and Roger took the next group astern for their tours. The last group began their tour with Jack and Scott at amidships. The tours went smoothly and at about 3:00 PM Teddy and Percy went below to change into cutoffs and prepare for their repair duty on the hull's cracks.

As the two sailors prepared to go over the side with their dive masks and flippers, several guests approached and questioned them about what they were about to do. The boys followed their instructions and merely explained they were going to do some minor repairs to the hull, smiled and climbed over the side.

Soon it became obvious that Percy and Teddy were the objects of attention. The sight of the two sailors splashing around between the port side hull and the Town Pier drew a lot of attention. Guests began to wander from their tours and crowded around the railing above Percy and Teddy to watch the activity in the water.

Smitty noticed the growing crowd and broke it up. "Please folks, let the boys do their work. We need to keep the tours on schedule and there are more guests waiting to board." The crowd slowly dissipated and went back to their tours. The same scenario arose with each group of guests. The largest group was toward the end of the day when Percy and Teddy climbed up the rope ladder and onto the deck. There were questions from all the onlookers. One older gentleman asked if they were fixing a leak, another asked if the ship was sinking. Others wanted to know why they weren't using scuba gear.

Percy and Teddy continued to be very vague in their answers and smiled as they headed for the aft hatch to see the captain to report the completion of their assignment.

Murdock sat in his cabin awaiting news from the repair crew. Suddenly there was a knock at the door. Murdock looked up, "Come."

Percy and Teddy walked in to the captain's cabin wrapped in towels. Murdock put his pen down and smiled. "So, what's it look like down there?"

Percy frowned and tipped his head to one side. "The hull still had tar on it and one of the tarred splints was missing so we replaced it."

Teddy added, "We checked the bilge level, Skipper. Looks like it's still leaking but not like before."

Murdock nodded his head in approval. "Good job, boys. We'll send another team over the side tomorrow just to see how today's fix went. Thank you. Go get some dry clothes on. You're done for the day. That's all." The boys nodded and went to the crew's quarters.

▽

Day two in Wellfleet Harbor went without incident. The day began with tours and the next repair team went over the side and inspected Percy and Teddy's work from the day before. They followed up by checking the bilge level and reported their findings to Captain Murdock.

Jack stood before Murdock and reported their findings. "The plank repairs from yesterday look okay, Skipper but the ship hasn't been under way. I don't know how it's gonna' hold when we start sailing. There's a lot of tar smeared all over that part of the hull but I think it's only slowing the leaks. The wood splints don't look very secure so I don't know what would happen if we got into rough seas."

Murdock stood from his desk and rubbed his chin. "What about the bilge level?"

Scott replied this time, "The pumps are still running and keeping the bilges at an acceptable level but they've been running at capacity for a few days now. I hope they can keep up."

Murdock sat back down at his desk. "Okay boys – thanks. Get cleaned up and tell Smitty I want to see him." He looked back up at the sailors. "Good job. Dismissed."

Twenty minutes later, Smitty sat in the captain's cabin listening to what Jack and Scott had reported. Murdock finished by saying, "So, considering that the problem hasn't gotten any worse, and that we can band aid our way to the next port of call, I've decided to continue with our planned schedule and go to Provincetown Harbor before continuing home to Gloucester. Boston Harbor is no longer a consideration."

Smitty stood from his chair. "Skipper, I respectfully disagree with your decision. We have six inexperienced sailors working this ship, not to mention their ages. I feel we have an obligation to their safety, as well as the ship's, at the very least."

Murdock raised his eyebrows at Smitty's sudden attitude. "Sit down, Mr. Smith. I have not considered this situation lightly. As captain of this ship, I have considered all of that – crew first of course, and also the degree to which we are impaired. The season is at the beginning of the summer doldrums, so I don't expect there will be much in the way of high winds or high seas." He looked away from Smitty for a moment before continuing. "We are not out to sea but are within the confines of Cape Cod Bay where, if need be, could ascertain help very quickly." Murdock paused as he locked eyes with the first mate. "We will sail for Provincetown tomorrow at 8:00 AM." Murdock shifted his gaze to the paperwork on his desk. "That's all, Mr. Smith."

Smitty turned and left the cabin as he thought. *Yeah right. Hope for light winds and fair seas. That's a comforting thought. Shit!*

CHAPTER THIRTY SEVEN

Saturday morning saw the Defiant and her crew preparing to depart Wellfleet Harbor. Josh walked over to Smitty standing behind the helm. "There's no wind, Smitty. We can raise the sails, but they're just gonna' luff and make noise. Do you want me to fire up the Diesel engine?"

Smitty shook his head. "Nope. We have too much water sloshing around down there. I don't want to take the chance on shorting out the system. Launch the dinghies – both of them. I want three sailors in each, with you and Louis in either one of them. We'll tow the Defiant out to the bay where she can pick up some wind."

Josh nodded his head. "You got it, Smitty."

The dinghies were two wooden nine-foot-long row boats with a capacity of five people each. They had oar locks on the gunnels next to the two middle benches and were powered by four oars, operated by four rowers. Included on the small craft, was a wooden keel that ran its length to help with steerage in choppy seas.

Josh assembled the crew at Defiant's stern and explained the age-old practice of towing a tall ship out of the harbor in no wind conditions. "Okay guys, there's no wind today and we have to get the ship out of the harbor. Smitty wants us to tow her out into the bay using the dinghies. I'll have three of you in my boat and three of you in Louis's boat. The captain will be at the helm to steer her out of here and Smitty will be directing him around boats and other obstacles in the harbor. Any questions?"

No one said a word, so Josh continued. "I want Jack, Teddy, and Percy with me in Boat 1. Scotty, Roger, and Wally will be in Boat 2 with Louis."

Immediately, Roger spoke up and complained. "Wait! You can't put me in Boat 2 with Louis. He gonna' give me so much shit and be on me about not oaring hard enough. He thinks I'm a slacker."

Josh just smiled, "Well, prove him wrong and oar your ass off. This isn't a popularity contest Roger. You shouldn't even be thinking about who's boat you're in. Your first priority is the ship...and then your shipmates."

Josh waited for questions. When there weren't any, he turned toward the dinghies lashed to the stern's raised transom. "Alright boys, get those dinghies into the water. Lower them off the starboard side. We'll tow the ship stern first, to back her out of the pier. Once we get clear of the pier, we'll row around to the bow and attach tow lines there so we can tow her out to the bay where there will be more wind."

The sailors spent the next half hour unlashing the dinghies, loading them with oars and life jackets, and finally dropping them over the Defiant's starboard side, into the quiet water of Wellfleet Harbor. Josh supervised the work and was very patient. "Okay, keep the dinghies' bow lines attached to the ship's railing and climb down the rope ladder. We're gonna' need two lengths of towline for each boat. Make each of them about a hundred feet." He looked to the stern and pointed. "Make sure somebody hooks those up to the ship's stern cleats before we leave the ship. Just let them hang in a coil where we can reach them from the tow boats." The boys followed Josh's directions to the letter, and welcomed the chance to get off the ship.

Finally, both dinghies were in the water with their assigned crews. Each boat approached the Defiant's stern, uncoiled the hanging tow lines and lashed them to the stern of each dinghy. Josh stood in Boat 1 and shouted his instructions. "Boat 2– row out to about a thirty-degree angle to the ship's centerline while letting the tow line out as you go. We'll do the same, but to starboard. When we're both in position, we'll begin to tow. Listen to Louis' stroke calls so everyone rows together."

Finally, the dinghies had stretched out the tow lines so they were about one hundred feet from the Defiant's stern. Josh signaled Smitty in the Defiant's bow to let go the ship's mooring lines. Then he looked to Louis in Boat 2 and gave them their signal. The boys began to row against the tow lines. The Defiant remained motionless for several minutes while the boys rowed in place trying to keep in sync with one another. Josh shouted encouragement to both crews.

Percy grunted as he looked back at the tall ship, "She's not budging."

Josh assured the crews. "Keep rowing and stay in sync with each other. Dig in hard. She'll pull free soon enough." Then, as if on cue, the struggle eased and the big schooner relented to the tow boats' efforts. The Defiant slowly began to move toward them and the tow boats started to make way into the harbor.

Louis sat in the front of Boat 2 next to Scott, and Burt sat behind them in the tip of the bow. Everyone was beginning to sweat, and the strain of pulling a 25 ton wooden schooner through the water began to show on their faces. Louis grimaced as he rowed. "I'm gettin' too old for this shit."

Scott replied as he pulled on his own oar. "It feels like it's getting easier."

Louis spoke in breaks between breaths. "Yeah, it'll get easier as soon as the ship starts to get some way on. Don't worry about it running us down though. We'll probably get her to about two knots – if we're lucky. If we stop, she'll glide to a stop in just a few feet."

When the ship was clear of the pier the boats unhooked from the stern and rowed to the bow where they once again attached their tow lines to turn the Defiant and tow her out to the bay - bow first.

Smitty stood in the Defiant's bow to direct the tow boats and point out areas for Murdock to avoid as he tended the helm. Slowly but surely, the Defiant made her way out to the harbor's entrance. The activity attracted groups of onlookers along the harbor's docks who stopped to watch the ancient technique of towing a tall ship. The local newspaper had been notified and took pictures of the ancient practice as she slowly made her way to the harbor entrance. Defiant had made her stay in Wellfleet known.

Smitty signaled Josh and Louis to detach and get the boys back on board. He shouted to the two boat captains, "Hook the dinghies up one behind the other for now and we'll tow 'em behind us until we get to Provincetown."

With the boys back on board, Murdock let the boat crews rest and get some water before raising the sails. The entire crew congregated about amidships and Louis made an announcement. "You're all getting haircuts before we get into Provincetown. One by one, and by sailing station. You will be relieved from your post and come to see me right here at amidships. The kind of haircut you get depends on how cooperative you are. There are no options." A look of fear momentarily crossed everyone's face, but as Louis said, they had no choice.

When the crew had recovered from the long pull, Smitty ordered all hands to sailing stations. As hoped, there was a light but steady breeze out of the northwest. When everyone was in position, he glanced over to Murdock who was still behind the helm. Murdock gave him a nod and Smitty shouted, "Raise the mainsail."

Jack and Scott pulled hard on the halyard and winched in the mainsheet to keep the big sail close-hauled since they'd be sailing so close to the wind. The Defiant began to move on her own and soon had way on. She was only making about eight knots, but she was underway. Smitty called to the bow. "Bow team – fly the big jib sail." The big jib slid up the foremast and snapped open. The Defiant was on her way.

Provincetown Harbor lies fifteen miles north of Wellfleet as the crow flies, but the Defiant would need to be tacking frequently as she would be sailing so close to the wind and fighting confused currents in the bay. There would also be two main ferry paths to cross before getting to the famous harbor, but for now the crew was grateful for the smooth water and whatever wind was present.

Defiant sailed flat and steady for the next hour. The coast of Truro, Massachusetts appeared off the starboard side. Murdock looked over to Smitty standing by the starboard railing. "When we get abeam of North Truro, get Scotty up in the cross trees – only for boat traffic. It's a deep harbor, so I'm not worried about brown water. We've got two widely used ferry lanes to pass through. It could get a little busy. Have him watch for Long Point Light and call me when he has it in sight."

Smitty nodded, "Aye, Skipper."

Presently, Louis came up the aft hatch with a towel, comb and scissors. He placed an old wooden stool at amidships just aft of the cabintop. Louis looked forward and called to the bow, "Roger Bower – to amidships!"

Roger heard the call and looked back at his bow team. No one said a word, but a worried smile crossed everyone's face. Roger dropped his coil of line before reporting to Louis. "Yeah, well you guys are next."

Louis cut Roger's hair and wore a nasty grin as he worked. Roger was quiet until he began to notice the size of the locks falling from his head. Finally, he expressed his discontent. "How much are you going to take off, Louis? There's too much hair on the deck. I should've been finished a while ago."

Louis kept cutting. "Shut up and stay still. You keep moving and it causes me to make mistakes, so I have to cut more off, just to balance it out."

Scotty watched the haircut from his sailing station by the mainmast. "Hey Jack, look what Louis is doing to Roger's hair."

Jack glanced over and covered his mouth, turning away just in time to hide a muffled laugh. "He's giving him a crewcut! Roger is gonna' be pissed."

"Okay, you're done." Louis handed Roger a mirror and the same nasty grin returned to the cook's face.

Roger looked into the mirror. "A crewcut? You cut all my hair off! Aww, shit!"

Louis shook his head from side to side. "It'll grow back, Hollywood. Everyone's gettin' one. Now get back to your sailing station." He looked back to the bow and shouted, "Teddy Brinks! Get over here for your haircut. I'll try to do a better job than I did on Roger."

Teddy reluctantly left the bow and walked to amidships as a condemned man would walk to the gallows. "Be gentle, Louis. I'd like to have a girlfriend someday."

Louis threw the towel over Teddy's shoulders. "Don't worry, son. It'll grow back in a few months."

One by one, each sailor took his turn with the burly cook. A pile of multi colored hair lay on the ship's deck. A result of Louis' handiwork. He laughed and swept it into the bay.

Another hour passed as the Defiant sailed into the tropical breeze. Murdock nodded to Smitty, "North Truro off the starboard side."

Smitty stood by the port railing. "Scotty, get up in the crosstrees. Keep an eye out for Long Point Light to port, and boat traffic. We have two ferry lanes to get through, so be alert. Don't worry about brown water, it's a deep harbor."

Scott climbed up onto the port side railing and began to climb the ratlines. The breeze was still light, but it felt good to get up higher, away from the deck, where it would be cooler. Once he settled into the crosstrees he looked ahead and noticed busy water ahead of the ship. There was a ferryboat approaching from port and another leaving Provincetown Harbor and approaching their starboard side. In addition, several small crafts and fishing boats dotted the area ahead. He shouted down to Murdock. "Ferries to port and starboard at 1000 yards. Starboard ferry seems closer and faster."

Murdock maintained his course which would put him in the middle of the ferry lanes. A ship under sail possesses the right of way under all conditions, but it doesn't always work out that way. Murdock kept his focus on the horizon ahead. "Smitty, get up to the bow and watch those ferries. The one to starboard is coming on hard."

Smitty jogged to the bow and held onto the forestay that came down from the foremast to the prow. He scanned the water dead ahead of Defiant's path as they sailed further into the ferries' travel lanes. "Bow team, get ready to raise another jib sail - the small one. There's still not enough wind for the mainsail alone, so we have to keep enough way on, especially with the wake we're about to sail into."

Smitty looked to port to see the approaching ferry was close, but coming on slower than the one to starboard. Neither vessel was slowing or changing course to accommodate the Defiant. Smitty realized what the next few minutes would bring. *At the rate they're approaching, the port side ferry will cross our bow just as the starboard ferry passes our stern.* He looked up into the crosstrees. "Scotty, get a good grip up there. There's not enough time for you to get back down to the deck. We'll be taking both of their wakes – one from the bow and the other from the stern." He turned and cautioned the helm. "Steady as she goes until they pass. Prepare for wakes – bow and stern."

Murdock waved his right hand to indicate he understood.

Scotty shouted from the crosstrees, "Long Point Light dead ahead, two miles. Port side ferry at twenty yards, crossing the bow. Starboard ferry, about twenty-five yards by the stern."

Smitty turned to face the crew. "Brace for wakes – fore and aft. Tighten all sheets!"

The crew pulled the mainsail in closer to the ship and the bow team pulled the big jib sail taut. As the two ferry boats crossed the Defiant's bow and stern, there were only seconds before the ship encountered their wakes. Keeping the sheets taut would lessen the amount of luffing in the sails as she crashed into the oncoming waves. The crew awaited the inevitable as the bow plowed ahead into the ferry wake, violently shaking the mainsail and spars. About the same time, the wake from the ferry passing behind the Defiant, rolled under her stern, lifting it to a steep angle and plunging the bow deeper into the wake forward of the ship.

Another huge wave came over the bow and covered Smitty and the bow team, followed by the bow pitching upward to a steep angle causing some of the sailors to lose their footing. The bow action caused Defiant's stern to dip lower into the bay, as another ferryboat wave washed over the aft end of the ship and around Murdock standing at the helm. The dinghies that had been in tow, rolled wildly in Defiant's wake. The confused waves caused the tiny crafts to take on water, swamping both of them. The dinghies now acted as anchors to their mother ship, and had an immediate effect on her forward momentum.

Murdock shouted to Josh by the port railing. "Josh, make your way to the stern and cut the dinghies loose."

Water washed over the Defiant's deck from bow and stern and crashed together at amidships. The violent wave action caused the ship to heel from side to side as it rode over and through the ferryboat wakes. Scotty held on tight up in the crosstrees as he rode the mainmast that tipped wildly in every direction. He kept one leg wrapped around the mast and the other around the cross tree brace he sat on, while clinging to the shrouds within his reach with one hand and the mainmast with the other.

Back at the stern, the dinghies fell away from the ship when Josh cut them loose. They seemed to go from thrashing wildly and refusing the force of the wake, to suddenly calm and quiet, as they settled into the bay. Only the gunnels and tips of their bows were visible above the water.

The ferries left the Defiant and continued on their way with no recourse as to what had just happened. The Defiant began to shed water from her deck through the scuppers along her deck rails, and seemed to rise back up out of the bay. Her sails snapped back to their taut position and the ship slowly began to regain her balance as she settled into the otherwise calm waters of the bay.

Murdock looked around the deck and into the crosstrees. Everyone was still on board…soaked and somewhat relocated by the onrush of water. The crisis was over. He shouted to Scotty. "Any ferryboats in sight?"

Scotty panned the entire horizon. "Nope. Just a few fishing boats."

Murdock had the entire crew's attention. "We have to go back and get the dinghies. Prepare to come about."

Everyone stared at one another in disbelief. They couldn't believe the skipper was bringing them back for round two.

Murdock knew what the crew was thinking. He explained. "We can't leave those dinghies partly submerged. They're a hazard to other boat traffic in the area. We'll have to work fast." He called Smitty back to the helm. "I don't want to be in these ferry lanes any longer than I have to. We'll sail by the dinghies and come around again. I'll pull up to them and point the ship into the wind. When we're dead in the water, get Josh and Jack to snag the dinghies and get as much water out of them as you can so we can tow them out of the area. We'll pump 'em out when we get to our pier."

The dingy recovery went without incident, but the ship's ferry experience caused everyone to be unusually aware of all the boat traffic in the area.

Bruised and battered, the Defiant continued toward Provincetown Harbor. It was late afternoon and the sun was in the west. The Defiant sailed smoothly toward the harbor entrance and as she passed Long Point Light, Murdock considered the ferry incident earlier that afternoon. He looked over at his first mate by the port railing. "That couldn't have been too good for the cracked hull planks."

Smitty shook his head from side to side. Then he stepped away from the port railing and headed for the aft hatch. "I better go check the bilge levels."

CHAPTER THIRTY EIGHT

The Defiant rested at her new mooring in Provincetown Harbor, with her deck quiet and abandoned. To a unknowing passerby, the ship appeared disheveled and neglected. Her ordeal with the two ferryboats had left the deck in shambles. Loose lines and sheets hung from various locations about the ship, and the deck was awash with deck equipment like wooden stools, buckets, sail bags, and equipment lockers. The cluttered and disorganized deck was the result of the forceful rush of water that had found its way over Defiant's bow and stern.

It had only been a few hours but the sun was beginning to fall below the horizon. There was still no wind to speak of, and for once, Murdock had approved the use of the diesel engine to maneuver the ship into their mooring. Smitty made his disapproval known and warned the captain about the use of the engine with the amount of water below decks, but Murdock felt that under the conditions with increased flooding, the condition of the crew, and the compromised hull planks, he'd take the chance.

The crew was exhausted after recovering and pumping out the dinghies, so Murdock had sent them below for a rest before dinner. When they were alone, Murdock and Smitty sat in deck chairs by the aft hatch and discussed Defiant's condition. Murdock tipped his head to the side and asked. "What are the bilge levels at?"

Smitty frowned, "We have a lot of water down there, Skipper. Levels are all higher than our measured marks. We're lucky the engine sits on a platform higher than the below deck passageway. Pumps are still operating, but I've started to run them at alternate times, so at least one of them will get a chance to cool down." He paused a moment and shook his head, "We took on a lot of water because of the ferries' wakes. I don't know if it's the water that ran down the fore and aft hatches, or if it's because of water coming from the cracked hull planks. In any case, we are over max levels."

Murdock was leaning forward in his chair and stared at the deck. Without looking at the first mate he said, "There's that much water down there?"

Smitty frowned and nodded. "Yes, sir. It's getting to a serious level. That pounding we took from the ferries' wakes must have opened the cracks in the hull planking."

Murdock pursed his lips and slapped his thighs. "That's it then! I'm going to the harbor repair office in the morning. I think they'll be okay with pulling us out and into dry dock to make some emergency repairs. We can't risk the hull condition any longer. If they pull us out, we'll make our own repairs, and if we haven't been too badly damaged…sail for Boston Harbor as planned."

Smitty smiled for the first time in a long time. "I think that's a good decision, Skipper. It's probably going to hold us here in Provincetown all week…or more, but I think it's the prudent thing to do."

Murdock stood from his chair, "Okay, it's decided then. We'll go to dry dock at the earliest opening, make emergency repairs, and sail for Boston Harbor at our earliest opportunity." He turned to the aft hatch. "Okay, that's all. Have a good night, Smitty." He ducked into the aft hatch and disappeared down its steep ladder.

▽

Murdock had convinced the harbor authorities that Defiant's situation was dire, regarding schedule and a young and inexperienced crew. They granted her an emergency place on the dry dock list with the understanding that Defiant's crew would do their own work. The problem was that the Defiant's extraction from the harbor would be delayed until Monday morning. That meant two more days of downtime for the ship and its crew. Tours had to be cancelled and the crew sequestered to the ship until further notice. Sunday was their day off so the captain allowed them on deck for the day. They read or wrote letters, picked up the deck from the day before, played cards or had checker tournaments.

Scotty lay in his bunk and stared at a letter from his mother. She had written back personally, as he requested. He wondered what the letter's contents may reveal. *Would she be truthful with him? Would she tell him what was going on in the family?*

Suddenly, Jack popped his head into the crew's quarters. "Hey, buddy! You gonna' read that or study it?" Scott looked up, but didn't answer. "Well, hurry up. We're waiting for you topside. We need a fourth in a setback game."

"I'll be up soon. This is from my mom. I've been waiting for it, ya' know? I have to read it."

Jack's face suddenly went serious. "Yeah, sure. We'll play something else until you're ready. Take your time." Jack nodded at Scotty and went topside again.

Scott opened the envelope slowly and carefully, as if he was afraid to damage it. He unfolded the letter and began to read.

My dearest, Scott. I was so sorry to hear that you thought we might have been keeping things from you. I have to say that I'm not surprised you suspected something was afoot. You have always been a very observant and sensitive boy, one who could read between the lines, so to speak. We didn't want to worry you while you were out sailing around the Atlantic Ocean. God knows you have enough on your mind, getting used to this new sailor life and moving from port to port.

So, here it is. I have been diagnosed with ALS, short for Amyotrophic Lateral Sclerosis. It's just a big word for something everyone used to call Lou Gehrig's disease. Remember Lou Gehrig, the famous Yankee baseball player? Well, he had it, and it's named after him, so I'm in good company.

Anyway, it's a neurological disorder that affects nerve cells that control my voluntary muscles. Eventually, as the cells are affected, I'm told I can expect more weakness and tiredness, which will probably lead to some level of disability. But don't worry, it's not supposed to affect my mind or how alert I am, so I'll still be able to give you a piece of my mind when you mess up.

So that's about it. It just happened. It came on very slowly and I thought I was just tired. Right now, I'm in the early stages, but there are treatments that we're looking into with my doctor. Don't worry, it's not something you can inherit. They don't know what causes it, but I'm just going to see it through…and you can bet I'll be waiting on that dock when you finish your time on that ship and come sailing home. You have to do your part and keep yourself safe with all that dangerous sailing you're doing. Come home to me safe, Scott. I want to see my little boy again, so handsome with those blue eyes and curly hair.

The rest of the family is doing fine and Dad has been good about keeping you informed along those lines. We look forward to your next letter. Make us proud. We all miss you terribly, Love, Mom.

Scott crunched the letter in his hand as the tears streamed down his cheeks. *That's why they busted their ass to see me in Plymouth...and where was I? Out on the town getting drunk. Aww shit, what an ass!*

Scott lay there for a while and considered the entire situation. He realized the only thing he could do, was to do everything possible to get through his sentence on the Defiant. That meant staying out of trouble so his sentence didn't get extended, and anything else he could to support her situation, which for right now, was as she asked...to make her proud.

▽

On Monday, the crew was asked to debark the ship and meet at the dry dock area. Only Smitty and Josh remained on board to motor the Defiant over to the dry dock ramp. Just as they had experienced when they launched Defiant in Gloucester, a similar ramp and railing, was positioned near the harbor's repair and maintenance section. Smitty guided the schooner up to the ramp, while a maintenance crew attached cables and a temporary cradle around Defiant's hull. A huge winch began to groan, the wooden ramp creaked, and metal cables squealed and whined as the schooner was pulled from the harbor.

Murdock stood by the end of the ramp and signaled the winch operator to stop the pull when the ship was far enough out of the water where the damaged hull could be accessed, and the ship sat on fairly level ground. Temporary supports and braces were placed against the ship's hull, and Defiant was in dry dock.

Murdock called the crew over to see the damaged hull planks. The cracks had gotten longer, and the gaps wider. When everyone had seen the damage, Murdock turned to the group of sailors and explained what the next few days would entail. "Okay sailors, we have our work cut out for us. We're going to be sitting in dry dock …probably for the week. Later this morning, Smitty and Josh will go into town and secure the materials to repair the hull, and then we'll make the fix I spoke of in Wellfleet…with treenails. It's going to take a few days to do it right." He paused and looked into their faces. "Just like in Gloucester, you'll be living right here on the ship. No one leaves the ship unless it's to work on the hull. The only difference is that you'll be climbing that ladder to board or debark her. Because of the emergency pull out, this is the only place they could put us on short notice, so we're sitting a little higher off the ground. Just be careful climbing up or down. I don't need any sailors with broken bones."

Murdock walked over to the ship's temporary ladder. "Okay boys, everyone back on board. Spend the rest of the day cleaning up the ship from Saturday's ordeal with the ferries. You all handled yourselves very well through that and stayed at your stations, so I let you retire early that afternoon. We'll spend the morning getting everything back where it belongs, dried out, and checking for damage to the decks, sheets and sails. When Josh and Smitty get back with the repair materials we can start to clean up the affected hull area in preparation to tomorrow's repair." He pointed to the ladder, "After you, gentlemen."

One by one, the crew climbed the ladder back up to Defiant's deck. It was going to be a long day.

Josh and Smitty headed off into town to buy the tar, wooden dowels, and fresh planking to make the temporary fix to Defiant's hull. Since the ship was clear of the water, they planned on getting some seamer and fresh caulking too.

Their idea was to use the ship's current dry dock status as an opportunity. It was also their chance to buy some good materials with the ship's petty cash.

The boys worked non-stop under Murdock's supervision. In the afternoon, Murdock met with the crew on the ground near the damaged hull. "Okay sailors, we have to get all of the damaged area clean. Scrape it down good and clear away any excess wood splinters. Don't worry about sanding for now. Tomorrow we'll make the repair."

CHAPTER THIRTY NINE

Tuesday morning began as a hot day. There was no breeze to speak of and no shade for the sailors to shelter themselves from the late July sun. Josh and Smitty had set up a tent and work platform next to the ship, and organized all the repair materials and necessary tools. Murdock walked up to the platform and explained the process.

"We're going to do this in shifts. I only need three of you at a time working on the hull. After I explain the process, the other three can go back to swabbing the deck and working on the sails." Murdock stopped and went over to the work platform. He picked up two pieces of new wood planking. "After we boil the wood and bend it close to the shape of the hull's profile, we'll take these lengths of wood and use them as patches. Tar the back of them and secure them to the hull. They're only temporary until we can get back to Gloucester. When we get them in place, we'll use the braces to drill some holes through the wood patches and into the hull. After you drill the holes, hammer the wooden tree nails into the holes with the wooden mallets. We'll let everything set for a few hours and then throw some water on the tree nails. That 'll cause them to swell so they won't leak. I want to wait for everything to dry before the next step, so once that's done, we'll stop repairs for the day.

"Tomorrow, we'll apply some caulking to the new planks and hit that with some plank seamer. By afternoon, everything should be dry and you guys can come down here and paint the whole repair." He looked at the group of disinterested sailors. "Any questions?"

There were none so he called the first team to work. "Roger, Percy, and Teddy! Get to work and start boiling the wood patches. Once they're done, we'll bend them on the work table, and start slapping tar onto the back of them. In a few hours, switch with Jack, Scotty and Wally." He looked at Jack and Scott. "I want you guys to drill the holes with those braces. Take your time and do a good job. That's our hull you're gonna' be drilling holes in."

Murdock began to climb back up the Defiant's ladder leaving Smitty to supervise the work crew.

Smitty stepped up to the group of sailors, "Okay guys, you heard the captain. Let's get to it."

The Defiant's hull was constructed of the plank on frame type and curved below the waterline that ended at the keel. The damage was only a couple of feet from the keel, and on the curved portion of its carvel hull. For the most part, the repair area was within two feet of the ground surface. Access to the area was difficult and required one to lay on his side to get to it.

Smitty stood by a barrel of water and an open fire that heated a large pot of water and reiterated Murdock's process, but in more detail. "We're going to boil the wood due to our limited resources out here. Just put the wood patches in the big pot before you tar them and make sure they stay under water.

Then we'll cover the pot with this piece of sheet metal and put a large rock on top to hold it down. After boiling the wood for a while, take the wood out and try to bend it to the profile of the hull with these clamps I attached to the work table." He looked at the focused sailors. "These are just patches, guys. You don't have to get the bend perfect...just close. It'll all pull together when Jack and Scotty hammer the tree nails into them."

It wasn't an operation that was expected to go easily, or neatly but the boys gave it their best. Cutting and bending the wood patches took the most time as they tried to match the curve of the hull and bend the wood to the approximate profile.

When the repair team finally had some acceptable shaped lengths of patches, they attempted the patching process. Roger laid on his side and tried to position the tarred patch while Percy held it in place. The boys were in each other's way as they fought for position to apply the patch to the hull. After a few hours of struggling, it seemed as if there was as much tar on them as on the ship. Smitty sat under the tent and laughed. "You guys are going to have to throw those clothes away. I hope you wore your worst work clothes."

After lunch the second repair team came down the ladder and switched with the first team. Roger threw down his tar laden brush and wiped his forehead. "Good luck guys! This is a friggin' dirty ass job!"

Jack, Scott and Wally set to work preparing the braces for drilling, and choosing the areas to drill through the new patches. Wally's task was to push against the new patches while the tree nails were forced into the newly drilled holes.

Finally, the work was complete. They picked up their tools and stowed them in the tent for the night. As they stood at the bottom of the Defiant's ladder summoning the strength for the last climb of the day, the ship's bell clanged eight times. It was dinner time. Jack acknowledged the bell.

"There's your motivation guys. One last climb. Food and rest are waiting."

No one answered Jack. Wally went first, and one by one, they climbed the ladder back to Defiant's deck. Louis stuck his head out of the forward hatch and pointed at the three dirty sailors. "Get those shitty clothes off before you come down into my galley! Leave them in a heap by the gangway and you can put them in the trash tomorrow morning. Supper will be on the table in five minutes." The cook's head disappeared into the hatch as swiftly as it had appeared. The boys shook their heads, scanned the area to ensure no one was watching, and left their work jeans and shirts on deck. The day was done.

$$\triangledown$$

Supper that night was quiet. The sailors were too tired for their usual banter. It was the result of the last three days. All of the activity and experiences had finally caught up with them. Playing catch up with the ship's maintenance, coupled with the cracked hull repair had finally got the best of them. Working in the hot sun with no breeze also added to their discomfort and fatigue. Everyone retired to their bunks early and read or dozed. Teddy and Roger seemed to have the most energy and played cards at the galley table.

The night droned on in the dimly lit crew's quarters. Half of the sailors were asleep in their bunks, and the card game had finally come to an end. Scotty watched Roger and Teddy pick up their chips and pack the cards away. "Are you guys finally done? You've been fighting and taking each other's money for the past three hours. I have to say, I'm glad to hear the end of the bickering and name calling."

Teddy waved Scotty off. "Ah, we're just tired and bored, Scotty. Roger didn't mean anything he said to me."

Roger turned to face Teddy. "Yes, I did! You little shit! I caught you cheating twice."

Suddenly, Scotty raised his arm in the air as if he was trying to hear something. He perked up his head and stared at some unknown point in the room. Everyone was now awake and listened for what Scotty might be trying to hear. Scotty turned toward the boys in the room. "Where is Jack?"

Everyone shrugged or said nothing. Percy, rolled over in his bunk. "Haven't seen him in a while. He left crew's quarters about an hour ago. I thought he was going to the head."

Scotty raised his hand again. "Listen! There it is again."

There was the muffled sound of several people talking and laughing outside of the ship. It sounded like several female voices coming from the laydown area the Defiant rested on. The other voice sounded deeper but came from above and more aft on the ship.

Scott slid out of his bunk and stepped on the side of Jack's empty bunk. "I'm going topside through the foreward hatch to take a look. You guys wait here until I call you."

Scott climbed up the foreward hatch ladder. The hatch was open and the voices became more intelligible. One of the voices was definitely Jack's. Scott climbed another rung on the ladder to see Jack leaning on the port side rail talking to three scantily clad ladies dressed in bright colors of red, pink and black. Scotty shook his head, *I can't believe it. Leave it to Jack.*

One of the ladies noticed Scotty's upper body as it extended from the foredeck hatch. "Hey there's another one them! Come on out here, honey." She looked back at Jack. "How many more of those sailors do you have in there? We can have a real party now."

Scotty climbed out of the hatch and walked over to Jack. "What's going on, Jack? Who are they?"

Jack raised his eyebrows. "I don't know. They're obviously

some prostitutes from town that heard about us and decided to come down here and party with us."

Unfortunately, the rest of the crew were crammed together in the foreward hatch ladder space, listening to Jack's exchange with the ladies on the ground. Roger stood on the top rung with half his upper body exposed. He called down to the others standing below. "Guys, come up here and get a load of this!"

One of the ladies called to Scotty. "Hey cutie, go get the rest of the boys. It's time for a party. We got the booze…you guys bring the money."

The boys on the foreward hatch ladder heard the women's invitation and came spilling out of the hatch like ants from an ant hole.

Another one of the women stepped back as she watched four more shirtless twenty-year old boys dressed in nothing but cutoff jeans, stumble and trip over each other, as they made their way to the railing. "Whoa! Jackpot girls, …and not a one of them looks over twenty-one!"

The boys crammed the port side railing as they peered down at the beautiful women. Percy was shocked. "What in hell?"

Jack frowned at the naive sailor and answered, "They're whores, Percy…prostitutes!"

The lady in red shouted up to the railing. "Come on down here, pretty sailors. We came down here to party…and we got booze. You just get yourselves down from that ship and we'll take you for a ride like you've never had before."

Jack smiled at the three women. "We can't. We're not allowed to leave the ship."

The lady wearing red was quick to reply. "Then, we'll come up there. Throw that ladder down and we'll be right up."

Suddenly, a voice came out of the darkness near the aft hatch. "Good evening, ladies." It was Louis. The burly cook came out of the shadows and showed himself. "We are flattered that you came down to visit us, but it's eleven o'clock and my sailors need to get their rest. We won't be doing tours until Saturday, so I'm afraid we'll have to say good night...ladies." Louis wore a smile that was both friendly but intimidating at the same time.

The three women stood on the gravel and said nothing as they stared at the huge cook. The woman wearing all black stepped forward and addressed Louis. "Well, what about you, big guy?"

Louis looked over at the boys standing by the port side railing. "Sailors! Get below right now, unless you want me to report this." He looked back at the three women on the ground. "Unfortunately, it's not a good time for either of us. You see, this is a ship of detention, and I wouldn't think ladies of your stature would want any part of...detention." Louis gave them the same uncomfortable smile as he did a few minutes before.

The women shook their heads and walked away. Louis laughed as he went back to the aft hatch. *Happens every cruise.*

The next morning Louis walked into the galley to start breakfast only to find all six of the boys still asleep in their bunks. He stood in the entrance, shocked and unsure of the boys' behavior. They were all there...just still asleep.

Louis reached up, grabbed his large soup spoon and began striking the pots that hung from the overhead. "Out of those bunks! Let's go you bunch of Nancys!" Louis shouted at the top of his lungs as he walked about crew's quarters hitting everything in his path with the spoon, and pulling blankets off the sailors' prone bodies. Roger's right foot hung over the side of his top bunk. Louis saw it and pulled it hard. The waking sailor came out of the bunk and fell to the hard deck.

Roger rolled onto his right side and rubbed his left arm. "Shit! Okay, Louis! We get the message. You sound like an old fish wife!"

Louis heard the remark, turned, and pointed at the fallen sailor. The look on the cook's face said it all. Roger refrained from saying another word.

There were more groans and specific expletives, none of which were directed at the enraged cook. Louis continued, "I'll not have this on my ship! You guys should have been dressed and topside an hour ago, swabbing the deck and readying the ship…and don't forget you have to get back under the ship and paint that repair today."

The boys slowly climbed out of their bunks and searched for clothes to wear while Louis stood by the galley entrance with an expectant stare. The cook blocked the entire opening, arms folded in front of his chest, with his spoon still in hand. "Well, this is how it's gonna' play out. Scotty, you're cooking the bacon and eggs, Teddy and Wally, get the mugs out and get the coffee goin'. Percy set the table. Jack, you have the clean-up. Roger, go topside and start swabbing the deck!"

No one said another word. The boys went about their assigned tasks and grumbled as they did so. They made their own breakfast and cleaned the crew's quarters, as Louis expected they would. He came back in an hour to inspect, and promptly sent them topside to begin their daily chores.

Up on deck, the sailors found it to be another hot day with no breeze. Each sailor went to his sailing station and began tending to lines, sheets and shrouds. Lines that hung loosely were coiled up tight and hung appropriately. Brass and steel accoutrements were polished, and mooring lines were adjusted.

Everyone set to swabbing the deck to finish what Roger had started earlier. Just before lunch three quick bells sounded about the ship. All eyes went to amidships. Smitty rang the ship's bell three more times, while Captain Murdock stood forward of the helm and raised his right arm in the air, twirling his hand in a circular motion. A ship's meeting was being called…and no one wanted to be late. The sailors dropped what they were doing and hurried to the widest part of the ship.

When the crew was present, Murdock stepped forward into the semi-circle of sailors. "Good morning, sailors. I'd like to discuss the schedule for the next few days." He paused, and paced from one side of the ship to the other, before speaking. He stopped and scanned the anxious faces of the crew before him. "I'm planning on launching the Defiant back into the harbor tomorrow…first thing in the morning. The painted hull repair will be more than dry by that time and we have to ready the ship for tours on Saturday and Sunday." The crew's faces dropped immediately and Murdock noticed it. "I'm sorry guys, but we'll have to change your day off to Monday. If we get the ship ready on Thursday and Friday, we'll have little to do on Monday before we depart Provincetown on Tuesday."

Murdock looked over to his first mate, "Smitty, take a couple of the boys and make sure the bilges are completely drained. The bilge drains have been wide open since we got into dry dock so there can't be much left."

Murdock glanced back at the crew, began to pace the deck again, and continued. "Once the tours are over, I have decided to cancel Boston Harbor and proceed north toward Smutty Nose Island, which is part of the Isles of Shoals chain off the coasts of New Hampshire and Maine."

Murdock watched the boys faces closely. "As you know, we are getting into the part of summer called the 'summer doldrums.' You've already experienced a little of it when we departed Wellfleet Harbor last week. The doldrums mean that winds are light to non-existent and very unpredictable. We'll have to watch for intermittent puffs and freak tropical storms, so report any unusual weather patterns or colors in the sky, while you go about your duties." Murdock paused for a moment as if in deep thought, "Fog is one my greatest concerns. I don't have to remind you that we don't have radar or radio on board, so we have to rely on natural weather conditions to forecast any upcoming weather or sea conditions. In any fog condition, I want lookouts fore and aft, and also in the crosstrees. If there is any boat traffic in a foggy situation, we won't know how close another vessel is, until he's upon us, and we may not have the wind to move out of his path in time." Murdock stopped pacing and looked at the crew, "This is serious stuff, sailors. You will hear that big ship coming, but you won't be able to tell where he is until he breaks through the curtain of fog and is right on top of you...so be on your toes."

Murdock clasped his hands behind his back and nodded his head, as he stared into the deck before him. He looked up, "Any questions?" No one moved. Murdock nodded once again. "Good. We'll go back over my expectations of your sailing responsibilities again before we depart Provincetown. That's all." The captain turned and disappeared into the aft hatch.

Smitty waited for the captain to go below and addressed the crew. "Okay, sailors. We have a ton of work to do before we launch tomorrow." He began to assign work tasks. "Teddy and Wally...go below and check the bilges...bow to stern. Pull the bilge planks and make sure they're dry. Look at the bilge pumps and clean them up. Make sure they're operational." Smitty turned toward the rest of the crew. "Roger and Percy, get everything in its place, topside and below. Make everything ready for tour status." The crew began to head to their assigned work areas. Jack and Scott remained. "I want you two to get under the ship and paint that repair. Inspect it first, and look for gaps and cracks. If it's okay, get it painted up. I know you guys will be meticulous. When you're done, come back aboard and help get the ship ready for tours."

The day proceeded without incident. It was just a hot day with hardly a breeze to offer the sailors a reprieve from the hot, end of July sun. It was especially miserable below deck where Teddy and Wally toiled, pulling up bilge planks.

Eventually, Louis went below with some water. "Okay, that's enough, you two. Take this water and go topside. Get some air and start helping with the tasks up there. I'll finish up with the bilge pumps." The two sailors looked at each other in shock. Louis interrupted the moment. "Get goin' before I change my mind."

By day's end, the ship was back in an organized state and up to tour status. The bilges were dry and the bilge drains closed. Lines and shrouds were inspected and tightened, and the hull repair painted to match Defiant's black hull. The ship was seaworthy once more.

After dinner, Murdock and Smitty walked around the hull for a general inspection, anticipating the morning's launch back into the Harbor. Murdock knelt down and ran his hand over the finished hull repair. He chuckled as he inspected the work. "The boys did a good job, Smitty! Did you inspect this yet?"

Smitty half smiled as he stood behind the Captain. "Yes, I did, Skipper. I hope it holds. They worked hard on it."

Murdock nodded his head. "They did a pretty good job bending the wood planks and seaming the gaps. It'll hold. I'm not expecting any rough weather in the next week anyway. It should be a slow but smooth sail to Smutty Nose."

Smitty stepped back and folded his arms in front of him. "Yeah, I've been meaning to ask you about that."

Murdock stood and faced Smitty. "Of course. What is it?"

Smitty continued, "Why the sudden change in plans from Boston Harbor to Smutty Nose?"

Murdock ran his hand through his short brown hair. "Well, I gave it a lot of thought, Smitty. At first, I wanted to defer to Boston Harbor because of the ship's hull damage, but once I was granted the time in dry dock, I knew we could get a good fix that would last the rest of the summer. Aside from the fact that Smuttynose was a scheduled port of call, I considered the fact that we are entering the summer doldrums. I felt there would be less stress on the hull with the lighter winds and calmer seas, so a longer cruise wouldn't be a concern."

Smitty watched the ground under their feet as the captain explained his decision. He said nothing except to nod his head.

Murdock smiled and continued, "I have to admit that I thought a long sail to Smuttynose would be good for the crew too. It's sixty-seven and a half miles as the crow flies, not including tacking. It'll probably be a nine to ten-hour sail with intermittent winds and currents."

Smitty still kept his focus on the ground. "Were those your only reasons, Skipper?"

Murdock gave Smitty a confused glance. "Smitty, you don't know me as a softy of any sort, and I'd be the first to deny it, but I'm damn proud of this crew and how far they've come. Yeah, they've had their moments but they're twenty-year old boys that have been sequestered to this ship since May. I've never heard a complaint or had anyone disobey an order. They're a bunch of good lads in my book."

Smitty finally looked up to meet the captain's gaze. "What are you saying, Skipper?"

"I'm saying the summer is coming to an end and before we go to Gloucester for repairs, I want to give them a special sail. I think they'll enjoy the history and legends that the island has. You know…the whole murder mystery that continues to hang over Smuttynose and its islands. It'll be a fun trip without me telling them that. I want them to come away from this experience on the Defiant that it was a lot of hard work but also special, in the way that they experienced some neat things along the way…that it wasn't all hard work."

Smitty frowned. "Skipper, they are being punished for juvenile offenses. They couldn't expect that it would be a good time."

Murdock turned toward the ship and leaned against the Defiant, resting his right hand on her hull. "I know, I know.

But remember, I was once one of them...a Tall Ship Sailor. I can identify with what they're feeling and how they look at things...where they think this experience may be taking them. I don't want them to look back at their sailing experience in a negative way."

Smitty raised his eyebrows. "I'm glad to hear you say all this, Skipper. It's how I feel too."

Murdock turned back to Smitty. "After the repairs in Gloucester, we've got a few more scheduled ports of call north to Newfoundland, and then our sailing orders are to go south toward the Chesapeake Bay area with scheduled ports of call until April. I want the first part of their sentence to be meaningful and wholesome."

Smitty nodded to end the conversation. "Okay, Skipper. You got it." Smitty turned and walked toward the Defiant's ladder. "Looks like we're ready for launch in the morning. Have a good night, Skipper."

Murdock smiled and said nothing as he watched his first mate climb up to the ship's deck.

CHAPTER FORTY

It was Thursday morning, launch day. The dock yard hands arrived bright and early and stood by the Defiant's hull sipping coffee until the crew was ready and off the ship. Smitty took his usual position behind the helm and Josh stood in the bow to ready the lines. The portable stanchions were removed and the Defiant settled into her cradle.

When the crew was a safe distance from the ship, Smitty stepped to the port side rail and shouted, "Clear! Away all lines!"

The yard hands released the winch cable and slowly the Defiant began its slide down the dry dock's temporary ramp. She moved slowly at first, then faster as her momentum built on the angled set of tracks. She hit the water stern first, throwing up a huge stern spray. Upon hitting the water, Smitty engaged the small diesel to motor the ship over to the public pier she had tied up to, almost a week before.

Once they had finished securing the mooring lines, Smitty signaled the crew. The boys accompanied by Louis, walked over to meet their ship and asked permission to come aboard. Smitty granted their request and as the crew crossed the gangway, Smitty reminded them. "It's 8:00 AM, sailors. Get settled and check your sailing stations. The captain is in town, at the Harbor Repair Office, to pay the dry dock bill. He wants a ship's meeting at 10:00. Don't be late!"

The boys set to work readying the Defiant for Saturday and Sunday tours. There was literally no breeze as the crew raised the ship's pennants and the American flag. Eventually, the mid-morning hour arrived. Captain Murdock crossed the gangway at 10:00 AM to see the crew waiting at amidships. He stopped and stared for a moment. He nodded his head and smiled as he walked over to the crew. "Good morning, sailors. Thank you for being so punctual. I called a ship's meeting because I want to inform you of a change in our schedule. As you know, the next two days will be tours for the public. Be ready to accept guests tomorrow at 8:00 AM sharp...in dress whites."

Murdock paused and paced the deck as usual before continuing. He also wanted to make a distinction between the weekend activities and the upcoming cruise. "Get some rest on Sunday night as we'll be preparing the ship for a nine to ten-hour sail to the Isles of Shoals on Tuesday, August 1. Our destination is north to a small set of islands in the Gulf of Maine, located about six miles off the New Hampshire and Maine coastline. Any questions?"

There were none so Murdock continued. "We'll be anchoring in Gosport Harbor, off Smuttynose Island in the midst of those little islands. It's about sixty-seven and a half miles from here as the crow flies but we'll be sailing into the wind and tacking, so our total sailing distance will be about ninety miles." He paused and panned the entire crew. "That means you're going to be busy trimming sails and coming about when I call for it."

Murdock paced the deck again and continued. "They are expecting us Tuesday evening and the moorings there are hard to come by, so if our slip gets taken before we arrive, we'll have to anchor out in the harbor. Actually, I prefer that. I want to anchor where the island's original schooner, Clara Bella anchored, just off Smutty Nose."

Murdock stopped pacing and looked the crew over again. "There is a story about this place, gentlemen. It's a little grisly but I'll give you the condensed version when we drop anchor there. For now, just focus on the weekend of tours. On Monday morning, I want the ship prepared for a long sail to the Gulf of Maine, Isles of Shoals." He scanned the crew's faces and waited for questions or comments. No one moved or said a word. Murdock nodded at the crew and said, "That's all," then turned and disappeared into the aft hatch.

The crew watched the captain leave and milled about amidships discussing the new schedule and the mysterious, Isles of Shoals. Smitty let the boys talk for a few minutes and then brought order to the group of sailors. "Okay sailors, that's enough. I know you're excited about the upcoming cruise, but as the captain said, 'for now, just focus on the weekend of tours.' Set up your sailing stations, get your dress whites in order and ironed, shine your shoes, and think about what you're going to say to your guests. This will be your easy day, since you'll be working on Sunday, which is usually your day off."

The crew broke up and went their separate ways. As expected, the boys followed Smitty's suggestions and the afternoon passed quietly and slowly.

The next morning, Saturday tours opened at 8:00 AM. The Defiant was moored at the extreme end of the town's Public Pier so guests had to walk a good distance to get to her gangway. The pier was crowded with vessels of all sizes. Tall ships, fishing boats, yachts, power boats, and small boats of all varieties, were moored there. Shops, restaurants and even a museum adorned the perimeter of the pier's wharf. It was a happy place and usually attracted a large amount of people.

Guests began arriving around 10:00 AM and crowded the end of the pier. Smitty walked to the Defiant's railing and greeted her guests. "Good morning, everyone! Welcome to the wooden schooner, Defiant. If you'll all form a line by the gangway ramp, we'll begin taking visitors. Groups of five to six would be best.

The crowd organized themselves into a long line that snaked about the pier, and the day began. It was very routine and the crew handled their responsibilities, as if they had become old hands on a sailing ship. Tourist traffic was sporadic and the day progressed slowly. Finally, eight bells rang as the last guest left the ship. Supper was uneventful, as the crew was more interested and excited about finally leaving Provincetown.

Sunday tours were more of the same. Vacationers to the town either stumbled onto the opportunity to see the Defiant or accidentally saw the ship's posting on a restaurant wall they had just visited for breakfast, and included it in their daily schedule. Surprisingly, the afternoon became quite busy, and a line of waiting tourists extended from Defiant's mooring at the extreme end of the pier to the end of the wharf, and onto the historical banks of the harbor. The ship and crew had gained a reputation over the summer from Cape Cod Bay's ports of call, and people waited anxiously, in a long line to see and hear the Defiant's complement of young sailors serving out their sentence for rehabilitation.

Smitty began changing the boys' sailing stations to ward against the crew's monotony. The sailors felt like celebrities on one hand, and did their best to accommodate the onslaught of guests, but by mid-afternoon had enough of questions and offhanded comments from the public. They came to feel as if they were becoming more of a spectacle than an interpretive demonstration.

Finally, the day was done and the last guest left the Defiant's gangway. Smitty called the boys to amidships and told them that they had weathered more guests in one afternoon, than any other crew in the history of the ship. He told them he was proud of them for how they handled themselves and sent them below for supper and to get some rest. As a special reward, Smitty granted the boys time afterward, to spend topside until 10:00 PM.

During supper, the boys talked excitedly about spending time topside. It was a hot night and there were no fans below deck, so being anywhere but in the crew's quarters was acceptable. As they finished their meals, the boys cleaned up the galley, and went up on deck. Percy brought a harmonica he didn't know how to play, some brought old letters or magazines to read in the waning light, and others just went to get out of the ship.

As the boys settled into their favorite places on the ship's deck, the sun settled into the western sky. It was a beautiful sunset with colors of yellow, orange, and red slipping into the horizon of Cape Cod Bay. A small breeze, the first in two days, floated across the Defiant's deck and into the young sailors' hair. The boys welcomed the change, and smiles crossed their faces for the first time in days.

The night grew dark, but remained clear. Jack and Scotty laid on the cabintop and stared into the western sky. Neither of the boys had seen so many stars before. The sight was mesmerizing and almost forced one from looking away. Suddenly, a flash of light to their left, caught Jack's eye. He pointed into the southeastern sky. "Scotty, look! It's a shooting star!"

A star angled across the sky trailing a small tail of light and seemed to plummet into the dark somewhere above the Bay's quiet sea.

Scotty had never seen one before and sat up on the cabintop. "Wow! Is that an omen or something, Jack? I hear shooting stars are kind of rare."

Jack nodded and answered from his prone position. "Yeah, sure is Scotty. According to ancient sailing lore, it can be a good one or a bad one, depending on what might be going on."

Scotty laid back down on the cabintop. "I don't understand, Jack. It's got to be a good omen or a bad one."

Jack remained still and focused on the starry, night sky. "We'll see, Scotty. We'll know soon."

CHAPTER FORTY ONE

Tuesday morning arrived with the long-awaited breeze the sailors had been hoping for. Unfortunately, it was an overcast day with light fog. The boys were up early and readying the ship for their long sail, north to the Isles of Shoals. Monday, had been spent swabbing decks, stowing tools and equipment, and lashing down items, topside and below deck. The boys were anxious to leave Provincetown Harbor, where a lot of their time had been involved with ship maintenance. None of them had ever been to an island before and the idea that their new destination held an interesting history, played on their minds.

Smitty and the captain came from below and stood by the helm conferring with one another. Smitty looked at his watch. It was 7:00 AM. Finally, they both nodded, as if in agreement to something, and Murdock took the helm. "Sailors to sailing stations! Ready to cast off."

The wind came over the Defiant's starboard side as confused air that had just spilled over the tip of Provincetown's land mass. Fortunately, the ship was moored with its bow facing southwest, and her starboard side parallel to the very end of the pier, so departure would be easy. Murdock watched the boys as they got into position and bellowed, "Away all lines, fore and aft. Raise the small jib sail."

As the sailors cast their mooring lines to the pier, the bow team raised the jib halyard. The jib sail filled and snapped open. Murdock held the helm hard over to port, and the Defiant began to fall away from the pier, bow first. Once away from the pier, Murdock straightened out his course and asked for the mainsail. "Raise the mainsail, ready on the mainsheet."

The mainsail climbed up the mainmast as Jack, Scotty, and Josh hauled down on its halyard. The northerly breeze filled the big sail and Murdock shouted to the two boys and Josh, "Half travel for now…until we get out of the bay." The mainsail travelled halfway out to port and about forty-five degrees to the centerline of the ship, to catch as much wind as possible. Scotty ran over to the mainsheet and cleated the line off. The ship responded by heeling slightly to port while picking up speed. The Defiant was on its way to a new destination and adventure.

Murdock sailed the ship out of Provincetown Harbor and southwest past Long Point Light. Smitty stood at his usual perch on the port side railing holding onto the ratlines. "Scotty, get up in the crosstrees. We've got fog and we're in the ferry lane. Keep a sharp eye forward and to port. Call down to me when you see us approaching Wood End Light to starboard."

Scott climbed the rat lines to the cross trees from starboard, as the Defiant's port side leaned into the harbor. It was a little disconcerting as he climbed toward the cross trees with the ship heeled to the opposite side, but he continued, and tried not to look down. The water rushing by the ship below could cause an optical illusion and cause the climber a mis-step, possibly resulting in a fall.

The bay was fairly smooth and the Defiant had good way on. The ship had been cruising unrestricted for several minutes along the coast of Provincetown's, Wood End. Scotty shouted down to Smitty, "Wood End Light five hundred yards off the starboard bow."

Smitty looked over to Murdock at the helm. "Wood End Light, Skipper, five hundred yards."

Murdock nodded and replied, "Ready for starboard turn on the port tack...two minutes."

Wood end Light came up on the Defiant's starboard side and Murdock kept the ship on a port tack but turned starboard a bit to sail northwest before sailing into the wind. "Heel to port. Steady as she goes." The wind, out of the north, no longer confused and weakened by the Provincetown land mass, heeled the ship further over to the port side increasing the angle of the deck. Murdock looked aloft to the cross trees. "Hold on, Scotty. We'll be on this tack for a while. Give us a shout when you see Race Point Light off the starboard side."

The Defiant continued on a northwesterly course keeping Provincetown to starboard, and sailing as close to the wind as possible. The fog still consumed the area and Scotty was having trouble keeping the coast of Provincetown in site. Defiant's course was about a mile west of Wood End. Murdock's plan was to sail until they were about a mile north of Race Point light, and come about to a starboard tack. The new course would put them out about one mile north of the Cape's most northern point. His only concern was about the confused currents that were common to that area. The only way to push through that situation was to increase the ship's speed and keep the course as steady as possible.

The Defiant maintained her northwesterly course for another two and half hours. The fog began to lift, but limited the visibility to about one-half mile. He looked aloft to the crosstrees. "Scotty, can you see Race Point Light yet?"

Scotty strained to see any sign of land starboard of the ship's course. "Not yet, Skipper. I think I can see what looks like a dim moon in the fog. Can't be sure though."

Murdock looked over to Smitty on the port railing. "That must be Race Point Light he's seeing through the fog." Murdock glanced in the direction of what Scotty saw. "Check your watch, Smitty. We're doing about eight knots, so if that is the light house, we need to sail another mile on this course so I can come about to starboard and pass Race Point's coast by about a mile. We'll stay on this course for another ten minutes and come about to starboard." Murdock paused as he looked east into the fog. "Okay, mark the time...beginning now, and get a lookout on the bow to watch for traffic dead ahead."

"Aye, Skipper. Ten minutes...marking now." Smitty climbed up on the port railing and held onto the ratlines. When he was in place, he shouted to the bow team. "Percy! Get a lookout on the bow and watch for traffic dead ahead."

Percy put Teddy at the Defiant's prow and turned back to Smitty, giving him a thumbs up signal.

Smitty kept an eye on his wristwatch and turned to Murdock. "Okay, Skipper. Coming up on ten minutes...Mark!"

Murdock gave the order and swung the helm over, "Coming about to starboard!"

The Defiant slowly responded to Murdock's course change. The bow began to move in a northeasterly direction across the foggy horizon and the mainsail luffed for a minute until the wind from the north began to fill the large sail again. Suddenly, an audible snap could be heard as the mainsail filled, and drove the mainsail's boom to the starboard side. Murdock shouted above the breeze, "Trim the mainsail! I want her close to the wind." Josh and Jack hauled the sail's mainsheet in until any further trimming would cause the sail to luff and spill wind. The spars, booms, and mainmast creaked and groaned in response, and the deck heeled over to starboard. Percy's bow team knelt low to the deck and let the small jib sail move to starboard as the ship changed direction. Defiant's sails once again filled with the northerly breeze and moved the ship out of Cape Cod Bay.

Defiant sailed into the morning fog with about a half mile of visibility. Murdock steered the ship to keep her course north of the light Scotty had seen, and as close to the wind as he could. As Defiant sailed, the silhouette of a land mass began to take shape off the starboard side. The fog continued to lift and soon the shadow of a tall cylindrical structure rose from the horizon. The dim moon Scott had seen was, in fact, Race Point Light's beacon. Defiant was right on course and right where the captain wanted her to be.

Murdock looked over to Smitty. "Okay, we're clear. Take the helm and stay this course for another twenty minutes. That 'll give us another two miles to the east…then come about to port. The wind is picking up as will our speed. Continue tacking into the wind every twenty minutes, until we get the Isles of Shoals in site, then call me. I'll be in my cabin."

Smitty got behind the helm, "Aye, Skipper." He looked at Murdock and smiled, "The boys are going to be busy today."

Murdock raised one eyebrow and nodded matter-of-factly, "I told them they would be busy today. They'll be tired tonight. Tell Louis to give them a hearty supper."

Smitty looked at his watch and nodded. "Aye, Skipper. I'll call you up on deck when we have the Isles of Shoals in sight."

Murdock turned away, and before he went below, looked aloft and said, "Get Scotty out of the cross trees. The fog is lifting and the sun is trying to burn through. Tell him, he did well." He looked ahead of the ship one more time before he turned and went below.

When the Defiant was abeam of Race Point Light, Smitty noticed a drag on the ship, and steering became difficult. He knew the area well and thought, *We're getting into the confused currents off Race Point. Gonna' need to increase speed to get through it.* He shouted to the sailors tending the mainsail. "Scotty, Jack! Go forward and make ready to raise the foresail. We have a confused current situation here and need to increase steerageway."

Smitty struggled with the helm and fought what felt like several currents from different directions at the same time. The boys in the bow noticed the waver in the ship's course and looked back at the first mate. Smitty shouted to the bow team in response. "Ready to fly the medium jib sail."

When Scott and jack were in position, Smitty gave the order. "Raise the foresail and trim it tight!"

Jack, Scott and Josh pulled hard on the foremast's halyard and the foresail rose, slowly at first, then faster. When it reached the top of the foremast and began to fill with air, Smitty shouted to the bow team. "Fly the medium jib sail!

The Defiant now sailed with her two large sails and two jib sails. She heeled further to starboard and the sea passed just below her starboard railing. She was almost at her maximum heel angle. As the ship lurched forward, her speed increased through the water and Smitty found the steering easier. "Steady as she goes. We'll drop those last two sails when we get through this area. Wait for my order."

The sea was calm, except for the confused currents below, that the ship sliced thru at her increased speed. Smitty let Defiant continue northeast for another twenty minutes as Murdock had requested. He figured the drag on the ship caused by the currents, slowed her to about the same speed she would have been going at eight knots without currents. He looked at his watch. "Ready to come about!" The sailors scurried to their sailing stations and Smitty shouted above the light breeze. "Coming about to port!"

The Defiant responded to the sailors' efforts and Smitty's steering. Gradually, the bow began to move across the horizon in a northwesterly direction. The mainsail and foresail booms travelled across the ship's centerline and out past the port side of the ship, while the jib sails hung for a moment before catching the new breeze. The usual creaks and groans of stressed wooden timbers was noticeable above the wind in the rigging, and the sound of the sea as it splashed against the Defiant's hull. The ship heeled to port and Defiant began her new tack to the northwest, slowing chipping away at their intended travel to the Isles of Shoals.

Time after time, Smitty ordered a course change. The twenty-minute intervals between tacks became routine for the sailors and the cruise continued in a smooth and efficient manner. As the morning wore on, the sun began to burn away the fog and gradually turned the grey, dismal surroundings into a clear and bright day. The sea remained calm and reflected the new light and warmth onto Defiant's sails and crew. Eventually, Percy pointed into the water just ahead of the Defiant's bow. "Hey, we got dolphins swimming with us on both sides of the bow…three on each side."

Smitty smiled and told the bow team to switch off with the rest of the crew so everyone could see the dolphins as they jumped and dove just ahead of the ship. He explained they were Atlantic White Sided Dolphins, common to the area, but usually found further out to sea. He let all of the sailors get a look at the pod of dolphins as they swam just before the bow, and then ordered everyone back to their sailing stations. "Okay, that's enough, sailors. Everyone back to work. You'll see a lot more of them when we get to the Isles of Shoals. They're especially common to that area, probably due to the abundance of fish around the islands."

The dolphins swam at the Defiant's bow for some time and suddenly, almost at once, disappeared. Percy looked into the water and back at the bow team. "They're gone. All of a sudden." Then there was a noticeable difference in the ship's speed. The foresail and medium jib began to luff and the ship began to slow. Smitty looked aloft to see the pennants that flew at the top of the main and fore masts no longer flapped vigorously in the wind. The wind was dying.

Smitty tried several kinds of positioning for the ship and sails, to no avail. Within the hour, the breeze was gone and the Defiant experienced what mariners call 'dead calm.' Even the pennants at the top of the ship's masts hung, without so much as a flutter, in the dead air. The sea was like glass…no swells or waves…not even a ripple.

The boys stood at their sailing stations and looked back to the helm for instruction. Smitty reached over to the ship's bell and rang it three times. The crew was confused. A ship's meeting in the middle of the Atlantic Ocean? "Jack, go below and get the captain. Tell him we're at dead calm at our halfway mark in the middle of a starboard tack."

Jack ran to the aft hatch and disappeared. Smitty waved everyone back to amidships. "Come on back. Looks like you guys are going to get a break. Sit on the deck and wait until the captain comes up."

Murdock came up the aft hatch within minutes, squinted at the bright sunshine and walked to the starboard railing. The sky was deep blue, the sun was bright, and there was no noise. The silence was deafening. Nothing flapped or strained against its restraints. The masts stood as dormant pinnacles that reached up into quiet air, that usually played the ratlines and rigging like a guitar. It felt like sitting on a large pond.

Murdock walked back to the sailors seated on the deck and scratched the back of his head. "Well, boys, were at dead calm. That means we're in a spot where nothing is moving, except for maybe a small current under the ship. This is only more of what you experienced before we left Provincetown, except that was sporadic because it was only the beginning of the summer doldrums. I had hoped to get a jump on that and get to the Isles of Shoals before this, but being laid up in dry dock for a week didn't help."

Murdock walked over to the port side and looked east toward the Massachusetts/New Hampshire coast. The coastline was barely visible. He walked back to the helm and said, "We're about twelve miles off the eastern seaboard. Lucky for us the currents aren't too bad here. The ship will drift a little, but to us it'll look like she's dead in the water. There's nothing to worry about. We're just going to have to wait it out."

Murdock glanced at Smitty and raised an eyebrow. Smitty returned the look with a wink of his right eye and Murdock looked back to his group of sailors. "I see this as a gift from the sea, and the only thing we can do is to take advantage of that." The boys looked worried as they waited for Murdock's next words. "You guys are just going to have to experience this first hand, so go for a swim, dive off the ship, soak in some rays… have a little fun."

There was some shouting and certain expletives, but Murdock contained that. "Sailors, watch your terminology. Enjoy the afternoon but don't stray too far from the ship… especially if you're swimming. When the wind picks up, we have to be able to go." The boys started stripping down to their cutoff jeans. Murdock smiled before he went below and got the boys attention one more time. "Oh, and watch for sharks. Remember, we are at sea."

CHAPTER FORTY TWO

The boys raced to the starboard railing, as their shirts and sneakers landed on the deck. In a dead run, Jack hopped up onto the railing, planted one foot on its top, and pushed off into a clean, arcing dive to the water below. The rest of the young crew followed. Some dove from a standing position and some jumped. Murdock wasn't even at the bottom of the aft hatch ladder when he heard the first splash.

Josh walked over to Smitty. "I'll watch the helm if you want to keep an eye on the boys, Smitty."

Smitty waved off the offer. "Nah, we'll just lie ahull. Tie off the helm to starboard so the rudder is in a fixed position. That might help us drift in one direction. It's so calm, I don't see a need to do anything else."

Louis came up on deck followed by Burt the dog, and saw the boys splashing about in the sea. "What do we have here…a mutiny?"

Smitty laughed, "Nah, Murdock gave them free time while we're at dead calm.

Percy noticed the new arrivals on deck and shouted. "Hey, Burt is on deck!" He waved his arms and called the dog. "Hey, Burt! Abandon ship!"

Burt's ears went erect as he heard the sensitive command. He pointed his tail and broke into a run, jumped up onto the ship's rail, and lept into the sea.

Everyone clapped and cheered as Burt swam over to Percy. The boy held the dog at a distance making sure to keep clear of his paddling paws. "I bet you've been waiting the whole cruise to do that, Burt. Good dog!"

Smitty threw a small two-man life raft over the side. "Put Burt in the raft when he gets tired. He'll want to stay out there with you guys."

The boys swam and floated in the cool sea, and let the afternoon sun bathe their bodies. It was a feeling of careless freedom. They dunked each other and climbed back up onto the ship, just to jump off again. Roger climbed back on board and shouted to everyone in the water, "I'm going to the bow and dive off the bowsprit."

That action gave Jack an idea. He climbed back aboard and climbed the ratlines to the crosstrees. Instead of sitting, he stood on them and held onto the nearby shrouds with his hands. "Scotty yelled from the water, "I dare you, Jack. You don't have the balls to jump from there."

Jack shouted back down. "If I jump…you have to follow."

Scott shouted back, "Done. You'll never do it."

Jack braced himself and pushed off hard from the crosstrees, high above the Defiant's deck. Everyone was shocked. "He jumped!" Someone else shouted, "Jack really did it. He actually jumped from the crosstrees."

Jack cleared the side of the ship by several feet and hit the water, making a huge splash. When he came up from underwater, he looked to Scotty. "Get up there, buddy. It's your turn now."

Reluctantly, Scott swam to the ship and climbed the ratlines. Carefully, he got his feet into position and stood on the two timbers that made up the crosstrees. He held the shrouds in his hands as Jack did, and finally looked down. The deck looked so far below…and so small. He tried to distract himself and slowly turned his head toward his crewmates in the water. The boys all floated in a tight circle about thirty feet away from the ship and began their cat calls. "Come on, Scotty. You have to jump now." Teddy cautioned Scott, "Don't hit the railing on the way down. We'll have to feed you to the fish." Scott stood on the crosstrees and knew he had to jump, yet he really didn't want to. He knew that If he jumped out too far, his feet could get out in front of him causing him to land on his back. If he didn't jump out far enough, he could hit the side of the ship.

The rude urgings from his crewmates kept up and Scott knew he had to go. He braced his feet and prepared to jump. As he looked out to his waiting crewmates, he appeared as if he had just noticed something in the water. Scott leaned forward a bit to get a better look, and then let go of one of the shrouds with his right hand to point at an area of water just behind the circle of boys. "Hey…shark! I see a dark shape moving toward you guys…and there's a fin too."

Simultaneously, the circle of boys turned to look. When they did, Scott let go of the shrouds and gave a huge push off the crosstrees with both legs. He landed in the same area as Jack did, feet first, raising a huge plume of water. Hearing the splash, the boys turned back around, and Scott was gone. Percy looked up and saw the crosstrees were vacant. "Where is he? I heard the splash."

Wally scanned the surface of the water, "He probably went too deep and is still swimming to the surface." Still there was no sign of Scott.

Thirty seconds passed and the boys watched the area where the splash came from. Suddenly, Percy screamed, "Shark! It's got my leg!"

Frantically, everyone but Percy, swam for the Defiant. It was chaos in the water. In their haste to get to the ship, they swam into and over one another. Then, Scott's head popped out of the water as he let go of Percy's leg. "You guys are such wimps! Someone says shark and you freak out."

They all turned around to see Scott laughing as he continued to duck Percy under water. Someone shouted, "It was a trick! He swam under us. Let's get him!" The boys felt as though they had been duped and swam after Scott.

Jack yelled above the thrashing swimmers, "You're gonna' pay for that one, Scotty!"

The swimmers caught up with Scott where there was a lot of wrestling and dunking of heads. Amazingly, it was all in fun and the good times continued.

After Scott paid for his practical joke, the laughter and enthusiasm began to wither. The effects of the cool Atlantic began to take its toll. The boys were tiring and began to shiver, so they gave up on Scott and headed back to the ship to lie in the sun.

The whole crew lay on the Defiant's wooden deck and absorbed the afternoon rays. After only a few minutes of inactivity, the sun's warmth had rejuvenated their young bodies and brought new life back to the crew. Percy had an idea. "Hey, let's launch the dinghies and have jousting matches."

Jack sat up from his prone position on the cabintop. "What are you talking about, Percy?"

Percy pointed to the dinghies lashed to the aft end of the Defiant. "We'll put the dinghies in the water, with two guys in each dinghy. One guy rows, and the other guy stands on the front bench seat with a broom handle. The two boats head for each other and try to knock the other guy into the water."

Everyone sat up at once and concurred with phrases like, "Yeah, I'm in," or "I got the broom handle first," or "Let's do it."

Smitty sat on the cabintop and shook his head again. "I hope you guys are going to have enough energy to sail the rest of the way to Smuttynose after all this." The boys paid no attention to the first mate as they prepared to launch the dinghies.

They drew straws for the first contestants. Circumstance had it that the first two teams were Percy and Scott against Jack and Roger. The joust seemed quite innocent at first, but since there were no rules, things got out of hand in a hurry. The jousters began climbing aboard each other's boats to wrestle the other guys into the water. Eventually, Smitty had to step in. "Okay, guys, it's getting too violent out there. Tie the dinghies to the back of the ship and we'll tow them behind us when we get underway. Find something else to do."

The crew decided to have races up the ratlines. Smitty sat on the cabintop with his head in his hands, shook his head, and waited for the outcome.

Once again, they divided their group in half with three boys on each side of the ship. On Smitty's call, two sailors raced each other to the crosstrees from different sides of the ship. The first one to touch the crosstrees' timbers was the winner. After an hour of bare feet against the rough ratline hemp, and several near falls to the deck, Smitty told the boys to sit quiet for a while. In minutes, the deck was strewn with sleeping sailors. Some lay on the deck and others leaned against the ship's railing. Louis came out of the aft hatch with a tray of lemonade and Smitty put a finger to his lips. "Don't wake them. I'm feeling a slight breeze starting and they're going to need every bit of strength to sail this ship the rest of the way." Louis nodded and set the tray down on the cabintop.

▽

Late in the afternoon, the pennants began to flutter until they flew straight out from their masts, supported by a new breeze. The huge mainsail slowly moved out to starboard as it filled with air. Smitty removed the lashings josh had fixed to the helm and then rang the ship's bell three times. The sleeping crew awakened with a start, followed by a few derogatory remarks.

The ship began to move and Smitty shouted, "Sailors, take your sailing stations!" Reluctantly, the boys struggled to their feet and ran to their positions. The new breeze was light but apparent enough, so the sailors could feel it against their skin and face. Smitty watched the pennants at the top of Defiant's masts and turned the helm over until the sails began to fill with air. The ship responded and slowly began to get way on. Smitty shouted into the wind, "Pull the main sheet in tight. Bow team - tighten up on the jib sheet."

Slowly, the Defiant responded to the crew's efforts, and was once again on her way to the Isles of Shoals. The seas were fairly flat with minimum swells, and according to Murdock's calculations, the Defiant was about three hours out from their destination if they continued to have a steady breeze.

The Defiant continued tacking into the wind against a northerly breeze. As the afternoon wore on, the wind picked up to moderate. The ship and her crew were making good time. Smitty looked west to see the sun begin its slide into the flat horizon, and hoped they could make it to Gosport before nightfall. Their new anchorage was nestled in the middle of the Isles, just west of Smuttynose Island, and between Appledorf and Cedar Islands. Star Island would be to their south.

Defiant continued to sail in a northerly direction for the next three hours. By nature of their intended destination and the lay of the New England coastline, their course came increasingly close to the New Hampshire/Maine coastline. The

Isles of Shoals are approximately six miles off the coast of those two states and shares the borders of both.

The sun was low on the horizon and the wind began to subside. Smitty sighted the Isles of Shoals in the waning sunlight and knew it was going to be close. Normally, anchoring at night is not a big deal but Gosport Harbor is fairly small, and space would be tight between the islands and the moored vessels. He knew there would be no available slips but he had preferred to anchor where the inhabitants of Smuttynose had anchored their schooner, the Clara Bella, one hundred years before. He thought it a unique opportunity for the boys, and that it might add to the sailing lore of the island's history.

He called Jack over to the helm. "Jack, that's the Isles of Shoals about a mile off our starboard side." He raised his right arm and pointed. "Get up in the crosstrees and watch for rocks and shipping. The sun is going down so be alert. There shouldn't be much traffic at this hour but pay special attention to whitecaps where there shouldn't be any. If you see something like that out there, it's probably a rock or ledge just below the surface, so give me a shout…immediately."

A worried look crossed Jack's face, so Smitty added, "We're coming in at high tide, Jack. That should give us some extra water above the rocks but keep a close eye anyway."

Jack smiled and nodded his head as he began to climb the ratlines. Smitty continued, "We'll be at the harbor entrance in about thirty minutes. I'll call you down at that point and then you can help Scotty with the mainsail."

The wind was still firm and stable, so Smitty stayed on a longer port tack than usual because the entrance to Gosport was from the west. As soon as they came around the coast of Star Island, Smitty came about and took the starboard tack all the way into the harbor entrance. He called Jack down from the crosstrees and shouted to the bow team. "Lookouts! I want one of you on each point of the bow! Watch dead ahead, port and starboard. There's a lot of rocks just under the surface around these islands."

Smitty told the boys to let the mainsail out to its furthest travel to slow the ship. Then he shouted forward, "Bow team – drop the medium jib sail." The Defiant responded and its speed slowed by half. Cautiously, the first mate picked his way through the coastlines of the tiny islands. As the ship came around the south side of Appledorf, Smuttynose Island lay dead ahead. Smitty smiled and looked to Jack and Scott. "Ready to drop the mainsail! Bow team ready on the bow anchor. Teddy, go astern and ready on the stern anchor."

The Defiant was almost at a crawl. Smitty used landmarks on each of the islands that surrounded him. When he was almost lined up, he knew he had arrived at Clara Bella's anchorage. "Drop the mainsail and jib. Teddy, drop the stern anchor!"

The Defiant's anchor sunk to the bottom and grabbed the sandy bottom. Everyone felt a slight tug as the ship glided to a stop. Smitty shouted to the bow, "Percy, drop the bow anchor." Percy released the latch on the anchor's winch and the heavy anchor dropped to the bottom of Gosport Harbor. The Defiant was finally at anchor.

Once the sails and sheets were secured, Murdock came up on deck and rang the ship's bell. A tired crew stood before him and he smiled. "Welcome to the Isles of Shoals, sailors. You did a great job today and you've sailed through supper time. I'd like you all to go below and get something to eat. Louis has fixed some sandwiches for you. Bring your food back up here and I'll tell you the story about where we're anchored," Murdock paused and pointed east over the Defiant's bow, "...and what happened in that lonely house over there on Smuttynose, one night, a hundred years ago."

The boys all turned their heads to look in the direction Murdock had directed and saw a small house on the horizon of a tiny island. It was dusk, so the structure's detail showed as a silhouette against a darkening sky. The island seemed barren and abandoned, as the last breeze of the day whistled through the ship's rigging.

After the crew had retrieved their sandwiches and returned to amidships, Murdock began telling the tale of the legendary hatchet murders on Smuttynose. He walked about the deck as he spoke, and pointed to the harbor entrance to explain the murderer's path, as he rowed a small dory six miles from the mainland out to these isles in the dark of night.

Murdock pointed again toward the lonely house on Smuttynose and continued. "A couple of murders happened in that house over there one night a long time ago...like in March of 1873. There were just a few people living on that island making a living as fishermen. In fact, they worked off a wooden schooner like ours to support a fishing business. The schooner was called the Clara Bella and it was anchored right where we are. Of course, the ship is long gone, but the house is still there. Evidently one night, someone the family knew, rowed the six miles out from the mainland to Smuttynose, and killed two of the three women...one of them with a hatchet, and robbed their house. No one knows why he did it, but the murderer was eventually tracked down and hanged in Thomaston, Maine.

Murdock was very animated in his story and detailed the alleged murderer's break-in on the house, that at this moment lay only a few hundred feet in front of them. The boys ate and listened to the grisly tale as darkness consumed the schooner. It was better than watching a movie. They were right there, where it happened, only at a different point in time, yet they could see everything first hand, right in front of them, and feel the ship as it gently rocked in the small harbor.

It was dark as Murdock finished his tale. He turned to look at his audience. They were tired but wide awake. He smiled and said, "That's about it. Now you know the story...and you can say that you were there." He paused and looked at his watch, "It's time to go below and get some sleep, so you can say you slept here too."

As the boys began to rise from the deck, he pointed over to Star Island off their starboard side. "That island is a bit of a tourist attraction, so we'll be going ashore in the dinghies tomorrow. Wear your dress whites as we have been invited to tour the village. They have advertised our arrival so people are going to want to talk to you about what you do on the Defiant. Be polite and informative."

Murdock paused, "Any questions?" There were none so he nodded and said, "That's all." He turned and disappeared into the aft hatch.

Smitty waited for the captain to go below. "Okay, sailors. Time to turn in. You have a busy day tomorrow. Make sure your dress whites are clean and ironed."

Some of the boys went down the aft hatch and some went forward to the forward hatch. The ship's deck was suddenly quiet aside from the occasional squeaks and groans, a result of the harbor's tidal action. In the dark, the ship's noises were a little eerie, but at the same time comforting. They were natural in their cause, and to a sailor, meant the ship was alive.

Thirty minutes later, the small gas lantern in the crew's quarters went out, and on this night, there were no lingering conversations in the dark. The night was on the cool side and the boys drifted off to sleep in minutes.

CHAPTER FORTY THREE

The boys awoke the next morning to heat and humidity. The air felt damp and still, as did the sheets and blankets that loosely lay upon their wooden bunks. The clock in the crew's quarters showed 6:00 AM and Louis was already banging around in the kitchen, brewing coffee and preparing bacon and eggs. "Let's go you guys. Get out of those bunks. You gotta' be on deck in an hour to get the ship in order, and prepare the dinghies to go ashore."

Slowly and reluctantly, the crew rolled out of their bunks and sat down to Louis' breakfast. When they went topside and climbed out of the forward hatch, everyone was shocked to see the close quarters the schooner shared with the surrounding vessels that were moored to piers or anchored nearby. The proximity of the islands around them and their rocky shores seemed uncomfortably close. It was amazing they had anchored so successfully in so little sunlight. The dinghies still trailed behind the Defiant and kept an amazingly straight-line relationship to the stern of the ship. Jack pointed out that the current that passed under the ship and out of the harbor was responsible for their organized orientation, and that was probably why Smitty hadn't insisted on pulling the dinghies aboard for the night.

The crew milled around on Defiant's deck for a few minutes and studied their surroundings before getting to work on the ship. It was indeed, a unique place to be anchored. Overnight, a fog layer had moved in and obscured the house on Smuttynose and most of the other islands around them. Portions of vessels protruded from the thick fog while only the tops of bare masts from other tall ships poked through the gray layer. Somewhere, a foghorn bellowed its lonely warning. The boys weren't quite sure where the foghorn was, as fog tends to distort sight and sound. The fact that they were anchored in the midst of four islands also helped to disguise the horn's location.

The boys stood along the starboard railing and stared into the soupy fog. Percy spoke in a low tone. "It's so quiet…like the fog just absorbs everything around it."

Jack commented on Percy's observation as he looked into the fog. "It can cause optical illusions and even confuse sound, especially when there are structures or a nearby landmass." He chuckled and added, "We have all of that, not to mention the rocky shorelines of these islands."

Wally peered into the gray curtain as if he was trying to focus on something. "It's so overcast and quiet, and all those silhouettes from the ships and boats make it look kind of ghostly."

Scotty laughed and started over to his sailing station. "Well, I've heard enough. We don't have to worry about the foghorn because we're not going anywhere. But I do know that if we're not done with our morning chores, we may be risking our chances of going ashore this afternoon."

The rest of the boys followed Scott's example and set about deck maintenance, checking the sails, and coiling lines. They swabbed the Defiant's deck and wiped down any metal surfaces for the next two hours. Finally, Murdock and Smitty came up on deck. Smitty rang the ship's bell and everyone went to amidships for a crew's meeting.

Captain Murdock began. "Good morning, sailors. I hope everyone slept well in our little anchorage." Before waiting for anyone to answer he went on, "Everyone did a great job at anchoring the ship last night." He half turned and swung his arm around horizontally. "We did that in the last light of day and I know visibility was tough…and as you can see, we didn't have a whole lot of extra space to play with. You guys have come a long way."

Murdock walked over to the port side and faced Appledore Island as he spoke. "The sun will be breaking through this fog layer shortly. Finish up your deck chores and get the dinghies over to the gangway. We'll be going ashore after lunch to tour the village on Star Island, and entertain tourists about what you've been doing on the Defiant. Tonight, is our last night here and tomorrow we have an early departure for Gloucester. We're heading home for repairs, so be up on deck at 6:00 AM. I want to set sail by 7:00." He paused and turned around to look at the crew. "It'll be foggier than it was this morning, so I want a lookout on the bow, one in the crosstrees and one at the stern." He continued to stare at the crew for a moment and said, "See you in a couple of hours…in your dress whites. That's all." Murdock turned and went below.

The morning passed and everyone was excited about getting off the ship. Josh and Smitty helped the boys get the dinghies over to the gangway ladder. This time, they'd have to climb down to the tiny boats.

At 1:00 PM, Murdock appeared on deck ready to go ashore. The crew stood by the port railing ready to disembark. Josh was already in the first dinghy holding it and the other one, close to the Defiant's hull. Murdock turned and looked the crew over. "You're a good crew, lads. I'm proud of you. Do your best today and be friendly and courteous."

Murdock climbed down into the first dinghy and everyone followed, one at a time. Louis watched from the railing as the two dinghies rowed around Defiant's stern to get to the starboard side, where Star Island lay, only a few hundred feet away.

The boys rowed the dinghies to Star's rocky shore and tied up to a public pier. They proceeded to a long walkway through a beautiful country setting of grass and exposed rock with quaint structures that dotted the landscape. The village had set aside two tables with chairs in the midst of the village, where the boys would get the most exposure. As they entered the village, A banner hung from two poles, WELCOME SCHOONER DEFIANT AND ITS TALL SHIP SAILORS.

Murdock stopped and looked up at the banner for a moment. "That's an honor boys! I guess they're going to be happy to see you. Have fun with this."

The crew took their places and stood by the tables in groups of two. They stood out from the usual attractions in their dress whites – six young handsome and sun-tanned young men from a tall ship.

At first, only a few people wandered over to the sailors to say hello or ask a question. By mid-afternoon, the boys were swamped with tourists. They wrote autographs and told stories about their experiences on the Defiant. They talked about everything from the hull cracks, to the ferry experience. They spoke about how to boil wood to bend hull planking, to towing a ship out of the harbor with their dinghies, and the experience of having waves wash over them in the bow during rough seas. People snapped pictures of the crew and tried to tip them for their time – acceptance of which was not allowed. It was a terrific afternoon in the sun.

As the crew finished their day and walked through the village, Roger began to take note of the different shops and small variety stores. He tried to look discrete as he thought, *Cigarettes and beer...all available here! Maybe I can sneak away in one of the dinghies tonight and buy some of this stuff before they close. Hopefully, Murdock will leave the dinghies in the water again.*

The sailors, accompanied by their captain, boarded their dinghies and rowed back to the ship. It had been a good day. Everyone felt a sense of satisfaction in that, so many people were interested in what they had been doing, and how much they had accomplished over one short summer. They felt like celebrities and compared the number of autographs each had signed. Roger had remained quiet. He had been secretly planning his little sortie back to Star Island in the dark.

After dinner, the boys read or had quiet conversations about the day. Roger slid out of his bunk and said he'd be back. He had been lucky as Murdock had decided to leave the dinghies in the water and tow them to Gloucester on their departure from Gosport. Quietly, Roger climbed the forward hatch ladder and snuck over to the ship's stern. First, he looked astern and forward to make sure no one was around. Then he pulled the dinghies in close to the Defiant's stern by their tow lines, and tied off the lead dinghy. Carefully and quietly, he slid over the stern railing and climbed into the trailing dinghy. He thought reconnecting the dinghies would be easier on the way back, if he only had to attach his to the one already secured to the ship.

Captain Murdock sat behind his desk reading charts and weather patterns in preparation of the morning's sail. A thud resonated from the aft end of the ship. He looked up and listened harder. *Can that be the dinghies bumping into the stern?* He thought for a moment and listened. The bumping was definitely coming from the stern. He shook his head, *It can't be the dinghies. They should be at their maximum lead away from the ship. The current out of the harbor is directly under us.* Then he pursed his lips. *Unless someone is trying to run off with one of them.* Murdock stood from his desk and grabbed his flashlight. *Ah, I better go check it out. We can't afford to lose one of those dinghies.*

Just as Roger set his oars into the oarlocks and reached forward to unclip the tow line, he was blinded by a bright light. He sat back on the dinghy's bench seat and rubbed his eyes. A flat, serious, voice came from the deck of Defiant's stern. "Keep your hands off those oarlocks, son. If I have to get wet to come and get you, I promise there will be hell to pay."

Roger closed his eyes. *Oh shit, it's Murdock! Out of the four regular crew, it has to be Murdock.*

Roger sat in the dinghy not moving. The voice from the black stern came through the darkness again. "Okay, Roger. Put the oars back and secure the dinghy." Roger complied. The voice without a face continued, "Now, hop out of the dinghy and swim over to the gangway ladder."

Roger quickly replied, "Skipper, it's dark and the water is cold. I'll just get the dinghy up to the stern and climb back aboard."

Murdock's voice came sharply through the darkness. "Don't make it worse for yourself. Get in the water and swim over to the ladder. Now!"

Roger reluctantly obeyed and swam to the ship's ladder, wondering what might be swimming around him in the black water. He climbed back aboard the ship and stood before Murdock. The captain blankly stared into the shivering youth's face. Roger apologized, "Sorry, Skipper. I thought I'd just go ashore to get some cigarettes and come right back."

Murdock kept the light in the boy's face. "Really, Roger? Just cigarettes?" Murdock paused and a wicked little smile crossed his face. "Haven't you heard? They're bad for your health?"

Roger didn't move. He just stood there dripping on the deck. Murdock finally broke the silence. "Go get some dry clothes on and be in my cabin in twenty minutes. Do not speak to anyone. Just get changed and report to me. Go!"

Roger ran for the aft hatch and down the long narrow passageway to the crew's quarters. The boys were surprised at the condition of Roger and his haste in getting dressed. Jack asked, "What happened? Did you fall over the side or something?"

Roger said nothing. He merely raised one hand in the air as if to stay stop, and finished dressing. The rest of the crew quietly looked on as Roger pulled on his wet sneakers and ran out of the crew's quarters.

When he reached the captain's cabin, he paused and took a deep breath before knocking. A voice from within came through the door, stern and flat, "Come." Roger entered the cabin to find Murdock seated behind his desk while Smitty, Louis, and Josh stood on either side. Murdock began, "Stand up straight, Roger and look me in the eye." Roger did so, and took a deep breath. "You don't seem to learn, son. You just keep trying to break the rules, so this is how it is. I don't want you on my ship right now. In the morning, when we set sail for Gloucester, I want you off the ship."

Roger pleaded. "But Skipper, you can't just leave me out here in these Islands."

Murdock smiled, "Oh, I'm not leaving you here! You like that dingy so much," Murdock paused for effect, …"that is where you'll be for the remainder of the trip."

Roger looked confused. "I don't know what you mean, Skipper."

Murdock replied, "You are relieved of your sailing responsibilities...as of this moment. When the crew prepares the ship to sail, one of your crewmates will help you into the rear dinghy, and you will ride there, as we tow it back to

Gloucester." He glanced at Smitty, "Make sure he's wearing a life jacket."

Smitty nodded back at the captain.

Roger was astounded. "Are you serious, Skipper? That's a half-day's sail from here and if it's rough, it could be dangerous."

Murdock nodded his head. "That's right Roger, but you earned that place. We call it a tow behind...and that will be your place for the next leg of this trip. Your responsibility will be to see that you don't founder." He paused and then nodded at the youth. "That is all, Roger. Better get some sleep...and don't talk to the rest of the crew about this." Roger looked to Smitty, who just waved him to the cabin's door.

CHAPTER FORTY FOUR

The next morning arrived dark and overcast. The fog was especially thick and there was a cool dampness in the air. It was the day of the Defiant's departure from Gosport and the long-awaited trip back to Gloucester Harbor for repairs. It was only a twenty-seven-mile trip, which meant a three-hour cruise under a moderate breeze, but Murdock had insisted on an early departure. The winds were favorable and out of the northeast, making it an easy exit for Defiant to catch the breeze, pivot on her stern anchor, and reverse her direction.

It was 6:00 AM. All of the Tall Ship Sailors stood at amidships awaiting a ship's meeting. Captain Murdock came up on deck from the aft hatch and stood in front of the helm. He said nothing and looked at no one while he waited for everyone to be present, which included the regular crew of Smitty, Josh and Louis. It was quiet and uncomfortable, not only because of the weather, but because of the attitude the captain exuded.

Finally, everyone was on deck and Murdock began. "Good morning, sailors. As you know we'll be leaving Gosport Harbor in a short while. We'll be sailing for Gloucester Harbor for repairs before moving on to our scheduled ports, north to the Canadian coast." Murdock paused and looked at his crew before continuing. His face was solemn and serious. "There will be a change in our sailing regimen as one of our sailors will not be sailing with us...and I'd like to bring that to the crew's attention."

Murdock paused and looked at his sailors, "Last night, I discovered one of our crew," he paused a moment and then continued, "Roger Bower... was trying to take one of the ship's dinghies back to Star Island. He said he was only going to get some cigarettes. Keep in mind, it doesn't matter what he was going there for. The fact of the matter is, he was topside without permission and off the ship preparing to leave the anchorage when he was stopped. Because of that, he will be riding in that same dingy, towed behind the Defiant, all the way to Gloucester." Murdock stopped and looked at Roger. "It is my hope that he gets a safe ride. It won't be smooth or dry, but he will get that ride to Gloucester. I will decide on what to do with him once we get settled in port. Therefore, his sailing responsibilities will have to be shared between the rest of you."

Murdock stepped out from behind the helm and walked across the deck watching the boys. "I need to know if Roger was put up to this, or if any one of you had a part in having him secure cigarettes, or whatever he was going to get."

Murdock stopped pacing and faced the crew. Their faces showed surprise and bewilderment. "If Roger was not alone in this, and anyone else admits to it, this is the time to tell me. If there were other people involved, and they admit to it, I will let Roger ride below with that person or persons, until we get to Gloucester. Then a decision will be made as to whether you will be punished or be put off the ship and sent elsewhere."

The captain paced the deck in silence a few times and came back to the helm. The crew remained quiet. "Okay, that's it then. It appears Roger was in on this scheme on his own." He paused to look at the pennants flying at the top of the masts. "Everyone to their sailing stations. Jack and Scotty, bring Roger to the stern, bring up the trailing dinghy, and help Roger into it."

The boys did as they were told and escorted their condemned shipmate to the stern railing. It was an awkward moment. Jack handed Roger his lifejacket and Scotty put his hand on Roger's left shoulder. "Hold on tight, pal. We'll all be watching over you. See you in Gloucester."

Roger kept his head down in shame, and managed to nod in acknowledgement.

When Roger had his life jacket secured, and his dingy had drifted back behind the lead dinghy, Murdock began shouting orders to raise anchor. "Okay everyone, we are going to swing off the wind, just as we did in Plymouth Harbor." He swung the helm hard over to starboard and shouted, "Bow team... pull the bow anchor. Percy...raise the small jib sail when that anchor clears the water."

Once the anchor was up and the jib sail filled, the breeze began to push the ship, bow first, to starboard. The stern anchor, still secured to the harbor's bottom, held the Defiant in place, and the entire ship pivoted about her stern anchor. As the ship continued to turn, the breeze now passed over the starboard beam. Defiant had completely reversed her direction and was pointed out of the tiny harbor. Murdock ordered, "Pull the stern anchor...raise the mainsail!" The mainsail came to life with an audible snapping sound and the Defiant was on her way out of Gosport, Isles of Shoals.

As the ship turned, the two dinghies trailed dutifully behind, and at a safe distance from the ship's stern. Roger sat in the middle of the furthest dinghy from the ship, wearing his lifejacket, with his hands clamped to the boat's gunnels. It was going to be a long ride.

CHAPTER FORTY FIVE

The Defiant left the confines of Gosport Harbor at approximately 6:30 AM. Visibility was only about one hundred feet and the sky was overcast, so Murdock turned on the running lights for safety. There was still a following breeze from the northeast and the ship was making about eight knots. The slow speed was acceptable to Murdock because of the dense fog they were experiencing, and he wanted to be able to slow the ship in the event of unforeseen circumstances.

The boys had all the sails trimmed in tight, and they were well out of Gosport, so Murdock ordered lookouts. "Jack! Get up on the bow sprit and watch for ships. Shimmy out there about halfway and listen, as well as look. This fog can distort sound. Give us a shout if you see or hear anything."

Jack nodded and went forward. He climbed out over the bow railing and onto the bow sprit, locking his legs into the safety netting below.

Murdock looked to Scott sitting by the mainmast. "Scotty, get up in the crosstrees. Jack is watching for traffic dead ahead and off the port and starboard bows. You keep an eye aft, and to port and starboard quarters. Shout if you see or hear something."

Scott looked aloft to the crosstrees and frowned. He knew it would be miserable up in the crosstrees, given the present weather conditions, but he also knew Murdock wouldn't ask him to do it if it wasn't necessary. "You got it, Skipper." He ran over to the starboard railing and begin to climb the ratlines.

The Defiant sailed on for about an hour. There was no need to tack as the wind came from astern and over the port quarter. Suddenly, the mainsail began to luff. Murdock looked aloft to see the pennants no longer flew straight out, but continued to droop. The jib sail in the bow kept spilling wind too.

Smitty felt the change in the ship and came topside. "Everything okay, Skipper? I felt a noticeable change in the way she was sailing."

Murdock nodded toward the mainsail. "The wind is dying. I looked at the weather charts last night and we should have been okay until noon. It's starting to come in puffs too. I'm considering pulling the sails down and just ride the engine in."

Smitty looked aloft to the pennants and then to the luffing sails. "That would be my choice, Skipper...especially in this dense fog. Man, it's like pea soup out there."

Murdock nodded, "Yeah, I have jack on the bow sprit and Scotty in the crosstrees. I'm going to send the rest of the crew below to take a break. I don't need them up here, once I go to engine-only."

Smitty pointed toward Roger in the trailing dinghy. "What about him? He's got to be feeling it about now."

Murdock turned and glanced at Roger. "Ah, he's fine. I've been keeping an eye on him. The water has been pretty flat and he's been adjusting his position in the dinghy. He hasn't hailed the ship or complained, so I think he's toughing it out. I hope this is the last time I have to do something like this, but he's on this ship to learn."

Smitty nodded as he looked back at Roger. "He seems okay, but he's got to be pretty board though. Has he got water?"

Murdock nodded as he tried to turn the helm to squeeze out the last bit of wind coming from behind the ship. "He's got a few bottles of water in that dinghy. I had the boys show him where they were."

Smitty stepped to the helm. "Skipper, why don't you go below for a while? I'll take her from here."

Murdock reached down to the helm's console and pushed the ENGINE ON button before he left. "Have the boys drop the sails and go below for a while. I'll send Josh up here, to keep an eye on Roger."

Smitty took the helm with both hands. "Aye, Skipper!" Then he shouted, "Bow team! Drop the jib sail and come back here to drop the mainsail. You can go below and take a break after that."

Percy dropped the jib sail and stuffed it into its sail locker while Teddy and Wally came aft and dropped the mainsail. The boys didn't ask any questions. They were happy to get out of the cool mist and get some time below. They disappeared into the forward hatch, leaving Jack on the bow sprit.

Smitty shouted some words of encouragement to the lone sailor on the bow. "Steady as she goes, Jack. Let me know if you hear or see anything."

Jack didn't look back. He just waved his right arm in the air.

▽

The Defiant cruised through the flat water bare masted with lookouts on the bow and in the crosstrees. The dense fog somehow seemed to make it more quiet than usual. Scotty and Jack were very focused on their assignments. They felt they alone were responsible for the ship's safety. That thought alone seemed to give them extra motivation despite the cool and misty conditions.

The ship had been under 'engine-only' power for thirty minutes when Jack thought he heard a fog horn. He leaned forward from his position on the bowsprit, as if it would make a difference. *There it goes again*, he thought. Suddenly, the silhouette of a tall, pointed bow appeared as a huge, wedged shaped wall about one hundred feet off Defiant's port bow. The size seemed immense and was approaching fast. Jack shouted back to the helm. "Ship at the ten o'clock position…coming fast!"

Jack turned around to see if Smitty had heard him, and shouted again. "Ship coming in fast off the port bow!"

Scotty was watching the aft end of the Defiant and heard Jack's warnings. He turned to see the huge dark shape knifing in toward the Defiant's port side. His heart sank. At their rate of speed, there was no time to maneuver. Then, the silence was broken by a loud and long bellow from the approaching ship's horn. First, there was one loud blast, followed by several short blasts. It was so loud it pieced one's ears.

Smitty watched helplessly, as the huge shape emerged from the fog layer. It was a large ocean-going freighter. He knew the Defiant was only making about six knots and the freighter's bow was now within one hundred feet. If he tried to turn into its path, he might risk a head-on collision, and if he turned to starboard, he'd expose the Defiant at amidships for certain impact and seal Roger's fate in the dinghy. Hopeless as it was, Smitty shoved the engine throttle to full ahead.

The freighter was on top of the Defiant in no time. Smitty looked aloft to the crosstrees, and shouted to Scotty to hold tight. The huge bow of the freighter struck Defiant at an angle, on the port side, between its two masts, just forward of amidships. The sound of metal crashing into wood followed with a sickening sound of wood planking groaning and snapping, as the Defiant's wooden hull splintered and exploded at the sudden impact. Wood planking flew into the air with the sound of shroud lines snapping and whipping the air like a buggy whip on a horse drawn carriage.

The freighter's horn seemed to draw the life out of the entire moment as it continued to blast its warning. In just a few seconds, the freighter had sliced through the schooner, taking down the foremast with it.

Scotty was still in the crosstrees and held on as the mainmast slowly tipped toward the sea. Smitty held onto the useless helm and shouted to Scott. "Hold on and ride it down. Swim clear when you get to the water."

The freighter continued on, leaving a path of destruction and debris in its wake. The wooden schooner Defiant was cut in half and lay on its starboard hulls. The bow was pointed toward the sky as the crew's compartment filled with seawater. The aft end, from the mainmast to the stern, was almost flat on its starboard hull with the very top of the mainmast still above the water.

Once the stern wake from the freighter subsided, Smitty crawled up onto the Defiant's hull and looked for survivors. "Yo, sailors! Can anyone hear me?" Smitty repeatedly called for his sailors. He called in every direction. Still no answer.

Finally, Scott answered and began swimming toward the stern, then Teddy's head popped up from between the sections of the broken ship. Wally followed and came up to the surface coughing, near the overturned bow. Percy swam around from the front of what used to be the bow, and hailed Smitty.

When everyone got to the overturned stern, Smitty helped them up out of the Atlantic's cold water. He looked around frantically, "Where's Jack?" He put his hands to his mouth and began shouting for Jack.

Finally, Captain Murdock swam up to the sinking stern and was obviously injured. His right arm and leg seemed twisted in a strange manner and were probably broken. Josh had found Louis struggling to keep Burt, the ship's mascot, afloat amongst some of the Defiant's debris and helped both of them over to where Smitty and the rest of the crew waited.

Once Murdock was pulled onto the floating hull, and was able to catch his breath, he asked. "Where is Roger?" In the midst of what had just happened, everyone had forgotten about Roger in the dinghy. No one said a word. Murdock asked again only louder and more demanding. "Has anyone seen Roger?"

There was a dismal quiet amongst the wreckage and crew. They sat floating on their overturned stern staring into the fog, trying to digest what had just happened. Only the sound of the sea lapping against the stern's wreckage could be heard. A few minutes passed and suddenly a new voice pierced the fog and quietness. "Hey, is anyone out there? Anyone?"

Smitty smiled as he looked into the fog. "That's Roger!" He cupped his hands about his mouth and answered. "Roger! We're here! Keep rowing toward my voice."

In a few minutes, Roger and the two dinghies emerged from the thick fog. He was rowing one dinghy and towing another. He rowed up to the wreckage to transfer the sailors from the stern's hull to his dinghies. "I've been looking all over for you guys. The towline snapped during the collision and we got separated. Is everybody okay?"

Scott shook his head. "Jack is missing. He's not answering our calls."

Roger helped people into the dinghies and asked, "Where was he when the freighter hit?"

Scott answered. "On the bow sprit. He was the one who saw it, and he was the one who warned us.

Once everyone was seated in the dinghies, Smitty had the two boats row around the wreckage in search of Jack. They poked at the sinking pieces of Defiant's bow and stern, and Smitty dove into the water several times and under part of the wrecked hulls to see if Jack might be trapped inside. Despite his best efforts, Smitty found nothing. The young sailor from Plymouth Harbor was gone.

The boys tied the dinghies together and drifted for a while with the sinking wreckage. The fog was still present and the crew was disoriented as to which way was toward the coast.

Roger pointed to the Defiant's remains, "Hey, look at that!" The bow pointed straight up into the air amidst a rush of air bubbles and went straight down into the sea. The bow sprit Jack had used as his lookout position was the last part of the bow to pass beneath the surface.

Within minutes, the stern began to sink from its aft end and also disappeared in a rush of air bubbles. The Defiant was gone.

The boys watched the last of their ship sink into the sea in silence. It was a sad moment. The ship that had brought them from boys to men had perished without a trace. Percy broke the silence. "Why didn't the freighter stop to help us?"

Murdock answered in a fatherly tone. "They probably didn't realize the damage or the severity of the collision, especially in this fog."

Scotty added, "Come on Skipper, they carry radar on a ship that size. They had to know they hit us."

Murdock shook his head. "Not necessarily. Wooden ships have little to no return on radar. They might know by a visual sighting from their crew, but they wouldn't stop because they can't stop within a reasonable distance to help."

Scotty looked angry, "So, they just say the hell with it and continue on their way?"

Murdock adjusted his bruised and broken body in the dinghy and replied. "It's pretty common for a ship of that size to call the Coast Guard with the coordinates of a suspected mishap. Right now, we're about ten miles off the Massachusetts coast. It's pretty standard for a captain to call in a suspected collision and have the Coast Guard check it out." He paused and added, "That freighter wouldn't be outfitted for a rescue operation anyway."

The dinghies drifted for another hour and the fog began to break up. The sun began to poke its way through the grayness and take some of the chill away from the wet sailors. It was a good feeling. At least, there was light, and that annoying mist had dissipated.

Smitty pointed off into the distance. "I guess those freighter sailors aren't so bad after all."

A white helicopter with an orange stripe on its fuselage was headed in their direction, only a couple of hundred feet off the water. Murdock smiled as he lay against the front of his dinghy. "I guess they called it in, boys. The Coast Guard is coming. We are so lucky!"

$$\triangledown$$

The memories of a well spent youth passed through Captain Scott Muldoon's mind, as he closed his book of memoirs and photographs. He closed his eyes and let all the years of sailing, and all the different crews, and of course, all the different escapades he'd been through, filter through his sixty-year-old mind. There was only one crew and one ship that lay at the forefront of his memory, and that was the crew of the Defiant, and his first ship as a green, Tall Ship Sailor.

He opened his eyes and looked about his study. He sat back in his soft desk chair and took another puff on his pipe.

The room was fashioned in a nautical theme and dimly lit with various ship's lamps. Maritime memorabilia adorned the walls and decorated some of the wall's shelves.

The aroma of his tobacco smoke wafted through the room. Hanging from a small wooden nautical stand that stood on the right front of his desk was an old, worn and stained, rope bracelet given to him by an old shipmate named Jack, on his first cruise. It stood for teamwork, companionship, trust and safe travels. He removed it from the stand and put it on his wrist. It still fit. He remembered Jack with a smile, and a feeling of happiness, still overshadowed by sorrow, filled the moment.

He looked around the confines of his wood-furnished study and realized he had lived a life worth spent. Pictures hung from the walls, sailing trophies adorned some of the shelves, and several certificates of commendation for the Youth of America Campaign were posted on the wall next to his cherry mahogany desk.

Scott, now in his golden years, nodded his head and pursed his lips, as he realized his life was spent in meaningful way. His eyes settled on a large framed picture of the schooner Defiant. She had been long gone, but in her day, was the main tool in contributing to the needs of truant youth…those young people that were a little too old for community detention or service programs, and too young for the harshness of prison walls.

His role as a schooner captain played a major role in turning around some gifted youths that would otherwise have succumbed to inner city pressures and temptations. He instilled hard work and determination in his sailors, so the knowledge of responsibility would go further than themselves. Scott realized he had taught his young sailors that whatever they did on that tall ship would result in the benefit or demise of their shipmates and ship. It was a true team effort on board ship and in life itself.